Every Good Thing

JESSICA SHERRY

Published by Jessica Sherry
Copyright © 2024 by Jessica Sherry
jessicasherry.com

ISBN (Print): 979-8-9887254-6-6
ISBN (eBook): 979-8-9887254-4-2

Book Cover Design by Ink & Laurel

Printed/Published in the United States of America

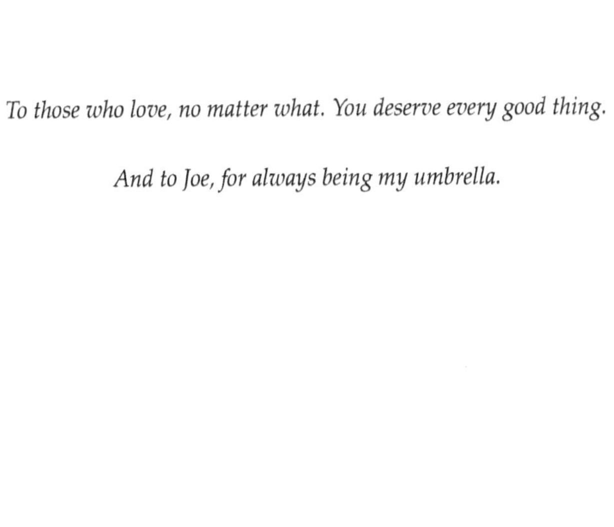

To those who love, no matter what. You deserve every good thing.

And to Joe, for always being my umbrella.

Author's Note

Dear Reader,

You're about to read an emotional, feel-good contemporary romance that features realistic, wounded characters and sensitive subject matter that may upset some readers. Lena suffers from anxiety, and Ben struggles with mental health issues and indecision about his career in law enforcement. If you don't want spoilers, please skip to the prologue with my thanks for reading.

For those who prefer to know, this book deals with the following complex topics: a marriage in trouble, discussions of infidelity (no cheating), anxiety disorder, panic attacks, PTSD, grief, child abuse, physical scars, and hearing impairment. There are also mentions of the COVID-19 pandemic and suicide. There is profanity and sexual content.

Please be assured that I have done my best to handle these topics with respect and sensitivity. Thanks for reading.

Jessica Sherry

1. Wrecked - Imagine Dragons
2. Daylight - David Kushner
3. Fuck, I Luv My Friends - renforshort
4. Say - John Mayer
5. Past Life - Trevor Daniel, Selena Gomez
6. Boss Bitch - Doja Cat
7. Kill Bill - SZA
8. Don't Give Up On Me - Andy Grammar
9. Please Don't Go - Joel Adams
10. Beautiful Things - Benson Boone
11. All I Need - Mat Kearney
12. You're Losing Me (From The Vault) - Taylor Swift
13. Next To Me - Imagine Dragons
14. Feel Like Shit - Tate McRae
15. Slow Fade - Ruth B.
16. People I Don't Like - UPSAHL
17. Till Forever Falls Apart - Ashe, FINNEAS
18. Iris (Acoustic) - Adam Christopher
19. If You Love Her - Forest Blakk
20. Exile - Bon Iver, Taylor Swift
21. I Miss You, I'm Sorry - Gracie Abrams
22. This Is Me Trying - Taylor Swift

Ben

PROLOGUE - SUMMER 2020

"PLEASE, TALK TO HER, BEN," my sister's voice echoes as I twist the steering wheel. "Let her *see* you."

The idea sounds horrifying. It's like undergoing a full bedroom inspection without cleaning it first, except the bedroom is my head. And I can't clean it; I can only move things into corners or under beds where I hope she never looks. Or never wants for the full tour.

Love is too damn complicated.

I huff at my sister. "She sees me enough without a history lesson. It's too much."

Becca chuckles. "Too much for Lena? The woman gracefully handling an anxiety disorder, unemployment, a house falling apart around her, and the loss of her mother during a pandemic? She's Wonder Woman, Ben. *Nothing* is too much for her."

"We've only been… together a few months," I remind her, unsure how to classify us. "I don't want to ruin a good thing."

"You love her, right?"

"Yes." My quick answer surprises me and makes my twin giddy, clapping and hooting like she's won a prize by securing my admission. It *is* a significant milestone, one I never expected—at thirty-seven years old, I've only been in love once before, and that felt nothing like this.

"Then, you won't ruin anything. You've said it yourself—*she's* different." She groans at my hesitation. "Falling is the fun part. Grounding the relationship with a true soul connection is harder, especially for you.

If she's the one, you have to let her in. Otherwise, you're half-assing it, and it's bound to blow up just like—"

"Don't." My stern voice strikes my twin silent. "That's off the table."

After an annoyed sigh, she regroups. "Remember what you told me when I asked what you love about Lena? I mean, after her hot bod and gorgeous bits?"

"Not after. Alongside. And I didn't use *those* terms. But, yes," I relent, knowing where this is going. "Her openness."

"Then, give her what she's so freely given you, Ben. Give her a chance to *really* know you."

Though not keen to give my sister the satisfaction, she's right.

I end the call with a definite, "I'll think about it."

Pulling into Lena's driveway for probably the hundredth time since we met, I'm atypically apprehensive.

In law enforcement, there's an expression we use when a suspect evades capture and drops from our radar—he *gets small*. He shrinks his existence until he's nearly invisible and can hide in plain sight, surviving only by one careful decision to the next.

That's what I've been doing for the last seven years. I've gotten small.

In my conversations.

In my personal life.

In everything.

With Lena, I don't want to be small anymore. I can't be. Not with the warm, full, generous person she is or the enormous life she's determined to get when she eventually turns her family home into a working farm and bakery café—a dream she's only shared with me so far.

The Jeep bounces easily over the rough terrain of her driveway, slightly muddy from recent summer storms. The blackened scar of a strange roof patch catches my eye—I guess she's applied some epoxy to seal a leak, but I don't want to offend her by asking. She thinks I don't notice the concerning state of her family home, but I do. I notice everything, especially when it comes to her. Her home is one power outage or plumbing situation away from being uninhabitable. When I'm not here, I'm stressed that she'll fall through the floorboards or get shocked by a bad breaker. Voicing my concerns would embarrass her, though, and I want her to feel comfortable and trust me enough to ask for help when she's ready.

Partnering with her to renovate her family home and turn it into a business could be my dream, too, if she's willing to share it.

The driveway is lined with narrow, leafy trees, stretching upright like guards in full salute. The trees end when the path curves, and the cedar and brick house comes into view. It's worn down from neglect, but its former beauty remains evident in its grand arched roofs on either side, double fireplaces, partial wraparound porch, and large, gabled windows. Wood-boring bees have made a feast of the cedar, the roof has reached its limit, and the porch is too unstable to walk on. Still, it's large and lovely, despite its defects.

The entire property is like this—broken down but beautiful. Maybe that's why I like it so much.

And why I like her even more. She not only wants to save it, but she hopes to make it a place for everyone.

The driveway curves around the house like a backward question mark, cutting between it and what Lena affectionately calls her middle finger garden. Tall shoots promise it'll thrive by late summer with tomatoes, cucumbers and squashes, herbs of every kind, carrots, and potatoes. It's more food than she needs, but she'll likely donate it, as she's done with her baked goods.

Bookending the garden is a forgotten, rusty playground missing its swings. Beyond that, former horse pastures await a new life, their fences broken and the weeds thick.

Behind the house, the carport and expansive backyard appear. It's as if the driveway's end divides the property into two parts: home and farm. A football field away from the house and carport, the barn is larger and newer—ten stalls occupy the bottom level, along with an office, tack room, and horse shower, all filled with junk. Above it, the barn loft holds decades of her family's history, from furniture to photos. Lena's parents never threw anything away, a fact that's as inefficient as it is endearing.

Lena's spent the pandemic meticulously sorting and salvaging her diverse inheritance. She calls it her parents' legacy, and she's taking good care of it, as she has with everything.

I keep hoping she'll find something of value that'll help her get back on her feet. We joke about her discovering a Picasso in the attic, but it's unlikely that any treasure would be in suitable condition, given the state of things.

Behind the barn (or through it, as it's always open) is a gorgeous, acre-sized pond teeming with catfish and turtles, surrounded by a lush bank and her mom's favorite tree, a sprawling live oak that seems ancient considering its size and artful in the way it curls, bumps, and sways with Spanish moss.

That's where I should tell her.

When I park, the buzz of an electric sander draws my attention to the carport. Lena is removing decades of dust and grime from another salvaged piece—this time, a dresser. Her back is to me, and her toned arms and legs flex as she runs the appliance over the surface.

God, she's beautiful. The thought upticks my nervousness.

But it also reminds me of the first time I came here to help her responsibly get rid of her parents' firearms, a part of her inheritance she didn't want. Then, she was restoring her first piece—a chestnut-brown hutch that once housed her family's china. The noise kept her from hearing me arrive, leaving me wondering how to approach without scaring her. I already knew she was the same woman I pulled over for speeding weeks earlier. Her amusing confession, distressed smile, and humor produced a warm sensation inside me, long forgotten. I let her go with a warning and a note:

Things will get better

I never expected to see her again. Receiving her call weeks later stirred something else that had been dormant in me. Hope, I guess.

On my first visit, I settled with a gentle tap on her shoulder, and yes, I scared her. But that didn't keep her from smiling when she saw that it was me.

This time, I approach in stealth, slipping my arms around her before she realizes I'm there. She laughs, relaxing into me as she turns off the sander. Her hair smells like vanilla, mixing with the sawdust in the air. With a twist, she faces me, edging upward on her rubber boots for a quick kiss.

The fact that we've finally moved into the kissing stage of our relationship makes me very happy.

It's a recent development. One rainy day aside, we hadn't been physically affectionate until a recent beach trip pushed me over the edge—I couldn't hold back any longer. That kiss firmly and finally bridged the gap from friends to something else. I like the slowness of us. Nothing moves forward until we're both comfortable, and talking takes priority. It's been good for her anxiety.

Good for me, too.

"Yay, it's a Ben-day. I'm glad you're here," she says, though I see that already.

"Me, too."

"What's it going to be today, Ben?" She grins, pulling away to wave her arms across the carport. "Sanding? Painting? Laser tag?"

Laser tag tempts me, but I suppress it. "How about a walk?"

She dusts her hands on her jean shorts before slipping one into mine.

I don't lead her directly to my destination—her mom's Saddletree, nicknamed that because it held her dreams for this place like a perch for a saddle.

We traverse the garden first. She turns on the soaker hose she's set up for a good watering. We cut through the field, over rough brambles and dried weeds, until we reach the property's edge. A thick line of trees surrounds the property like strong fingers holding it together. Long-leaf pines are most prevalent, towering over us and providing a blanket of needles for our path. The air is noticeably cooler, and wrens and crows create a pleasant background for all the words I should be saying. A warm-up conversation might ease me into it, even something insignificant about the weather.

But words don't come.

Words have always given me trouble. On paper, my dyslexic mind jumbles them confusingly. In speaking terms, I've always believed staying quiet is better. I've never minded being the quiet one —not with a boisterous twin who talked enough for two, or in school when speaking up could've revealed my reading problem. Pulling fire alarms to get out of class eventually said what I couldn't—I needed help.

After struggling through high school, military life appealed to me. The only words I needed were the orders I had to follow, and not letting emotions get in the way made that easier. There's need-to-know, and nothing else matters.

But I love this woman, and there are things she needs to know. More than that, she's probably the only person on earth who might truly understand me. If I give her the chance, that is.

Silence settles between us—we've gotten good at those. Once, we went over two hours without talking—a new record for her. She always breaks it, as if her not talking prevents a rushing river from falling over a cliff when there's nowhere else for the water to go. Compared to Lena, I'm a verbal desert—words have to be extracted from deep underneath if found at all. She's grown accustomed to this about me. At first, she'd carry on our conversations like an overzealous waitress, refilling a water glass whenever it got the least bit low. Now, she's comfortable enough to let the glass sit. Comfortable enough to be silent.

"Let's see if the fish are jumping," she decides, pulling me away from the wooded trail to the back of the pond near her mom's tree. The light blue sky, nearly matching her eyes, reflects in the water like a mirror. The water is perfectly still, which seems to disappoint her.

Lena, I need to tell you something. I think the words, but don't speak them.

It's easy to blame my inability to communicate on my dyslexia, my childhood, or the military, and certainly, they're all contributing factors. But they aren't the primary cause. The day I truly went silent and got small is, ironically, what I need to share with her.

That day, I put on my tight and heavy armor, zipped it over my chest, and never took it off. The one time I tried real vulnerability with someone other than my sister or my shrink ended badly, but it taught me a hard truth. Most people prefer the armor. They prefer wounds hidden, difficulties undiscussed, and tears sucked in. So, now that I've finally found someone I want to take off my armor for, someone who isn't like that, the zipper is stuck.

Lena's eyes catch mine, silently asking the same question she's put to me hundreds of times. *What are you thinking?*

It's been her go-to question since we started to ease me into conversations. She always wants more of me, and, honored by that sweet sentiment, I vowed to always answer. To let those words chisel away at my rough exterior and bring us closer.

I imagine her saying them now, and it helps.

I motion to the swing hanging from her mom's tree, and she sits.

With her back to me, I gently send her forward, releasing the words with her ascent. "I want to tell you how I was injured."

The story emerges from me in choppy pieces that come together as roughly as the scars covering my chest. But I don't care. I don't need eloquence, only to get it out. I catch side views of her expression as she sails back into my arms—she keeps her eyes forward as if she knows it's easier for me. So is telling her like this—on a tree swing—something innocent and lovely softening what's dark, dirty, and painful.

I describe that day in the Wardak province of Afghanistan as if I were reporting to my higher-ups. Positions. Armaments. Bystanders. Cargo inventory. Time of day. Estimated time of arrival. The names and ranks of those with me. Jargon she surely doesn't understand. Every fucking detail. No half-assing. I see the village ahead and catch the worried eyes of a woman pulling her small child away from the building.

"Something's wrong," I said immediately before glass shattered against our Humvee and burst into flames. The diversion preceded the main event—a shrapnel-packed IED that ambushed our unit's convoy, killing two and injuring seven.

I tell her about the god-awful ringing in my ears, how I couldn't make sense of bullets flying by me when I couldn't hear them.

I tell her about Sergeant Adam Ricks, dying next to me, and the young family he left behind.

I tell her my armor all but failed me, letting hot metal embed in my chest. How it burned. How I bled.

I tell her we barely made it out, and often, I wished I hadn't.

Her boots find the ground then, resisting the force until the swing mostly stops. She pops off, filling my arms in an instant.

"Damn it, Ben. That belongs in the fire barrel. Never think it again. I mean it." Her forceful, desperate words don't match the delicacy of her fingers falling on my cheek and tracing my scar, but I savor both.

I don't know what I expected from Lena, but her bypassing unwanted sympathy for anger and concern strengthens my love for her. It's the reaction I didn't know I needed—it's her, honest as ever, loving me through the pain, now and in hindsight.

I wondered before, but no longer. *This woman loves me.*

"Our heads play mean tricks on us—I know," she says. "And, yes, we're all expendable and can't control explosions or viruses or anything, really. But you belong here. With me." She nibbles her bottom lip, making me desperate to kiss her. "I need you, Ben. You're not expendable. Not to me."

Her hurried confession inspires me to smile, my pent-up tension leaving with every word she says. I grip her waist, pulling her into me. Her hands rest on my chest, lightly tugging my shirt. She relaxes against me, fitting perfectly.

My relief is palpable, like it could liquefy, pour off me, and feed the roots underground. "I need you, too, Lena. I won't think it again."

"Just like that?" she asks, breathless.

"Not just, but yes." I hold out my hand and mimic dropping the thought into our fire barrel, where she recently burned the remains of her past life—her mom's medical bills, a stack of Garbage Pail Kids, including the one she said was her, Nervous Nellie, and most significantly, her wedding photos, which took beautiful courage, I thought.

Now, she laughs at my gesture, our private joke, and I hold her closer.

"You're the best reason," I say. "Every good and terrible thing we've been through makes strange sense now. That's why I told you. I want you to know everything. No holding back."

I mean it—I want only honesty between us.

But there's more I could say. That day didn't happen in a bubble—it set off a chain of events, costing me my hearing and my profession, wounding me physically and mentally, and stealing my ability to love and be loved.

Until now. That day also brought me here. *To her.* And for the first time, with Lena in my arms, I'm grateful. It's like getting lost in the woods for seven years only to find a vast and unbelievable treasure before being rescued.

A treasure I'll do anything to protect.

Five Years Later
Ben

Rain gently taps the hood of my patrol car and pings objects that shouldn't be outside—used plates and cups on a ragged picnic table, a ripped open case of Miller Lite, and a plastic bin of action figures. It's a wonder there are toys.

Motherfuckers.

The scene unfolding around me is more solemn than most—it's always like that when children are involved. The CSI team works in relative silence. Officers speak into their two-way radios in hushed tones. Another speaks on the phone to the Jehovah's Witnesses, who requested a well-check at the residence after hearing noises inside, but didn't call until later when they decided the whimpering sounded more human-like than a dog, as they had first thought. The location feels remote, even though it's in a large trailer park. The property looks carved into the woods, like a hovel at the back end of the neighborhood, far enough from neighbors not to get much attention. There are no signs of life except a naked doll sitting upright on the picnic table, occasionally saying, "Mommy," in a drawn-out slur when anyone comes near it.

And, of course, the kid.

I finger my temples, feeling pained and nauseated.

Detective Ed Gentry has taken over; it's now an investigation. We've had our differences, but although the guy's an old-school asshole with no filter, he's like a bulldog with cases like these. I have no doubt that he'll apprehend the suspects forthwith and without leniency.

He approaches, hands fixed on his belt, flashing his gold badge. "Okay, lieutenant? You look a little green."

"Fine."

"Found our suspects tying one on at the Copper Penny downtown. Got 'em in custody. The boy's parents and uncle. All three occupy the house, so they'll all go down for it. That and the meth they were using and selling," he reports, glancing at his black notebook.

"Any other relatives to contact?" I ask.

"Nope. There's no one else."

"He'll have to go into the system," I sigh. "Call Olivia Jones. She's good with kids like this. Have her meet him at the hospital."

"Already done," he says. "Go home, Wright. Your shift ended hours ago, and it's a tough one. I got this. We'll get the kid to the hospital and take good care of him."

"About that," Officer Pam Gay chimes in, rushing over. "He's anxious about going." She motions toward the nearby ambulance. "He keeps asking for *the big guy*."

I cross the littered lawn, leaving them to handle the scene. At the ambulance's open doors, I find the kid huddled under a blanket on the gurney, sitting slouched and curled rather than lying down, like he's lived his life in a tiny ball. *Small.* His hair is matted with scum, his face smudged with dirt, and his eyes look icy with fear. Each cheek boasts a long scar, scabbed over and red with infection. His fingers are skeletal, gripping the blanket tightly around his neck and holding the flashlight I gave him—inside the trailer was unnaturally dark.

The paramedic attempts to coax him to lie down while the other holds an IV, ready for application.

The kid only stares over their heads, his mouth open and lips trembling.

"We need to secure him," she says when she sees me, "but he's…"

Scared shitless.

With a languid glance to see who the paramedic is speaking to, the kid notices me. He scurries on all fours to the end of the gurney and reaches out to me, his stick-like arms and legs latching around my neck and waist, regardless of my belt, vest, and radio. He did the same after I broke down the trailer door and unlocked the dog crate holding him inside.

All I said to him then was, "You're safe now."

It's hard to believe that ten hours ago, I dropped Ruthie at preschool. I still feel her chubby cheek pressing against mine for her "goodbye, Dad" hug. She smelled like apple juice and laundry detergent and gushed about her noodle-necklace art project, presently rubbing my chest under my shirt. She'd colored each macaroni differently to create a rainbow, which she said would keep me safe before making me promise to wear it.

Now, my hand goes to brace the kid's back, and I feel his ribs under his filthy, adult-sized t-shirt. He feels like a heavy coat, not a child. My heart, my fucking soul, feels shredded.

"It's okay, Adam."

"Don't go," he whispers, his voice so low and raspy I'm surprised I hear it.

"Ride with us?" asks the relieved paramedic. "So we can stabilize him?"

My brow pinches atop a developing migraine, but I nod. I relinquish the keys to my patrol car to Officer Gay. I climb aboard, ducking to avoid hitting my head. I tug Adam from me, setting him gently on the gurney—a move he allows, though he grabs my hand as if I'll abandon him. I think of Lena and how her hands shake when she panics—it hardly happens anymore.

I wish she were here. She'd know how to put this boy at ease. She'd make him feel at home, even if he no longer has one. Not that he did. Not that he even understands what home is.

"Look at me," I tell him as the paramedic readies the needle for the IV. He doesn't even wince as it punctures his dainty forearm between dark finger bruises where someone has gripped him and squeezed.

Motherfuckers.

The paramedic hands me a pack of cookies while asking Adam if he's hungry. He doesn't answer. I rip open the pack, take a bite, and offer the rest to him. He gobbles it up like he's starved.

He *is* starved.

I hate this fucking planet sometimes.

At the hospital, I hold Adam's hand through his medical evaluation. Color returns to his face as the IV bag empties, and he relaxes. He's malnourished, dehydrated, and covered in cuts and bruises. His fingers shake perpetually as everything happens, making me wonder how he has the energy. Whenever he's asked a question, he looks to me for approval.

I don't know what to say to him. It's a frequent problem for me, but it's worse right now. I can't talk video games or school or TV shows with a kid who's spent an undetermined amount of time locked in a dog crate and probably years suffering his family's abuse.

But Adam seems okay with my silence, especially as hospital staff move in and out, each trying to connect with the kid but failing. He clicks my flashlight on and off, shining it around the room.

My contact at social services arrives. Olivia Jones is a family friend, and she'll keep me updated on Adam's situation. She brings a colleague, Mira, who will handle Adam's case.

My paternal instinct wants to take Adam home, be his dad, and show him the love and care he's never had. But that's not how things work. Besides, I trust Olivia Jones to find him the ideal situation and get him the help he'll undoubtedly need.

They consult with the doctor while I stay with him.

In the quiet between visitors, Adam plays with my hand, comparing his with mine. He's older than Ruthie, but his hand is only slightly bigger. He seems to marvel at my size; kids often find me amusing that way. I remember the first time I held Ruthie—she felt like a football in the crook of my arm, and I felt larger than normal holding her. Peering up at me with her bright green eyes, watching every move I made, I felt like a hero.

Adam sees me that way, too. He imprinted me with the label the moment I unlocked the dog crate. But I'm not. *I'm no fucking hero.*

He gives me a curious look and motions to my neck. I feel along my collar and find the string of Ruthie's macaroni necklace peeking out. I pull it free and take it off to show Adam. He smiles, running his tiny, nail-bitten fingers over the multicolored noodles, touching each one in strange delight. He shakes the necklace, and it rattles. Then, he hugs it to himself before returning it to me.

"I can't stay much longer," I tell him flatly.

He nods, his smile falling.

"But I promise you'll be well cared for, and you'll never go back to that house again. They can't hurt you anymore."

His slight shoulders release as he nods again.

I hand him the necklace. "My daughter made it. She said it would keep me safe. I want you to have it."

His smile perks as I slip it over his head. He holds up the flashlight questioningly. "For the dark?"

"Keep it, too."

"Thank you, Officer Wright." His voice is raspy and unsure, but he forces the words out. "I'm lucky you found me."

"I'm the lucky one," I tell him.

Lucky. The word clangs in my head and burrows under my skin on the way home. It's after midnight. Rain drenches the windshield. The streets are empty, but the drive feels long. My head pounds, and pressure tightens my chest. The day's reality hits me—I almost didn't save him, almost left him there to die, almost failed him like everyone else in his life, almost left him behind.

My hands strangle the steering wheel. Gunfire whizzes by my ears, but it's not real. It's *that* day, surging through my usual fortress. "You got lucky, Wright. Could've been you," I remember a medic saying under the helicopter's roar as we were lifted away. *Lucky. Lucky. Lucky.*

It should've been me.

I reach home but don't remember getting here.

I climb the stairs but don't feel the cool night air or the rain drenching my clothes.

When I enter, the dogs bark softly, stirring Lena on the couch. She glances at the clock on the microwave.

"Ben, you're so late. Everything okay?"

I peel off my belt, radio, vest, and shirt as I make my way to her, dropping them as I go, like burdens I can't carry for one more second. Finally, I kneel before her place on the couch, aching with exhaustion and run ragged with emotional bullshit.

She grabs onto me, shifting her legs to pull me into her chest. It feels so good to be here—to be home—that I crumble. My arms lock hers to me, and I bury my face in her warm, soft neck.

I don't know how long we stay this way. Today mixes strangely with *that* one like they're the same event, replaying on a wicked loop, dragging me into a familiar dark place.

But Lena grounds me. I hold her as tight as I can until I feel anchored again.

When I finally drag myself off her, she smiles softly, running her fingers along my damp cheeks.

"Want to talk about it?"

"No."

She nods. "Okay. Tell me what you need."

My forehead drifts to hers, creating a small pocket between us. "I-I don't know."

"Come with me." She tugs me along lightly by the hand. We cross through the kitchen, picking up my leftover pieces. She stops at Ruthie's door and motions me inside. "Go kiss your daughter."

I do as I'm told, tearing up as I lean down and graze her chubby cheek. She's warm and fast asleep—she doesn't even flinch at my kiss.

Returning to Lena in the hall, she leads me to our bedroom. She puts my things away and starts the shower. Zombie-like, I follow her lead, kicking off my boots and undressing. I let the hot water pour over my head, ridding me of the misery of the last few hours. Or pushing it aside, at least.

When I emerge from the shower, she hands me a towel. Then, she helps me into bed, pulling me to her chest. She rubs my head, delicately massaging my temples as if she sees my migraine underneath.

"You're home. You're safe. Everything's okay." Her words reach me even without my hearing aids.

And I want to believe them.

But in a few hours, she'll leave for work. I'll wake alone. And she'll be so busy with the million and one tasks of Saddletree Bakery and Café that even when she asks what happened today, I won't be able to tell her, for all the chaos and noise. Why would I darken her bright, beautiful world with that anyway? It'll be locked away, where all my unsaid words go to fester but not die. The memories will return, forcing me to get small in fear of the day when my luck runs out.

CHAPTER 1

Lena

FIVE MONTHS LATER... NOW.

MY PHONE RATTLES on the nightstand. Four a.m. I tap the screen. *Just another ten minutes.* A window glance confirms it's still dark. This tops my shortlist of peeves about being a baker and business owner.

But when you love something, you have to work for it.

Burrowing into my pillow, my packed schedule streams like an unwelcome dream, and to-dos poke me. I don't *have* another ten minutes.

Rolling over, I spy Ben lying on his side, facing me. Watching him dissipates my rising tension. He extinguishes so many mental fires—he has no idea. Seeing him every day, being privy to that almost imperceptible smile, those penetrating green eyes, hearing his mild but strong voice, having that sweet marital permission to touch him whenever I want, waking to him beside me, *anything Ben*, his mere presence calms me like nothing else. It whispers to me. *Everything's okay.*

He twitches suddenly, jerking his head. His fingers tighten into fists against his chest. Another nightmare.

I wiggle closer, nestling in the crook of his neck and shoulder. My fingers wander his bare chest, drifting across familiar terrain and rough edges. The lumpy gashes made by hot metal shards, the textures of burns, scrapes, and divots driven into him by flying debris, healed but never forgotten—this is his survivor story, like cave drawings etched into a mountain.

I relax against his warmth as his arm drapes around me. With a heavy breath, he settles again.

Drifting away in his comfort, I know my alarm will erupt again at any second. A slight turn and glance at my phone confirms what I already know—I'm late. My anxiety bitches, those panic-inducing voices in my head that rarely shut up, are quick to nag me with their usual spiel.

Falling behind means never catching up.

There are cakes to bake, orders to fill, people to feed and make happy.

They're counting on me.

What am I still doing here in bed? There's no time for this.

I kiss his stubbled chin and whisper that I love him before dragging myself away. But with his hearing aids on the bedside table, I know he doesn't hear me.

With my teeth brushed, clothes on, and minimal makeup applied, which at forty is a step I *cannot* skip, I tiptoe from my bedroom and peek into Ruthie's. Her constellation nightlight swirls stars over the ceiling—she knows all the main ones, thanks to Ben's patient teaching. She's also well-taught in animal care, baking, reading, simple math, and construction. The latter is thanks to her godmother and my best friend Dot, who runs her own construction business and considers Ruthie her assistant. She's also just started preschool with the confident air of a college student, like school is only a formality and she must do her time. Our daughter is four going on thirty, as I often joke.

Beside her ruffled daybed, I lean down for a quick peck. Her green eyes, identical to her father's, peel open.

"Mom, don't forget my dress and boots," she says, drifting off on the last syllable.

Shit. I forgot.

In my defense, Ruthie's wardrobe revolves around only three dresses—one pink, one yellow, and one apple green—so keeping up with her laundry is challenging. Purple rubber boots with umbrellas complete her outfit. If she'd had it her way, hers would be black and dotted with pink-bowed skulls, like mine. But stores tend to shy away from skulls for four-year-olds.

Both wait for me in the mudroom. Now, I'm further behind.

We created Saddletree Farm and Bakery Café from my once-dilapidated family home, where I cared for Mom during the last years of her life. With its flickering power, plumbing issues, roof leaks, and old wood stove sourcing the house's heat, living there was constant work and worry for me.

It still is, but in totally different ways.

Thanks to Mom's coin collection, the Saddletree renovation project took place five years ago. Since the main house was in terrible shape then, we first renovated the enormous barn loft to create a home for Ben and me. We needed a space to call ours (gratefully away from the business) while most of the restoration happened at the main house.

Cherry, my other best friend and now Wilmington's premiere interior designer, calls Saddletree "the best reason to spend a day in the country." Of course, that's also because she's more of a city girl. Dot, the project's lead contractor, brags that it's "her favorite place in the world, guaranteed to fix everything." She may be *slightly* biased, but she has a point. Saddletree fixed our three careers in one transformation.

To me, it's simply home. It's where I grew up, and Ben and I fell in love and built our lives together. Our gorgeous home over the barn, also designed and renovated by Dot and Cherry, serves as a private oasis amid the chaos.

But unless I'm there, I'm working (and sometimes, even then), and our beautiful enterprise is incredibly overwhelming.

My former family home is now Saddletree's bakery (my favorite part), serving nearly every church function, birthday, and anniversary within a twenty-mile radius. The café supports our rural area, hosting hundreds of farmers, shift workers, and retirees daily, who'd otherwise have to travel fifteen miles to reach the nearest Starbucks (they prefer my home cooking, anyway).

Families visit Saddletree every weekend to enjoy our scenic picnic spots, walking trail, fishing pond, horse pastures, wraparound porch, playgrounds, bunnies, chickens, massive garden for picking fresh veggies, and weekend tractor-pulled hayrides.

It's a retreat for organizations, too. We host everything from AA to wounded vets, book clubs to bike clubs, therapy groups to yoga classes. We cater their meetings and give them a peaceful place to connect. Our spaces are booked (occasionally overbooked) most evenings.

Since the family home also has completely renovated bedrooms, Saddletree could be a bed and breakfast, but I haven't invited overnight guests yet (other than family). Keeping up is hard enough already.

Like Mom's best friend, Mrs. Moore (Aunt Barb to Dot and Ruthie), says, "It's a basket with too many eggs."

Eggs that often end up on my face.

Though I have a firm grasp of what Saddletree *is*, my grip on managing it is tenuous. I'm always busy, constantly learning, and often fucking up.

I gather Ruthie's dirty clothes and start a quick cycle. If I get them in the dryer before leaving, Ben will handle the rest. He gets her ready for preschool and drops her off before work—he's a Wilmington police lieutenant and supervisor of his division's second shift. He's also a training officer and assists with the K-9 unit. It's a strange comfort that I'm not the only one with a busy career.

The difference between us is that when he's home, *he's home*. Work is left behind for what he loves—spending time with Ruthie, our dogs, Hugo and Penelope, and helping with the support groups, his favorite part of Saddletree.

When I'm home, I'm still at work, always working. Never ahead and always behind.

In my gorgeous custom white kitchen that makes me go *ahhhhh* every time I enter it (Cherry truly is a magician), I start coffee and make their lunches, thinking about the fifty-plus lunches I'll make when I get to the bakery. And cookies. And biscuits. And cinnamon rolls. And three cake orders. Oh, and cupcakes. I still have muffins from yesterday, and soups are slow-cooking, thanks to last night's prep. But the time saved won't matter because it's Thursday. I'll spend a few hours delivering calming homemade animal treats to local farms and vet clinics and dropping off free baked goods to local charities—something I used to have plenty of time for during the pandemic and before Saddletree opened. Now, it's a time-suck I can barely afford. But I love supporting the community that's loved and supported me.

With at-home prep done—lunches made, boots cleaned, coffee in hand—I stand by the window in the laundry room, lights off to calm my mind while the washer fills for its final spin. It's still dark outside, but the barn lights stretch across the backyard like fingers, gently tickling the pond's edge.

It was Dot's idea to turn the barn loft into our home, which I initially thought was bonkers. In my defense, Dot *is* somewhat bonkers, and we were far from besties then. Our friendship grew slowly, like a book that didn't get good until the eighth chapter, and now we can't put it down. Our story helped create Saddletree with our treehouse home in the center overlooking the kingdom.

When it's light out, anyway. Right now, it's a black ocean.

"Lena." Ben's soft voice makes my shoulders jump.

He stands in the doorway. His broad shoulders and thick, muscular arms create a sexy silhouette with the kitchen lights behind him—a real-life Iron Giant. He's wearing only boxer briefs, and a mental *holy fuck* makes me gasp, seeing him that way.

Ben Wright is and always will be the hottest man I know.

An easy "hi" slips out with a wave. Remembering his bad dream, I ask, "Everything okay?"

"No," he breathes. "The bed's too cold without you."

A single stride brings him to me, front and center. Commanding and determined. He eases the mug from my hands and sets it on the laundry counter while keeping his gaze on mine. *Holy shit*—he hasn't even touched me, and I'm a breathy, hot mess for my thudding heartbeat and prickling skin.

God, this man.

Ever calm and collected, he takes me in as if scientifically registering my heightened anticipation to determine the most effective moment to—

His lips land on mine almost roughly. Hands grazing my cheeks, our familiar tangle deepens in a breath. Major tongue action has me tugging him closer by the shoulders, desperate for more of him. His hands travel down my backside, squeezing my ass before lifting me up and, pressed against him, I realize I'm trembling for him.

Fucking trembling.

I've learned many things about being married to Ben Wright—for one, *this* never gets old. I do whatever feels right (and it always feels right), but Ben is a sex practitioner. He turns me on in a blink, like a skill he's honed as we've been together. Hell, more than once, he's reduced me to mush with only a coy look from across the room. The slightest upturn of his lips and the laser focus of his gorgeous green eyes are enough to make me go wild and attack him with tongue-laced kisses.

And *this* will have me tingling the rest of the day. How will I serve customers under these conditions, all flushed, blushing, and trembling with hot Ben aftershocks sure to come?

I tuck that in my worries-for-later file.

Why don't we start every day this way? I can't remember the last time we were together. Small things pile up between then and now, stretching and confusing my memory. Has it been *that* long?

That's another thing I've learned about marriage—the longer it is, the more you lose that beautiful urgency that once had you racing to the bedroom. Or you're too busy and tired to entertain it.

A soft moan escapes me when he sets me against the spinning washer and yanks off my shirt. My fingers rake through his short blond hair while his mouth slips warmly over my chilled skin. He nibbles my collarbone and grazes my shoulder. I love the feel of his stubble scraping down my neck and the familiar way his fingers knead my back, rough and delicate at once. He's about to peel off my bra when the wash cycle ends, interrupting our fun times with an annoying buzz.

He sighs and rests his head against my chest. Then, with a swift move that flexes all his incredible chest muscles, he scoots me against him, lifts me off the machine, and carries me out of the laundry room.

"What're you doing?"

"Taking you to bed."

Crossing the living room, my to-do list screams, taking center stage in my head. "Um, I don't have much time." *Or any, if I'm honest.*

Ben stops abruptly, his intent gaze diving into me and reading my contemplation. "I'll help with setup. Please, Lena. Just stay."

The soft desperation in his eyes fills me with love and worry in a breath as if one can't exist without the other. I'm about to agree—to give him a wild, wet kiss while mumbling for him to "take me to bed" in a dramatic, soap opera fashion. But as I quickly reshuffle my mental schedule, I glance at the oven's digital clock.

He stiffens. "Damn it, Lauren."

I gawk at him, breathless and devastated. His grip loosens, and my feet land gently on the cold wood floor.

"What? What did you say?" The words sputter out like I'm choking, but I know *exactly* what he said—*Lauren.* I sign my question, too, in case he can't hear me.

He looks frustrated and perplexed, as if *I'm* the puzzle here. His eyes drift from me to the floor.

"I'm sorry," he manages.

"Who the fuck is Lauren?" I demand stronger now with words and hands.

"No one. It's nothing. It's work-related. Don't read into it." He's calm, but irritation pools around his edges like a headache he's trying to thwart with all his mental energy. "I have a lot on my mind."

I bristle. "Yeah, someone named Lauren. How can I *not* read into it?"

"Because I love you, and you trust me." He runs a hand through his short hair and shrugs. "It was an accident. That's all."

Stunned, I stand there like he's turned me to stone. I trust him—he's not the cheating type. But saying another woman's name mid-seduction ranks high on the list of things a spouse should never, ever do. It's worse than forgetting a birthday or leaving the seat up. This offense falls uncomfortably close to marriage's cardinal sins—lying, stealing, manipulating, adultery. It feels too egregious to ignore.

I blink as tears fall out, and all of a sudden, I can't fucking breathe. *Lauren.* That it eased from his lips so naturally—lips that I claim as mine—shakes me to my core and instigates my anxiety. I haven't had a panic attack in years, and here I am, heart racing, fingers trembling, mouth going dry, and stomach twisting into tight knots. The sleeping predator inside me awakes with renewed vigor, uncaged and ready to pounce.

"Breathe," he says, and I obey in long, slow breaths. Ben sighs and locks eyes in that sincere, stern way he does that says he'll only say the next thing once. "I swear, it's nothing."

My eyes fix on his as he says it, though his hands move, too. Using American Sign Language is standard practice in our household, even when we speak audibly. Ben's hearing loss will eventually become profound, so it's good practice. Communication is a struggle for us, anyway—using both helps.

Now, it emphasizes his words like bold text in capital letters.

I believe him, *I think*, though my anxiety bitches don't. Cherry has filled my head with stories about her philandering ex-husband. She heard, "I swear it's nothing," for years before finally figuring him out. Similar stories float around the café whenever the ladies gossip.

It happens, and sometimes, to the best couples.

But this is Ben. The love of my life, Ruthie's dad, and my sweet husband. Under the sprawling pondside oak tree, the man who rarely shows emotion told me, "I do," with happy tears in his eyes. I still feel his gentle kisses on my forehead and his strong hand enveloping mine when I was in labor. If not for him, Saddletree would've been a lost dream, and my family's home reduced to farmland. He got me through my mom's death, joblessness, and the pandemic—I honestly don't know where I'd be without him. Probably in my brother Lucas's Malibu pool house, living a half-life, dependent and miserable.

Ben and I bonded over our brokenness, and we've healed and

strengthened each other ever since. He'd never jeopardize us, our beautiful love and history, for whoever Lauren is or anyone else.

Still, alarm bells ring in my head. Something's amiss and has been for a while.

But with Ben, finding out the problem isn't as easy as asking. He never says ten words when three will do and rarely volunteers that many, regardless. He keeps things close to the chest—a trait that's served him well in his military and law enforcement careers.

Silence isn't an asset in a relationship, though—it's a curse.

It's especially awful for me because I *am* a talker. Open conversations are the butter on my bread. The sugar that activates my yeast. Without information, I resort to worst-case thinking, and that's never good.

When we first got to know each other, I battled for more words from Ben with a simple question: *what are you thinking?* It became a rule between us to ask each other that and answer honestly.

But, when I ask him now, "What are you thinking?" he hesitates.

Why is he hesitating?

He shifts on his feet before folding his bulky arms over his scarred chest, and his words emerge choppily and broken, like I'm a stranger. "You're always in a million places, but never with me. I miss us."

"Of course, I'm with you." My defenses rise with the pitch in my voice and the flurry of my excited hands as they keep up with my words. "I'm here. I'm always right here. What do you mean?"

When he doesn't speak, I say, "*You* said the wrong name. How did this turn around on me?"

He huffs, brushing by me. "Go to work, Lena."

He disappears down the dark hall, leaving me crushed.

I plop against the table's edge in a full-bodied slump. Still breathing through my panic, I glance at the opposite wall. Amid family pictures, my eyes stop on the two framed hand-written notes at the center. First, a note I found in Mom's medication journal after she passed, words that inspired Saddletree.

Dream something better

The second is from Ben—a message he wrote on a warning ticket after pulling me over for speeding the day we met, words that, in my grief and high anxiety, I desperately needed.

Things will get better

His promise held true. With him by my side, I turned the shitshow remains of my life into a stable and thriving business, and my grip on that has been white-knuckled and fierce ever since. Saddletree isn't just *my* dream. It's our home, Ruthie's future, and our retirement plan. It's the safety net that will catch us if his hearing worsens and he decides not to work anymore. That was the deal we made when he supported me through Saddletree's creation—I'd be there for him if the situation ever reversed. *That's* why I work so hard.

But something's been lost.

Ten minutes ago, I thought I had everything I ever wanted. Now, for the first time, I'm left wondering, do I truly have Ben?

CHAPTER 2

Ben

WHEN I CAN'T GO BACK to sleep, I hit the shower, the water set to scorching. Steam fills the bathroom. My skin reddens under the heat, but I like that it hurts. The deadened nerves across my chest awaken, relieving the pain felt elsewhere.

But it's not enough.

My fist slams into a wall tile, cracking it.

"Fuck," I breathe out into humidity so thick it steals my voice.

I hover under the showerhead, skin red and aching, water filtering over my face into my mouth. Sometimes, I still feel grit in my eyes and taste the damn sand—I could never get clean over there. Sometimes, the pain returns, too—heat eating through my nerves and burning metal slicing paths into my skin. Ghost pain joins the live ones. The searing water, my aching fist, and Lena.

Damn it, Lena.

I promised myself I wouldn't let the past infect the present, but it's infiltrated without my consent. A lone sniper lying in wait. A devious mole, sneaking around and assessing weaknesses. A damn toxin, slipping into the bloodstream. Anyone who believes the past can't hurt them anymore is living in a fucking fairytale.

The past hurts me every day. It's a desperate perp rummaging through my life and taking whatever it can get, an addict, feeding off me, eating away at my peace of mind, leaving destruction behind.

Lauren's the perfect example.

I wish she'd never come back in my life. I'm dealing with enough shit already. There should be a statute of limitations on former relationships—any long gap in communication should forfeit future contact. *Lauren fucking Riley.* Before her call, it'd been twelve years. Was it guilt that made me finally take her call? Anger? Or just simple curiosity?

Regardless, that was my fault.

I want to blame Lena for the rest, but I shouldn't. I went to her with my sensitivities already primed, forcing me to overreact and then fuck up. Dropping her name instead of Lena's feels criminal. I needed her this morning. Not sex, exactly. I wanted her comfort, her kiss, and all those small, beautiful things she does that build, shield, and better me. Closeness with Lena comes with a full-bodied, emotional recharge—I *need* her.

Especially today.

But I sabotaged us.

I turn off the water and swipe the moisture over the cracked tile. It's not broken enough to replace, but a layer of caulk will reseal it properly.

A task for later.

I dry off, straining to listen for any signs of Lena lingering or Ruthie waking. It doesn't matter—I can't hear a thing. Without my hearing aids, I'm more likely to feel their movements—the door vibrating at Lena's exit or the soft reverberations of Ruthie's feet plodding down the hall. I've even told her to use heavy feet so that I'll "hear" her better. It's a game for her now.

I exit the bathroom in a steam cloud, retrieve my hearing aids from the bedside table, and slip them into place. Faint morning sounds fill my ears—Hugo and Penelope barking as they accompany Lena to the café, chickens cluttering from the pen, and a delicate ensemble of birds serenading the rising sun. My shoulders drop. I'll miss those sounds.

Most of all, I'll miss Lena's voice. And Ruthie's. She sounds a little older every day. I hate that I'll never hear her as an adult. Hell, even our game of heavy feet won't work forever.

My head droops. The temporary relief of the hot water is gone. My hands claw and fist, imagining a silent future when my career is no longer an option and dependency shifts from my capable shoulders to theirs. Their words will be replaced with touches and gestures drenched in sympathy, and I'll be no more useful than one of Ruthie's bunnies.

I take a breath, centering myself.

Bullshit circumstances corner me and impact those I love. I can't even get a quickie right.

I stare at the unmade bed, where half-asleep, I imagined Lena with me, curling close and kissing my chin. That's what drew me from bed to find her.

It's no surprise she looked at the clock. Lena chooses work over me all the time. She doesn't even realize it anymore.

I make the bed. Tight corners. No wrinkles.

Then, I extract my navy-blue suit from the walk-in closet. I haven't worn it since Will Harvey's wedding last year. Lena said I looked like "a badass Secret Service agent," which still makes me smile. Impressing her pleases me.

I miss that feeling and don't understand where it's gone.

Planes need lift to fly. Lights need electricity. Sailboats need wind. Jeeps need fuel. And love needs presence.

She misses most of the meals I prepare and the outings I plan. Saddletree steals ninety percent of our time together because she cannot say no or manage her time. Every disappointment prompts me to tell her that her failure to make time for us bothers me.

But when the moment arises, I freeze. I don't want to ruin what little time we have with a conflict or cause her anxiety. More than that, I don't want to hurt her.

Only I just did. Twice. Saying Lauren's name and following it up with *I miss us* was a double-hit she didn't deserve.

But she asked our question, and I had to say it.

I've wanted her to ask me that question for months, but she hasn't had time.

Everything about Lena is honest, from her over-the-top efforts to keep this place going to her anxiety disorder to her beautifully expressive face. She is the realest person I know, and I love her for it. My admission crushed her, evident in her watery eyes, pinched brow, and entire body drooping like a wilting flower.

Shit.

I set up the ironing board, let the iron heat, and retrieve my white button-down. Running the warm iron over the shirt's creases makes me shake my head. Lauren Riley doesn't iron clothes. She has people for that—a fact that blew my mind in high school. Lauren doesn't clean her toilet or wash her car, either. As a teenager, I found her life amazing.

After becoming a soldier, I found it superficial. There's something that feels disingenuous about living such a charmed life. Her world is soft, clean, and uncomplicated.

But having sampled her easy life, it's hard not to miss it sometimes.

Hanging my crisp shirt on the door handle, I fumble over Lena's discarded nightgown. I tidy her side of the closet and put the ironing away.

Sipping coffee on the front deck, I take comfort in the lights coming from the bakery's kitchen. It glows with activity like a lighthouse amid rough seas. It glows with *her. Everything's okay.* Lena's working, and that's where she'll be when I return later. Then, I'll tell her everything— I'll insist. I should've insisted sooner.

Talking is a challenge I avoid. Discussing feelings or anything that matters feels foreign and uncomfortable for me. I endured combat for a decade, yet therapy has been my most challenging experience to date.

Therapy *and* marriage. Talking to Lena used to be the exception— our game of telling each other what we thought in the moment helped in the early days. I didn't have to plan what to say, only reveal it. But she rarely asks anymore. Not that I need a prompt to talk to her, but the things I need to say get snuffed out every time she glances at the clock. Noting the time is Lena's signature move these days.

I need to pull us together again. *Pull it in. Pull her in.*

Five years ago, I told Lena about the IED that caused my injuries, but I didn't tell her everything. I left out the aftermath. Now, it's come back on me. I'm even having the fucking nightmares again.

Talking to Lena then relieved and centered me. If I let her in again, I know it'll help.

I lean against the deck railing with a deep breath. Why is it so hard to do?

Words forced into me from my Ranger days make me shudder. *An emotional mind is a distracted mind. A narrow mind. Drink water. Drive on. Do your fucking duty.* I pull my thoughts in.

Headlights bounce up the driveway. Mr. Wickers's 2014 Prius quietly enters its spot next to Lena's 2005 Honda Pilot. He exits the vehicle and tosses me his usual wave, which I return. He shows up every morning before the bakery opens to keep Lena company—a distraction she doesn't need, not that she'd ever let on. My wife is too good-natured to turn anyone away. He raps his knuckles on the sliding glass door. She lets him in a moment later, waving a hand towel like a flag to usher him inside.

Our rural community believes that Lena saved Gus Wickers from his retirement depression just by being herself—warm, funny, welcoming… present.

In the early days of our relationship, I recall showing up at that same door and being awed by her beautiful, easy manner. Lena makes everyone feel at home, a truth I love and sometimes resent.

Still, it would've been a much better morning if I'd kept my mouth shut. And people wonder why I'm so quiet.

I return to the house, listen for Ruthie, and mentally review my day.

Breakfast.

Prepare Ruthie for preschool.

Clean.

Leave no later than 8:30 for my 10 o'clock meeting.

Say goodbye to Lena at the bakery.

I pause, leaning against the couch to reevaluate my plan. I *can't* say goodbye to Lena in my suit. She'll ask too many questions I'm not ready to answer. I hate the idea of breaking our routine to postpone a conversation, hate that it will hurt her.

When faced with limited choices, people resort to the unthinkable. I've seen it a thousand times. I shouldn't be one of those people, but I feel myself getting small, wanting to hide.

So, here I am. About to do the unthinkable. For the second time.

Lauren called four times before I answered. *Someone must be dead*, I thought. Why else would she reach out after all this time? No one was, though—a relief, considering I once cared very deeply for the Riley family. Now, three conversations later, she's stuck in my head like a fucking migraine.

The morning progresses as planned, except for uncharacteristic nerves gnawing away at me from the inside like embedded termites. I shouldn't have agreed to this, but I'm already committed.

The bakery is across the expansive yard, visible from our elevated barn house, but we drive the distance because it puts us closer to the driveway and our exit. I park outside the kitchen door, which provides easy access to Lena while avoiding interactions with customers in the dining room. We aren't antisocial, just on a schedule. It's our morning routine, stopping in to say goodbye, and one of the few moments I get with her.

But I can't today. "Ruthie, run inside and say goodbye to Mom."

"Aren't you coming, Dad?" she asks, unbuckling her booster seat.

Guilt joins my growing unease. "No. Go on."

She climbs out of the Jeep and bumbles through the back door, her skirt askew in her undershorts. I'll address that problem when we arrive at preschool.

Identify the problem. Solve the problem. Simple.

Yet, I've created multiple problems this morning with no easy solutions. Hiding in the Jeep to avoid Lena creates another. I should've told her about Lauren, but the pressure mounted every time I considered it until I couldn't breathe, let alone talk. It doesn't make sense—this fear of talking to my wife.

I adore Lena. My intense affection borders on unhealthy, as if it should be moderated like carbs and beer. Sometimes, I play a mental game, challenging my devotion: *what wouldn't I do for that woman?*

Sacrifice a kidney?

Easy.

Crawl across the Sahara?

Yes, though beach sand is the only good kind.

Naked?

Damn. Yes.

Show up to the station naked?

That'd be rough, but yes.

The answer is always the same. It's a dumb game.

Point is, I'd do anything for her.

That's why it's hard to talk to her. I don't want to hurt her. I don't want to be her burden. If she sees me as I am, it'll do both. Five years ago, she was a new beginning. She replaced my dark past with her warming light and made it all worth it, every scar.

I don't want to go back. But I can't move forward, either.

I close my eyes, gripping the steering wheel and twisting as tightly as my hands allow. My red-knuckled right hand is sore from punching the tile. I take a breath, again centering myself.

The immense pressure that's been building for months shows no sign of lessening. I'm suffocating, especially in this damn suit.

Ruthie races from the kitchen door, carrying her prize—cookies in a sleeve. Her skirt is fixed, but I'll inevitably have to shake her free of crumbs before preschool. But that's another solvable problem.

She jumps into the Jeep, and I assist, buckling her up.

"Dad, Tessa made me these," she reports excitedly. "Mom says she loves you."

The vise tightens, killing me slowly.

CHAPTER 3

Lena

"WHO THE FUCK IS LAUREN?" Dot's voice blares through my phone on the stainless-steel counter in the kitchen. She sounds much more awake than when she answered my 5 a.m. call with a weak, "You okay? Ruthie okay?" After assuring her everyone was fine, the confusing story poured out of me.

Now, I take a breath. "I don't know. He said it was no one, work-related, not to read into it."

Her heavy sigh scratches through the phone. "Then, don't. Lauren sounds like Lena. Ben works with a lot of people. He probably just had a brain fart. Besides, he's obsessed with you and not the cheating type. I get the emergency wake-up call, but I'm sure it's nothing. Trust me."

Her response is stern and quick—exactly what I need.

Once, Dot, Cherry, and I made a promise over a dwindling Chardonnay box, and we've kept it like a blood pact.

Always tell each other the truth, even if it hurts to hear it.

That promise got us through Cherry's divorce when she was too bitter to hear reason unless it came from us, Dot's off-the-wall ideas when she was getting her business off the ground, and my pregnancy when I was perpetually hangry. We rely on our friendship like the internet—it's there for whatever we need, when we need it.

That understanding flows between us now. If Dot says it's nothing, I should believe her. I take a deep breath, my nose filling with cinnamon and vanilla from the batter I'm mixing.

But my shoulders sink when she adds on a belabored, "But something's wrong. Not cheating, but something."

"He also said… he misses us."

"Yeah, that makes sense." Clattering ensues on her end. "Are you freaking out?"

"A little. Yes."

"What's the anxiety meter at right now?"

"Eh, six. Seven. Ish. I'm already late and so far behind."

"Threat-level-midnight," she says. "Take a breath, get to work, and I'll be there shortly with reinforcements."

"Not Cherry, right?" I ask, loving my friend but knowing I don't need her men-only-think-with-their-penises lecture today.

"God no, she'd jump all over this like a drunk spring breaker on a mechanical bull. Just me. Hang in there, babe."

We end the call, and I feel slightly better. But Ben's words still haunt me as I make the coffee, preheat the ovens, and let Mr. Wickers in.

He bows his glossy bald head. "Morning, Lena. Ready for the day?"

"Is the day ready for me?" My usual reply sounds somewhat weaker today.

He inhales deeply and looks alarmed. "Nothing's baking yet?"

"I'm getting there. Everything okay with you?"

"Fine and dandy. Saw your beau out there." He motions toward the barn. "He's as dependable as your mailman. No fuss. No muss."

Mr. Wickers and Ben once bonded in relative silence over a stalled car in the parking lot. Ben had jumper cables. Mr. Wickers had WD-40 for the caked battery acid on the terminals. The rest is history.

"Yes, he's a keeper," I say with an uneasy chuckle.

"I'll turn on the lights and check the bathrooms."

He leaves me for his self-assigned tasks. Soon, he'll take his usual table—the two-top by the window—where he'll tackle his crossword and wait patiently for coffee and a bran muffin. He's the only reason I make the bland things. No one else buys them, but I don't mind that or his arriving so early. He's become a welcome fixture around here.

I watch Ben's shadow disappear into the house through the kitchen window. *Everything's okay*—it has to be. Still, a familiar undercurrent hums through me, tensing my shoulders and turning my stomach, so I engage the mantra that helped me fight anxiety while caring for Mom: make *one* thing better. Focusing on what needs to get done will eventually lead me back to Ben. He's my end goal today. I'm determined to spend time together and talk like we used to.

Determined to find out more about Lauren, too, if only to satiate my anxiety bitches. She must be more than *nothing* to be on Ben's mind.

I concentrate on the jobs at hand—cinnamon rolls, bagged lunches, and special orders. I flip open my black, half-sized spiral notebook, similar to the one I used to keep track of Mom's medications. Loose pages fly to the floor. I scoop them up and turn to today's list, scribbled in shorthand that only I understand. Along with the usual, I have to make two bundt carrot cakes for the Thursday ladies' Bible study and a dozen limoncello cupcakes with purple icing for Millie Lewis's girls' night—special request, extra boozy.

The papers flutter in my trembling hands. Nerves claw at my insides like skittish cats. Damn it—these are not the Ben aftershocks I wanted.

Upbeat piano melodies drift through the kitchen. Mr. Wickers must be in a good mood—he doesn't play every day. But when he does, I usually move faster and smile more.

Not today.

Tessa, my baking assistant, arrives as the carrot cakes are baking and the cupcakes are about to go in. I start packing lunches.

"Am I on cookies again?" she asks dully, tying her apron.

"Would you rather make sandwiches?"

She shakes her head. "I'll make cookies."

Tessa wants to be a full-time baker when she graduates high school. She comes in every morning before school to help with the morning rush. She calls me her mentor, and I've taught her some basics. But there's little time for proper instruction.

"I promise I'll teach you something more intricate when things slow down. Macaroons, tiramisu, oh, mirror glazes."

She smirks. "How about fancy sugar work? And a chocolate soufflé?"

"You got it," I say, wondering if she's watching too much of *The Great British Baking Show*. I can't blame her—I adore that show, too.

Satisfied, she tackles the cookies.

The piano music comes to an abrupt, clattering halt—my signal that Trisha's arrived. A sixty-year-old widow with tattoos, piercings, and a bohemian wardrobe, she catches everyone's eye, especially Mr. Wickers's. She flips her long gray braid to the side as she puts on her apron.

"Don't stop on my account, Gus," she says, and he hurries to pick up the song again.

Trisha sets up the dining room and serving area. Then, she helps me finish the sandwiches.

"You're a little behind," she says, "but we'll get it done."

By seven, the café bustles with locals. Trisha handles the front, along with May and June Taylor, sisters and retired teachers who took the job to stay busy and gossip.

But I need all the help I can get. Turns out, food service and farm work don't top most people's employment wish lists, especially since our rural location isn't convenient to anything that might bring more employees my way, like neighborhoods and apartment buildings. It's all farms, woods, and swamps out here. So, though I pay well, working here most likely means a long commute, and interviewees usually decide it's too far to drive.

A hot pan of oatmeal raisin cookies clatters to the floor, face-down. I wince at the lost cookies and the angry red mark now stinging my arm.

"You okay?" Tessa asks.

Not okay. "Yeah, just another burn to add to my collection." I hold up my right arm, covered in small scars from kitchen mishaps. "You better head to school."

Tessa unties her apron but reluctantly looks at the tall metal rack of unfinished cupcakes, bundt cakes, Danishes, and cookies. "How will you get all this done?"

My *it'll-be-okay* smile flashes automatically. "With my usual magic… by taking one thing at a time."

"Mom!" Ruthie rushes into the kitchen, her rubber boots flapping together. I take in her apple green dress, sensible pink cardigan, and shorts, visible only because her dress is tucked into them on the side. I insist on under-dress shorts for playground time. I crouch for a hug and fix her fashion faux pas. She smells like syrup and feels like sunshine.

"Good morning, sweet girl." I tug her sweater together. "Got your lunchbox and backpack?"

"Yes, Mom." Her dainty hand extends for her usual drive-to-preschool treat—two oatmeal raisin cookies straight from the oven. My shoulders slump at the mess on the floor.

Tessa hands me a sleeve of cookies—two peanut butter delights pulled from the display case. "Let me know if you like these, Ruthie. Made them myself."

Ruthie beams.

"Thanks, Tessa," we say together.

I straighten Ruthie's collar, pushing her long curls behind her shoulders. "Be a good girl. No taking over story time again. Okay?"

Her pout tells me this will be a challenge—she loves hijacking her teacher's story time by reading the book herself more dramatically. Her classmates love it—her teacher, not so much. But she nods. "Okay, Mom."

I glance over her shoulder, where Ben usually waits for a goodbye kiss. "Where's Dad?"

"In the Jeep."

I downplay a gasp at his newest slight. This hurts almost as much as hearing the name Lauren. That was an accident. This is totally on purpose. Why didn't he say goodbye? He always says goodbye.

Ruthie's expectant gaze brings another forced smile. "Oh, um, he doesn't want you to be late. Love you. Tell Dad I love him. Have a good day."

"You, too!" She skips out the back door, her boots slapping together.

On second thought, I follow her to confront Ben with, "What the hell?" before demanding his usual soft kiss and monotone, "See you later."

But May yells through the serving window. "Lena, you mixed up Mr. Haywood's ham and cheese with Reverend Jenner's BLT."

"We're out of oatmeal raisin cookies," June adds, gasping at the inner kitchen. "This place is a disaster! Did a tornado come through here?"

"It was a tornado out here, too," May says. "I didn't think we'd ever catch up with the morning rush. You had us scrambling, Lena. I don't like to scramble."

All I do is scramble. Through the small window, I see the Jeep pulling away.

"Hello? Earth to Lena?" May calls, snapping her fingers.

My automatic smile reappears, though their sisterly glares give off a creepy vibe, like the twins in *The Shining*. "Sorry. Running a little late this morning."

June's lips pinch. "Now, so is everyone else."

My chest tightens with invisible pressure. She's right. The long line of construction workers, farmers, and factory workers who stop in before heading to their shifts might be late because I was.

"She's doing her best." Trisha breezes between the sisters, sizing me up with her sea-blue eyes. "But there's a shadow over your aura. Something's wrong."

"Aura, bora," May huffs. Her penciled brow shoots up her forehead.

"I'll help clean up," Trisha offers.

"Oh, no, you don't." June's hands plop against her impressive hips. "You're needed out here. We don't do clean up, anyway."

"What do you mean? You don't *do* clean up?" Dot's boisterous voice fills the restaurant as she enters the kitchen through the swinging door. My three employees return to work—or at least, their version of it— while I clean my workspace. Dot chomps her Flamin' Hot Cheetos as her glare moves from my employees to me and my mess. "Shit, it's worse than I thought."

"He left without coming in to say goodbye," I say softly.

She leans against the counter, shaking her head like she's watching a disaster movie. "Text him and tell him that was a dick move."

"Can't. Won't. I need to think and… clean this shit up."

"Why don't they *do* clean up?"

Her question makes me grunt. "June says no one over sixty should work in the kitchen because of wet floors and other hazards, so they don't clean up. Or bake. Or cook. Or take out the trash. Or mop. They handle the front—that's it."

Dot chuckles, tossing back another Cheeto. "Sounds like they're the bosses here, not you."

"Feels that way sometimes. Trisha's great, though. I'm lucky I have her and Tessa."

"You need to hire more help."

I grab the broom. "I would if I could. Most people don't want to work thirty minutes outside the city. The gas money alone works against me. Did you sign Alice's petition for the city to add a bus route out here?"

Dot grins. "Of course. Can't say no to Alice Harvey."

I smirk. "Wouldn't dare. Let's hope the city can't say no to her, either. A bus route would save us both."

Jack and Alice Harvey are the formidable and quirky owners of the farm next door. He specializes in corn, soybeans, and sweet potatoes, and she in all things lavender. She makes lavender sachets, soaps, lotions, candles, pillow sprays, and teas. Her lavender chamomile blend is my favorite, and Ruthie adores her lavender bubble bath. Five years ago, they nearly bought my property to expand her Lavender Fields Forever business, but when that fell through, we settled on a partial land lease.

We've been the best of neighbors ever since, and that's funny because I once wondered if they were serial killers. In my defense, Jack's larger than Ben, and wears dirty coveralls and boots like Michael Myers. Alice dresses like a 1950s housewife and gets things done like a mafia boss.

Raised voices pull our attention to the serving window where May and June bicker, each vying to roll silverware rather than clean tables. They argue at least once every morning.

"I usually separate them." Resting my broom against the table, I check the schedule on the clipboard by the door. "Shit. I messed up. I wrote them all in today. I have no one for tomorrow." I vaguely remember composing this schedule between helping Ruthie with her homework, ordering groceries for pick-up, and making dinner.

Multitasking is one thing. All-tasking is another. I do neither well.

Dot hovers over my shoulder, peering at my rudimentary, pencil-sketched schedule while crunching Cheetos in my ear. "Did Ruthie draw this?"

"Very funny. Ben wants me to upgrade, but I haven't had time to research it. Besides, the sisters might revolt if I put their schedules on an app."

"Who's running the show here, Lena? It's *your* business. Do it *your* way."

"*My way* would be to focus on what I'm best at—baking. I haven't created a new recipe in years." I lean against the counter, exhausted, though it's not even nine. "Sometimes, I miss making do in my mom's shit kitchen, scrounging for grocery money in the couch cushions, and spending entire days experimenting with recipes. Ben would come over and sample everything, and we'd spend the night talking. He always encouraged me, always said the exact thing I needed to hear."

"Holy shit, are you crying?" Dot huffs and tucks her open bag of Cheetos into her baggy pocket. "Lena, babe, take a breath."

I swipe under my eyes. Ben's right. Even when I'm with him, I'm not. I miss us, too.

Dot catches my gaze sternly. "Is it time to feed the animals?"

I chuckle lightly. That's Dot's code for getting me out of the kitchen, a wink-wink between us. Plus, she loves driving the ATV I use for feeding. She calls it a tricked-out golf cart, but it's much tougher and faster. "I'd love to, but—"

"No buts, Lena. I got this." She pushes through the swinging door and converses with Trisha.

Then, she drags me out the back door and slips into the driver's seat.

"What did you tell her?"

"The truth—that you needed a mental health moment. I also got her to clean the kitchen and come in tomorrow."

"Ah, thanks."

"They don't call me Boss Bitch for nothing." She motions to the lettering proudly displayed on her cap.

I snort. "Only *you* call yourself that."

"Only because it's true. I'm living proof that business owners don't have to work themselves to death. I choose my schedule and my clients and never work past five or on the weekends."

"Our businesses are completely different. I don't have the luxury of choosing my clients or not working weekends."

She revs the engine and shifts it into gear. "Choices, Lena, babe. Set some damn boundaries. If you don't have room to breathe, you'll suffocate."

It's hard to breathe already, I think, but don't say.

Mud kicks up from the back tires as she jerks the ATV into action. I grab the oh-shit handle over the door. Hugo and Penelope race and bark beside us, like engine noise cues them that it's time for farm work.

Saddletree is a frequent topic of discussion with my business-owning friends, but my issues are unique.

Ben understands, and his advice is always concrete and direct—I should close two days a week "like other reasonable businesses" and upgrade to business software, so I'm not "overwhelmed with paper-work." He wants an entrance gate and better security to prevent people from showing up when we're closed or wandering into off-limits areas —that happens a lot. He tells me that good software and better planning would prevent my "frequent mistakes," like overbooking the support groups.

He's probably right, and his advice is always welcome. We made most of Saddletree's original decisions together, like partners.

But it's hard to change what's been established—not that I have time. I'm hanging on, maybe by a fraying thread, but getting the job done. Mostly. Some days are hard, that's all.

We feed the chickens and the bunnies before taking grain to the horses. Shadow, my elderly Appaloosa, looks annoyed when we approach, as if we're intruders on his property. He flicks his half-tail and turns his gray ass toward us. I chuckle—he's always been a grumpy horse, but five years ago, he was an integral part of my reinvention after Mom died, building my confidence and teaching me to breathe again. Shadow helped me rediscover *me*. I long to tack up and go for a rigorous ride.

But, like so many things I want to do, there's no time.

The water trough overflows, so I close the faucet. The other horses wander over—River, a beautiful thoroughbred, Maxie, another gray Appaloosa, and Coconut, Ruthie's pale brown pony. Dot sets down the grain buckets, spacing them apart to give the horses room to feed.

Leaning against the fence, we watch them eat. Dot retrieves her unfinished Cheetos and frees a second bag from her other pocket, handing it to me. "Reinforcements. Comfort food."

I'd argue her definition of comfort food any other day, but not today. I pull the bag apart, toss a Cheeto into my mouth, and my taste buds alight with the synthetic flavorings.

"I checked his social media," Dot says while munching. "No Laurens. I don't think you should read into a bad morning. It'll only make you anxious. Just rely on what you know about Ben."

What I know about Ben. Her words flip a switch, flooding me with Ben-isms.

He likes a schedule and thrives on routines. He even schedules time to update the schedule (Sunday nights before bed). He's a meticulous record keeper, and since he's dyslexic, keeping everything organized and correct is like slaying his personal dragons. He updates a detailed family calendar app that syncs on our phones with his work shifts, car maintenance, doctor's appointments, and Ruthie's school schedule.

I don't always check it, but I try to remember.

Ben does what he says, says what he means, and never says more than necessary. This sometimes comes off as unfriendly to new people. But underneath his rigid composure, he's compassionate and kind. He understands brokenness and trauma better than most and has a soft spot for anyone who needs help.

He always knows what I need. He's surprised me with hot baths, beach trips, back massages, late meals, flowers, and often, the horses, all tacked up for a family trail ride. He promised to always romance me. Only lately that's fallen to the wayside.

Or maybe I've been too busy to make the time for it.

Ben shows up. He's dropped everything over fevers, flat tires, scheduling mess-ups, and once when our dog Penelope got into a thorny bush, requiring an emergency vet visit.

He may be short on words, but he's strong on commitment.

He's my perfect partner.

But lately, he's been distracted and irritable. His hearing has worsened—he hasn't told me this, but it's obvious given his frequent headaches and how often he asks me to repeat myself. Cochlear implants are the next step, but Ben seems reluctant.

So, he puts up with more migraines when he's overstimulated or has a rough day. These debilitating, stomach-turning, pounding headaches blur his vision and piss him off.

Sometimes, he lets me help. More often lately, he doesn't. The last time, he got frustrated with me for offering to rub his head despite the relief it usually gives him.

He didn't want my help.

Work adds more frustration. He received a complaint from a witness because she misconstrued Ben's inability to hear her as his refusing to listen.

Days later, a well-check call led him to find Adam—an eight-year-old, locked in a dog crate. The night it happened, he came home after midnight and held me tighter than ever, so tight I could barely breathe. He shared the upsetting story later, a bare-bones version anyway.

Adam now lives with an amazing family. His foster parents, Jack Graham and Rowan Mackey-Graham, have become good friends. But despite Adam's happily-ever-after, Ben seems disillusioned by the community service he once loved doing. That's what I suspect, anyway.

It's hard to know for sure.

What I do know about Ben, and what Dot reinforces, is that he's honest and loves Ruthie and me more than anything.

"You're right," I say finally. "It's a bad morning, but Ben loves me."

"Whatever's going on with him, he's having trouble talking to you about it. Work your magic and get him talking."

"Easier said than done."

Dot motions toward my phone pocket. "Text him. Get the conversation started."

I take a breath and do as she says.

> I'm sorry about this morning. Let's talk tonight. Dinner under the stars?

A moment later, he texts back.

> Yes. I'll be home early.

A long exhale releases my tension. "He's coming home early for dinner tonight."

Dot snaps her cheesy fingers and scrolls through her phone. "How about I take Ruthie for one of our epic sleepovers? Huh? I'll feed her nothing but junk food, show her all the scary movies, and keep her up all night."

She smirks, and I laugh—she'd never do that to Ruthie.

"Lena, babe, just kidding. We'll watch the latest Pixar and play cards with Aunt Barb. Ruthie's becoming quite the poker player."

I sigh. "What's cute today will be hell for us when she's a teenager."

Looking over my shoulder, Dot's eyes go from amused to deer-in-the-headlights. She grips my bicep, yanking me to her like a human shield and spilling my Cheetos. "Holy shit, is that *her*? Is this a set-up? What's she doing here?"

CHAPTER 4

Lena

THE COOLEST PERSON I've ever met approaches like she's on a mission she believes she'll win—squared shoulders, a determined gait, a tiny smirk, and enviable confidence. Jaye Kent is otherworldly awesome. As a graphic novelist and actress, her imagination alone puts her on a different creative level than other mere mortals. But so does her unique beauty and general ease.

"Did you know she was coming?" Dot demands nervously as Jaye moves closer up the lane. "Why didn't you tell me?"

"I didn't know. Be cool. Not weird."

She rolls her shoulders and her eyes. "How? It's Jaye Kent. What the fuck do I say?"

"Follow my lead... Hey, Jaye, it's great to see you again."

She eyes our Cheetos bags. "Ah, the breakfast of champions."

Dot's Cheetos fall to the dirt like she's lost all motor function. I scoop it up before the dogs get it. "Yep, we run on caffeine and Cheetos around here."

Her head tilts toward the stone-like woman beside me. She extends her hand. "Hi, I'm Jaye. You must be Dot?"

Dot stares in stunned disbelief at her gracious offering. *Does she not know what to do?* At her side, I push her arm out with mine like she's my puppet.

A quicker, limper handshake has never happened.

"Um, I've heard a lot about you," Jaye says, her confidence dipping slightly. "Ruthie loves your monster and alien collection."

Shadow grunts when Dot doesn't answer—even my grumpy horse understands her social awkwardness.

"Dot's a horror and sci-fi expert." An arm pinch pulls me into Dot's whisper. I roll my eyes. "And graphic novels. She loves your books."

"Thanks." Jaye's cheeks redden. Her bronze shoulders bounce lightly, bringing my eyes to the delicate inked flowers stretching over her upper chest and disappearing into her shirt. "Writing's my passion. I don't feel happy unless I'm in front of my laptop."

"I'm the same way about baking." Another violent pinch brings me closer to Dot. "For Dot, it's building or fixing things."

She confirms with a brief nod. I can't wait to tease her relentlessly about her crush.

"So, Jaye... here for your usual? There's a hot cinnamon roll with your name on it."

Her hands slip into the pockets of her high-waisted army-green wide-leg pants. She wears a buttoned-up, silky blouse that gathers at her waist, revealing glimpses of tattoos and her tight abs. This woman works out—her muscular arms make me want to join Ben for weightlifting. She's my height, around five-eight, but her short haircut makes her look taller. She gives off a serious professional vibe, softened by delicate gold jewelry and her heeled sneakers, which I hope aren't getting too muddy.

"I'll never turn down your cinnamon rolls," she grins, "but that's not the only reason I'm here."

"As I suspected," I say, stifling my bother. *I don't have time for this.*

Her pleading brown eyes land on mine. "It's down to the wire, Lena. Nothing suits us like Saddletree. The only thing close is two hours away in Kinston. Will you humor me and listen to one last pitch?"

I met Jaye last month when she showed up with a team from Diamond Studios to scout locations for their next feature, *Hunter, The Return*. My property has everything Jaye's movie needs—a beautiful country house, horse pastures, a pond, a barn, and a thick tree line.

"It's the perfect vibe—gentle beauty, rough and wild, with an undercurrent of anticipation like anything can happen here," Jaye said then (and many times since), which made Saddletree sound like the Australian outback or Grand Canyon.

Knowing little about graphic novels or horror movies, I turned to my expert, Dot. After happy cursing and ecstatic screaming, Dot explained that Jaye's best known for her graphic novel series, *The Watchers*, about a ragtag team of oddballs (some with powers) who fight supernatural forces when they aren't working their day jobs.

The Hunter franchise is semi-based on that series. The team's mentor, archaeological anthropologist Dr. Jim Hunter, investigates "haunted" artifacts and places for his research. He's like Indiana Jones, but with horror. In the first surprise mega-hit movie, *Hunter*, he investigates a demon possession. This time, he investigates a farmhouse based on rumors of witches and lore about an ancient relic that summons them.

They offered me a deal.

I turned it down multiple times. As amazing as it sounded (and as much as Dot begged me to do it), I couldn't.

Three hundred grand to film a horror flick here sounds like a jackpot, but it means closing Saddletree for two months. Too many people count on me and this place for food, peacefulness, and connection. I can't let them down.

"One last pitch," I agree, only for Dot's sake. "As long as you can pitch on the move. I must get back to the kitchen."

Dot practically dives into the driver's seat. I give Jaye the passenger seat, slightly cleaner than the open trunk littered with hay and oats.

The ATV sputters and stalls when she turns the key. A second try produces the same disappointing result.

"We're out of gas... just like you, Lena, babe," Dot says.

"Shit. Another thing I forgot this morning. Sorry."

"Let's walk and talk," Jaye says, sounding upbeat. "It's a gorgeous morning."

Our dogs greet her as she exits, and Jaye gives them enthusiastic affection, showing no intimidation over our two German shepherds. Hugo and Penelope take our sides as we stroll, barking like they have opinions on our conversation.

"Great dogs," Jaye says. "I've always wanted one, but I travel too much."

"Aw, wish you'd been here to see their puppies. UNCW adopted them for service training. Well, except one—Samwise Gamgee went home with a little boy named Adam. If Ben had it his way, we'd get all the retired service dogs and horses—"

"Lena, let her do her pitch," Dot whispers sternly beside me.

"Right, the pitch. Just don't be too disappointed when I say no again."

She smirks. "I appreciate the chance. You can't blame me for falling in love with this place."

"Before the renovation, it felt like living in a horror movie, but not after Dot and Cherry got through with it," I chuckle. "Filming a horror movie here doesn't fit the peaceful retreat we've worked so hard to create."

"Horror isn't your brand—I get it. But that's exactly why Saddletree's perfect for the story. Dr. Jim Hunter is trying to save a beautiful place and a close-knit family from dark forces. The retreat you've built here will be respected in the story and completely restored by the movie's end. And—bonus—a nice side effect of opening your home to celebrities is that they'll rave about Saddletree on social media. Your customers will be more excited than ever when you reopen."

"Maybe, but I don't want Saddletree synonymous with witches and battles against evil. This is a happy place, a safe place, free from darkness."

"No place is free from darkness. That's the first mistake people make in any good horror movie—thinking they're safe. Complacency breeds trouble."

Dot's voice surprises Jaye and me, bringing our light stroll to a quick stop.

I gawk at her, stopping short of the eye roll and arm punch I want to give. She has a chance to flirt, and this is what she says? Cherry may need to give Dot a flirting tutorial.

"It's true," Jaye says. "The moment you relax into thinking everything's okay is when it probably isn't…"

My throat tightens. *Everything's okay.*

"You have a tight grasp of the horror genre."

Dot's cheeks go brick red. This is so unbelievably cute.

I stifle a laugh. "This isn't a horror movie. It's my life. I can't shut down for two months. Too many people count on me."

"The community adores you—they'll understand. Why wouldn't they want Saddletree in the limelight?" Her bangs slide sideways as her head tilts. "If it helps, I've discussed your situation with the execs. They've authorized me to up the offer."

Dot grips my arm so tight it cuts off my circulation. *I really don't have time for this.*

She says a number I don't understand.

"What?" I ask, sure I didn't hear her correctly.

"Five hundred grand. A cool half-mil, Lena, and all you have to do is..." Jaye shrugs her muscular shoulders. "Say yes to a two-month vacation."

Hugo sits beside me and barks shortly—he doesn't believe her either.

"Um, that's ridiculous," I say, ready to argue that the studio should be more fiscally responsible.

"That's more than double what Matt Kirby made starring in the first movie. He's the actor who plays Jim Hunter," Dot says for my benefit, though I know who Matt Kirby is. Before he was Jim Hunter, he played a detective in *Nightshift*, a police drama Mom enjoyed. She compared Kirby to *"that adorable Matt Damon"* and called them both *"casually hand-some."* I never argued.

A gentle smile finds my lips, imagining what she'd say about Hollywood magic and Matt Kirby descending onto her homestead, let alone the 500-grand. Mom loved TV, crime shows, and treasures.

"Well, the original *Hunter* was a low-budget film. No one expected it to become a mega-hit. The studio's more generous this time," Jaye explains before locking eyes with me again. "They understand your concerns regarding the support groups, too. They don't want to displace anyone, either. If you agree, they'll build a new structure with bath-rooms near the pond as a bonus. And we'll keep to a schedule during filming to share the spaces. You won't have to turn them away. What do you think, Lena? Will you reconsider?"

My phone pings, and I glance at Trisha's text.

> May and June are arguing over the tip jar again. 😐

I groan.

> Please confiscate the tip jar and separate them until I get back. OMW.

"Everything okay?" Jaye asks.

"Just issues with the children," I sigh.

She looks confused. "I thought you only had one child."

"Me, too. Look, I appreciate all that you're trying to do, but—"

Dot yanks me aside, earning a stern bark from Penelope. "Don't be so hasty, Lena."

"I'm not shutting down Saddletree for your love life, Dot."

Her hands go to her hips. "It could be good for yours, too. Talk to Ben first, at least."

"I don't need to talk to Ben. He'd hate it. Plus, there's Ruthie. Do you want her having nightmares over the horror movie being filmed outside?"

"Are you fucking joking? She'll be a badass for life with this kind of street cred. Besides, seeing behind the scenes and knowing how things work will make her less scared of shit."

I shrug, knowing that's probably true.

"A half mil, Lena. Ben should know *before* you refuse it. What's the harm in asking for a little time to think? Come on. For me."

Her hopeful gleam karate-chops my resolve. Dot rarely asks for anything except time with Ruthie and free baked goods. How can I refuse? She side-eyes Jaye, who sweetly tries not to listen by playing with the dogs, and Dot's clear admiration sways me—she *really* likes this woman.

A deep breath and a quick step bring me back to Jaye. "You're right. I need more time to consider it. And, um, since Dot's my contractor and official property advisor, you should exchange numbers. She'll have many, many questions on my behalf. Dot'll let you know my final answer."

A glance between Dot and me confirms that I've scored a lifetime of favors. *Who's the boss bitch now?*

She bobs on her black Timberlands, back and forth, with authority. "Yep. I'll handle it. While you're here, Jaye, can you walk me through the studio's construction needs for the project?"

"Absolutely. Join me for coffee and cinnamon rolls?"

Blushing, they leave me. It's up to Dot now.

I pass the vegetable garden, well picked over and nearing its seasonal end. Jack Harvey helps me with spring planting—it's a massive undertaking now. In exchange, I cater his monthly poker nights (Alice refuses to host on religious grounds).

It's a rule of country life—we help each other out.

But there's no one to help me get back on schedule.

Returning to work, I race to complete everything necessary to make my deliveries, gulping coffee between tasks like a marathon runner hitting a water station. When the lunch rush ends, I load my twenty-year-old Honda Pilot with baked goods and hit the road.

I don't start to relax until I'm on my last delivery—Millie's neon purple cupcakes for her girls' night. I check the time. If I do a quick drop-off at Millie's, I'll only be a few minutes late to pick Ruthie up from preschool.

Or maybe I'll make it on time. I press the accelerator, curving quickly around the familiar country roads.

My mind drifts into planning for tonight. I'll set up the table on the back deck overlooking the pond with candles and soft music. I'll make a pit stop to Sunny's Beach Market for his favorite beer and make shrimp scampi. We'll watch the sunset and talk—*really talk*. I'll bring down his shields with funny stories and gentle questions. The more I imagine our reunion, the more I need it.

I miss him.

His small, one-breath laugh that feels like a win every time I hear it.

The way he holds my hand under the table whenever we go to dinner—maybe he'll do that tonight.

His deep, gentle voice that mesmerizes me when he talks.

I long to feel close to him again and feel ashamed that we've drifted apart in the first place.

My speed sneaks up on me, as does the sharp curve around Clayton's Swamp. I've driven this road thousands of times at higher speeds and in unfavorable weather conditions, but I'm hellishly preoccupied.

"Distraction can be deadly." Ben's words from previous driving lectures flitter my thoughts like an omen.

I take the narrow, tree-lined curve too fast and feel my rear end fishtailing behind me. *Shit, shit, shit.* I slam on the brakes too hard and overcorrect the wheel. The car jerks in nonsensical directions as the steering wheel refuses to turn where I tell it. Tires screech against the pavement, joining my screams when the car twists, and I feel inexplicably weightless.

No, no, no. Oh, God, no.

Airbags whoosh, but a brutal hit breaks against me, anyway. Sharp pains lightning bolt through me, and immense pressure pins me to the seat.

I can't breathe.

Then, darkness.

CHAPTER 5

Ben

MY HANDS STRANGLE the steering wheel hard enough to form blisters in the Riley Trust Bank parking lot. I'm nervous. I don't *get* nervous. I bump up the Jeep's AC to combat my damp palms and beading forehead. This morning still bothers me. Distracted over Lena, I failed to prevent one of Ruthie's classmates from grabbing my leg with his glue-covered hands. Preschoolers view me as a rock wall, ready for climbing, which is fine when I'm not in a suit. Wet spots linger on my pants' legs from my rigorous cleaning in the preschool bathroom.

Nothing is going right. My gut instinct assures me this won't either.

Nervous. Irritated. Distracted. The evidence is clear—I shouldn't be here, but I've already committed. *Drink water. Drive on. Do your fucking duty.*

I shake out my sore fingers and roll my head around my neck.

Refocus and assess the surroundings.

The Riley Trust Bank campus is impressive. A twelve-foot-high black iron fence surrounds the property, not unlike the type I want for Saddletree. Lena doesn't think we need it, that we're too far from the city to worry about robberies and break-ins.

But everyone thinks it won't happen to them. Until it does.

A uniformed security officer checked me in at the gate and provided a temporary badge. Top-of-the-line 4K cameras perch on every lamppost leading into the sprawling, meticulously maintained thirty-acre campus. Majestic pines and thick-leaved magnolia trees shield the area from the main roads, hiding the business like a secret. Most people probably don't know it's here—no cut-throughs or main roads.

Several buildings occupy the grounds, but I stare at the tallest one—a glass structure a dozen floors high with small trees surrounding the top floor. That's where my party awaits me.

Thirteen minutes early, I wait and reread Lena's text. Dinner tonight is just what we need, and I'm relieved she suggested it. She isn't upset with me, and tonight, I'll tell her everything and hope she'll forgive me for putting it off this long.

I silence my phone and tuck it into my jacket pocket. I repeat my rules for this meeting: *listen as promised and avoid anything personal.*

This will be a challenge. The Rileys make everything personal.

I exit my vehicle in an unwelcome train of memories—glasses clinking across the Riley's large dining table, the glass of a Molotov cocktail breaking against the Humvee that day in Afghanistan, wine glasses shattering over Lauren's hardwood floors.

Fuck. There's no way to keep this from being personal.

A cleansing breath moves me forward. *Focus.*

Cameras occupy the corners, and security guards man the doors.

The restaurant is named after Lauren's mother, Jillian, a vibrant woman consumed by fundraising events and perfectionism—her house, her wardrobe, and her daughter. At least, when I knew her. The upscale restaurant on the top floor resembles its namesake. It's elegant, expensive, and intimidating.

Scanning the room, my eyes magnetize onto Lauren like a predetermined target. Feelings surge, so I force my usual unresponsive demeanor. I prefer not to react.

But it's difficult.

Twelve years have passed since I last saw her, but closing in on her from across the room seems to pull the time together like a drawstring. She's barely changed.

My anger isn't as sharp as I expected, *as I wanted*, seeing her again. Faded memories stream in bright technicolor—good more than bad—and I hate myself for entertaining them like old friends.

This woman reminds me of everything I lost that day in Afghanistan, everything I'm *still* losing.

She stands when she sees me, straightening the baby-blue dress that clings to her slender frame like it was made for her. It probably was.

She intercepts me halfway to the table, and an awkward beat passes in mutual examination.

"Hey, stranger," she finally says, side-smiling.

Her familiar greeting tightens my throat, making it hard to swallow.

She leans in for an embrace, but I extend my hand, pushing it awkwardly into her tight stomach. She recovers with a knowing look and accepts the compromise.

"Lauren."

"Ben, it's good to see you."

The soft upturn of her smile seems genuine, but it's difficult to fathom how that can be true after our last encounter.

I can't return the sentiment. It's not good to see her. It's weird and disconcerting.

She directs me toward the table. "The years have been good to you. How come men get more handsome as they age? Hardly seems fair."

She sits first. I tuck her chair in behind her.

"Ever the gentleman. Just like the old days," she says, as I sit opposite. She leans forward, elbows on the table—something her mother often ridiculed her for—and seems to contemplate me.

"Should we address the elephant in the room first? Or should we waste more time feeling curious and awkward?"

I feel both awkward and curious. "Fine."

Her hands open submissively against the table. "We share a beautiful history. It ended in a way neither of us wanted. But it's done, and we're better people for it. Agreed?"

My eyes narrow, considering each point. "Yes."

"Let's not complicate it, then… You're here for a job. Not a tug-of-war down memory lane. Yes?"

I smirk. "Yes."

She holds her hand out again. "Lauren Riley, head of human resources."

Her fingers press softly against mine. I play her game, comforted by it. "Lieutenant Ben Wright, Wilmington Police Department."

"Alright, L.T." She grins.

My smile rises slightly at her informal use of lieutenant.

"Let's talk business." She motions for the waiter. "Comfortable with wine?"

"One glass."

She instructs the waiter. Once he leaves, she reaches for a leather binder beside her and holds it in her lap. "I've planned a light lunch to review the position's responsibilities and benefits. Then, we'll have a tour and visit Dad. He designed your incentive package himself."

"I appreciate the itinerary."

She waves a dismissive hand. "You like knowing the plan—I remember."

My nerves retreat, and my shoulders relax. I *do* like knowing the plan.

The waiter brings a charcuterie board with meats, cheeses, grapes, olives, crackers, and figs—Lena makes similar arrangements for groups at Saddletree. He pours pinot grigio into long-stemmed glasses.

She takes a healthy sip. "I heard you're married."

So much for avoiding anything personal. Still, it's good to be clear. "Yes. To Lena. We have a daughter, Ruthie." A glance at her left hand confirms the absence of a ring.

She catches me looking and holds up her bare hand. "I never married. Finding that perfect someone is not as easy as people make it seem. All the good ones are taken, and what's left are bitter divorcees or unscrupulous dolts after my family's money." She chuckles again. "Occasionally, I'll meet a nice guy, but he always ends up too clingy or untidy. You know I can't abide disorder."

Picking up Lena's discarded clothes comes to mind. "With the right person, you'd be surprised."

"It's all okay, though." Her wide smile returns but seems forced. "I love my independence. I do what I want when I want, and no one but Mom and Dad complain about it."

I say nothing, not that she expects a response.

"I have two sons." She grabs her phone, prompting the home screen with her pink-nailed fingers. Then, she shows me a picture of herself standing between two tall, well-built young men with toothy smiles.

"That's Frederick and Omar. Twins. They're Haitian." She smiles adoringly.

This information floors me. "Um, excellent."

"Shocker, right?" She tucks her phone away, sheepishly. "After… us, I took some time for myself." She sets the binder aside and adjusts the linen napkin in her lap. "Through Riley Trust's humanitarian efforts with Doctors Without Borders, I traveled to all the places we support: Indonesia, the Philippines, Nigeria, Yemen, and Iraq."

Her oration falters at the mention of a country she knows I spent time in.

She clears her throat. "It was eye-opening—you were right, Ben." Her brow twinges with regret. "I *was* sheltered and selfish... what did you call it? *Blissfully ignorant*."

"No, Lauren, I'm sorry. I regret saying those things to you. I was..." I don't know how to finish my sentence, words getting stuck in my throat over the shame and anger I still feel.

She waves this off. "It's okay. If you hadn't, I never would've gone. I met Frederick and Omar at an orphanage in Haiti. They were rambunctious eight-year-olds, and we hit it off immediately. They did that twin thing you and Becca used to do... they had their own language."

I nod. Becca and I still enjoy our warped pig Latin. It drives Lena crazy when we do it around her.

"Best thing I've ever done. I replaced you and me with Cub Scouts and soccer. They were my rebound boys." She laughs. "They're at Duke now. Omar's pre-med, and Frederick's pre-law—he's great at arguing."

"Rob must be thrilled at the prospect of a lawyer in the family."

A robust laugh erupts from her. "Uncle Rob's on his fourth wife... so, yeah."

I nod—he was on his second when we were together. I expected more. I sip my wine and sample the meats, trying to hide how her laugh pleases me. It's a relief to hear it under the circumstances.

She clinks her glass to mine. "Thanks for making this easy. I was so worried."

"Me, too."

After a long sip, I decide this is okay. I set my glass down, and my eyes find hers again. Gray in this light, like they might be invisible.

The slight rise of her bare shoulders and hopeful smile take me back to when she'd rush from her house when I pulled into her driveway and raced into my arms as soon as I exited my car. She'd wrap her legs around me and lavish me with kisses.

Lauren made me feel like the most important person in the world.

Until she didn't.

She opens the binder upside down so I can read it. "We're very excited about the prospect of you joining our team. Let's discuss what's in it for you."

A confident professional replaces the nervous Lauren of moments ago. I like her much better. She goes over health benefits, life insurance, vacations, and personal time. She gives detailed answers to my questions and elaborates on stock options and financial planning—incentives the bank provides its staff.

The proposed salary is nearly three times what I make now, but I'm not surprised.

Spare no expense is the Riley family motto.

"We've launched our new charitable giving program. Dad calls it The Lauren Project," she says, rolling her eyes. "We want to make giving easy and support the charities that matter most to our work family. It's an automatic payroll deduction for your favorite charity that we match every pay cycle."

"That's generous."

"We value our community roots and love supporting local charities. Dad claims it's the reason we've been so successful. Karma, I guess."

I nod, impressed. "You used to say you'd never work for Riley Trust." *Nothing personal. Shit.*

"I didn't appreciate it then. Didn't appreciate many things... I thought it was all about numbers and software, but it's about people. Relationships and connections are imperative to a positive work environment—that's the part I love. It's my job to nurture that for Riley Trust."

Her soft smile stirs memories of why I was drawn to her in the first place. Everyone wanted Lauren Riley back then. Her world felt larger than life, yet she was the girl next door—sweet, beautiful, and friendly. It surprised everyone that she chose to be with me, *me* most of all.

Sitting across from her, that familiar feeling of disbelief returns. "Why me, Lauren? Why now?"

"Our head of security is retiring, and he recommended you," she says quickly. She expected this question. "Remember Captain Lawrence Tenor?"

"My former training officer."

"He heard that you might be looking for a change."

I don't like people discussing my private matters, though it doesn't surprise me. News travels fast in law enforcement, and my captain knows of my recent concerns. I've requested fluff assignments lately because I no longer feel confident going on calls. It's clearer to me by the day that I *need* this job. "A coincidence, then?"

Her shoulders slump slightly. "Not entirely. We need people we trust, and your name still comes up often at family dinners. You were everything to me once—"

"Times have changed—"

"Ben, I know… but when your name came up, it felt like a chance to set things right. I've never forgiven myself for what happened. It's good knowing that you're okay. Might help me let go of the past."

"You should. I'm better than okay. I have Lena and Ruthie. It's been over a decade."

"Oh, I've missed your directness." She chuckles while catching the dampness under her eyes with her fingertips.

"Please, understand—I'm *only* here about the position. Not reconciliation. If the offer is genuinely extended, it should be because of my skills and experience, not because of us. I don't want it if you're the reason I'm here."

"You're here because you were recommended." Her mouth twists into an awkward smile. "But I understand your reluctance. We will rarely run into each other here if that helps."

"It does." *Pull it in.*

Her jaw shifts like she's been punched, compounding my regrets. Though still angry, I didn't come here to hurt her. I barely think of her anymore. She's locked away with everything else that I prefer to stay hidden.

But jobs like this don't come up often.

Her translucent eyes skip over my expression, hunting for emotion she won't find. Not because it isn't there. She's one reason I became so excellent at hiding it.

A beat passes.

"Okay. I understand and appreciate your honesty." Lauren closes the binder. "We're overdue for the tour."

We traverse the extensive campus on a golf cart. It resembles Googleplex—peaceful, amenity-rich, and more resort-like than a business. Playgrounds, picnic tables, and gardens soften the glass and hard corners of the buildings. Small groups work on whiteboards under park-like shelters. Picnic blankets speck the expansive lawn, where people work on laptops while eating.

"We like to think of it as a home away from home," she explains as she drives. "We have a small convenience store and pharmacy, cafeterias, fitness facilities, a hair salon, dry cleaner, massage therapists, a library, a daycare center, basketball and tennis courts, a swimming pool, and even a small movie theater on-site. Whatever our staff needs, it's right here for them."

The security offices delight me, though I don't let on. Everything is state-of-the-art, from the full wall of touch screens revealing every corner of the property to the fingerprint readers and bomb detection equipment. Riley Trust Bank has better resources than the police department.

"We rarely have problems here," she says. "But that's because we're prepared for them. Complacency is the worst mistake an organization can make."

"Agreed."

"Should you take the position, you will be expected to hire and spend as needed. You'll have a handsome budget." She motions me into a large office with two walls of windows overlooking gardens and a koi pond. "This is where you'll work when you aren't out with your team."

It is spacious and minimally decorated—just as I'd prefer it.

We enter her father's suite, one floor up and down the hall. When he sees me, Mr. Riley pops from his desk chair and crosses the room for a warm embrace. I don't mind. I've always had the greatest respect for John Riley, and when I was with Lauren, he was a second father to me.

"Ben, it's been too long, son." His thick arms tighten around me. "I've missed you."

"Thank you, sir."

"You look well," he says, giving me a once-over. He scratches his shaved chin. "Staying fit, I see. How old are you now?"

"Forty-two, sir."

"Hell, wish I looked that good at forty-two. Come in. What can I get you to drink?"

"Water is fine, thank you, sir." Before joining him and Lauren in the sitting area, I admire a wall of pictures. Younger Mr. Riley stands outside of the Blackhawk helicopter he once piloted. His sister, Miranda, poses from a Coast Guard helicopter. Their father stands by the guns of an aircraft carrier. Military service is a tradition in this family, and I followed in those honorable footsteps.

But maintaining my composure proves difficult when I find my formal Army Ranger portrait hanging next to theirs. The picture was taken after Ranger school, and I can't help but remember how accomplished I felt, donning my tan beret and the Airborne patch on my arm.

I was hopeful then, unscarred, and committed to two things—the army and Lauren.

It's strange seeing my portrait with theirs, though. A thin line of dust along the frame's top edge assures me this wasn't hung in preparation for this meeting. It's been here.

John puts his heavy arm around my shoulders again. "Things happened—I understand. But I never stopped considering you family, Ben. Thank you for your service."

My stone-like demeanor cracks as our former connection returns. We *were* family once. His war stories, combined with the distinguished and admirable man he is, led me to consider the military in the first place.

"It's good to see you again, Mr. Riley."

"Call me John," he says, slapping my back. "Come. Sit."

He directs me to the plush leather chairs, where Lauren occupies the long couch opposite. I sit across from her, looking away as she crosses her legs and tugs her skirt down around her thighs. She's always been self-conscious about showing too much skin—a sweet quality, I used to think.

John rattles instructions to his assistant before sitting next to his daughter.

His determined brown eyes lock on mine. "So, has Lauren dazzled you into signing yet?"

"No, sir. I don't make snap decisions."

"Of course not. You're a smart man."

He updates me on their family and asks about mine, condensing twelve years into twenty minutes. My phone vibrates repeatedly in my jacket pocket, but it'd be rude to take it out. Not wanting to offend John, I ignore the faint buzzing and soon take my jacket off and drape it over the couch beside me.

He asks about my injuries, but in a way that I don't mind, before commending me on my excellent reputation with the police department. "You've always had a heart for service."

"A mission you inspired, sir. I mean, John."

"I can't take credit. When I remember the last time I saw you at Walter Reed..." His head shakes, and he looks away as if overcome. "Anyway, your recovery has been impressive. Not many soldiers bounce back like you have, though I understand there are still some repercussions."

"My hearing. Yes, sir."

For the first time during our conversation, he glances at Lauren. "Did you discuss that part?"

"Not yet."

"We take care of our wounded vets at Riley Trust," he says. "As part of your package, we'll supplement your medical costs. I hear you're considering cochlear implants. With us, you won't have to settle for standard-issue care. You can get the Rolls Royce of implants if that's what you want."

Acute uneasiness overtakes me. I should've consulted Lena. It feels wrong to discuss this with them when I haven't with her. A headache pecks my temples. My neck burns with frustration, and my palms sweat.

People discussing me.

My hearing being a subject for conversation.

Lena not knowing anything, even that I'm here.

I stand to refill my empty water glass at the bar. The room spins. I stumble against a winged chair. The glass falls and shatters on the hardwood floor, a new memory mixing with the old.

"Ben!" Lauren rushes over and wraps my midsection, holding me up.

"Edward! Get the nurse up here!" John calls to his assistant.

"That's unnecessary."

"I insist, Ben." He helps me into the nearest chair. "Let us take care of you. Lightheadedness should be taken seriously."

Lauren fans me with papers. John gets me a fresh glass of water. The nurse arrives and performs tests—all my numbers are fine.

The spell passes, and I rise. "My apologies. I should've mentioned my occasional balance issues before discussing this offer. Forgive me for wasting your time."

"No, son, wait. That doesn't change anything," John assures me. "Tell us. What will it take to get you on our team?"

That he still wants me here after my embarrassing display stuns me.

I'm not one to allow my feelings much space. I prefer evidence to supposition, facts to thoughts, and the present to the past. But I'm besotted with emotion.

Gratitude—my employment opportunities will soon become increasingly limited.

Relief—seeing Lauren again wasn't the nightmare I imagined.

Regret over Lena and all the words I have trouble saying.

And, most unexpectedly, pleasure.

I remember what it was like to be a part of the Rileys' inner circle. They heard me out on matters I couldn't discuss with my family. For a young man with a learning disability, unsure about his future, the Rileys held up a mirror that revealed my true self and put me on a better path.

Surrounded by their familiar care and attention, I wouldn't mind being a part of their circle again. Taking this job would give me that.

No more noisy traffic situations, disgruntled citizens, or children imprisoned in dog crates.

Like he's reading my mind, Mr. Riley says, "You've done enough out there, son. You deserve something better."

John Riley understands service, family, and me in a way few people could. His words feel like permission.

Dream something better. The framed note from Lena's mom comes to mind. It led Lena to imagine Saddletree. I wonder if this position at Riley Trust could be *my something better.*

"Dad, don't be so aggressive." Lauren squeezes my arm. "Ben needs time to think about it and talk to Lena."

John raises his hands submissively. "Of course. Forgive my impatience, but I've had my mind made up since Larry mentioned you. Take all the time you need, Ben."

"I will give it my utmost consideration." I emerge from their protective cocoon and reach for my jacket.

My phone slips from my pocket and slides onto the couch.

Terror seizes me like a hand squeezing my throat. Twenty missed calls. Forty-three missed texts… Forty-four… Forty-five.

The screen alights with Jack Harvey's name. I answer.

"Ben, Lena's been in an accident."

CHAPTER 6

Lena

"HEY THERE, LITTLE LADY," a faint but familiar voice encourages my eyes to flutter. "Lena, do you hear me?"

My eyelids feel weighted as they peel open. Jack Harvey looms over me, upside down. He wears his usual dirty overalls, dingy baseball cap, and a wide-mouthed smile.

Through an incomprehensible haze, I say, "I used to think you and Alice were serial killers."

"Did ya now? We get that a lot," he says. "How ya feelin', sweetheart?"

"This is a weird dream."

"This ain't a dream. Don't you go fallin' asleep, ya hear?"

"What're you doing here, Jack?" I ask faintly, though I don't know where *here* is. My eyes don't seem to be reporting properly to my brain, like the connections have been shaken loose, probably thanks to my massive headache.

Upsidedown Jack is on his phone, murmuring to someone else while talking to me—it's very unlike him. "Is that Alice? Tell her I said hi… and thanks for Ben. Always, thanks for Ben."

Alice's extensive contacts led me to call Ben Wright to help with my parents' firearms after Mom died. Fuzzy memories swirl of bonding with him over grief and cupcakes. "He eats them in two bites."

Lightheaded, I close my eyes. Now doesn't seem the right time to talk cupcakes. *Silly goose.* I smell them in the air, though. Scents of lemon and cream cheese mix faintly with swamp and gasoline.

"Lena, stay with me, hon."

His stern words force my eyes wide open. What the fuck am I seeing?

"Holy shit!" I gasp. The dark cave I somehow imagined is my car—twisted, broken, distorted. Reality is a funhouse mirror. Everything's wrong. It's a nonsensical tangle of nature and car—tan plastic and leather, dark metal pieces, and glass everywhere, juxtaposed with ditch water, a dirt mound, and thick tree roots pushed into the side like a passenger.

The cracked windshield lies against black mud, murky water seeping through the gaps. The dashboard is crinkled like a can underfoot and spotted with purple icing and yellow cake bits—Millie's cupcakes. The dashboard and steering wheel are jammed into my lap with a deflated airbag in between. *Too much pressure.*

And blood.

There's fucking blood! Smeared against the airbag, on my shaking hands, splattered over the gauges. My hair dangles against broken roots, cutting through the car over my head.

Not over me. Under me.

Jack's not upside down—I am! My seat belt holds me in place.

"Call Ben." My voice sounds unsteady and unfamiliar. "Please, call Ben."

"Stay calm, Lena. We're trying to reach him. Everything's fine, but you shouldn't move. Help's comin'. Okay, darling?"

Where am I?

My head throbs, just trying to put the fuzzy pieces together. *Driving. Dinner plans. Ruthie.*

"Jack! Jack!"

"Right here, Lena." His massive frame blocks the sunlight as he leans in.

"Call Dot, please. Ask her to pick up Ruthie from preschool. Tell her to haul ass." Tears flood my eyes that I can't do it myself. I wriggle in my seat, desperate to pull through the smashed driver's window. I'm too cramped, too constricted, and panic surges through my broken fortress.

Ignoring the pain sharply cutting up my body, I squirm to reach my phone, lying on the dashboard. "Use my phone, Jack."

He fishes it from the dashboard nook by its charging cable. Then, with a grin, he holds it up to show me its intact screen.

"Lucky break, huh?"

I tell him my code, and I'm grateful to see the home screen appear. With his phone tucked against his ear, he scrolls through mine. He calls Dot, who answers on the first ring, and relays my instructions.

When he is done with her, he calls Ben on speaker.

No answer.

"Try again, please. Keep trying."

He obeys, saying, "Her head seems to be working, kinda, but she's startin' to freak out," into the other phone.

No answer. His voicemail clicks on. "Ben, it's Jack Harvey on Lena's phone. Call us back. It's an emergency."

A million fears rush me at once. *Why isn't he answering? Has something happened to him? Is he hurt? Or is he avoiding me? He's mad about this morning. He doesn't want to talk to me.*

I know not to listen. *These thoughts aren't my reality.* Ben wouldn't intentionally snub me. More likely, he's on a difficult call that's keeping him occupied. Years of therapy have taught me to focus on what I *know*, not what I *think*.

But Ben's never failed to answer before.

Jack laughs as he juggles the phones and eyes the mess around us. "If you'd gone one foot to the left, we wouldn't be having this conversation right now. It's a dang miracle."

One foot to the left—tree branches would've impaled my head. This doesn't help. I brace my right hand against the steering wheel to keep it from shaking.

I can't move my left hand or feel anything but immense pressure on my legs.

The pain intensifies with every passing second, like my body is catching up. Or maybe it's in my head. That hurts, too. My headache makes me woozy. Sirens echo in the distance, growing closer.

Jack narrates the action quickly. "Police are here. Fire truck, too. They'll have you out in a jiffy, Lena."

"Ben's on duty downtown. Ask the police to contact him," I say.

Jack steps away. I see booted feet coming together around the pavement's edge.

"Hey, Lena," another voice says. "You've gotten yourself in quite the pickle here."

"Donny," I say, remembering the fireman from the numerous times I called 9-1-1 when caring for Mom. "I can't reach Ben."

"Officer Bennett is contacting Wilmington PD right now. How you feeling, dear?"

"Um, anxious. My head hurts, my legs, I can't move my arm."

"Let's get you out of there, huh?"

An embarrassingly strenuous and complicated effort ensues—six firefighters with a slew of tools, two police officers directing traffic, and Jack Harvey navigating two phones and a chainsaw, which he keeps in his truck, of course. When they finally brace my neck, pull me onto a straight board, and lift me onto a gurney, I expect a squishing suck-noise, like a sardine freed from a tin.

Instead, I hear collective sighs and muted praise as they congratulate each other on a safe extraction.

"Dot's got Ruthie," Jack reports. "They'll meet you at the hospital."

"WPD says Lt. Wright took PTO today," Officer Bennett adds. "He's off duty. Is there anywhere else I can call?"

My mind blanks. *Off duty? PTO?* Maybe it's the bump on my head, but these words don't make sense. It's Thursday—Ben works on Thursdays. "Um, I don't know."

Jack checks the family calendar app on my phone with my help. Ben might be at the dentist or getting his hearing check-up.

"Nope. It says he's at work." Jack's perked brow and I-don't-know expression incite more anxiety, like we're both thinking the same thing. *This isn't like Ben.*

Donny squeezes my shoulder. "Don't worry, Lena. We'll find him. Let's focus on you right now, huh?"

They roll me toward the ambulance, rattling off questions and taking vitals. But my thoughts are on Ben, as if my racing worries might force him to materialize.

"I'll be right behind you," Jack says as they slide me inside the ambulance. "I'll stay with you at the hospital until Ben arrives—Alice's orders." He tucks my phone into my good hand.

On the drive, Donny affixes me to an EKG and oxygen. He reports his findings to me and the hospital. Elevated heart rate and blood pressure. Possible concussion. Multiple abrasions and minor lacerations. Suspected fracture. But everything he's saying and doing is secondary. I stare at my phone, willing Ben to call.

Arriving at the hospital and undergoing care feels like background noise, like I've left the TV on in the other room while I'm busy with something else. My fears compound the more time passes without hearing from him. Jack checks the hospital to ensure Ben isn't there, too, in some weird coincidence. No. He calls Ben's captain to see if he has more information. Nothing. Alice drives to Saddletree and looks for Ben on the off-chance he's home and lost his phone. Again, nothing.

With every lull, I send wonky, one-handed texts and try calling, only for it to go straight to voicemail.

I add up the time since the first call. One hour to two and now three. Desperation forms in his silence. I remember this feeling from my first marriage—that sickly unease of worry and suspicion when Mark started communicating less and coming home later, until both stopped altogether.

I'd been so ridiculously devastated, like a clown, not expecting the pie in the face, though I'd seen the pie, sensed the pie, and knew it could happen.

But no one ever thinks it'll happen to them. Then, it does.

The hospital curtain waves as shadows move by it. "Lena!" Dot's voice is unmistakable.

"Here! I'm here!"

She strong-arms the curtain and gawks at me before dropping Ruthie's hand and rushing into my arms.

"Gentle," I whisper into her pitch-black hair. "I'm okay."

"You fucking scared the shit out of me," she whispers back sternly. She pulls away and takes a long look at me with an expression that's a strange cross between seething and ecstatic.

"Sorry," I say, sinking over what I've put her through. I spot tears in her eyes as she takes me in—actual tears—and Dot prides herself on her impenetrable outer shell. *"You're the crier; I'm the badass,"* she often jokes.

She entangles me in a second hug before stepping away. "Is that mud… and purple icing in your hair? You look like shit, babe."

Ah, there's the Dot I know and love.

"Auntie Dot, bad word!" Ruthie's hands go hip-side as she gives Dot a parental stare-down—I've taught her well.

Dot raises her hands submissively. "My bad."

Ruthie's boots squeak as she climbs into my bed for a gigantic bear hug. "Mom, are you okay?"

I breathe her in and hold her close despite the aches it causes. With a warm smile, I say, "Yes, I'm fine, honey. Bumps and bruises, that's all. Thanks for being a good girl for Auntie Dot."

"Eh, Auntie Dot's being a good girl for me, too. Mostly." Ruthie gives a dismissive wave. "Your hair is messy, Mom."

I tug on my purse, thankfully salvaged by Jack from the wreck, and search for a scrunchie. It's not until I attempt to put my hair up that I realize I can't one-handed. Dot comes to my rescue, sweeping my dirty ends into a high knot.

"That's what I call a *messy* bun," she says, and Ruthie giggles.

Down the hall, Cherry calls out in her cheeriest business voice, "Thanks, Elaine!" before the confident clicks of her signature stilettos bang closer. The curtain whooshes aside with her dramatic entry, like she's taking the stage at a fashion show, especially in her silky green Ralph Lauren halter dress and strapped black heels.

With her typical swagger, she says, "Lena, you little witch! You scared us to death! Just talked to Elaine... I mean, Dr. Langston. I designed a... um, playroom for her last year—very inventive."

Her wink-wink clearly indicates a sex room. Dot and I share a glance before looking at Ruthie, who seems distracted by the buttons on the side of the hospital bed.

"Anyway," Cherry says, crossing the room for a brief hug. "She says slight concussion and probably a broken arm. Glad you got her—she's a great doctor and a *fascinating* client."

Cherry's chuckle perks my curiosity. Though Dot and I love hearing about Cherry's *fascinating* interior design clients, we'll have to save that story for a wine night.

"Sounds like you were lucky, kiddo," Dot reiterates with a gentle slap on my back.

Then, we all ask each other at once, "Heard from Ben?"

Everyone huffs and shrugs.

"No one has." Cherry holds up her phone. "Your weird neighbor started a group text. *For the friends and family of Lena Buckley-Wright— there's been an accident.* She's been updating everyone on your condition. I have to hand it to her—she's thorough. How did she get *my* number? And your brother Lucas's? And twenty-four others? How many friends does she think you have?"

I check my phone. Still nothing but a text from Millie saying not to worry about the cupcakes. "Why didn't Alice include me?"

"Didn't want to bother you, babe," Dot says. "She's organized a team to help at Saddletree with cleanup and the support groups tonight. Maybe *she* should be your manager, eh?"

I roll my eyes but can't argue.

Cherry sighs, scanning her phone again. "Can't you track Ben on your phone?"

"No, why would I?"

She scoffs. "Tracking apps keep men honest. Wish I'd had one on Warren. Could've saved myself a few years, at least. If only they made tracking apps for penises."

"Cherry!" I scold in a hushed tone while turning the TV volume up on SpongeBob for Ruthie.

"Like an activity tracker?" Dot asks curiously.

"Precisely. It'd send alerts whenever it entered restricted territory. A man-tivity tracker."

"Penis-dar," Dot offers. "That'd make bank."

Cherry puts her finger up. "It could truly make a better world, knowing what all the penises are up to—"

"Not another word about that," I spit through gritted teeth, eyeing Ruthie's distraction level. SpongeBob is doing his job, thankfully.

Cherry smirks. "Sorry, Lena. Just trying to keep things light."

"Yeah, besides, you wouldn't need that app for Ben. He's already honest. He'll be here," Dot assures us.

I relax somewhat. Cherry always defaults to distrust, anyway. I don't envy her ongoing experiences with her cheating ex. She still sees him at parties and business events, sometimes with his former mistress, Olive. Sometimes, with someone else. It's hard to heal when you're continuously exposed to the one who hurt you. Though she won't admit it, Cherry still feels broken from having her heart bashed into roadkill by that asshole. She won't be comfortable enough to love someone else anytime soon, if ever again.

"Dot's right," I say, trying to call him again. "He's just... I don't know."

"Daddy had a meeting," Ruthie shares incidentally as she leans against my pillow to watch SpongeBob.

"What meeting?" I ask.

Ruthie's shoulders bounce. "I dunno."

"How do you know he had a meeting?" I try, squeezing her against me.

"He dressed nice. In his suit." She giggles. "Jeremiah got glue on it this morning."

Worry pecks at me again, like a bird rooting in the ground, hunting for worms.

"Sounds suspicious," Cherry says, one brow cocked high on her forehead.

"Everything sounds suspicious to you," Dot returns.

"I'm a realist," Cherry defends, but her doll-like face softens when our eyes meet. "But we're talking about Ben here. It's nothing, I'm sure. He's got the least game of any man I've ever met."

I gape. "He's got *some* game."

"Must save it all for you, Lena, babe," Dot grins.

Cherry huffs. "He probably had an important meeting and silenced his phone."

"I bet he dropped it while diving into the Cape Fear to rescue a dog," Dot laughs.

"No, he lost it chasing a purse snatcher on roller skates," Cherry chuckles.

"Roller skates?" Ruthie giggles. "That's funny."

Though the laughter feels good, my thoughts wander as I try to fill in the blanks Ben's left open. I try him again. Nothing.

"Hey, Ruthie, let's hit up the vending machine," Cherry offers before winking at us, "and check out that handsome nurse I noticed on the way in here."

"Ugh," she groans but slides off the bed and takes Cherry's extended hand.

"Everything'll be okay." Dot plops beside me. "The important thing is not to panic."

"I need to know he's okay. This isn't like him."

"He's fine. Let's focus on you. Do that breathing thing," she instructs. "And the wrist thing."

I scoff but smile. During anxious moments, Ben massages the pressure points at my wrists to relieve anxiety. I can't do that now, I remind her with a look toward my immovable hand.

"Just breathe, then," she says, demonstrating a deep breath as if I've forgotten how to do it.

Maybe I have.

I take deep breaths, determined to fight back the anxiety zombies rising inside me and chomping at my reason. My husband had something important going on today, and he didn't tell me about it.

Jack pops into the curtained room. "Hey, little ladies. The nurse is 'bout to take you to x-ray. No word from Ben."

"You're still okay to stay?" I ask.

"Alice'd kill me if I didn't."

"Dot, take Ruthie home to pack a bag for your sleepover. Make it a fun night for her. I'll be here a while, and Ben'll be here any minute. Jack's here to take me home if not." When she gives me a concerned look, I force a smile. "I'm fine. Promise. Or... I will be."

Dot lets me crumble onto her shoulder long enough to breathe and scrape together my leftover bits of composure.

"I've got Ruthie," she says finally. "And *he* better have a fucking good explanation."

Soon, they leave. The room quiets. Missing Ben so sharply, I feel desperately alone. *Not fine. I am definitely not fine.*

CHAPTER 7

Lena

CATCHING sight of Ben's tall, imposing frame outside the imaging department vanquishes my fears. *He's okay.* Not lying in a ditch somewhere (like I was). Not trapped in a wood chipper. Not on a plane, extraditing himself to another country far away from me. He hasn't spontaneously combusted or been abducted by aliens.

My anxiety bitches may be troublemakers, but they have impressive imaginations.

Ben stands with Jack down the glowing florescent hallway, hands perched on his hips under his suit jacket, a stark reminder of my remaining worries. *Where was he today?*

He paces, running a hand through his hair at every turn—it's another relief to see him nervous. Not that I know what he's nervous about. Me being hurt? Or having to explain his absence?

When our eyes lock, I order myself to save my worries for later. *He's okay. I'm okay. We're together.*

Two long strides bring him to me, and I crumble into his arms, tucking my wounded arm between us like a broken wing. His strong shoulder pillows me while he breathes into my hair. Melting in his strength and familiarity, I bask in all the small, delicious things I love. His deep, gentle voice, the tickle of stubble grazing my cheek, and the soft smell of Ivory soap along his neck.

"I'm sorry," he whispers. "You needed me, and I wasn't there. It won't happen again."

His brow knits with concern as he assesses me, hands gently gripping my cheeks as he takes in my head wound. His green eyes land on the nurse behind me. "Has she been tested for a traumatic brain injury? CT scan? MRI?"

"Ben, I'm okay," I say, craving his attention. "I'm good—a mild headache and probably a broken wrist. I just had an x-ray."

My personal Superman eyes my wrist like he has x-ray vision and can see the broken bones underneath the swollen, red exterior.

"Let's get you back to your room. Dr. Langston will be in shortly." The nurse scoots ahead, leading us down the hall.

Ben takes my side, latching my good hand around his arm for support. His six-foot-two frame, wide shoulders, and crisp suit look impressive, especially with his tie still taut to his neck.

I'm a complete mess beside him, but that's our normal state. He's so *together* while I'm a walking cartoon of a woman ramming her finger into a wall socket.

Our differences stand out worse today. Mud, blood, and purple icing stain my peasant's blouse, jeans, and rubber boots. Not my best look. Certainly not with him trying out for the cover of *GQ Solider* beside me.

Ben doesn't mind our disparity, though. His hand slips over mine, pressing me closer to him as we slowly follow the nurse.

"Looks like my shift's over," Jack grins, kicking himself off the wall as we approach. "Glad you're okay, Lena."

"Thanks, Jack."

"Ben, keep us posted, eh? Take good care of our Lena."

"Will do. Thanks."

I turn to Ben when we're alone in the curtained room again. "Where were you?"

He takes a breath, watching me. "What's your pain level?"

"Moderate. Where *were* you?" There's no tone in my voice. I'm calm. But he steps back and shoves his hands in his pockets like I've accused him of something.

He matches my even voice, but my defenses skyrocket when he says, "Let's talk later when you're up for it."

"I'm up for it. It's a simple question."

His furrowed brow softens slightly. "Job interview."

"A job interview?" I repeat with surprise and relief. But it quickly translates into sadness that he didn't tell me.

He looks expectant of my typical response—an energetic, frustrating game of twenty questions to get answers that he has trouble volunteering in advance. Ben's minimal communication is endearing *sometimes*, but I've had to meld myself around it like batter in a baking tin. I shield him from social encounters I know he doesn't want. Then, I carry the conversations that happen regardless. Our private ones, too. All so he doesn't have to.

That's what couples do, right? Balance each other like a see-saw? I thought it made us a team.

But this news yanks me off the see-saw and kicks me while I'm down. I am *incredibly* hurt. An interview means job hunting, which means leaving the job he's loved for twelve years, and *I* knew nothing about it. He's making huge decisions without me. I'm *pretty* sure you're supposed to tell your spouse such things... *before* you actually do it. At least as a courtesy. Another basic marriage rule snaps and lies broken between us.

So, tears replace the questions I should be asking like they're flushing out the bothersome specks in our relationship.

"I'm your wife," comes out instead. I sign the words, too, but it's wonky one-handed.

Three words summarize my hurt feelings better than a long speech or playing twenty questions.

They get a reaction—he's surprised, and his brow knits with what looks like regret.

He closes the gap, edging between my legs, which dangle sideways off the bed. He grazes my cheek with the outside of his hand, and more tears slip over his tenderness and concern. In our warm huddle, he whispers another apology before resting his forehead softly against mine.

"You scared me," he says.

"You're scaring me," I say slowly as he watches my lips. "Why the secrecy?"

"Not secrecy. I delayed telling you. That's all."

"Why?"

"I needed to form my opinion before including yours," he says. "And..."

Behind him, the curtain's metal hooks drag along the upper bar, followed by a voice. "Okay, Lena, let's talk about your x-ray... Oh, hello."

Ben doesn't hear Dr. Langston enter. Still cupping my cheek, he says, "Talking to you is difficult."

Difficult? Another pain rips through me. No one in the history of my life has said that before—it's always the opposite. Most days, I struggle to get out of personal conversations with customers. Trisha and I have a code—*don't forget the sourdough*—for her to break me free from long customer engagements (I don't make anything with sourdough). Hell, just last week, Alice Harvey revealed her trouble keeping things spicy in the bedroom with Jack. People love talking to me. Too much. How can my husband make such a claim?

I redirect Ben's intense stare with a forced smile over his shoulder. "Hey, Dr. Langston. This is my husband, Ben."

"Ma'am. I mean, doctor." He's surprised and obviously flustered he didn't hear her.

Dr. Langston gives him a quick once over, her pink lips rising as she does. "Either is fine. Or Elaine is good, too."

Shit. I immediately think of a sex room. *Damn it, Cherry.*

My six-foot-two husband presents well, especially in a suit. It accentuates his broad shoulders and wraps his muscular arms, highlighting them. The jagged four-inch scar stretching from his left brow to his ear gives him a rugged look, especially when combined with his near-always stoicism. Dot calls him a cyborg, and he definitely gives off a robotic vibe.

What he lacks in friendly humanness, he makes up for in stature and sincerity.

Given Dr. Langston's coy smile, she thinks so, too. I wish the girls were here to see this. *No game, my ass.*

"What's the prognosis?" Ben asks, clearly missing her coyness.

She prompts her tablet. "Two impact injuries. Mild concussion—no indication of severe trauma." She points to my illuminated bones. "Two wrist fractures—"

"Intra or extra-articular?" Ben asks like he's a fellow doctor.

"Extra-articular, not touching the joint." She sounds surprised. "You know your fractures."

He shrugs indifferently and doesn't explain. The injuries he sustained as a soldier and the ones he sees every day as a police officer managing accident scenes give him a decent level of medical knowledge.

"Distal radius and distal ulna," she says, pointing them out. She unwraps a splint from under her arm and carefully sets my hand, making me cringe and tear up as the pain from moving it claws me. The Velcro and black brace reaches around my thumb and stretches to my elbow. She gently encloses it, but it still hurts like hell. She attaches a fabric sheath around my shoulder to hold the splint against my chest.

"When will I be able to move my hand again?" I ask, trying to keep my tears at bay. "And work?"

"Two months," they say together.

"Maybe longer." She side-eyes Ben like he's a man-sandwich. "You'll experience pain, bruising, and swelling. The splint will limit movement but adjust as needed. We need the swelling to go down before putting on your cast—that'll happen next week, and it'll be on for six. You may need physical therapy. What work do you do?"

I consider puffing up my resumé for her. But all that comes out is a weak, "I'm a baker."

"Take a leave of absence… unless you can bake one-handed."

My eyes narrow. *I can bake one-handed. Can't I?*

"Understood," Ben says. "Pain medications?"

They review my pain management schedule and care like they're the adults here.

That fits since a pained haze of anxiety forces me to zone out.

How can I *take a leave of absence at* my *business?* I brainstorm my simplest recipes and how I might finagle them, barely using my left hand. Dumping my bag, I find my black notebook and awkwardly flip through the worn, loose pages until I come to tomorrow's orders and events. It's a light Friday, thank God. Two cake orders and two groups are scheduled—a dog training class and a trauma support group. It won't be easy, but I'll find a way to manage. I *always* do.

But my lofty plans disintegrate as I struggle to return my notebook to my bag. *Fucking hell, how will I do this?* Just making the lunch boxes feels like a Herculean feat. So many people are counting on me—how could I let this happen?

Worse, Ben finds me "difficult" to talk to? Who cares about an inoperable left hand or the work catastrophe it'll cause when my husband can't talk to me?

Millie Davis just went through a rocky divorce—hence, the boozy girls' night cupcakes slathered inside the Pilot. She'd focused so entirely on her three young boys that she hadn't noticed her husband drifting away from her. Over macadamia nut cookies at the café, she told me they hadn't had sex in a year.

An entire year!

"Didn't you miss it?" I asked when she overshared. "The sex? The closeness?"

"I was too busy to miss it," she admitted regretfully. "By the time I realized something was wrong, he'd already fallen for someone else."

My eyes close as my thoughts spin into an anxiety tornado. *I can't let that happen to us. I can't make fifty to seventy-five sandwiches one-handed. I can't make myself less difficult, whatever that means, or make Ben talk to me. I can't—*

"Lena." Ben's voice stills my mental storm.

I open my eyes to find him staring at me.

"Breathe." His hand latches over my good one—I hadn't realized it was shaking or that my breathing had become hurried. I flush with panic and embarrassment as Dr. Langston looks on, assessing me.

"Are you alright, Lena?" she asks.

I nod, taking deep breaths in and out, slowing myself down, and feeling even more disappointed. The panic I've battled all day has finally won.

Ben presses my good hand to his chest under his tie. He holds it there flat so that I feel the gentle rise and fall of his breathing. He glances over his shoulder at Dr. Langston. "She's fine. Are we done?"

"The nurse will be by with your follow-up information and paperwork."

"Thank you, doctor," Ben says as she leaves. The room quiets again. "Focus on me. Everything's okay."

"No, it isn't. Nothing's okay if *we're* not okay."

His brow knits. "We're fine. Just breathe."

I match his breathing—slow, steady, and calm. Just like him. Soon, I no longer need to tell myself to do it.

"Been a long time." He sounds proud. Going from a panic attack every few days to every few years makes me proud, too. But it stings, resetting the sign in my head—*Days Without a Panic Attack, 0.*

My therapist, Dr. Reese, would say I'm being hard on myself. That's a problem for me and probably most women who give a shit about anything. Pushing too hard. Thinking too much. Trying to please everyone.

That's not living. That's doing. Look at the facts, she'd say. *Rough morning. Car accident. A long recovery ahead. And sudden uncertainty. Give yourself a break.*

Ben often says something similar when I get like this, especially when I have so much to do that I don't know where to start. "What's most important?" he usually asks, clearing my focus. Right now, it's this —us, together.

"It's been sneaking up on me all day, even before the accident," I admit, still breathless. "It's a wonder I lasted this long."

"Tell me about it," he urges. "Tell me everything."

"You first, when we get out of here. Please."

"Yes. Understood."

My hand slips down his chest, bringing me back to this morning when I only wanted to stay tucked against him in bed, safe, warm, and uncomplicated. "Tell me you love me, Ben."

His left brow perks in surprise at my request. But the nurse comes in before he gets a chance to say it.

CHAPTER 8

Lena

THE RIDE HOME begins in silence, which is weird, considering we have so much to say. The pain meds kick in, making me mellow and inexplicably sad. I don't have the energy for our usual communication games and shouldn't have to wrestle it from him. He knows what I need.

"You should close Saddletree temporarily." His knuckles protrude against his tight grip on the steering wheel, and his right hand is red and swollen.

"What happened to your hand?" I ask.

His fingers stretch against the wheel, and he looks almost surprised. "It's nothing."

I huff—it's the answer I should've expected. "I can't close. Alice has tomorrow covered with a bare-bones menu. I'll figure things out then."

"What's to figure out? You can't bake like this, and you don't have enough staff to compensate for your absence."

"I'll make do. Somehow."

He doesn't like my bullshit answer, but it's all I have right now.

We stop at Sunny's for my prescriptions. While I wait in the Jeep, he runs in and returns with the pills, a Dr. Pepper, and Reese's Peanut Butter Cups because he says, "Your blood sugar might be low."

When he learns I haven't eaten since breakfast, he detours to Elizabeth's Pizza for carry-out—not the dinner I planned, but nothing about today has gone right.

Heading out of Wilmington, he finally says, "Riley Trust Bank wants me to be their new head of security for their Wilmington campus. Outstanding benefits. Better hours that'll align with the family schedule. Nearly triple my current salary. Incredible healthcare. There's an on-site preschool. Ruthie could go to work with me."

"Ruthie loves her school, and she helps me in the kitchen in the afternoons. It's our time."

"It'd be there *if* we need it," he amends.

I peel open the peanut butter cups and shove one into my mouth. "Riley Trust Bank, as in Riley Trust Park with the baseball fields and the Riley Trust Amphitheater downtown? That's a big deal."

"Yes. Thirty-five hundred employees. A thirty-acre campus. I'd manage all their security systems from their campus to their network, handle employee background checks and situations, and provide private security for the family." He smirks slightly. "It's nothing like being a mall cop."

"I wasn't thinking mall cop. You'd hate that."

"Say again?" He leans closer, keeping his eyes on the road.

I repeat myself louder, and he nods.

"I wouldn't even wear a uniform. Business casual."

A smile drifts up my cheeks, imagining Ben in khakis and button-downs every day. "You sound interested."

"I wasn't initially, but I am now."

"It sounds amazing… if leaving the police department is what you want. Is it? It must be since you're job hunting."

"I wasn't job hunting. They approached me." He twists the wheel like he's wringing a wet towel. "I know the family."

"The Rileys? Are you hobnobbing with rich socialites behind my back?"

"No," he answers quickly, unamused.

"How do you know them?"

I expect a work story. He met Alice Harvey after she pulled her pepper spray on a purse snatcher at Independence Mall. The first time we met, he pulled me over for speeding. *And erratic driving*, he's quick to add whenever I tell the story. Ben meets many people through work —it's the nature of what he does.

So, hearing, "I dated their daughter," makes me choke on chocolate and peanut butter. I scramble for the Dr. Pepper but fumble with it one-handed. Ben opens it for me. I take a long swig.

Through Dr. Pepper burps, I sputter, "Let me guess… Lauren?"

"Yes."

"Ben…" His short name sounds longer with disappointment trailing in my voice.

"It was a long time ago. It doesn't matter."

"Yes, it does. An ex-girlfriend offers you a dream job, but you can't tell me about it because *I'm* suddenly difficult to talk to?"

"You're difficult to talk to because you never have time," he sighs.

"I would've made time. All you had to do was ask. I shouldn't be blamed for your *deliberate* deception."

"Deliberate?"

"Yes, not coming in to say goodbye this morning because I would've asked about the suit. Not telling me about the interview, let alone any history with Lauren Riley, and brushing off who Lauren was this morning when you said her name instead of mine. You *deliberately* mislead me."

He hesitates, rubbing his temple with his left hand. "I… yes. I did. I'm sorry. It seemed easier not to tell you."

His shoulders slump as he turns into our driveway. Every bounce along the well-worn gravel and dirt path sends pain ricocheting up my arm, enough to bring tears to my eyes, though that's not entirely why they're there.

Easier not to tell me? Like I'm his parent, and he doesn't want to get in trouble. Or his boss and he's been slacking off. Or maybe it's because I'm his wife, and he still holds feelings for Lauren Riley.

Why else wouldn't he share this with me?

Pain splits through my injured hand as my swollen digits tremble. Another wave of panic crashes over me, knocking me into a spin. *Breathe.*

Control your emotions, or your emotions will control you. My therapist's words flood into me.

I twist toward the passenger window, wrestling tears. Again. *This isn't me anymore!*

I fixate on the world outside the window. The late summer sun sets behind the property, highlighting the glistening garden, the peaks of the house and barn, and the pond. I spy Jack Harvey on his ATV, refilling my empty gas tank and feeding my horses. Alice's minivan assures me that she's inside, helping with clean-up. Mr. Wickers stands sentry-like on the café's patio, holding a bin of dirty dishes while Trisha fills it. I toss them a weak wave as Ben drives by.

My neighbors are fucking adorable. Like Dot and Cherry, they're people I wouldn't have hand-selected but who make me eternally grateful that I'm not in charge of such things. They've slipped into the empty spaces left behind by those I've lost, shoring up my foundation and making me stronger with their love and support. I don't know what I'd do without them.

Ben's the family I chose—a decision I've never doubted. We found each other exactly at the right time, and everything changed for the better.

Still, a bad feeling wriggles inside me, like a demon baby struggling to break free of its tethers to cause mischief and destruction. I don't like comparing my previous marriage to this one—they're night-and-day opposites. But I'm reminded of my first struggles with Mark. *He's keeping things from me. Pulling away. Blaming me. Letting irritation overrule love.*

This isn't us. And it scares me to death.

"Pain level?" Ben asks as he turns off the engine.

"Moderate but worsening... It hurts more that you couldn't talk to me."

His emerald eyes squint as he studies me. *Is he concerned? Regretful? Annoyed?* I can't tell.

And—another first—I'm tired of asking. Getting him to talk feels like an endless game of tug-of-war that I'm losing. It's okay that he'll never be one for small talk, that he views socializing as a task, not a pleasure, and that I have to soften his unfriendly vibe by assuring people that he's just quiet—Ben will never be the life of the party. But until now, I never thought his distance extended to us. To me.

He says nothing, as usual.

I exit the Jeep with a huff. It definitely won't be the night I planned. He's not even the husband I know—*my* Ben isn't dishonest. He doesn't attend events without logging them on the family calendar. He doesn't keep secrets or stay in touch with old girlfriends. He never even talks about them, as if meeting me moved them into his *don't-care* file, lost and forgotten.

Of course, I know they're out there—nameless, faceless, lucky beings who had their chance to kiss those lips and touch those muscles and lost it. That's how I like to keep them—nameless, faceless—because those lips and muscles belong to *me* now.

Lauren. This morning's failed encounter inflicts fresh stabs into my sore gut. Is it wrong to hope she's an ogre who smells like beer cheese and cat litter?

Maybe. Yes. But it's not wrong to expect more forthcomingness from Ben. *Wait, is that a word?* It damn well should be.

I trudge up the circular staircase leading to our above-barn home. Ben follows, carrying the pizza and meds, saying nothing. Hugo and Penelope join us, ready for dinner and relaxation.

But I can't relax, not with my head spinning.

I kick my boots off in the mudroom and retreat to the bedroom, closing the door behind me. All the things I should be doing ping through my thoughts—shower, plan for tomorrow, and reach out to my staff. I plop onto the bed's edge instead and cry. A gigantic purge to wash this shit day away.

Too many feelings. Too much pain. Too many anxiety bitches. It's all too much.

I tell myself it's a simple miscommunication, and couples get over these minor mishaps all the time.

But this feels more substantial than that. Like the ground is shaking under every good thing we've built together.

Of course, that could be my exhaustion talking. Or the pain. Or the meds.

The door opens. I swipe my tears one-handed, wishing he'd stayed away long enough for me to be less of a mess. No wonder he calls me difficult to talk to—I turn into this.

He sits beside me, sliding his hand over mine. "I'm sorry. I should've told you."

"You've always been so honest with me—that's what drew us together in the first place. If you'd asked me yesterday to name my top five things Ben Wright would *never ever* do, lying to me would be first, and hanging out with an old girlfriend would be a close second." I twist on the bed to face him, bringing my knee up between us. "Help me understand why you thought leaving me out of this was okay."

"It wasn't." He sighs. "I didn't want complications over a job I didn't think I'd want and a past better left alone. That's all. I planned on discussing the job tonight over dinner once I had all the information."

With a deep breath, I feel slightly better. This sounds like Ben. He prefers to keep things simple. "So, I shouldn't worry about Lauren being an ex-girlfriend?"

He recoils like I've said something ridiculous. "No. If I could remove her from the equation, I would. I'm considering the job. Nothing else. My heart belongs to you and Ruthie."

Through a relieved smile, more tears emerge, cleansing me of these preposterous ideas. I've given my anxiety bitches too much room to speculate.

"I'm sorry," I breathe out.

"No, it's my fault. I should've talked to you." He locks eyes with his sternest, most sincere expression. "Forgive me for creating doubts and not being forthcoming."

"You're forgiven." The words fall from me like I have no choice. It's such a rare occurrence that forgiveness is automatic when Ben asks for it. I can't think of anything I'd deny him. "But will you tell me all about it? I need more information."

"Understood. Whatever you need." He fiddles with the loose scrunchie and tugs it out, sending my purple and mud-stained locks around my shoulders. "You'll need help washing your hair. I'll draw a bath."

I'm about to protest—a shower would be quicker, and I'm tired.

But, he adds, "Soaking in warm water and Epsom salts will be good. You'll hurt like hell tomorrow."

"Really?"

"Yes. The soreness is always worse on the second or third day."

"Something to look forward to, then." I try loosening the knot that holds my sheathed arm in place but fail.

Ben takes over. "Let me help."

He presents like a tank but is incredibly gentle. I love this about him. His careful attention reminds me of him braiding Ruthie's hair, his big hands weaving the pieces together so delicately that she never flinches.

I don't flinch now, even as he maneuvers me from the sheath and my shirt. He traces the reddish lines crossing my chest—marks from the seatbelt. My chest feels sore with their discovery, reminding me that it should hurt, too.

With a heavy sigh, his eyes trail the marks on my arms and shoulders—not ugly bruises yet, but they will be. He kneels and removes my jeans next, finding more of the same.

"You're right. A bath is a good idea." I nibble my inner lip, anxiety rising and tears streaming as he tallies up my injuries.

He holds me around the waist, resting his head against my stomach. "It'll be okay."

"It's going to be tough on me," I admit.

"Tough on us," he corrects with a wry smile. "But it'll bring us closer."

A chuckle eases from me. "That almost sounds romantic."

He smirks again. "I *am* helping you get undressed and drawing you a bath."

I tug at his tie one-handed. "Will you get in with me? And bring the pizza?"

"That's already my plan."

My tension releases. This is us—casual, sexy, messy us.

We rarely argue, anyway, and never with raised voices—an eye-opener given my volatile marriage to Mark. He and I mastered shouting matches the way other couples do team sports—with intense practice. All those fights and yelling only led to something worse: absence. Marriages die the moment a couple stops talking and spending time together. The only thing left after that is giving up.

With Ben, I've learned the rules of a good marriage. For one thing, yelling isn't necessary or helpful. Talking and listening work more miracles than fighting ever could. His calmness offsets my anxiety, and my personality eases him into talking. *Usually.* Marriage is a delicate balance of two personalities, and we appreciate rather than resent our differences. Our disagreements don't follow us, either. Letting go is better than keeping score. And we're like-minded, most of the time.

Today was a blip on an otherwise clear radar. We'll get over it quicker in the tub.

That's another rule for a good marriage—never miss an opportunity for closeness. I haven't been good about following that one lately, but I'm determined to make up for it.

He holds my good hand as I step into the bath, the almost-too-hot water easing me at once. He cushions my splinted hand with a towel on the side edge. Then, after handing me a slice of pizza, he climbs in with me.

CHAPTER 9

Ben

TUB LENA RELAXES INSTANTLY. In two minutes, she scarfs down an entire pizza slice before twisting and backing herself between my legs. My hands slip around her, freely roaming over her familiar places. Naked Lena is one of my favorite versions of her.

I love all her versions. Lena is beautiful, sexy as hell, funny and warm in a way that brings comfort to any situation, intelligent, creative, and a good person—everything I want.

She's also a multiverse, complicated and intense, ruled most often by Busy Lena—my least favorite and most difficult to handle because she tends to overthink, overwork, and overplease.

I like things simple. Busy Lena makes things hard.

This applies especially to Saddletree. She feels she has to do it all, from the day-to-day to the deliveries to the damn dishes. When I suggest automating aspects of Saddletree's management, delegating more to her employees, or cutting back on hours and offerings, I'm met with frustration. No time is her most frequent excuse. Already spread thin, she's pulled in too many directions, incapable of making necessary changes. Her people-pleasing and unrealistic expectations come at a cost.

That cost is usually me.

I don't require much. But closeness with Lena has become a natural necessity for me. I almost lost her today—a stark reminder of how much I love and need her. I need more of this. More of her. And enough love and connection with my wife to feel like we could handle *anything* together.

Because *anything* is coming.

I should've told her everything long before today, but my confidence in us has slipped. What holds me back from her *is* her. How am I supposed to feel secure in us when I barely see her? It's hard to feel good about the woman you love when she constantly chooses everything over you and doesn't notice that it's been weeks since we've had a real conversation or even been naked together.

She doesn't have time to miss me, either.

But it affects her, too. Busy Lena is all about tasks and forced smiles. She doesn't relax or slow down. Busy Lena gets by but barely breathes. I help with that when she lets me.

Right now, though, I glimpse the Lena I love most—Present Lena, radiant and smiling. Holding her like this comforts me and makes me think everything's okay.

It isn't, though. I fucked up today—my deception *was* deliberate—but, to her credit, she's here, naked in the bath with me.

"When do you have to decide?" she asks as I shampoo her hair. "Or have you already?"

"I won't decide anything without you. We have a few weeks, but I can ask for more time if needed."

"Wow, that's generous of them."

"They're motivated." Before she asks why, I add, "But it's a major decision. Without your full support, the answer is no."

She leans her sudsy head against my shoulder and peers up at me. "I want you to be happy. Will this make you happy?"

"Happiness isn't a factor. You and Ruthie make me happy. Work is work."

Even upside down, I decipher her expression—the cocked brow and her bold, questioning eyes. She dislikes my answer.

"Ben, working to live is one thing, but no one wants a job that makes them miserable. Be honest—you haven't been happy being at work in a while."

"I've had some setbacks."

She scoffs and twists in the tub to face me again. "No, you've had struggles. The headaches. The hearing issues. Seeing people at their worst. Don't understate what you've been through."

"Fine. Struggles." I pick up Ruthie's watering can and rinse Lena's hair. Still facing me, she closes her eyes to keep the soap from getting in.

Clearing her face of water, she says, "It's okay to make a change if you want one. And there's no rush to figure out what that should be. If this offer excites you, let's talk about it. But you don't have to work for the sake of working. Or take a job you're lackluster about for a larger salary. Saddletree's doing great—"

"That could change," I point out, motioning to her arm. "I appreciate that we live comfortably, thanks to Saddletree, but I provide consistency and stability."

"*Always*, even without a paycheck." She grins. "But you're a police officer—anything could happen to you, too. My point is, you don't have to work. Let me be your sugar mama."

I groan.

She laughs knowingly. "You have breathing room, Ben, and you've earned it. Why not just… retire?"

Retire? Retirement is for seniors, not mostly capable, highly qualified, and self-sufficient forty-two-year-olds with a family. She claims I have breathing room, but it doesn't feel like it.

Tub Lena morphs into Anxiety Lena as she studies me. "Okay, don't retire. Work at Saddletree. You could take over all the support groups. I know how much you love them. I could really use the help—"

"No. I mean, yes, you do. But no."

"No?" Her face contorts at my quick and curt response. "Why not?"

"I… just can't." I don't want a handout, and I shouldn't have to accept one just because I'm losing my hearing. Besides, butting heads with her regarding Saddletree might strain us, and I don't want the chaos.

But I can't tell her this—she'd only argue. I deal with conflicts every day and usually diffuse them. But, when it comes to Lena, disagreements make me feel vulnerable and unnerved, overrun with fears of saying or doing the wrong things. I long to get small, to avoid either of us getting hurt.

Now, I see the pushback coming. Worry lines shadow her face. She removes herself from my grasp and leans on the end of the tub again, as far away as possible, while watching me intently.

"Can't because?" she pushes again. "Saddletree is *ours*, remember?"

Saddletree hasn't felt like *ours* since the business grew, and Busy

Lena took over, shutting me out—another thing I can't say. "I'm proud of what we started, but…"

She leans forward. "When did you stop telling me what you're thinking?"

"When you stopped asking."

She recoils again, filling me sharply with regret. *When did I stop talking to her?* It happened slowly. One less conversation here, fewer words there. Then, all at once, after Adam, I went silent.

"Lena, I'm sorry. I love Saddletree, but I don't belong here. *Professionally.*"

It's a vague truth. I don't elaborate. It's better for her to come to her own conclusions, and there are plenty of obvious reasons to choose from.

That I'm a cop, not a business owner.

That food service isn't my skill set.

That I'm socially awkward and terrible at chitchat.

Even organizing her groups could be handled by purchasing appropriate software if she'd take the step.

There isn't a real place for me, and she seems to understand that because her face softens as she considers it.

"Fine." She drifts closer. "Tell me more about Lauren and the Rileys. How did this happen?"

"A phone call."

Her eyes narrow. "From Lauren? When was the last time you heard from her?"

"Twelve years."

"How long were you two together?"

"A few years."

"Years?" Her blue eyes go wide. "How come you've never mentioned her?"

"Seemed irrelevant. Why should I?"

"Um, because knowing about significant exes provides an important backstory in a relationship."

"No, it isn't. What does it matter?"

"It matters now," she protests. "And because you haven't told me about her, I have to play catch-up. Where did you meet her?"

I grab a washcloth and soap it up. "High school. The Rileys were family friends."

Her eyes go even wider. "High school sweethearts?"

"No. Well, sort of. We were friends first. I was older so—"

"How much older?"

"Two years. I waited until she was eighteen."

She gawks. "What? Why? That never matters in high school."

I shrug. "It mattered to me. It felt like the right thing to do."

She groans. "Friends first. First love. Together for years. It sounds perfect, like one of Cherry's romance novels."

"It was far from perfect."

"Well, tell me about her."

She inches closer, her legs butting softly against mine under the water. Still, she gives me a cock-eyed glare. It's her *go-on-Ben* look—I see it often. But this territory seems fraught with landmines. I don't want to discuss Lauren tonight—or any night.

Lena and I have varying views on what's need-to-know. She told me too much information about her former marriage to Mark, unsolicited. I would've preferred not to know.

But Mark isn't a factor in our lives, and Lauren suddenly is. So, the day's guilt catches up to me.

"Fine, we were good friends," I say, gently running the washcloth over her cheeks and neck. "She helped me with algebra. We connected over unrealistic family expectations. She didn't want to go into her family's banking business. I didn't want to go to college. The Rileys have a long history of military service that I admire—her aunt, father, and grandfather. That influence led to my decision to enlist."

Her mouth drops. "So, you didn't *just* date their daughter. How can you call your history with her irrelevant?"

I wince. "My relationship with Lauren set me on a path, yes. But my decisions were my own. I'll have little contact with her if I accept the position." I slip the washcloth over her shoulders and chest, hoping to distract her.

She moves closer but narrows her eyes, dissatisfied.

"Please, can we just drop it?"

"No. Tell me how it ended."

"We broke up."

Her eyes narrow. "*That*, I figured out. Why?"

"Forget it. I won't take the job. It's decided."

Lena scoffs and gives me her serious look again. "Ben, if she's irrele-vant, why is she hard to talk about?"

"I didn't say *she* was irrelevant. I said our history was. We didn't work out. That's all."

She nods, biting her lower lip like she's processing the information. She pulls the washcloth away and runs it over my chest with her good hand, softly soaping my scars and defects with the same admiration she always has when she sees me.

This woman loves me.

With all her versions and complications.

Deeply and intensely.

I knew she truly loved me the first time she saw my chest. I'm not easy to look at. I'm rough and deformed, a patchwork pieced together. But Lena had nothing but love in her eyes. Still does.

She'll never fully understand what that meant to me. What it still means to me. To feel loved and accepted in one look.

In unaware affirmation, she grins sweetly as her hand circles my shoulders. "Wish I had two hands for this."

I tug her closer by the hips. "I'm supposed to be taking care of you."

"We take care of each other. I trust you. If you say the relationship doesn't matter, it doesn't."

Still, disappointment creases her brow as if she knows I'm holding back.

"Just... Is there anything else I should know about her or your past? Anything... I don't know... significant?"

Answers ping in my head like ricocheting bullets. "No. Nothing."

She accepts my answer with relief. "I'm here for you. Maybe it doesn't seem like it sometimes, but say the word, and I'll stop everything. I'll stop the world for you, Ben. Nothing's more important to me than you and Ruthie. If there's anything we need to talk about—"

"There's nothing."

It's been a tough day. The focus should be on Lena's recovery— not Lauren Riley or my bullshit.

But, yes, there are things I need to say.

My hearing has worsened, pushing me toward surgery I don't want.

My days on the police force are numbered because I no longer feel I can do the job to my standards and have lost motivation.

The offer is timely and the best I'll get, but complicated. I don't know what to do—a rare and unsettling situation that makes my chest tight with pressure.

And Lauren Riley dredges up unwanted feelings.

I don't want to think about it anymore tonight.

Lena sighs, scooting closer and awkwardly holding her injured hand above the water. She moves the washcloth under the surface, running it along my stomach and over my legs. "Okay. But we should talk more about the offer. It's worth considering."

My hand drifts up her leg under the water. Her smile returns like the sun peeking through dark clouds.

"Later."

Her lips coil into a coy grin. "I just want what's best for you."

I reclaim the washcloth and gently pull her into my lap. She straddles me, nestling like she's made to fit there. With her wounded arm secure on my shoulder, she slips the other around me. Her fingertips feel like flower petals over my old scars.

Lena has always loved me just as I am.

"You're best for me," I say, studying her. I love looking at Lena. Her damp hair messily frames her oval face, highlighting her expressive eyes. I imagine millions of thoughts circulating behind them like stars in an expansive universe. "I almost lost you today."

Her forehead falls against mine. "I'm sorry."

"Promise me, you'll drive the speed limit from now on. Please. I don't mean it as a judgment, just a request. I see too many accidents, Lena."

"Yes, okay. Promise." She tucks her bottom lip under her teeth, practically forcing me to kiss it free.

My lips drag over her determined chin and that place on her neck that makes her breath hitch every time. Her body melts against mine the more I kiss and touch her. Relaxed Lena—it's been too long.

"Pain level?" I whisper between us.

"I'll hurt tomorrow," she says breathlessly before easing me inside her. "Promise me… no more lies."

A low rumble rises through me at how good she feels. She could've asked me anything, and I would've said yes. I only hope she never asks the wrong questions. "Yes, I promise."

Water sloshes between us as she rides me, her leg muscles squeezing me into her. She cries out when I grab her ass and bring myself deeper.

Sex with Lena isn't just a highlight, but a need that five years together hasn't stifled. The closer we are, the longer we're together, the better it gets.

But our closeness proves elusive most days. It's a fluid thing that slips through our fingers and evaporates with every missed opportunity. The more we ignore it, the less often it appears.

It's here now, though, and not to be wasted. Tonight's about her healing *and* ours.

My fingers graze her stomach and then go lower, touching her exactly the way she likes. Her back arcs, her eyes roll before they close, and she nibbles her bottom lip—I love turning her on. Watching her, feeling her, delighting in her little trembles, I can tell she's as starved as I am.

Our distance lately isn't because she doesn't want me. It's *never* that. Just like my secrecy isn't because I don't love her—it's the opposite, really. Her breathless smile and her dilated eyes, bright blue and seeking, prove her devotion. She looks almost giddy, laughing over the rough waves of the tub water and taking me like a rediscovered treasure.

Lena loves me. Almost securing the thought in place so I won't forget it, she leans over me, kissing the scar on my forehead, my cheek, my lips, and slides her good hand around the back of my neck, pulling me closer. She keeps her eyes on mine, smiling, with her climax like it's a journey she wants to take me on. I soon follow, deep and full.

Later, in bed, holding her to my chest, I know I have to trust her with everything. She's the heart of me, and she deserves the truth.

Tomorrow.

CHAPTER 10

Lena

RUTHIE GIGGLES when my eyes flutter open. She lays against my pillow, our noses nearly touching. She smells like syrup and apple juice —her typical perfume—and grins like she knows a secret.

"Tell me what I was like as a baby again," she requests, her green eyes giddy-wide.

A groggy second passes before my usual spiel emerges—she likes this question. "You were born on a rainy Tuesday in the middle of the night—you've always been a night owl. You didn't take naps or sleep through the night like other babies. You were too afraid of missing anything, like we were having parties when you were asleep—we weren't. We were sleeping when you were asleep, silly goose, but FOMO was real for you. Books have always been your favorite toys. You used to stack them and make book teepees. Once you made a book tower that reached higher than you."

She giggles again with a low tummy rumble. "Book Jenga."

"From day one, you've loved animals, even the squiggly, buggy kinds, and rap music—for the beats, not the bad words. Late at night, it's the only thing that soothed you. Your first audible words were "Dada" and "Dot," though I try not to take that personally. Then, you said "taste" when helping me in the kitchen. But you were signing before that. You've always been smart and sweet and a handful of sunshine."

I tickle her belly with my working fingers, and she laughs, writhing in the bed covers. The bed moves, and pain rips up my hand and arm like the slip of a sharp knife. *Shit.* Ben's right—I hurt like hell. Every muscle aches like I spent yesterday doing advanced CrossFit.

Confusion hits me next. Bright sunlight streams in the sliding glass doors leading to the back deck.

Groaning, I reach for my phone, careful not to jostle my slung arm. Instead, I find a glass of water and a pill vial with a sticky note attached.

Take two immediately

is scrawled in Ben's handwriting. I obey quickly.

"Daddy tricked you," she reveals, laughing.

"What time is it? Are you late for preschool?"

"I'm playing hooky."

A glance at the wall clock near the door has me whipping back the covers and popping painfully from bed. "Fucking hell! It's after nine? Shit, don't say Momma's bad words."

I breathe, trying not to freak out. I find clean jeans in a pile in the closet. Pulling them on one-handed is an awkward, clumsy dance that makes Ruthie laugh again.

I should've expected this. The first time I spent the night with Ben, he commandeered my phone so I'd sleep in. During Ruthie's up-all-night baby years, he did the same thing. He knew what I needed.

I'm not sure that's true now, not with Saddletree to consider.

"What about the bakery? Is it open?" I ask my precocious four-year-old.

"Yep." Ruthie hops to my rescue when I get tangled in my shirt. I lean down so she can help me get it on properly.

"I like helping you, Mom. It's funny."

"Sometimes, we all need a little help, and it's always okay to ask for it. Remember that. Where's your dad?"

She shrugs. "At the bakery."

More frazzled than usual, if that's possible, I step into the bathroom and stare blankly at my toothbrush. I can't pinch my left fingers together, let alone apply toothpaste without making a huge mess. An anxious wave of what I can't do floods me...

Mixing and pouring batter...

Lifting heavy pans from the oven...

Delivering coffee and a cinnamon roll to a customer at once...

Buttering bread…

My shoulders slump achingly into resignation—this'll be a nightmare. Jaye's movie comes to mind. Who needs a coven of witches to cause problems and wreak havoc when a broken wrist is enough of a horror show?

"Ruthie, help."

She giggles and obliges, pinching a toothpaste glob onto my bristles. Then, she leaves me to finish getting ready.

Stepping onto the front deck, I bathe in the sunlight. It hadn't been a perfect night's sleep—not with the pain in my arm waking me every hour or so and Ben rousing me at midnight for more pills.

But it was more sleep than I usually get, and restful, nonetheless. I've forgotten how refreshing it felt.

Spending time with Ben, too. I want to lasso Ben, pull him to me, hog tie him, and keep him there forever. Last night felt like an excellent start to our revitalized us-mission.

This feels pretty good, too—Saddletree appears to be running fine without me. The usual cars occupy the lot—Trisha's Subaru, June and May's bright red Hyundai, Mr. Wickers' Prius, and Alice's minivan. Dot's work van is wedged between a white BMW and an old pick-up truck. Regulars dot the patio while Jack Harvey strolls the garden in his usual overalls and baseball cap. With the breakfast rush over, it's a quiet Friday.

The anxiety knotting my stomach loosens in a breath. Ruthie's hand slips into mine.

Hugo and Penelope greet us as we traverse the lawn, demanding Ruthie's attention. She races them to the playground by the garden. The restaurant isn't the five-alarm fire it feels like every other day—it stands and operates without me. A smile eases over my cheeks. Everything's okay.

My serenity is whacked with a wrecking ball when I walk inside.

Everything stops—restaurant noises, air circulation, conversations, heartbeats—and not in a good-to-see-you way. Their wide-eyed, gaping stares make me think I've caught them doing something naughty, like giving away free pastries or reporting to the health inspector that I don't always wear a hairnet.

Dot's ginormous brown orbs find mine. Her oh-shit expression alarms me as she mouths *fuck me* and points not-so-discreetly to her left.

Ben stands with probably the most beautiful woman I've ever seen in person. Her Swedish-esque blond hair makes mine look dirty, as if she's a descendant of elves in Rivendell and I'm a hobbit. She has the sweet girl-next-door charm of Anne Hathaway combined with a strong vixen vibe, as if she studied sex appeal under Nicole Kidman's tutelage and was her best student. She wears a white linen sundress showing off her silky, sun-kissed skin and Barbie curves, and she doesn't have a *single* worry line on her forehead. *Not one.*

This is Lauren Riley. Her icy eyes meet mine with strange relief. *No competition there,* I imagine her thinking. Her full lips curl into a beaming smile like her new best friend has arrived. Or her rival, and she's already one-upped me. She carries a soft bouquet, bride-like, and stands so close to Ben that my stomach twists into a hard, tight knot.

Ben needs close proximity to hear, especially here, where there is a lot of noise and few soft surfaces to buffer it. Still, he steps back when he sees me, breaking their tight circle. Any other time, I'd coo over how adorable he looks sporting an antique blue apron dotted with lemons and his hairnet, discarded in his hand. But not today. He looks perturbed. Whether at Lauren or me, I'm unsure.

My automatic smile shows up in record time. I approach, extending my right hand. "You must be Lauren."

Her dainty hand feels like expensive silk against my calloused, working woman's hand.

"Lena, I'm delighted to meet you finally." She looks and sounds like a Disney princess, especially when her nose scrunches with sympathy. "How are you feeling?"

"A little banged up, but good, thanks." I merge next to my husband. "Ben's taking good care of me."

Dot chuckles lightly, chomping on Cheetos and appearing on my free side as if expecting I'll need backup. She's not wrong.

Lauren pushes the flowers toward me. "These are for you."

An obligatory sniff has me wondering if their odor might be poisonous. Lauren could be a Disney villain disguised as a princess. "Thanks. How sweet."

Her tone shoulders bob in a gentle shrug. "Dad and I were so worried when Ben left yesterday. Car accidents are scary." Her eyes lock on Ben's again. "Remember Becca's in high school?"

"Yes."

"You never know what might happen," she says when Ben fails to reminisce about his twin's accident. "Glad you're okay."

I'm being insecure. Her goddess-like perfection doesn't matter; Ben's with me. My feelings aren't my reality. I sigh, replanting my best smile.

"Thanks, Lauren. Come sit down. Let me get you some coffee and a cinnamon roll." Then, glancing around, I remember—I haven't made cinnamon rolls this morning. "Or, um, something."

"That's kind. But, no, thank you. I've placed an order for the office and must get back."

Trisha sets two large pink boxes on the counter as she says it. She's practically bought out my display case.

Mr. Wickers appears from nowhere. "Would you like me to carry those to your car, madam?"

"Oh, yes, that would be lovely."

"The white BMW?" Dot asks with a rough nudge into my sore midsection.

"That's right," Lauren says.

A lightbulb flickers. "You've been in before," I say as it comes to me. She wore sunglasses and a baseball cap that day. Dot and I were shocked when she didn't ask for directions. We don't see many strangers on the weekdays—certainly not ones driving BMWs and sitting alone. "Coffee and a bran muffin."

"The bran muffins are my favorite," Mr. Wickers chimes in, holding the pink boxes beside us. "It's important to keep the body regular."

"Oh, right, yes," she says in a belabored breath. "Good memory."

"Lena loves getting to know her customers," Trisha adds, taking the bouquet from my hand. "I'll just put these in water, shall I?"

I nod, happy to be rid of them.

Alice Harvey strolls into our circle, carrying a clipboard and looking formidable in her fifties-style polka-dotted dress and a black-cat apron. She lowers her perched reading glasses and sizes Lauren up.

Then, she extends her hand. "I'm Alice Harvey of Lavender Fields Forever, the farm next door."

"Lauren Riley. Nice to meet—"

"Riley, as in the Wilmington Rileys? Riley Trust Bank?"

"Yes, that's us."

"Your Aunt Cheryl was in my knitting group once upon a time. The Knit Wits. Sign my petition? We're trying to get the city to add a bus stop out here. People need work—they can find it on our farms."

Lauren's dumbfounded look is replaced with a smile. "Oh, sure." She scribbles her signature across the rumpled page.

Dot tucks her Cheetos in her pocket, and her arms fold in a huff. "Funny that you've popped by before. What was that? A few weeks ago? Were you hoping to see Ben?"

"Oh, no. Of course not. I didn't realize Ben was connected to Saddle-tree until recently. Um, I was passing by and needed coffee," she says quickly.

Dot's *you're-full-of-shit* expression is unmistakable. Her dark eyes narrow with icy skepticism. "No one's just passing by out here."

Her elegant shoulders bounce again. "I was."

I nudge Dot's side, encouraging her to stop the interrogation.

"Um, I was telling Ben about Riley Trust's family picnic next weekend. Dad and I would love you to come. Food, games, live music, and I bet Ruthie will love our bounce houses and pony rides."

I chuckle. "She'd probably take over the pony rides."

Ben smirks.

"Right, I hear you're both quite the equestrians," she says.

Ben talked about that with her? "Well, we like to think so. Do you ride?"

She waves her hand dismissively. "When I was younger. All girls go through a horse stage. I showed a few times. Couple of blue ribbons. No biggie."

"Well, it was a late-in-life calling for me, for enjoyment, not competition. Ruthie loves it. She wants to be a farm vet one day."

"And an astronaut," Ben adds.

"And a contractor," Dot says.

A grin passes between us. We play Ruthie's Future Game often.

"I've got a doctor and lawyer myself," Lauren volunteers, not to be left out. "Omar and Frederick are at Duke."

I perk up. *She has kids. Probably a husband, too. Lighten up, Lena.* "Oh, that's great. You must be so proud."

She prompts her phone to show me their picture.

Dot leans in, too. "Handsome fellas. What's Mr. Lauren do?"

She chuckles, her eyes returning to Ben. "Oh, there's no Mr. Lauren."

Dot grunts, reading my mind.

"Anyway, I realize your weekends are packed," she goes on. "But the picnic's a great chance to get to know our work family before you decide."

"Decide what?" Dot retrieves her pocket snack and chomps on another Cheeto.

"Riley Trust has offered Ben a job," I tell her (and the rest of the room).

"Ben already has a job," Alice says with staunch disapproval. "He's a highly decorated and respected lieutenant with the Wilmington Police Department."

"I'm aware," she says.

"Doing what?" Dot asks.

"Handling security at Riley Trust."

Dot scoffs. "You want him to be a security guard?"

"Ben Wright is *no* security guard. He's too qualified for that," Alice says, a scary fire in her eyes.

"Is there a competitive benefits package?" Mr. Wickers asks.

"Guys, this isn't an open forum on Ben's future," I say.

"Does this job involve working beside you?" Dot asks.

"Our paths will cross. He'll work more with my father. He thinks the world of Ben. Always has. Not that he had much choice."

"How come?" Dot asks.

Lauren's shoulders rise slightly. "Oh, Ben and I were inseparable back then."

"Inseparable, huh?" Dot challenges with another Cheeto.

"Not true. My many deployments suggest otherwise," Ben says in awkward defense, easing his hand around my waist as if I need comfort. Or control.

Lauren shifts on her expensive wedges. "Dad took a great interest in Ben and his military career. Mentored him, even. They were close for years, even before we got engaged."

The word hangs like a noose dropped from the ceiling beams, dangling between us and waiting for a taker.

Dot's eyes burn a hole in my face. It takes every iota of fortitude I have not to break eye contact with Lauren. Or give Ben the angry stare-down he deserves.

Keep it together. A tense beat passes.

"Well, that's ancient history," she adds awkwardly. "I better get back. I hope you'll make it to the picnic."

"We'll consider it," Ben says while I belt out, "We'll be there."

"I'll text Ben the details. Nice to meet all of you. Feel better, Lena."

She floats toward the door with Mr. Wickers dutifully following. When the glass door eases shut, a collective sigh waves over the crowd as they stare at me quizzically. I'm rattled—they all see it. And I hate it.

"Keep your shit together," Dot whispers with Cheeto breath. "At least until she's left the parking lot."

"Um, thanks, everyone, for helping," I say. "Saddletree's in good hands, so I'll just, um… I have a… Oh, I forgot to…"

I want to run as far away from people as possible. But their watchful eyes, my rubber boots, and my insane soreness prevent me. As I descend the patio, the dogs rush up, and I lavish them with love. *Everything's normal. Nothing to see here.*

Ruthie plods up. "Can I feed the bunnies?"

"Yes, please. That would help."

She rushes to the pens. I can't get her to clean her room, but she loves farm chores.

Mr. Wickers meets me as I cross the driveway toward the barn. He waves a five-dollar bill in the air. "A tip! My first tip!"

"That's nice," I manage.

"Everything okay, Lena?"

"Fine, Mr. Wickers."

"Things are always fine until they're not," he says. "Anything I can do?"

"Um, keep an eye on Ruthie? She's feeding the bunnies. I need… a minute."

"Sure thing, Lena."

Mr. Wickers also loves farm chores.

I quick-step toward the house, hoping to secure myself inside before breaking down. Ben lied to me. *Again.* Harsh, bitter feelings circulate like poison in my bloodstream, sadness most of all.

I miss Mom. If she were here, she'd put her arm around me and give me all those magical assurances that only moms can give. *You're safe and loved and everything's okay.*

I bypass home for her tree, hoping to feel close to her, since I no longer feel close to my husband.

CHAPTER 11

Ben

"YOU WERE ENGAGED?"

Lena's voice trembles, sorrow seeping through her surprising calm. She sits at the base of her mom's tree—so much of our history has happened here. It's where I opened up about my injuries and the IED— something I hadn't done with anyone except my therapist and Becca. Her parents' ashes were spread here. It's where I asked her to marry me, where she told me she was pregnant, and where we had the ceremony a few months later.

It's too sacred a place for this discussion.

But, as Dot bluntly ordered after she and the others stared me down, I must "meet her where she is and beg her forgiveness."

"I'm sorry, Lena. Yes."

"How long were you with her?"

My hand drags over my mouth, unable to form the words. Lena's tear-streaked face kills me. *Lauren fucking Riley*—I wish I'd never taken her call, but how can I dismiss *any* opportunity knowing how limited my options will be when my hearing loss becomes profound? Sure, the department would find a place for me. So would many other fine institutions. But I already know those are jobs I don't want. Clerical. Behind a desk and a screen. Away from people.

A common misconception is that I dislike people. That's not true. Quietness does not mean disinterest. Often, it simply means I'm listening.

Now, I need to talk. Holding Lena last night, I promised myself I would. But everything's working against me. Lauren dropping our engagement as casually as a remark on the weather has upended my planned conversation with Lena, the one I've been prepping all morning in my head. Now, I'm forced to play defense. Lena's already hurt. Already pissed. And she has every reason to be. Her tears and disappointment make this much harder.

My mouth goes dry, but I force the answer free. "Ten years."

"Ten fucking years? That's more than *a few*, Ben."

"I was deployed for most of it."

"How come you never told me?"

"It felt unnecessary to discuss."

Her vivid eye-roll rivals those of busted teenagers, angry at me for calling their parents. Only with Lena it makes an impact. I sit on the ground beside her and absentmindedly drape my hand over her thigh. She shoves my hand away and tries standing, but her soreness prevents her. I assist her gently, though she quickly pulls her good hand free from mine once she's on her feet.

Now, standing under the same branches that have shaded so many fond memories, she glares at me with hurt eyes. My deception, *my very presence*, has heightened her anxiety. She radiates it like she's sourcing the humidity in the air.

It's hard to breathe.

"It should've been necessary last night when I *specifically* asked you if there was anything significant I needed to know. Why couldn't you tell me then?"

"I didn't want complications."

"Complications? The truth isn't complicated, Ben. I don't understand."

"We were both with other people before us—the *wrong* people. I don't understand why it matters."

"*You* matter. This is about you. You can't leave shit out because you don't want to talk about it—"

"Fine." I run a hand through my hair, handling my frustration like it's a door I'm holding shut. "Lauren and I were once engaged. We thought we loved each other, but shit happened, and we realized we didn't. End of story. I never told you because it didn't matter—I love you, and we're a good fit."

She scoffs. "A good fit? Like I'm a comfortable, old shoe."

"No. I didn't mean it like that."

"You've lied to me. *Twice.* You're making it impossible to believe there's nothing more to this than a job."

Heat rises inside me with her accusation. "Last night wasn't the right time to discuss it."

"Fuck that—I asked; you should've answered," she says, trying to sign the words as well.

"I wanted to be *with* you, to take care of you, not go through a fucking interrogation."

"A fucking interrogation?" she cries out. "*That's* what you think I do to you? If I didn't ask questions, you wouldn't talk to me at all. And that seems to be how you'd prefer it."

"No, damn it!"

Startled by our raised voices, a mallard nearby flaps with irritation before taking flight, forcing us both to pause and reset. *Pull it in.*

I take a breath. "I'm sorry, truly. I should've told you about her and her former significance. It's just that I've missed us. I didn't want to waste last night, or any night, on her."

Her brow pinches into what looks like sympathy. "I'm sorry, too. I don't mean to interrogate you. Or overthink things. It's just… I told you everything about Mark."

"Information I didn't need or want."

"Maybe not, but at least you knew he existed. And damn, I *wanted* to tell you, the same way I want to tell you when I have cramps or feel anxious or when Ruthie says something funny. I want to tell you everything—"

"I'm not like you—"

"You used to open up to me. Intimacy is more than having sex and sharing a bathroom. We're supposed to be partners. We're supposed to be close."

"Close? We haven't been close in months. How can we be close when we're never together? You don't have time for me." The pressure shifts away from me and onto her—a relief—but I hate how her shoulders slump and her eyes water.

"I'm sorry," she says sternly. "I never meant to make you feel neglected."

"I feel… alone." The word slips out, and I immediately want to reverse it, even if it's true. I want to erase this entire conversation.

Pale and pained, she gawks as if one word has stolen what her body needs, leaving her weak and faint. "Alone? How can you feel alone? I'm right here."

"You're never here for me. You give Saddletree 110 percent, and I respect you for it. But there's nothing left over. I average about five minutes of your time daily, and it's usually about Ruthie."

"That's not fair. I always have time for you. You have to ask."

"I've tried. Have you forgotten all the times I've asked you to have dinner or take a walk, all the horseback rides and beach days you've turned down? I've tried scheduling time with you, but you forget or back out. There's always something keeping you from us. Something has to change. I want our lives to center around us, not Saddletree."

She rubs her head near yesterday's bruise. "I want that, too, and I'm trying."

"Are you? You run your business like a dog park—you open the gate and let everyone frolic and play with little supervision. I offer help constantly, but you refuse to implement any suggestions. It's frustrating living with someone who prefers chaos."

"Ben, what the fuck? How can you say that to me? I don't *prefer* chaos."

"Your business is badly managed. You have little time for your family. Your head is always spinning. And you drive like a maniac to make your appointments. The evidence proves it."

She's devastated, eyes brimming with hurt like she doesn't know who I am. I'm not sure I know, either. I should be dropping to my knees and begging for her forgiveness, but fear prevents me.

"It needed to be said," I mutter weakly, trying to convince myself.

She exhales in a long puff that makes her bottom lip quiver. "So, I'm the Queen of Chaos, and my business is a shitshow. *That's* what you really think of me?"

"Um, well, that's not what I said, but—"

"You're an asshole for turning this around on me." Her finger goes up in a weak accusation. "Again! You blindsided me with your interview *and* Lauren. You've kept a decade of your life a damn secret from me. I looked like a clueless idiot in front of her, my staff, and my friends, thanks to you. This is about you, Ben. Not me."

"No, it isn't—"

"*You* lied. *You.* This isn't *my* fault. How can you blame me for the distance between us when you've held back the entire time?"

"Only about this one thing. I didn't think it mattered."

"That's not true, either. It matters so much that you've derailed this discussion by belittling my business and making me feel small and incapable—*that's* a first for you. I'll add it to the list of things I never thought you'd do. Lying. Spending time with old girlfriends—oops, no, fiancée. And now, making me feel like shit."

She stops to wipe her cheeks, though it's a pointless enterprise—the tears flow continuously. Still, she pushes her smile through them, almost like it's a robotic tick.

Or a defense mechanism.

"This isn't you," she decides tearfully. "Maybe instead of a business lecture, you should figure out why you don't want to talk to me about Lauren and whatever else you're avoiding. I can't be here for you if you don't tell me what's wrong. What do you *really* need to tell me?"

She awaits an answer—my head floods with them. I don't know where to start, even if I wanted to.

I don't. Not like this, especially.

Her pleading eyes shatter me. Her disappointment is another vise on my chest, tightening, adding pressure. I catch glimpses of our future, when it's not what I've left out of our conversations that frustrates her, but our difficulty communicating altogether. One day, Busy Lena will take on the responsibility of caring for me like I'm another Saddletree project, burying herself behind forced smiles and extra work. I'll be the burden I've always feared, weak and vulnerable. And Lena's one look of love and acceptance will be replaced with exhaustion and resentment.

She'll hate what I become someday.

The longer I'm silent, the more flushed and fidgety she becomes. She tries controlling her breathing, but it's hurried and irregular. I think to help her as I did at the hospital, but I know she'll reject my touch.

"I didn't mean to make you feel small or incapable," I say.

But before I finish my sentence, she turns toward the house. My weak-ass answer pushes her to her limit.

What should I tell her anyway? That my career is over? That I must consider their offer because it's the best I'll get? That the damn IED didn't kill me but stole my life all the same and keeps taking?

That one day, it'll take her from me, too, when she no longer sees me as the man she fell in love with but a burden she's stuck with, broken and unfixable? Unlovable and unworthy.

The dogs race to her side, followed quickly by Mr. Wickers and

Ruthie. Ruthie pushes a handful of dandelions and buttercups toward her, and Lena's good hand goes to her heart dramatically before accepting them. Her tears and panic move aside for smiles and gushing —Lena is good at redirection. She always makes everyone feel good, even when she doesn't.

How could I have been so hard on her? I love Saddletree and everything she's built here. People adore and depend on her. Local papers call Saddletree a community treasure, and TripAdvisor has deemed it a top pick for family fun in Wilmington.

Comparing it to a dog park was a dick move.

Not telling her the truth about Lauren was another.

Deflecting blame was easier. A burning self-hatred grows inside me, a tumor in my thoughts, malignant, and all I want is to get small and disappear.

But I can't. I'm a husband and father—I have to make this right.

After a brief interchange, Lena and Ruthie head toward the house while Mr. Wickers wanders over, hands in the pockets of his pressed khakis.

"Ben."

"Mr. Wickers."

"Lena doesn't seem herself today," he says.

"She isn't."

Mr. Wickers looks disappointed, as if his team has just fumbled what would've been the winning touchdown. "Things are always fine until they're not."

I respect Mr. Wickers, but I hope he doesn't press it further. My loyalty lies with Lena, and this is between us.

"She looked a little green. Tummy trouble, she said. She's taking Ruthie up to the house for food and a nap. She asked me to retrieve her phone."

"I'll take it to her."

"Good man." He pats my back. "Want me to hold down the fort?"

"Sure. Thanks." I don't know exactly what that entails, but it seems okay.

Mr. Wickers salutes and heads toward the café. I go home.

Marriages fall apart by a thousand small jabs—not one hit. *Usually.* I've seen it repeatedly when arguments between couples escalate and require police assistance. Domestic disturbances are my second-most-frequent call after car accidents. It's sad and humbling to watch couples go through that.

Whether a slow erosion or sudden destruction, witnessing such unkindness and cruelty between people makes me question how they ever loved each other at all. Love isn't a fixed constant. It either grows and changes with the couple or dies altogether.

Love is easy. Endurance is hard.

Until this moment, I never believed that could be us. One argument is nothing, but that's where it always begins. For the first time in our marriage, fear grows—that the subtle cracks in our foundation will lead to catastrophic disrepair if nothing is done. And she's right—I want to blame her, but *I'm* the problem, more than she realizes. If I'd been upfront, none of this would've happened. Lena doesn't need my criticism. She needs my help. My honesty. My everything.

I find her in the kitchen, supervising Ruthie on a badly executed peanut butter and jelly sandwich. A decisive stride brings me to her. Her breath hitches when I embrace her.

She stiffens in my arms but doesn't pull away. I can almost feel the anger and hurt pumping through her veins, the tension keeping her tight and unwilling to accept me. So, I do what I should've done when I found her at the tree—I hold her, whispering the same thing over and over.

"I'm sorry. I love you, and I'm sorry."

After ten attempts, her muscles relax. After twelve, she puts her arms around me. Finally, she pulls back so I can see her face, and a weak smile emerges through her tears when she mouths, "I love you, too."

Relief sweeps over my sharp regret.

A plan forms. To reassure Lena about my commitment to her and Saddletree, I must show her how much I believe in her and what she does here. I'll also show her how things can be improved, for both our sakes.

Watching her move slowly and sorely around the kitchen convinces me to extend my PTO and enact my plan tomorrow. Lena needs me.

CHAPTER 12

Lena

RUTHIE AND MR. Wickers show up at exactly the right time for me to avoid an embarrassing sob-fest slash panic attack. Ben's words—that I'm difficult, complicated, chaotic, and basically a terrible business-woman and wife—not only unleash my anxiety bitches from their weakened cages but give them free rein, like untethered ghosts whipping around in an old mansion. I'm tormented by them and his gorgeous former fiancée (*no game, my ass*). It's truly unfair that God makes people like her. That they were together longer than we've been means she might know him better than me—even now.

She knows his history, anyway. Set his path. *Broke his heart?*

Maybe it's my insecurity talking, but my woman's intuition hits red alert status. She reminded me of a little bird puffing out her chest and twittering around his words. Showing up here—*twice*—screams ulterior motives. First, she wanted to check me out. Second, she hoped I'd be dead.

Okay, that may be an exaggeration, but it's not far off.

Dot will back me up on this.

Lauren Riley hopes to fill more than a job vacancy—that's clear. Well, clear to everyone except maybe Ben.

That he turned all this around on me makes it all so much worse. He's never said such hurtful things to me—I never would've guessed him capable of it.

Unraveling this knotted tangle between my reality and my anxious thoughts challenges me—there's too much going on up there. I hate that I've reverted into this—a crying, panicky woman—like my Nervous Nellie persona is an annoying meme that won't die out. That used to be my nickname growing up, thanks to those damn Garbage Pail Kids cards. I'm supposed to be stronger now. Stable. In control-ish. Fucking therapized. I did so well that Dr. Reese changed our appointments to quarterly. This isn't me anymore.

But it only ever takes one thing. One hole to sink the ship. One day to question everything. One push to send you over the edge.

So, with my body aching and heart breaking, I take a page from Mom's book and fix PB&Js.

I try, anyway. Ruthie quickly takes over, giggling at my inability to do the simplest thing.

When Ben enters the house, I expect round two (a muted version for Ruthie's sake, anyway). I called him a liar and insinuated that this woman means more to him than he lets on, and neither accusation feels entirely accurate. I can't even look at him. I keep picturing a chaotic dog park with me trapped inside and Ben outside the opposite fence, bulky arms crossed and head shaking in irritation and disappointment while gorgeous Lauren dotes and twitters at his side.

I never thought he felt such disapproval of me. How can he feel so strongly against me when it was his support that led to Saddletree in the first place? I always believed it to be ours, not mine.

I'm so hurt and angry that I can't look at him but catch glimpses of his silhouette moving across the kitchen, like a soldier on a mission.

Expecting more unkind words, I'm shocked when his big arms lock around me. Irritated that he thinks a hug will suffice to earn my forgiveness after he called my business a dog park, I tense up, determined not to let him off so easily.

But then, he says he's sorry. He loves me, *and* he's sorry. Over and over. The more I hear those words, the longer he holds me, I melt, relaxing into his embrace like I did the tub last night.

Oh, Ben. He means it—I'm as sure about that as I am that we're standing in our kitchen over globs of peanut butter and jelly to a sound-track of Ruthie's laughter.

Ben's *with* me. My pain subsides, and clarity takes over. He's not keeping secrets because he has something to hide that'll change us. Whatever happened between them is difficult for Ben—*that's* why he hasn't told me.

The day he told me how he sustained his injuries in Afghanistan, he struggled to get the words out. Retelling that painful story was hard for him; he pushed me on the tree swing so he wouldn't have to look me in the eyes. He shared it not because I asked him a thousand questions but because he was ready to be vulnerable with me.

When he's ready, he'll tell me about Lauren, too. And everything else that's upsetting him. I just have to be patient and available, like he always is for me.

Until then, I *must* get my shit together. The dog park comparison was a shitty thing to say that will sting for a while, but he's not wrong. I don't run my business—my business runs me.

Ben's warm and persistent embrace makes me desperate for more of him. Rebuilding our closeness is my top priority. I can almost hear Mom's voice in my head. *Ben once gave you fireworks over a bad day. What can you do for him?*

Be more available, for starters. He *wants* to spend time with me. As long as that's true, we'll be okay.

He needs more tree-swing moments, when it's just him and me, no pressure, and he can open up naturally. I suspect he wants to say more, like things have been building in him with every opportunity I've missed. His dissatisfaction at work, his hearing, and his future—we're teetering on an uncertain edge of change. Time together will help us figure that out.

Finally, I release him and mouth that I love him back, just as Ruthie giggles.

"Are ya'll stuck or something?"

"Stuck like glue," Ben says and signs to her. He kisses my forehead.

A good marriage never hangs on to anger long.

He takes over my PB&J efforts, cuts the sandwiches in half, and serves them to us. Then, with that gentleness I adore, he takes my injured hand and looks it over. "Swollen. Pain level?"

I shrug. "Moderate. But I can help in the kitchen."

"No, I got it. You need to rest. Tomorrow's covered, too. After that, I don't know." He moves to Ruthie and gives her a side hug. "Enjoy your day off. Don't let Mom do any cartwheels or high-fives."

She flashes a peanut butter smile. "Or drum rolls or patty cake."

He smirks. "I better get back before your employees kill each other."

"Thanks, Ben."

He nods and sets my phone on the counter. At the door, he turns, catching my eyes with his, and a light smile eases up his handsome face. A warm surge bubbles in me, and with it comes a decision.

I know what I need to do.

The next morning, Ben sets up for Saturday at Saddletree and leaves with Ruthie—he doesn't say where.

I instruct Tessa on promised orders—she loves taking the lead on special bakes—and then post on social media that we'll be closed temporarily starting Sunday.

So, with everything under minimal control, I leave with Dot.

Cherry meets us at Diamond Studios, where she peruses the lengthy contract. Since her divorce, Cherry considers herself an armchair lawyer and skilled negotiator. She eyes me over the rim of her chunky reading glasses. "They've arranged for Saddletree's groups and compensated your employees. They've even added a bonus for the horses—they want to use them in some shots. They've thought of everything. It's a solid deal, but are you sure?"

"Ben needs me. I'm sure."

We review the contract, and, eventually, I sign Saddletree away for the next two months.

Two months to heal. Two months to research how to make Saddletree operate better. Two months for Ben and me. A chance for our lives to center around us, not Saddletree.

I can't wait to tell him.

CHAPTER 13

Ben

LENA and I wake up together on Saturday morning for the first time in years. I like maneuvering around her in the closet and bathroom and using both sinks as we brush our teeth. Our master suite was designed for dual occupancy, not tiptoeing around each other at odd hours.

She meets Tessa and Mr. Wickers at the bakery early to review orders and provide instructions. Her slow movements indicate her body aches today, and her hand is swollen like an engorged balloon about to burst. Soon, she'll return home to take over Ruthie's care while I handle the restaurant—an agreement I insisted on. I don't want her stressing her injury by doing too much. I watch from the balcony with coffee as I review my day.

Employee meeting at six sharp.

Set up for the morning rush.

Leave mid-morning with Ruthie.

Set everything right.

Stepping into Lena's life is like joining the circus trapeze team with zero knowledge of acrobatics. Or gravity. I ground her team with military precision that's met with grudging acceptance.

My presence doesn't allow for the restaurant's usual welcoming banter and relaxed atmosphere. Even now, as I hand-wash my fiftieth china plate—another area of inefficiency—I glance through the serving window and find the dining room uncharacteristically subdued.

That's acceptable as long as the work gets done. It's a business. Not a social event.

My phone pings, announcing an update to Saddletree's social media pages. Lena posted the light menu we agreed on and announced a temporary closure starting tomorrow. I feel better—she's listening to me.

Trisha, May, and June work the front end efficiently, though I could do without May and June's excessive chatter and occasional bickering.

I tell them this immediately. They don't like it, but they stop. Trisha appears grateful.

I assign tasks to ensure their continued focus. This also appears to be a surprise. Again, Trisha seems grateful. I suspect that these jobs typically fall to her. The other two are inefficient and lazy.

Lena's inability to find good help isn't her fault. Food service is difficult to employ, and our distance puts us at a distinct disadvantage despite offering above-average pay—a problem that will be rectified if Alice Harvey succeeds in her fight to incorporate a bus route nearby.

Identify the problem. Solve the problem. Simple.

I concoct a plan as I wash dishes.

A teacup breaks when it slips from my hands and falls against another dish. It's my third casualty. Lena's sentimentality in using her family's old china is understandable but misguided. She spends more time washing dishes than baking, which is a terrible business model. Her baking makes the business—not her grandmother's dishes.

I have two objectives today. First, I'll prove to Lena that there are workable solutions to reduce her schedule and increase her efficiency. She should be baking and creating, not taking out the trash and washing china.

By accomplishing the first objective, I'll achieve my second— restoring her faith in my commitment to her and Saddletree. I still can't believe I compared it to a dog park.

This will make up for it. After today, everything will be better.

With the café handled and Trisha (and Mr. Wickers) in charge, Ruthie and I leave for phase two of my plan.

"Where are we going, Daddy?"

"To see an old friend."

We travel downtown, and find Mr. Deakins loitering in the sheltered area of the Riverwalk downtown. It's almost September, but it still feels like summer, and the homeless and home-insecure residents do what they can to stay cool. Mr. Deakins, a.k.a. Shakespeare, was homeless but now lives in a men's boarding home. He cleans, does odd jobs for the landlady, and entertains his housemates with nightly poetry readings and karaoke.

He still uses the cane Lena gave him—a wooden antique once used by her mom. It thuds against the boards of the pier as he approaches.

"Ah, Ben Wright, what a joy and a pleasure… and this little sweetheart, what a treasure. Where is the love of my life? Your one, your only, your sweet, sweet wife?"

"Home. Recovering. She was in a car accident."

"Mr. Deakins, Mom broke her hand… on land… not near sand… and Candyland! Do you play?" Ruthie rattles off awkwardly. I admire her effort. It reminds me of the first time Lena met him and tried matching his rhymes, too.

Mr. Deakins laughs like she's told the perfect joke. "I do… on occasion. But it's been ages. Call me Shakespeare, if you please. And I'll say bless you, if you sneeze."

"Deal." Ruthie extends her hand, and he shakes it. Then, she fake-sneezes to test him.

"Bless you! Do you need a tissue? I have one right here; it's no issue."

She giggles dramatically. Nothing makes sense.

"Mr. Deakins, I have a business proposal for you," I say, ready for redirection.

"Oh, Ben Wright, you keep things real. Tell me about it, and let's make a deal."

I tell him my ideas, though his incessant rhyming is enough to make me reconsider it.

When we return to Saddletree a few hours later, it's busy. Scattered picnic blankets surround the pond. People tour the overgrown garden with baskets to get what's left of a dwindling crop. A small, neon-clad bicycle group meets at the carport, prepping for a long country bike ride. A line forms near the patio for the hayride, where Lena's weekend help—two teenagers who take turns driving the old tractor—organize the next round of guests.

I park near the barn, and Mr. Deakins, driving the small cargo van I've rented, pulls in beside me. He and four others exit the vehicle. I give them their assignments.

Ruthie and I don't find Lena upstairs. A quick text informs me that she's with Dot and will return soon, which is ideal. My plan can take effect before she arrives.

I can't wait for her to see.

Ruthie and I enjoy sandwiches and sodas on the café patio when Dot's van appears. They park near my Jeep, and Ruthie calls them over as soon as they exit.

Lena looks nice. Her summery dress immediately catches a breeze when she walks our way, tickling something in my chest. She's a beautiful woman. It's almost comical that she felt insecure meeting Lauren. Perhaps by the world's standards, Lauren is more traditionally beautiful, but I prefer Lena. She doesn't look salon-perfect most days (or any, for that matter), but I love her natural beauty. The way her nose freckles in the sun, the varying shades of blond and light brown in her hair, the fact that she looks pretty much the same with or without makeup, and her gentle strength when she rides horses, mixes batter, rakes the garden, or picks up our daughter.

She is and always will be the sexiest woman I know.

I stand when she approaches, the patio chair scraping the concrete under me. She smirks when I lean in for a quick kiss. "Hey. Everything okay?"

"Yes." I examine her braced arm—swollen and red. "Pain level?"

"High," she admits, slinging her bag off her shoulder. "Forgot to take my pills."

I open her bag so she can dig through it. A thick folder peeks from the top. She retrieves the pill vial and hands it to me—she can't twist the lid one-handed.

Ruthie giggles when Dot steals half a sandwich from her plate.

I give Lena my chair and move another from an empty table.

It's nearly three. Families spread over the acres like pegs on a map. Lena glances around, seemingly surprised that we're out here, enjoying the day when she'd typically be working her ass off on a given Saturday.

She tosses back the pain pills with a swig of my drink. I push my plate toward her. "Eat something."

Dot gives Lena an urging look.

"Um, I have news." Lena sounds nervous.

Before she continues, the tractor rolls up the driveway. From the driver's seat, Mr. Deakins waves his arm dramatically. "Alas, we reach our journey's end. We started as strangers, and now, we're friends."

The full trailer behind him breaks into applause, as they've done for every ride since he took over the position. He removes his hat and bows.

"Holy shit! It's Shakespeare!" Lena laughs. "What's he doing here?"

"He calls it *Poetry in Motion*. I call it *working*."

The delighted look on her face makes me swell with pride—I love that look.

Her head tilts as she grins at me. "What did you do?"

"I hired extra help for the day. Longer, if you approve. Mr. Deakins has agreed to be your new driver." I motion to the small cargo van parked beside my Jeep. "I rented a van for him. He has a clean driving record, and his landlord has agreed to allow it in her driveway. Four or five days a week, he could arrive in the morning *with help* and take over the hayrides and deliveries. I have one guy on dishes and cleaning tables. Others work the gardens, fields, and pens. After closing, he'll drive everyone home. They get reliable paychecks. You get the help you need if you agree."

She gawks as two men emerge from the garden carrying armfuls of weeds. In the distance, she spots another on the ATV, refilling the horses' water troughs.

"If you like the idea, we'll invest in a van. The Harveys might be interested, too. People want to work. This solves the problem of getting them here… at least until we get a bus stop. I also assigned Trisha as the temporary dining room manager. Your weekenders are helping Tessa and waiting tables—it's a much better use for them. May and June now have to compete for tips."

"Wow," she breathes out, glancing from the fields to me and back again.

"This plan will *significantly* reduce your workload. You can absorb the costs by charging for hayrides or renting picnic blankets—things you should do already. I have other suggestions that'll save you time and money… if you'd like to hear them."

"Of course, I would. Ben, this is amazing. I can't believe you did all this."

Lena operates on a default to doing everything herself. I don't blame her—I do, too. But if the last few days have taught us anything, we need each other. It feels good to see her faith in me restored. "I've also decided not to pursue the Riley Trust position."

"What? Why?"

I shrug lightly. "Hobnobbing with rich socialites just isn't me."

She smirks. "What's the real reason?"

"There's too much history there, and I prefer the present."

Her reaction confirms it's the right decision. My pride surges with her incredible smile. It reminds me of the night I surprised her with fireworks after she'd had a rough day—she couldn't believe someone would do something like that for her then, and she can't believe it now.

I slip my hand over hers under the table, locking it securely over her soft fingers. It's become automatic now, but fiddling with her fingertips reminds me of sliding the rings on her finger, making me grateful.

"Thank you, Ben. I'm sorry it took this to get me to listen." She holds up her braced arm, wincing.

"It's no trouble. I have other suggestions to make the next two months easier while you heal."

Lena's pinched brow quirks with a glance at Dot. "Um, I want to hear your ideas, but I've got it handled."

"Handled? What does that mean?"

"Ruthie, come on. Let's check out this poetic hayride, huh?" Dot stands and tugs at Ruthie's sweater.

Lena watches them descend the patio, appearing more anxious the further they go. When her eyes finally find mine again, a forced smile emerges.

With a no-big-deal shrug, she announces, "Diamond Studios wants to film a movie here. I'm closing Saddletree for two months. I signed the deal an hour ago."

She elaborates, but I fixate on two words—*closing Saddletree*. Unease festers in my stomach and a headache twinges behind my eyes. She explains all the positives in one long oration, the pros ramming uncomfortably against the bigger issue in my head, and try as I might, I can't see them beyond the underlying problem. Logic tells me that she did the same as me. She identified the problem and solved it—simple. But I didn't make any overarching decisions without her—renting the van and hiring Mr. Deakins and his crew for the day were only meant to show her what she *could* do if she agreed to make it permanent.

The fact that she did this without even a heads-up blindsides me and worries me about our future. I feel excluded and hurt that she didn't consult me before making such a drastic move. We used to make decisions like this together.

I can't believe she did this.

Without me.

Even worse, she did it *for* me. It's happening already, sacrificing Saddletree for me. Sacrificing herself for me.

"Ben?" she says finally, her voice shaky with anxiety. "Say something."

"I can't. Not now." I get up and leave her at the table.

CHAPTER 14

Lena

I FIND Ben an hour later in the barn, shoveling muck from the horse stalls while Hugo and Penelope watch. His button-down hangs on the half-door, and his white undershirt is smeared with dirt and clinging to his sweat.

He's using work as a focus to balance his emotions—a trick I pull thousands of times a day. Sometimes, the best thing to do is to stay busy, despite how taboo that word has become lately.

Choosing to retreat to the barn makes sense, too. It's off-limits to guests, and there aren't many quiet places at Saddletree on the weekends.

"Ready to talk yet?" I lean against the half-door, trying to look nonconfrontational.

"Yes. No. Maybe." He barely looks at me.

"It's an amazing deal, Ben. If you'd hear me out, read the paperwork—"

"How could you do this without consulting me?"

"You called me a chaotic mess. I wanted to prove otherwise and solve the problem myself... and I did. I need to heal, and you need me to be more available—win, win."

He grunts, looking everywhere but at me. "No. You refused to close when I asked you to. You would've found a way to keep the place running, even if it meant baking one-handed... and asking you to be more available didn't mean I wanted this."

I soften him with a light smile and trace the veins in his arm. "I told you I'd stop the world for you. That's what I did. I thought it'd be… fireworks."

"You did this for *me*," he summarizes, closing his eyes tightly. His face pinches, and for a second, I almost expect tears to spit from his eyes —not the good kind.

"For *us*. Surprise," I say, trying to be cute.

He remains blank, arms folded like a barrier between us, and shakes his head.

I square my shoulders and offer a soft smile. "This'll give us time. We could discuss job options, ways to run Saddletree better, whatever you want. I love you and want us to fix what's broken… I thought you'd be proud of me."

"You made a huge decision that affects us all and could ruin Saddletree over *one* argument? That's unreasonable."

I raise my good hand delicately between us, trying to turn this calm again when I say, "It wasn't unreasonable, Ben. And it's not *one* fight. It's *us*."

"You *can't* make these kinds of decisions over me, Lena. Not now. Not…"

He drags a hand down his mouth as if loosening his tight jaw and gritted teeth. A breathy pause brings his hands to his hips, but he seems stuck like he can't get the words out.

"Not what, Ben? Not for a two-month vacation that we both desperately need?"

"It won't be a vacation. It'll be a circus."

"You don't know that," I argue.

"Yes, I do. I see it all over Wilmington. They'll come in and take over. Saddletree belongs to them now."

"I thoroughly reviewed the details. It won't be like that," I say, though now tiny doubts fray my confidence. "You *said* I needed to do better with Saddletree. I made what I believe is a smart business decision that helps my family. That's why I did it, Ben. It's *for* us."

He scoffs. "No. If this were for us, you would've discussed it with me, like you always used to. Agreeing to it without me is retaliation."

The accusation makes my neck snap back in surprise. "What?"

"You're pissed about Lauren and the job, so you did this behind my back." He shrugs like this is obvious.

"That's not true. I'd never be so fucking petty. How can you say that?"

"The evidence supports it—"

"Evidence, *my ass*. I was upset, yes, but I got over it. Stop blaming me for every shit thing. You're only upset because I've hurt your pride. You thought you could show me how fucked up I run things around here, swoop in, fix everything, and play the hero. Well, guess what? *I'm* the hero. If you'd give it a chance—"

"Dictating a major decision concerning our household without me makes you feel heroic?" He huffs like he's seething. "I'm sick of living around your edges, Lena."

"What does that mean?" I barely manage to get the words out.

He steps closer, signing as he speaks. "We used to be different. I *wanted* things for us. Family vacations. More kids—"

"That's not my fault. I'm forty, Ben. Even Ruthie was a long shot."

"Yes, I know," he puts his hand in the air as if to soften his words. "But look at us. We're lucky to have her, lucky to have all of this, but we aren't together enough to enjoy it, let alone grow our family. We could've discussed adoption or fostering."

"Then, why haven't we?"

"We parent Ruthie in shifts as it is. You're constantly overwhelmed. How could I possibly bring up more kids or taking trips when—"

"When I turn into this?" I finish for him, waving my good hand in the air. "All my fault. Again."

"No, it's mine, too. I struggle to communicate on a good day. I know it's not easy living with someone so closed off, especially since you're so open," he explains, his hand motioning back and forth between us. "But you don't even listen to the small things. I exist in your periphery—your business, your schedule, and your anxiety. You must believe it, too, or you would've talked to me first before turning our home into a movie set."

"Fine, I should've talked to you. I'm sorry. I tried to do something good for us. It *will* be good for us."

"It's a Band-Aid, Lena. Not a long-term solution." His arms unfold long enough for him to rake a hand through his hair. "I don't want you giving things up for me. Not now. Not ever."

"Well, tough shit. I'd give up *anything* for you. Wouldn't you do the same for me?"

"Stop romanticizing it. This is different." He rolls his eyes and refolds his arms. "You can't take risks—not for me. Shutting down Saddletree puts it in jeopardy. Puts *us* in jeopardy."

"How? Saddletree will be fine, better than fine—trust me," I say, tears dripping and anxiety rising because how can I be sure of anything? "What do you want me to do? Hell, I'll sell the whole place if that's what you want. I'll do anything. Just tell me why you're so fucking angry?"

My words catch him like a hook, and his expression falls somewhere between hurt and stunned. His brow pinches at the top of his nose, and his lips part, like maybe the words he needs to say are right there, lined up in proper order, awaiting his final command.

But they don't come.

"Why can't you talk to me?" I say, tears dripping from my chin to the ground. "Lying, blaming me, being fucking mean... *this* isn't you. What's going on with you? Really?"

"It doesn't matter. Do whatever you want... that's what you'll do anyway." He brushes by me so fast that the breeze he creates ruffles my dress.

CHAPTER 15

Ben

I STORM AWAY from the barn, headed nowhere, just away.

I hate that she'd give up every good thing she's worked for over worries about me; I hate that she'd even consider shutting down for two months or closing altogether. This compounds my fears about our future when I desperately need her to be stable because I won't be. My probable deafness and unemployment will burden her constantly, and Busy Lena will be her norm, perpetually stressed and overwhelmed. She'll take on the responsibility of supporting our family alongside the daunting task of caring and communicating for me until it crushes her and strains or ruins her business. It's happened before; it's her modus operandi.

Lena gave up herself for her first marriage and business, only for both to fail.

Her devotion to her mom's care cost her her identity for three years and wrecked her mental health.

Saddletree operates on her blood, sweat, and tears—a beast that will never be satisfied. Still, she keeps giving it more, but her momentum won't last. She can't keep her manic pace forever, and she shouldn't try to, not for me.

How could she be so goddamned impulsive?

Pressure closes in on me from all sides—health, finances, home life, career, and now a future where one bad decision could end everything she's worked for, and I'd be unable to save it.

Ten yards from the barn, Lauren Riley calls. Feeling angry and like shit already, I answer.

"Yes?"

"Hi, Ben, how's everything going? Is Lena feeling better?" Her chipper voice grates on my raw nerves.

"She's fine."

"Great! I just wanted to check in. I've spoken with Dad, and we understand you're still considering us. Larry won't retire until the new year, so we're flexible. Take all the time you need. *Really.* But—"

I expected a *but*. My throat constricts as my stress skyrockets.

"He suggested you come in for a working interview to see firsthand what Riley Trust will be like. It'll alleviate any concerns you may have, and we'll have the chance to impress you with our thorough background checks, meticulous routines and record-keeping, and our over-the-top tech." She laughs. "What do you say?"

I don't want to say anything. The pressure has me in a stranglehold, my heart racing, and irritation climbing. My boots stop abruptly. I don't know where I'm going, just away from Lena. I hate that I've spoken to her harshly again, and desperate to regain my self-control.

I'm at the pond's edge, near her mom's tree. A family leans against the trunk while the children fight over the rope swing.

Nothing is sacred here.

I told Lena I'd refuse the position—*that's* the plan. But the words are held hostage by my frustration. How can I turn it down with Saddletree now at risk? Lena's decision has uprooted our one-sided stability and thrown our future into question. I can't rely on the hope that Saddletree will bounce back after a long closure.

"Ben, are you okay?"

Flashes of her appear—memories I don't want. Legs crisscrossed on her pale-yellow bed, making funny faces into her laptop on our video chats. Every exuberant, full-bodied greeting at the airport. Her jumping onto me for piggyback rides at the beach. The gentleness in her voice forces me to see the concerned tilt to her chin, the crease at the corner of her mouth, and her gray eyes expanding with the question. She must've asked me that a million times, especially when things got hard.

I always said the same thing. "Fine."

She pauses as if the answer hurts her.

"It's not a good time," I say after a beat. "I'll... think about it."

Then, I hang up.

Everything has gone wrong today.

I don't know where Lena is—maybe in the barn. I circle the property, telling each of Mr. Deakins' friends that their day is done, ending with him.

"Plans have changed," I explain, handing over money for him and his buddies. "I'll be in touch tomorrow about the van."

"Well, it was fun… we had a good run…"

I don't stay to hear the rest.

Inside the café, Dot and Ruthie play checkers at a corner table. I instruct Trisha to close as soon as possible before calling Ruthie over.

"Say goodbye. We're going home." I don't mean to sound angry, but Ruthie winces at my voice as if I've spoken too loudly. It's possible. It's hard to tell anymore. Even so, she obeys.

Dot and I exchange a knowing look—I don't want to talk, and she has nothing to say to me anyway. Her lips pinch before getting on her phone.

My breathing doesn't normalize until Ruthie and I are home, closing the door behind us. I want to be home with my daughter, away from the world. I need distance from the lingering families, job offers, movie deals, and residual bullshit.

Distance from Lena, too. I fear the changes ahead and worry she can't handle them.

I feel even worse forcing her to.

On the counter, the file folder from the studio protrudes from Lena's bag. I ignore it. My anger is a blanket, keeping me warm, and I don't want to be without it yet.

But settling onto the couch with Ruthie's head on my shoulder as we watch TV, my determination falters.

I said things I shouldn't have.

She's right—this *isn't* me. But the truth is, I haven't been *me* since that fucking bomb destroyed me. I'll never be that young man again, untainted and unscarred by such atrocities, powerful and capable—the *real* me. The me I so desperately want to be again, but I know I never will be. So many things were stolen that day. Lauren's reappearance rips the seams on my old wounds, gutting me again, especially since she inflicted many herself.

Not Lena's fault.

I edge out from under Ruthie and return to my spot a moment later, contract in hand.

I start reading, but the words soon swirl on the page. I move to the kitchen table for more direct light and get my reading glasses—another change I don't like. I pop my prescription migraine medicine with a glass of water and keep reading.

Soon, the front door clicks, and Lena steps in, carrying a paper bag from Sunny's. Dot must've driven her. I don't know what to expect, which unnerves me. We've never argued like this before. Since she's often fueled by anxiety, it's hard to know where this new road will take us.

Our eyes meet—hers are puffy but dry. Her lips upturn slightly—not enough to be called a smile, but an attempt at one.

She offers reassurance. I do nothing. Even so, I feel myself softening to her. Despite our second fight in as many days, she's home with a dinner plan and a hint of a smile. She always makes others feel good even when she doesn't.

"Mom, look. Dad's letting me rot my brain," Ruthie tattles, pointing at the princess movie on TV. Catching my stern gaze, she shrugs. "He told me not to let the princess part go to my head, though."

Her smile grows. "That's good. Hungry for dinner?"

"What're we having?"

Lena gives her a coy look. "A Ruthie special."

Her face goes wide with delight. She spits "spaghetti" in a single syllable. I laugh—I can't help it, and the room feels like home again—not a waiting room for an unwanted appointment.

Chuckling, Lena empties the bag one-handed, revealing each ingredient to her captive audience. Ruthie loves helping with dinner, but given my work schedule, I don't get to see their dinner game very often. With each unveiling, she steps toward the kitchen, until finally climbing onto a barstool and leaning half her body across the counter.

"First, we start the sauce," she declares, holding up a wooden spoon with authority.

Lena gets out a cutting board, knife, onion, and green pepper. She attempts to hold the pepper with her injured hand and cut it with the other, but it spins out from under her loose grip.

"Let me help." I rise from the table. My eyes need a break anyway.

Lena moves aside, saying nothing, and busies herself with a more manageable task—boiling water for the noodles.

I sympathize—the inability to do what should be easy poses a mental challenge. She's not used to it. Not like I am. Her frustration grows with each difficult action, even when I step in to help. No one wants to depend on help. At least her affliction is temporary.

Over dinner, not much is said. Lena seems reluctant to engage us like usual. But finally, she fills the void with, "Tomorrow's Sunday, and it's our first day off together in ages. Let's do something fun. I thought we could—"

"I'm working."

Her shoulders fall. "On a Sunday? You never work on Sundays."

"Making up for time lost." I don't tell her I called my captain and asked for a shift. I'm not proud of this. Or her disappointment.

But work provides a good distraction. Besides, she's done this to me a hundred times.

"What shift?" she tries, her voice duller than usual. "Maybe we could do something before or after."

"Mid."

"How about Ruthie and I bring you dinner, then? We could meet at the park like we used to."

"The one with the gators?" Ruthie gushes.

"Yes, gator park," Lena says. Her eyes land on mine, softly pleading. "Will you come gator spotting with us, Ben?"

A lump forms in my throat. "Can't. I'm working a concert at the amphitheater downtown."

"Oh, Ben. A concert? That won't be good for you," she says and half-signs together.

"I'll be fine."

"Can we go to church with Auntie Dot and Aunt Barb?" Ruthie asks. She shouldn't call them Auntie or Aunt, especially not Mrs. Moore, but I've given up correcting her. She's claimed Dot as her Auntie; by extension, Mrs. Moore is Aunt Barb.

"Sure." Lena collects dirty dishes and takes them into the kitchen, swallowing her disappointment.

She attempts no further discussion, even after Ruthie goes to bed.

No talking.

No interrogation.

Maybe she's broken.

Or simply tired of fighting.

After the things I said, I understand.

I continue reading the contract while she moves quietly around me —folding laundry, *sort of,* rinsing their boots in the mud room, and straightening Ruthie's toys in the living room. I drown her out, focusing on the convoluted lawyer-speak before me.

After reading every word of the contract (some parts multiple times), I realize it's a good deal. She'll make two years' profit in two months. Plus, she's thought of everything—maintaining our residency and normal routines, compensation for employees, parking allotments, spaces for support groups to continue meeting, our personal use of the playground, walking trail, fields, barn, and even protection of her mom's tree. She has the right to attend daily production meetings and offer input. There's even a stipend for the animals they might use in shots.

This wasn't a snap decision. She considered everything, even things I wouldn't have. Though her days often get away from her, Lena *is* a good businessperson, and Saddletree means the world to her. I should've trusted her to ensure that Saddletree is treated with the respect and care it deserves.

Glancing up from my reading, I expect to see her, but the open living room, kitchen, and dining are empty. Except for where I'm reading, the lights are low, as if she's gone to bed.

A sinking, empty feeling hits me with her absence, growing deeper and darker with every shit thing I said to her earlier. She tried to do something good for us—*for me*—and I answered with, "Why haven't you given me more kids?" What the fuck is wrong with me?

I find her in the dark bedroom, turned away from me, appearing asleep. But I feel the tension in the room and know she isn't. I quietly go about my normal routine, playing along. If she doesn't want to talk, I won't make her.

Soon, I slide into bed and curl around her, careful of her injured arm, propped on a pillow beside her. Her body stiffens, but she doesn't pull away. She always accepts me, even when she probably shouldn't. I ease closer, cradling her to me, hoping she understands my regret, that she feels what I can't seem to say.

CHAPTER 16

Lena

DOT, Cherry, and I nestle into our usual spots on Mrs. Moore's front porch, our white rockers creaking in unison. We sip on what Cherry affectionately calls "wine spritzers"—a mix of wine and Sprite. It's our post-church and lunch ritual when our schedules allow—not often enough for me. In the yard, Ruthie trails behind Mrs. Moore, a basket of freshly clipped blooms in her hands. Mrs. Moore's love for fresh bouquets is well-known.

"You should've talked to him before signing," Dot says for the hundredth time. "I told you."

"I thought it'd be a big romantic gesture, you know? Like Ben's fireworks."

Cherry cocks her head. "Remind me… what's the fireworks story?"

Memories rush in, bringing a wide smile. I love telling this story, and though I'm sure I've told Cherry it before, it spills anyway. "It was the shittiest day. I lost what I thought would be my dream job because of the pandemic, ruined the deal to sell the house to the Harveys, the living room ceiling was practically caving in, and I was panicked about my future and Lucas's because his husband Drew had Covid, and I couldn't be there to help. Everything had gone to hell. And then, Ben showed up—"

"And Lena attacked him," Dot laughs.

Warmth rises to my cheeks. "Yep, I did. I'll never forget our rainy first kiss… or what happened after."

Cherry coos. "Ooooohhhhhh. Give me all the sexy details."

Dot and I share a grin before I say, "We didn't do *that*, Cherry."

"Not for lack of trying," Dot added. "Lena basically played musical make-out spots all through the house before ending in the barn, unable to… close the deal."

Cherry gapes. "Why the hell not?"

"I couldn't relax," I admit. "Not in that house, the way it was. Not with myself, either. My anxiety took over, and I fell apart. I broke out crying."

"So, things were getting all hot and heavy, and you *cried*? What'd Ben do?"

"He held me." My hands drift up my arms, remembering the feeling. Not that it's hard. The same comfort warmed me last night when he fell asleep molded to me like icing on a cake. For a while, I lay there, confused and hurt. After the things he said, it's a wonder he wanted to touch me at all. But soon, I let go of my thoughts for the reality of his actions—he loves me and must've felt sorry.

"He held me as long as I needed… and later surprised me with *real* fireworks over the pond. Fireworks for fireworks, he said. He turned the worst day into the best night. It was the first time I imagined my family home could be something more… that he and I could be something more, too."

Cherry sighs. "Damn. I take back what I said about him having no game."

"As you should," I smirk. "No one had ever done something so beautiful for me. That's what I thought the movie deal would be for him —a way to show him everything's okay. I thought he'd feel loved, not pissed."

"Men are thick, anyway," Cherry decides. "If it doesn't involve food or sex, it takes time for them to get it."

"Ben isn't thick. He's just… hurting. I haven't been there for him." I take a deep breath as if sucking in confidence from the warm air. "That's going to change."

"I'd be more worried about Lauren," Cherry says. "Dot said she was the hottest woman she's ever seen."

"Not *the* hottest," Dot corrects, extending her hand submissively. "Top five, maybe."

"Oh, where does Jaye fall on that list?" I laugh.

She bites her bottom lip in deliberation. "Jaye, Jaye, Jaye… she's *the* hottest. She's fucking brilliant, too. The other night, we spent an hour on the phone just talking about alien excretions."

Cherry and I share a grimace. "Well, it must be love when you can talk alien excretions," I say. "Have you asked her out yet?"

Her shoulders bounce. "Eh, I've got time. The movie deal may not be a big romantic gesture for Ben, but it is for me—I'm going to romance the hell of out her."

My head tilts in skepticism. "What will that look like, Dot?"

"Yeah, stalking her and tugging on her ponytail?" Cherry giggles.

"I have serious game," she says. "You'll see."

"Oh, please tell me you're making her a mix tape," Cherry goads.

Dot blushes. "It's a *playlist*, grandma… but yeah, I'm creating soundtracks for her graphic novels. She'll love it. Assholes."

I laugh. "Well, you're welcome to steal Ben's fireworks idea. That was definitely the most romantic thing anyone's done for me. What about you, Cherry? Do you have a most romantic gesture ever story?"

Her red fingernail taps against her chin. "Brian Kennedy, fifth grade. He always had KitKats in his lunchbox—my favorite candy bar. One day, he brought an extra one for me."

"He gave you a break, huh?" Dot laughs. "That's sweet."

"He kept bringing them, too. We'd sit together, giggling over our chocolate fingers. He was shy. Sharing his chocolate bars broke the ice, I think." She shrugs, her grin wide with the memory. Bringing her phone to her face, she says, "Wonder if he's on Instagram."

"There you go, Lena babe. Just bring Ben his favorite candy bar."

"Well, you've already given him a Baby Ruth," Cherry laughs, "so I bet his next favorite is Mounds for those muscles. Or a bag of Kisses. He'll like that."

"Oh, a bag of Kisses," Dot says. "I'm stealing that for my romance list for Jaye."

"You have a list?" I ask, brow perched.

Her cheeks redden as she types into her phone. "So? It wouldn't hurt for you to have a list for Ben. Your romance game needs help, right?"

"Ugh, I guess so, if Ben was open to it. Candy and playlists aren't going to cut it."

Still tapping her phone, Cherry says, "Sending you both links from some influencers with ideas for romancing your significant other. Talk about game, though… that nurse I met at the hospital? Amazing." Her eyes go wide with the word. "He really knows his way around—"

"Hey, Ruthie!" I chime in as she approaches. Cherry clamps her lips shut. "Done collecting flowers?"

She nods, barely holding the wicker basket with her bounty.

Mrs. Moore smiles. "Ruthie's decided that hydrangeas are her favorite."

"They don't have petals, Mom. They have *sepals*—Aunt Barb told me. They're leaves that turn pretty."

"They start green but discover their true colors as they grow," she explains.

"Kinda like us," I grin, and Mrs. Moore gives me an affirming wink, flashing me back to her high school chemistry class.

"They're big and poofy," Ruthie says, "like lollipops."

"Oh, never eat them, though," Mrs. Moore says, holding up her finger. "Poisonous."

Ruthie salutes. "Aye, aye, captain."

"Now, let's get these in water." Mrs. Moore guides Ruthie inside.

"How's Mrs. Moore doing?" I ask Dot. "She looks a little…"

"Slow." Dot leans up in her chair and pulls her vape pen from her pocket. "She says she's fine, but I don't know. Sometimes, she needs a shot, and sometimes, she doesn't. I'll talk to the nurses when we go on Friday."

Six months ago, Mrs. Moore turned eighty, and her yearly blood-work revealed blood cancer. She goes in for a cell-boosting shot weekly but receives it only if her white blood cell count is low. Often, it isn't. Otherwise, the cancer has barely affected her. She keeps up with all her Bible studies, charity work, and gardening.

But Dot worries. Watching Mrs. Moore slow down worries me, too.

"So, let's get back to Ben and your plan. I know a great little shop, very boutiquey, for some ooh-la-la lingerie," Cherry offers. "Avery, the owner, is like my new best friend. I could get you a little discount."

"Hold up." Dot raises a hand. "Lena shouldn't have to doll up her sexy bits just because Ben's in a mood. This ain't the fucking fifties."

"Oh, *I know* that," Cherry says. "It's more about *her* confidence than his enjoyment. It's like wearing lipstick always makes me feel more powerful. Uplifting lingerie uplifts."

Dot nods her reluctant approval. "Lena could use the confidence."

"And the sex," Cherry adds.

"Thanks, but that's not what this is about."

"Connection is connection," Cherry says. "If you want to be close with him, that's one way to do it. Bonus—reminding him of what he has may keep him from looking elsewhere."

"Normally, I'd say don't project your bullshit on her," Dot says to Cherry, "but considering the Lauren factor, she makes a point."

"Ben's no cheater," I say sternly.

"No guy is… until they are," Cherry says.

"Ben's not a cheater, but Lauren Riley seems keen to make him one." Dot blows out a long cloud that dissipates in a breath. "She was making mad come-hither eyes at him the other morning."

"His eyes are the only ones I care about."

"Oh, he didn't look happy," she agrees. "But they have unresolved history… and there's that job offer."

"He's not taking it."

Dot gapes. "Damn girl, you dodged a bullet there."

"Absolutely!" Cherry agrees, sipping her wine. "Him working there every day… around her… protecting her… the bodyguard and the former fiancée, eesh. It sounds like a bad second-chance romance that won't end in your favor."

"What have I told you about reading those?" Dot snaps.

"Probably the same thing she says about my self-help books," I say to Cherry. "Not to read them."

"What's the harm?" Cherry coos.

"The harm? Oh, only that you'll have unrealistic expectations, either of yourselves or your significant others. No book will tame your insane schedule or give you more time in the day, and no guy'll live up to your book boyfriends," she says, motioning from me to Cherry.

"Oh, I know," Cherry says. "But see? That's the trick. I drop them *before* they ruin my fantasy, so real guys, book boyfriends… they're all the same to me. *Temporary.*"

Dot and I share a glance that's a mix between *poor Cherry* and *dang woman.*

"Anyway," Cherry says, before we can argue, "Ben taking that job would put you in a state of constant panic."

"It's a relief, I admit. One less thing to worry about… and fight over."

Dot leans over and rests her hand on my knee. "It'll be okay."

Cherry twists in her rocker, laying her soft fingers on my good hand. "She's right. You and Ben are one of those annoying couples that… *belong.*"

"You'll get through this and be a stronger couple for it."

"And you have us." Cherry shrugs her bony shoulders.

"Thanks, you guys," I say, feeling better.

Cherry's pink manicure slides away from my hand. "How can we help?"

"Just this... your support means so much to me. The next two months will be all about reconnecting with Ben. More lace won't hurt. Let's go see Avery."

CHAPTER 17

Ben

THE RILEY TRUST Amphitheater echoes with applause as the outdoor summer concert begins. Screeching guitars, banging drums, and a thumping bass have me on my two-way, requesting another officer to switch with my central position. She arrives promptly, glad for the swap. She gets to enjoy the concert while I monitor the food truck lot, away from the speakers. My hearing aids don't make loud noises louder, but it's harder to hear much else in these conditions.

A brief patrol along the food trucks reveals nothing concerning. It's a casual venue that rarely presents a problem.

But even the easy assignments prove challenging. The noise rattles in my head, increasing my sensitivity. A headache pings my temples. Lena was right—this isn't good for me.

"Ben?"

A light tap on my arm accompanies a muffled version of my name. I turn and find Lauren. Her white shorts and soft pink sleeveless top accentuate her tan skin and remind me of long summer days together on the beach. She holds a party box of tacos from one of the trucks.

"Wow, you always did look amazing in a uniform. Funny seeing you here," she says.

Best to ignore the uniform remark. "My captain assigned me here."

She shrugs and grins. "You say *assigned*. I say a *funny coincidence*. We were just talking about you in the booth."

"The booth?"

"Well, our version of a skybox." She motions sheepishly over her shoulder at the main building overlooking the amphitheater. "The Riley booth—a little perk to funding the venue. We attend most events. Dad calls it community spirit. The gang's all here… and hungry for tacos. Come say hello."

"I'm on duty." I assess my surroundings rather than her. But it's a challenge. Her hair is up, but loose pieces dangle on her bare shoulders, stirring memories I don't want to have. I straighten my back. "I'm turning down the position. Please extend my appreciation to your father for the opportunity."

A beat passes.

"That's it? You're not even going to tell me why?"

"I'm not required to explain."

"It'd be nice. If something's lacking in the offer—"

"There isn't. It's personal. I put you and the Rileys in my rearview long ago. I don't see a reason to go back."

She loses her smile and glances at the ground between us. When her gray eyes land on mine again, she nods. "Not even for my mom's weird handsiness or Uncle Rob's gross doctor stories?"

An unstoppable laugh rumbles from me. She routinely saved me from both at their frequent family events. Jillian would loop her hand around my arm and parade me around parties—her way of getting me talking. Rob, a well-known orthopedic surgeon, shared his worst ER stories; the more graphic, the better. Lauren would swoop in when she suspected I'd reached my limit.

But I never minded. The upside to spending time with the Rileys was that they made me feel I belonged there.

Until I didn't.

"Wow, I never thought I'd get another laugh out of you. It's good to see you smile." She tilts her head, scrutinizing me. "Well, I'm disappointed, but I understand. But is there any chance you could tell Dad yourself? He'll blame me, especially if I break the bad news."

She tips her head toward the booth again.

"I'm on patrol."

With an amused chuckle, she nods toward four officers loitering twenty feet from us. "I think this parking lot is covered. It'll only take a minute."

She steps away, leaving me little choice but to follow.

The booth resembles a large living room with a bar, couches, plush chairs, tables, and a windowed wall overlooking the concert. The music filters gently into the room via speakers built into the walls and ceiling, but it's barely heard over their conversations. I linger in the doorway with Lauren, reluctantly taking in the small group.

The people in this room once mattered to me. They filled the stands at my football games and cheered at my high school graduation. Seeing them again feels jarring, but so does their absence over the years, as if it just hits me.

"I got tacos!" Lauren announces, breaking their chatter. "And Ben!"

The room shifts toward me with wide-eyed familiarity. My timid wave doesn't satiate them. Rising from their seats, the Rileys pull me into their circle, wrapping arms around me and shaking hands. It's like I never left.

Their warm reception makes me wonder how Lauren handled her family after us. What she said to explain my sudden absence. I can only guess she told them the truth.

My headache worsens.

Jillian looks the same: elegant, poised, and beautiful. She tilts her margarita toward me before linking arms and steering me around the room. Lauren's grandmother kisses my cheek. Aunt Miranda, the former Coast Guard pilot, salutes me before introducing her husband and their kids. Uncle Rob also has a new wife, much younger than him, and several small children, who race around the room in a strange game of tag.

He slaps my back. "Heard your wife was in a fender bender. How's her arm?"

"Broken. Distal radius and distal ulna," I say.

"Cast yet?"

"No."

"Wrist fractures are tricky. If they aren't set right, it could mean a much longer recovery." He hands me his card. "Bring her by the office Monday morning. Around ten."

I consider refusing. I'm trying to distance myself from them, not become more integrated. But Dr. Robert Riley handles orthopedics for the Carolina Panthers and two local Olympic-level surfers. I can't say no if it means Lena receives better care. "Yes, sir. Thank you."

He slaps my back again and leans in. "I've got a court behind the office. Shoot hoops after?"

"Yes. Definitely." Basketball with Rob in the Riley's driveway was a distinct highlight to many family events.

Jillian tugs me toward her husband.

"Ben, working the event today? Must be fate." John shakes my hand and embraces me, not minding my gear and vest. "We were just telling them about you joining our team."

"Possibly," I correct, as the family cheers and claps. "I'm considering it."

I catch Lauren's small smile at my sudden reversal, but it's not the right time to do it. I decide to call John on Monday.

But talking and answering questions about my parents and Becca, I realize it won't be an easy call to make. I don't mind Jillian's doting attention. Regular pick-up games with Rob would be a welcome diversion. Working for John would be an honor. Until everything fell apart, I loved being a part of the Riley family. It felt like the one place I truly belonged.

His heavy arm wraps my shoulders as we talk, reminding me of a particularly shitty football game. An easy pass would've won the game if I hadn't fucked up the throw. Mr. Riley met me outside the locker room. He put his arm around me and said, "Everyone wants the wins, but the losses… those make us who we are."

His words stayed with me through each loss, especially in Afghanistan. There, the losses changed everything but, strangely, made me a better man—a *lucky* man, though it took me years to see it.

Lauren wedges between me and her mother with a knowing look. "Dad, don't monopolize him. He's on duty. And Mom, he's not your personal escort."

"Oh, Lauren, relax. Ben doesn't mind," Jillian argues. "Tell us about—"

My phone rings, and with the volume up, the conversation comes to a skidding stop. It's Lena, so I answer immediately.

"Hey, Ben. Is it a good time?"

"Everything okay?"

"Yes, we're great. We're at Greenfield Lake. Ruthie insisted on dinner with the gators, and Mrs. Moore let me borrow her MINI Cooper. We brought dinner. Any chance you can join us? We don't mind waiting."

She's talking a mile a minute, which tells me she's nervous, probably that I'll say no.

I try to interject, but she continues, "I thought you might have a meal break soon. I brought your migraine meds, too, if you need them."

"Is that Lena?" Lauren asks louder than necessary. "Tell her we say hello."

There's a pause before Lena says, "Was… that… Lauren?"

Lauren fucking Riley. My irritation spikes.

"Invite her to the booth, Ben," John tacks on. "Her and Ruthie."

"I have to go." I exit their booth before they can argue, shutting the door behind me. "Lena?"

She's no longer there. I call her back.

"I thought you had to go," she answers, her voice distressed.

"No. That wasn't directed at you. I'll be there in fifteen minutes."

I hurry to arrange my meal break and get to my patrol car. Lena likely feels suspicious, perhaps even betrayed—I can't blame her. Lauren has wedged between us for the second time in two days, creating doubts where there shouldn't be any.

Lena overlooks the lake and Ruthie from a park bench while our daughter gator-hunts safely behind the raised boardwalk's railings. They don't see me at first. I stop beside a bursting palmetto and breathe in with relief. It's quiet, a welcome change from the ringing in my ears. My headache subsides with the peacefulness.

Seeing them makes me grateful and more upset with myself. Her head sinks, and her shoulders droop, making me wonder what she's thinking.

And if she's crying.

She looks up when I move to the bench, her eyes sweeping over my uniform with guarded relief as if she worried I'd lied to her again. She swallows her distress, reaching for the cooler by her feet. "Hungry? Ruthie helped me make very messy subs."

She refuses eye contact as if she's overloaded emotionally. "I don't want to fight in front of Ruthie," she says, strained and desperate as she fumbles to open the cooler.

"Lena, I wasn't there with Lauren. I was assigned to the concert. I had no idea she'd be there."

Her eyes catch mine in a huff. "How do you expect me to…"

She can't finish her sentence, but she doesn't have to. *How can I expect her to trust me now?* I move beside her, setting the cooler aside. Her hand is limp in mine, trembling just enough to know that I've hurt her. Again. I grip it tightly.

"Forgive me, please. For causing you anxiety today. For everything yesterday. I was an asshole and said things I didn't mean. I let my frustration take over, and you didn't deserve any of it." I take a breath, words getting stuck in my throat. "All I do is fuck-up lately."

Her shoulders sink, and she smirks through her hurt feelings. "I know the feeling. We all fuck-up, Ben."

"Yeah, but you never take it out on me. I'm so fucking sorry."

She nods, forehead pinched with worry lines, but her hand locks around mine. "It's okay. We need to talk more. Tell me what happened today."

"Nothing. She was there with her family for the concert. The only reason I went to the booth—"

"Booth?" she interrupts with confusion.

"They call it a booth. It's a skybox. It's where rich people watch concerts."

"Oh."

"I went there to tell John I didn't want the job."

"Did you? Tell him?" she asks, perking with hope.

"It didn't seem appropriate around the family. I will Monday morning. He'll appreciate hearing it from me directly."

She absorbs the information and then nods. "You… like him. A lot."

"Yes."

She sighs, turning her attention to Ruthie, playing nearby. Her expression remains pained, though. I take her splinted arm in my hands, examining it gently. Brownish-blue bruises mix with the red areas. It's less swollen today, but her fingers stay fixed in one position, unmovable. She pulls her arm away, as if me looking at it makes it hurt more.

I take a breath and say what I wanted to tell her last night. "The studio's contract is a good deal. I understand why you accepted it."

Her eyes gloss over with potential tears, but she keeps them in. "Thank you for that. I should've consulted you. You always think of things I don't—"

"No, you covered everything."

"So, you'll accept the circus?" she asks with reserved amusement.

"Yes. Of course. Anything for you, and you're right. It'll probably be good for us."

Tears slip to her lashes, and I love knowing exactly how she feels.

Lena wears her emotions so freely, so beautifully, like a bold, colorful dress that moves with her and changes with her mood.

Loving me must be torture for her. I'm cardboard to her watercolor canvas.

"Ben, don't be hasty about the job. It's an incredible offer, working for someone you truly admire. You have time to consider it. Why not take it?"

"It's more trouble than it's worth, especially with Lauren involved." My teeth clench, considering her stunt when Lena called. It could've been innocent, but remembering how she occasionally manipulated her parents as a teenager, I can't be sure. Regardless, Monday's call feels easier to make.

Lena's weak voice cuts through my thoughts. "Do you still care for her? At all?"

"No, I don't. Not like that. She and her family influenced me greatly. We share some fond memories. That's all."

I hesitate, watching Ruthie play. She waves a large fern leaf and marches in a one-woman parade along the deck. A pained smirk brings me back to Lena, eyeing me intently with her big blues like she wants to dive into me and swim around until she gets the answers she needs.

Answers she deserves.

"Lauren hurt me terribly. She couldn't... handle my injuries." I scoff. "Neither could I." The words hang between us, and Lena stays silent—a relief. It's hard enough without questions. My brow pinches with the memory, inciting my headache again, and I want to get small and disappear so I never feel that way again. "I'm still... angry."

My head hangs at the admission. Angry *and* ashamed would be more accurate. Lena's fingers curl around mine, encouraging me without making a sound.

My eyes land on hers again—there's no judgment in her expression. Only acceptance. So, I tell her exactly what I'm thinking. "I didn't know love until you."

A smile joins her tears like she knows exactly what I mean. Of course, she does. The strength of our love passes between us, energized by my rare vulnerability and her usual Lena-ness. It's strange to say, but I love it when she's moved to tears, when she feels so much over something I've done or said that she literally can't hold it in. Tearful Lena is beautiful and genuine and adorably herself. Adorably mine, too. I run over the wetness with the pads of my thumbs. Her forehead settles against mine. Sharing the space in our pocket, I relax in us again.

For all I lost with the Rileys, I gained so much more. A complicated multiverse, yes, but a better one, too.

Her delicate fingertips slide up my cheek. "Thanks for telling me that. I see it's not easy to talk about it."

"It isn't." Talking about what happened to Lauren and me is the last conversation I want to have with Lena as if the toxic remnants might spill over from one to the other like ink spreading on a paper towel. I never want her to know the full story.

But she smirks tearfully, looking more hopeful. "I'm here whenever you're ready."

Ruthie bumbles over, waving the fern, and Lena sits up, regaining her composure. She grabs the cooler and sets it between us. "For now, let's just enjoy the day, huh?"

"Good idea." I hold down the notch and open the cooler. Inside, I find mason jars of lemonade and plastic-wrapped subs. I grab the top one, ogling the exorbitant amount of plastic wrap she used. The plastic is almost as thick as the sandwich.

Lena holds up her injured hand in defense. "I had trouble with the plastic wrap. It's hard operating with one hand."

A chuckle rumbles from me. "I understand... though the environment may not."

"The environment understands that I'm adapting... slowly."

"The cast will help. We have an appointment Monday at ten. Dr. Rob Riley wants to take over your care."

"Is he good?"

"He's the Rolls Royce of doctors," I reply, remembering John using the expression about my future implants.

She looks amused. "Is Rolls Royce still a thing?"

I grin. "In some circles... not ours. I love you."

"Love you, too." Her eyes catch the light as she looks toward me, and I think of firecrackers. "Now, eat. I don't want you returning to the mayhem without a full stomach. Otherwise, you'll get a migraine."

"Yes, ma'am."

CHAPTER 18

Lena

WHITE TRACTOR-TRAILERS STREAM down the old country road the next morning, slowly managing wide turns into the driveway and lining the field closest to the road. The parade lasts almost a full hour. Ben and I watch from the upper deck, sipping coffee and cringing whenever the long trucks twist into the fence's entrance. It's a narrow turn, but they make it.

The driveway and field suffer some damage, though. A late-night storm rendered the ground soft, and the heavy trucks leave deep lines and mud tracks behind them.

"We'll have to grate the driveway when this is over," Ben says.

"No, *they'll* grate the driveway," I say, adding it to a mental list to discuss with the production manager, Elsie Todd.

"I should be down there."

"We'd just be in the way. They're the professionals," I assure him. "I'm thinking of asking Cherry to design a logo for Saddletree… for the new van."

"Good idea." His green eyes latch on to me instead of watching the circus unfold. "We should go van shopping… but car shopping first. The Pilot's totaled."

I sigh. "I loved that car."

"Would you love matching Jeeps?" He grins.

I perk up. "Oh, and we could take them off-roading together. Let's go Jeep shopping after the appointment… or any shopping. We're wealthy now."

A bracing thud turns our attention back to the film crew, who have released the rear door of a tractor-trailer. A golf cart travels from the interior to the ground, followed by a forklift.

Ben grunts. "Looks like we'll have many tire treads to worry about."

"Not to worry about," I counter, but he turns away and goes inside. Maybe he doesn't hear me.

At ten, we meet Dr. Rob Riley in his swanky medical office near the hospital. He quickly examines my wrist—it's shaped less sausage-like today, though still blotchy with bruises. He reviews the x-rays and shows me exercises to do when possible. My fingers and hand barely move today, but he promises some range of motion in a week. I smirk at Ben, watching nearby, as Dr. Riley demonstrates the movements.

"It's ASL," I say.

"Similar. You know ASL?" Dr. Riley asks.

"Yes, we use it in our house along with audible speech," I say proudly.

Dr. Riley nods. "That's our Ben. He likes to be prepared."

I cringe internally at *"our* Ben" as if he's property belonging to everyone. Are all the Rileys this possessive over him?

"Ready to shoot some?" he asks Ben.

"Only if you remembered your calcium supplements today. Don't want you breaking a hip."

My head whips toward Ben with astonishment. *Playful banter?* I only see that at home, sometimes. Not that I'm complaining—it's good to see him loosen up.

Dr. Riley throws his head back in laughter. "Ah, man, I've missed that. Come on… Lena, Ebony will be in to set your cast. Think about what color you want."

They leave so quickly that my "have fun" gets drowned out by the closing door.

Soon, dribbling draws me to the office window. Ben and Dr. Riley shoot free throws at a portable hoop in the back lot, laughing like old friends.

They *are* old friends. The stoic tension Ben usually holds in his face vanishes into laughs and smiles like he's entirely different than the man who comes off as unfriendly to folks at Saddletree. He looks *himself* with Rob—a thought that's sweet and painful.

Does Ben feel like he can't be himself at home?

I scan my brain for anything that would counter that theory. But Ben rarely 'hangs out' with anyone except me, Ruthie, and the girls on canasta night at Mrs. Moore's.

Ben loves canasta.

Jack and Rowan, the couple adopting Adam, have become good friends. Jack considers Ben his hero for saving Adam, but even with him, Ben's reserved. His quiet nature makes casual friendships tough.

Dr. Riley appears to be an exception. Or maybe I don't know my husband as well as I think.

Ebony sets my cast. I go with purple, Ruthie's favorite color, and I hope it'll renew her respect for me since my inability to accomplish simple tasks has tickled her lately.

Thirty minutes later, I'm ready to show Ben my new bling. I leave the office and trek around the building. Me and my excitement stop short at the corner when I hear Dr. Riley say, "She wasn't the same after you left."

"Neither was I," Ben says, dribbling.

"She left for over a year, traveling. Trying to find herself again. Came back with the twins. We thought she'd lost her mind, but they're awesome. You'll have to play basketball with Freddy and Omar on break."

"Are they good?"

Dr. Riley looks stern. "Hell yes, and they don't need calcium supplements yet."

They laugh, and I feel bad for listening. But then Dr. Riley says, "She always thought you'd come back. See that she's changed. Forgive her."

Ben stops, one arm holding the ball while the other rests on his hip. "I never gave her that indication."

Dr. Riley shrugs. "You were with Lauren longer than any of my marriages to date. No one believed you'd give up on her, least of all her. One moment shouldn't have ended it."

"Why the fuck not? One moment destroyed me."

"That wasn't Lauren's fault. You took it out on her."

"No, I didn't. What happened couldn't be undone. I don't need the damn guilt trip. Let's play."

He laughs. "I've been waiting a decade to say this… shit happened, and you pushed her away, pushed all of us away. You're the king of self-sabotage, dude."

Ben shrugs lightly, tossing the ball into the basket. "Now, you're a shrink, huh?"

"You need one," he teases. "She needs your forgiveness, man."

"I told her. She has it. But that's her problem—nothing's ever good enough for Lauren."

Dr. Riley moves in and steals the ball. "Take the job. Let her have closure, and she'll move on. It's not like she has a chance with you anyway, right?"

So, she wants a chance with him. It's understood. Ben sees it, too. We stare at Ben, awaiting an answer that takes far too long to deliver. Dr. Riley grins, probably latching onto Ben's pause in a sort of victory. *He's considering it.*

Meanwhile, my heart palpitates, and my breath holds in fear over his delay. *Why isn't he answering?* The correct answer is something along the lines of *right, no chance, no chance in hell, what a dumbass question.* Instead, there's only silence.

Ben slaps the ball away and dribbles around him for another basket. "I don't operate by Rob Riley's rules of marriage—the more the merrier."

Dr. Riley belly laughs. "Hey, don't knock it till you try it."

Pressing myself against the brick wall so they can't see me, I take several deep breaths, replaying the gist of Ben's words the other day. *Hurt terribly. Irreparable. Angry. I didn't know love until you.* But my anxiety bitches pull their punches. She's one of the hottest women ever, and she traveled the world and adopted two boys, hoping, all these years, that Ben would come back to her? *God, it's like my anxiety bitches Frankensteined this woman out of my worst fears.*

Pull your shit together, Lena.

Many long breaths later, I stroll around the corner, flashing my usual smile and holding up my cast. "All done. What do you think of my new look?"

Ben only nods.

"Ah, purple. Fun choice," Dr. Riley says. "Did Ebony answer all your questions about cast care?"

"Yep. I'm all set. Get it? Set? Cast?"

Ben's brow quirks. It's a bad joke, but the best I can do.

Dr. Riley chuckles graciously. "Ah, you're *breaking* my heart."

I laugh. "Thanks for seeing me, Dr. Riley."

"Call me Rob. Ben has my number if you need anything. Don't forget those exercises."

Ben relinquishes the basketball, looking almost disappointed.

At his favorite brewery for lunch, he stares into his beer and holds the glass like it's a genie meant to solve his problems. Problems I wish I fully understood.

"Tell me about Rob," I say. "He seems like a real character."

Ben shrugs but doesn't meet my eyes. "He is. Not much to tell."

"Aw, come on. Surely you have a funny Rob story."

A tiny smirk edges his lips like he might have thought of one, but it disappears just as fast. "I don't know."

"Were you two close?"

"We were all close," he says with a pinched brow and an almost regretful tone, though it's hard to tell.

A beat passes with zero elaboration. He doesn't want to talk about it.

Hurt waves over me suddenly, thinking about how easy Ben was with Rob compared to the man sitting across from me now, grumpy, quiet, and winning a staring contest with his beer. I finally understand why he comes off as unfriendly to people at Saddletree—it feels like he doesn't want to be here. Worse, his quiet nature isn't just reserved for other people, like I thought. He uses it on me, too.

Strangling my napkin under the table, I go for old reliable. "What're you thinking?"

"I'm unsure about turning down the position," he admits, making eye contact for the first time.

My internal organs liquefy into an *oh-shit* feeling, but I manage a short smile. "Why the change of heart?" I ask, though I already know. Spending time with Rob has rekindled something he misses—perhaps the old Ben. Or even the *real* Ben.

He shrugs. "It's lucrative and reliable. The movie deal is risky in the long term. My income will be necessary if Saddletree suffers for closing."

My fault. Again. A quick breath eases my growing tension. I slide my good hand over his across the table. "Ben, Saddletree will be fine. It'll reopen better than ever under improved management. Don't do this for Saddletree. Do it for you... *if* it's what you want."

When he doesn't respond, I squeeze his hand. "Is it? What you want?"

A heavy sigh precedes his answer. "I don't know."

His frustration ripples across the table. His world is changing, and he doesn't know how to navigate it. Offering my opinion feels tricky, especially because I don't think he wants it. The job sounds perfect in every way but one. Cherry and Dot's words replay in my head—*around her… protecting her… her mad come-hither eyes.*

I don't believe Ben would cheat on me, but she'd put him to the test. Falling into old habits is easy. He may be angry, but he still cares for her. Love and anger are two paths along the same trail, right? His anger wouldn't exist without having loved her first. What if those paths cross again?

But letting my fears steal his opportunity feels horribly unfair. Like settling for Lucas's pool house would've been for me five years ago. He'd undoubtedly blame and resent me, just as he has with everything else lately.

I manage an encouraging smile. "Whenever I didn't know what to do, Dad would say to wait for the fog to clear. Advice I wish I would've followed more often. Ninety percent of my bad decisions were made too quickly."

"Time brings clarity—I know," he says dismissively. "But so does more information. John suggested a working interview."

The server brings our food, breaking our conversation. When Ben doesn't continue once she leaves, I launch into my questioning mode. He gives brief but efficient answers, explaining it as a day in the life of the position, with his former training officer showing him the ropes.

While I nod and smile, a full-fledged battle plays out in my head. Anxiety versus Reason.

What harm could it do to have a better feel for the place? Score 1 for Reason.

Ben is a committed husband and father. It's one day, not a lifetime. Score 2 and 3 for Reason.

She's one of the top five hottest women of all time (according to Dot), Ben's first love, and mysteriously missing any worry lines. *Anything* could happen. Angry make-up sex. A romantic reunion. A damsel in distress scenario. Ah, and he has to carry her? What if they get locked in a closet? Or a freaking bedroom? Or caught in the rain? Forced proximity, locked doors, grumpy meets sunshine, second chances, and rekindled love?

Damn Cherry and her romances!

Only it's not just fiction. These things happen. Even to the best couples.

What if he spends one day with her and decides he no longer wants me? That I'm a placeholder for the woman he lost? What if one touch between them sets off an avalanche of love and regret that buries them inside and takes him away from me forever?

And anxiety slides into home for the win.

Now, *I* stare into my beer, hoping for answers.

"What're you thinking?" His emerald eyes latch on mine in his thoughtful way.

"I won't lie—Lauren bothers me. I'm worried about you and don't trust her. It's hard feeling comfortable about this, especially since that time in your life caused you so much pain, and you can't even talk to me about it."

There, I said it. An understated version of it, anyway. But calling Lauren my worst, hellish nightmare and my anxiety bitches' new bestie seems too much.

My brow clinches, waiting for him to argue, blame me, or worse, fall into silence again, leaving me stranded in my overactive imagination.

Instead, he nods. "I understand. I'm asking a lot from you, especially with how things have been lately, but I'd like to explore the option. Not for Lauren. But for me. I'm asking for your trust—"

"You have it." The words roll out like boulders down a mountainside, unstoppable. "You deserve the opportunity, and I won't keep you from it. I'll be okay."

He looks surprised. "Are you sure?"

"Yes. I want what's best for you. You should do the working interview and see what it's like." I bookend my answer with another forced smile and slip my hand over his for good measure.

He seems relieved, even meeting my smile with a softer one of his. I have to trust him. But this might haunt me when he loves the job, and Lauren becomes a permanent fixture in his work life and my worries.

Worries-for-later file.

Determined not to let everything be about the Rileys, I steer the conversation toward Saddletree. Ben's remarks about my business hurt, but despite how poorly he said it, he only wants to help me and get his wife back. I need to let go of feeling offended and get to work.

His mood shifts, thankfully. He shares his ideas beyond Shakespeare and the van. Going completely digital tops his list—scheduling, inventory, ordering, and accounting—and he gets excited as he explains. Transforming my system, such as it is, fills me with trepidation. But he's narrowed software options to three, making it more manageable for me to research.

"Setting it up will be the most time-consuming part. Once it's in place, you'll be amazed at the time you save."

He texts me their websites, briefly explaining their pros and cons. I look forward to sitting on the deck overlooking the pond with coffee, my computer, and an open mind. If Ben gets excited about this, so should I.

He gives me a shortlist of security companies that install electric gates and cameras.

"That way, when we're closed, we're closed," he says. "We can enjoy Saddletree without interference... the way we used to. I miss how peaceful it was then."

"Me, too." Ben has pushed for this since the first "trespassers" wandered into the off-limits barn and drove down our driveway during off-hours. People show whenever they feel like it, as if Saddletree was public land paid for by tax dollars, and they're entitled to it.

"It'd be nice to have some privacy again," I say.

"So, you'll consider it?"

"Definitely. Saddletree is *ours* first. I'm sorry it hasn't felt like that lately, but I promise that'll change."

"Lena, thank you." He says the words slowly, oozing sincerity like it's exactly what he needed me to say.

We share a look that assures me we're thinking the same thing. *Everything's okay.*

But everything's not okay—Elsie Todd flags us down as we pull into the driveway later that afternoon. Ben stops and puts down his window.

"The bunnies," she gasps, "they've escaped."

Ruthie makes a strange wallop from the backseat while unbuckling her car seat. Ben puts the Jeep into park, mid-driveway, and we race to the pen. The door flops open, and the pen lies empty.

"I'm so sorry," Elsie gushes. "Someone wanted a cuddle but didn't latch the door properly."

"Here's one," a crewman says as he approaches.

"Chandler!" Ruthie coos, eyes full of fat tears. She follows the man inside the pen, where he releases Chandler.

"Ruthie, stay here in case any bunnies come back," Ben says. She plops on the tree stump inside, loving on the big ears of the rescued American Fuzzy Lop.

"Perimeter search," Ben says. "You take the barn. I'll take the chicken coop."

I do as I'm told, starting in the stall where the feed is kept. There, Monica, a checkered black and white bunny, nibbles on a feed bag. I scoop her up and return her to the pen, where Ruthie claps through her tears.

Ben finds Phoebe and Joey, the Rex Rabbits, near the chicken coop, looking lost and confused. Jaye finds Rachel, the fluffy cashmere, under the hay in an empty barn stall.

But we can't find Ross. After two hours of frantic searching for the pygmy rabbit, we take a fitful Ruthie home. She is devastated. Ben carries her upstairs, and she cries on his shoulder.

"Pygmies like to dig holes, remember?" I say, tearing up. "He's probably hiding in a hole."

"He'd never hide from me, Mom."

In bed, she curls into a ball and sobs. Ben gives me a look outside her bedroom that stabs my heart—anger, irritation, blame—and our good day vanishes.

"I'll keep looking," he says gruffly. "Stay here."

Ruthie soon falls asleep. Helpless, I stand on the deck with binoculars, hoping to glimpse the tiny bunny.

I don't find Ross, but my property is overrun with trucks and gear. A huge white tent has been erected near the tractor-trailers. Construction has started on the new shelter by the pond. Crews set up scenes on the walking trail, in the main house, and around the carport. Golf carts, a small pick-up, a forklift, and over a hundred people traverse the landscape like ants over an anthill.

They've come in and taken over, just like he said they would. My promise to make this place feel like ours again feels further away.

CHAPTER 19
Lena

PROBLEMS CONTINUE.

Damage along the back fence line by an overzealous truck driver meant a morning wrangling horses one-handed for me—not easy to do, especially with Shadow flicking his ass in my direction every time I tried.

Our first group meetings had to be rescheduled because of a misunderstanding with the film crew.

Ben was none-too-pleased to discover an entitled actor playing with the bunnies, even after we posted more signs not to enter. Ruthie's cried herself to sleep every night over Ross.

And someone ran through my garden with a golf cart, ruining my cucumbers and my plan to pickle them.

My "vacation" from Saddletree has only made me more stressed.

"Growing pains," Mr. Wickers says, tipping his coffee mug as we meet on the wraparound deck outside my house overlooking the pond.

I invited Trisha to talk dining room business, Alice Harvey about Ben's van idea, Dot and Cherry for moral support, Jaye because sets were in transition (and for Dot), and Mr. Wickers because, why not?

"It'll pass," he adds on. "All relationships have to iron out the wrinkles."

"The studio is extremely apologetic about the snafus," Jaye says as Ruthie hands her a teacup and splashes lemonade into it.

"Jack and I could do without the spotlights shining into our bedroom at all hours," Alice says, tidying her skirt around her knees, "but we're not ones to complain."

Ben has. With our bedroom at the back of the house, closest to the outer trail, we've dealt with the lights, too. And the noise. Between that and Ben's nightmares, it's a wonder we sleep at all.

"Don't everyone get your panties in a bunch. Dr. Jim Hunter is saving humanity from crazy-ass witches out there," Dot says as if it's real. "They're filming the most elaborate scenes in the woods first while the weather cooperates. Soon, they'll move to the house for the tamer stuff—out of sight, out of mind."

I doubt it, I think, but don't say.

"Am I right, Jaye?" Dot turns toward her, though they're close, like first daters in a movie theater. A magical spark fires when their eyes meet—lips upturned, eyes narrowed, cheeks blushing—as if Cupid has sprinkled love dust over their heads. Or banged their heads together.

"Absolutely right. We have some on-location days coming up. That'll give everyone a break, too," she adds with gentle enthusiasm.

"That'll be nice," I sigh. "Ben's been..." I don't know how to finish my sentence. *Irritated. Quieter than usual. Livid.* He blames his frustrations on me—all bitter fruit from the same poisoned tree I let take over our home. I broke out Avery's "surefire seduction lingerie" for Ben the other night—it misfired, and I'm still stinging from his rejection. For the first time in our marriage, he told me he was tired—*tired.*

With his working interview taking place as we speak, I'm hyped up on high anxiety.

Even so, I report my progress. We discuss the new software I've purchased with Ben's help, and make plans with Trisha and Mr. Wickers to learn it. Cherry agrees to design a logo, and Dot volunteers to take Alice and me van shopping.

Then, we agree to Friday afternoon meetings for future updates on our progress, which I promptly add to the family calendar.

When the meeting's over, Ruthie and I walk the group downstairs, saying goodbye at the barn's entrance. Mr. Wickers and Trisha leave together, and so do Dot and Jaye. My heart flutters, hoping that my sweet friends find love like me.

But my shoulders slump. Ben and I aren't exactly ideal models for happily-ever-after right now.

"Mom, ready to feed the animals?" Ruthie tugs my hand.

"First the animals, then us. Deal?"

"Deal. I'm starving."

"Hmm, what're you fixing for dinner?" I ask with a playful smile before glancing down the empty driveway and feeling disappointed that Ben's not home yet.

Ruthie taps her chin. "Waffles? No, wait… French toast?"

"Dinner, not breakfast—"

"Hi."

My shoulders jerk in surprise before twisting around and laughing at the man standing there. It's Matt Kirby. *The Matt Kirby.* I'm taken back in time to Mom and me in the shag-carpeted, wood-paneled living room where we'd binge-watch TV shows, his especially, to take her mind off how terrible she felt. Matt Kirby made cameos in my restless dreams back then, a calming presence amid the chaos. Few things made Mom giddy, but this would have.

"Hi," I repeat dumbly, taking in his boyishly handsome features. He looks exactly the same as on TV, from his thick, neatly styled hair to the light expanse of stubble along his strong jawline.

His hand magnetizes to mine, and he cradles it there softly. "I'm Matt. You must be Lena."

"Um, yes. I'm Lena." His blue eyes are mesmerizing. I drop his hand, fearing that I've held it too long. "This is Ruthie." She gives him a light wave, unimpressed. "I'm a big fan."

"Oh," he says, as if he never hears that. "Well, the *Hunter* series is—"

"No, not of *Hunter.* I mean, it's fine and all, but horror isn't my thing. I meant of *Nightshift.*"

His ridiculously handsome face lights up. "Wow, you humble me. That was my first real gig. I was… bad."

"No, you were awesome. Detective Mike Storm, the insomniac policeman hunting for bad guys while the world sleeps. Ah, Mom and I adored that show—it was one of the few we agreed on. *Who needs sleep?*"

I do a mock Mike Storm voice, and he laughs, his cheeks reddening. "You just dropped one of my catchphrases on me… nice."

"That wasn't even my favorite. I liked it when you were the voice of reason to your anxious partner. *We got this.*"

"Storm wasn't exactly a genius at one-liners." He looks surprisingly sheepish but amused.

"No, but there was something comforting about him. Mom and I would say that to each other every time we had a doctor's appointment… which was pretty often."

"Doctors' appointments?" The soft way his brow furrows makes me think he really cares… or speaks well to his acting ability.

"She was sick for a long time. I cared for her. Here. She passed away. That's how I came to own Saddletree."

My words are choppy and awkward. It feels unnatural to talk about Mom with a stranger, especially a *familiar* stranger.

He nods, shoving his hands in the pockets of his dark jeans. "I'm sorry for your loss." His blue eyes linger on mine like they're stuck. "My mom's gone, too. The world hasn't felt the same since, like I've lost my best protection."

"I'm sorry, too. I get it. I call it losing your umbrella, the shield that keeps you safe and warm against the elements."

"Huh, that's exactly how it feels. That's so insightful."

"Well, I don't know about that, but thank you." *Wow. Am I having a moment with Matt Kirby?* "And sorry for rambling. I didn't expect to find Matt Kirby in my barn. Um, what are you doing here?"

"Right, yes, sorry about that. I needed a walk and wanted to get a feel for where we'll be shooting." His eyes roll over the high ceiling of the barn. "Saddletree is amazing, so peaceful and beautiful. It's by far the best film set I've ever been on."

"Ah, I bet you say that to all the property owners."

"Yes, but this time I mean it," he grins, and a warm tickle stirs in my abdomen. "Truly, I'm a fan of everything you've done here. We're lucky to have found you."

I nibble my bottom lip to keep from gawking. *Is Matt Kirby putting on the smolder? For me?*

"Mom, the horses aren't going to feed themselves." Ruthie tugs my arm again.

"Right, we should go."

"*Night is coming, and the storm is almost here,*" he says in his Storm-voice.

Suddenly, a giddy twelve-year-old, I bust out laughing, leaning toward him. "Oh, my gosh, Mom would've loved having you around."

A good-natured laugh rumbles from him. "I get that a lot from the older ladies."

"Ha, younger ones, too, I bet."

"Lena." Ben's voice splits like an arrow, curt and sudden, his annoyance clear. His green eyes laser in on Matt as he approaches.

"Hey, I'm Matt."

The two meet with extended hands. Matt smiles warmly. Ben doesn't.

"Ben Wright."

"Good to meet you. Beautiful place here—I was just telling Lena."

Ben nods, emotionless. "Filming is supposed to be in the woods today."

A beat passes in an intense stare-down. I'm fucking mortified. I try to bridge the awkward gap. "Mom and I were big fans of Matt. He played a cop in *Nightshift.*"

Ben says, "I play a cop in real life."

My mortification upticks as I gape at my husband. *What is this?* His unfriendly vibe has leveled up to actual rudeness.

"Filming is supposed to be in the woods," Ben says again after a stinging pause.

Matt steps away, hands sliding into his pockets again. "I better get over there before they notice I'm gone. Nice to meet you."

He backsteps carefully like the barn is suddenly riddled with landmines.

Once he's gone, I give Ben a pained look, signing as I demand, "What was that? You were harsh."

"He shouldn't be in here."

Bored with us, Ruthie jumps into the driver's seat of the ATV and pretends to drive it.

"That's Matt Kirby. Mom and I used to love his show—"

"I don't care who he is. He shouldn't be in here."

"*You* shouldn't be so rude. I'd never be like that to someone you admire." My entire body prickles with anger at his deadpan, uncaring expression. A bad mood is one thing, but dismissing a memory of Mom feels like stabbing me in the heart. "Thanks for ruining a good Mom memory with your shit attitude, Ben."

I curve around him for the ATV and move Ruthie to the passenger seat. "Time to feed."

"Is Daddy coming?"

"Nope, he's had a long day."

"Go slow, Mom. For Ross," she advises as I start the engine.

Ben cuts me a cold glance—Ross is my fault, too.

CHAPTER 20

Ben

I ARRIVE at the Riley Trust campus fifteen minutes early to find my former training officer, Captain Tenor, waiting for me. He's also a man who appreciates punctuality.

"Ben, it's great to see you." He shakes my hand, his eyes glistening. I also feel unexpected emotions at our reunion. He was a good teacher.

"You, too, Captain."

"Oh, no," he says, wagging his finger. "We're friends now. Call me Larry."

"Yes, sir." My attire matches his, which is a relief. Lena's suggestion of dark blue chinos, brown shoes, and a checkered blue and red button-down feels appropriate. "You look well."

"Well-fed, you mean." He rubs his soft paunch, chuckling. "My Jenny knows the way to my heart is through my stomach. You look great, too. Still keeping in shape, I see."

"Jogging, biking, weights," I explain. "Routine is everything."

He laughs, though I'm not trying to be funny.

"Amen, brother. Your diligence pays off. It's like I was telling the Rileys—you're the most reliable and capable officer I ever worked with, dutiful to a fault sometimes. Course, they already knew that about you. I'm thrilled that you're considering Riley Trust. I'll feel better retiring knowing it's in capable hands."

"I'm undecided about the position," I clarify. "But excited to learn more about it."

He pats my back good-naturedly. "See? That makes you a good officer—you rely on facts and observations. Let's get to it."

He takes me through a typical day for him. He arrives by seven, chats with the security team, and then walks the campus perimeter, which seems unnecessary given the cameras. But he says that doing it himself—checking doors, examining the fence line, and considering weaknesses—is better than watching screens.

His method proves correct when I spot a campsite beyond the fence at the westernmost section of campus. It's barely visible from our vantage point—and inaccessible to the cameras—but we find a better angle to see it. The accumulation of trash and various implements—a shopping cart, buckets, and a rope dangling between trees with clothes pinned to it—shows the camp has been here for some time. This news irritates Larry.

He rubs his bald head. "Can't believe I missed it."

"Similar encampments are all over the city. The resident likely won't cause issues. There's no evidence to suggest he's breached the fence."

"You get one homeless camper, and more won't be far behind. They multiply like rabbits," he laughs. "The Rileys won't be happy. They like their ambiance. I'll make a call and get it taken care of."

"Instead of calling the police, may I suggest handling it ourselves?" I ask.

He laughs. "You always were a big guy with a bigger heart. Let's go."

We leave the Riley Trust campus in my Jeep to access the camper's position—it's only twenty yards from the main road leading into the property. We intercept the individual returning to his campsite. He's reluctant at first, but soon reveals that he's a former marine and that alcoholism and PTSD have cost him his job and family. Helping is better than displacing. With his permission, I secure him a spot in a treatment facility known for its work with veterans and, within the hour, he's moved in. Perhaps regretful for wanting to call the police, Tenor decides that Riley Trust will pick up his tab for as long as his recovery takes—a preferred outcome.

Identify a problem. Solve a problem. Simple.

Back on campus, we resume Tenor's normal day. His position isn't the boring upper management role I expected. He isn't stuck in his office behind screens all day. Nor is he merely an overseer. He is hands-on and involved. He's well-versed in the tech he manages—Riley Trust develops its systems in-house, and they make the WPD software look like an archaic joke from the sixties. The largest threat to Riley Trust is virtual: viruses, ransomware, masking emails, and scams. The head of security works with IT to monitor and respond to such threats.

When a computer technician approaches him about a ten-thousand-dollar expenditure, Tenor signs the paperwork agreeing to the purchase. There's no ten-month wait for approval from a litany of higher-ups, as there is in the police department. Results are quick and unencumbered by policies, permissions, or red tape.

I am dazzled.

The perks of a "normal" job impress me, too. I've never had the freedom to self-manage my time. I respond when and where I'm needed, and when the moment ends, so does my involvement. Most of the time. Here, tasks are concrete and efficiently handled, providing a feeling of accomplishment that's foreign to me. I'd be a person rather than a presence. I'd be valued for my intelligence and experience, not my uniform. It's become increasingly difficult to wear it in light of the department's attrocities. I want to *serve* my community, not represent those who have hurt it.

Not that I still feel qualified to serve. Fears that my hearing will betray me and make a bad situation worse spike every time my radio clicks on.

Other people's shit has worn me down, too. Is it wrong to want a job that doesn't include finding kids in dog crates? Adam's whimpers background my nightmares behind AK-47 pops and hellfire missiles. Doesn't seem right that the worst thing I've ever seen wasn't overseas in a sandbox but down the damn road, fifteen minutes from Saddletree.

At a late lunch at Jillian's with John and Larry, we swap war stories and review the job's logistics for nearly two hours. I can't remember the last time I talked so much. Lena would be astounded. I don't open up often to people around Saddletree. When she and I got together, I merged into her life, and I'm still trying to find my place in it like I'm the odd man out, awkward and uncertain, unable to relax. Or open up, even to her.

"So, Ben, what do you think about the job so far?" John asks, pulling me from my thoughts.

When I don't answer right away, Larry laughs. "Uh, oh, John. Looks like you stumped him."

"I'm unqualified for cyber-crimes," I admit.

"So, was I to begin with," Larry says. "But Riley Trust only hires the best and the brightest. The techies will get you up to speed real quick."

"There's no us-and-them attitude here at Riley Trust," John explains. "We support and learn from each other. Larry is a team leader more than he's a manager. So, don't worry about what you don't know. You're smart. Your team is smart. You'll learn. Focus on what you offer… like today. Well done, spotting that camp."

Larry huffs. "Still can't believe I missed it."

"It was a minimal threat," I say.

"Minimal for now, but a huge hassle later," John corrects. "So, tell us… what will it take to get you on our team?"

"Time. You've given me much to consider."

John wags his finger. "Come on, Ben. I know you—Riley Trust fits you to a tee. You won't get a better offer in the private sector, and certainly not one with a family you know and trust. What's the hold-up?"

"Lena." Her name falls out carelessly like those china cups slipping from my hands in the wash. "We'll decide together."

"Understood," John nods, "but surely she's supportive. What wife wouldn't want this opportunity for her husband?"

"A wife who understands it's not that simple. She wants what's best for me. We're not convinced this is it."

John leans forward, folding his arms on the table. "Because of Lauren?"

"Yes."

Silence ensues after my admission. The puzzle is scattered on the table, and we're each trying to make the pieces fit. After two hours of openly talking, it felt wrong to sidestep the truth. I would've already accepted the job if Lauren wasn't a factor. John's right—I won't get a better offer, and the position suits me.

But it'd be hard on Lena.

She says all the right things. I wouldn't be here now without her encouragement. Everything's gone to hell this week with the studio's occupation of Saddletree, and she's done nothing but try to appease me. Turning her down the other night when she wore that lacy getup was me choosing my bad mood over her—I've regretted it since. Taking this job feels wrong, too. It'd be a test of her faith in me that, however strong, she shouldn't have to endure.

It's a test I don't want to endure, either.

I could've lived out the rest of my days in sublime contentment without so much as a hesitant pause over Lauren Riley. Like she said, it's done, and we're better people for it.

Only after Adam and with the changes ahead, my self-assurance has taken a hit. I don't know who I am anymore—a debilitating feeling that I haven't had since six weeks after that damn IED when I lost Lauren and the Rileys in a blink, while starting over and recovering from physical injuries and PTSD.

It feels like history is repeating itself, except this time, I'm split into two versions—the man I was and the man I am now. I catch glimpses of me before my injuries and long to be him again. That guy had it all—an impressive career ahead, overwhelming family support, a bright, predictable future, and excellent hearing. The Rileys make me remember what it was like to be whole.

And wholly devastated. Lauren destroyed us, forcing me to get small. I screamed, cried, said things, and broke things. I let my anger shield my brokenness to keep her away from me.

I never wanted to see her again, let alone be able to see her daily.

"Your contact with Lauren will be limited," John says. "Larry, how often do you see Lauren?"

"Once in a blue moon. We handle HR's security checks but rarely communicate unless there's an issue."

"She refused my invitation to our lunch today," John adds. "She's only interested in finding the best person for the job. That's all… If Lena feels insecure, I'd be happy to—"

"Lena's not insecure. She has no reason to be. She doesn't want it to be a strain on me," I say, more defensively than needed.

"That's understandable. It was a difficult time. None of us handled it well. Lauren… it was hard for her to see you like that." He takes a long breath. "But it's all in the past now."

I nod, but it doesn't feel that way. I'm still *like that*. And with my hearing deteriorating, I'm even more broken.

On the drive home, I resolve to tell Lena everything. Pushing the past aside, going with Riley Trust would make my future feel less daunting. I *want* that security and support. To make the final decision, I *need* Lena's.

Finding her in the barn laughing with that guy thwarts my best intentions. He's clearly flirting, and she plays along, perhaps unaware.

Maybe encouraging it. Regardless, it's a violation. I don't know him. That he's alone in the barn with my wife and daughter pisses me off.

When she defends his intrusion and implies that she "admires" him, I cringe with jealousy, like she can't admire us both at the same time. She can't—I have a shit attitude and Kirby has a TV show.

Damn it. That's not fucking fair, and I know it.

When she drives off, regret swarms me—it's my headline emotion these days. I know how hard things were for her when she cared for her mom and how precious small pleasures are when you find them.

Why do I keep hurting her?

Then, I consider that taking the job means jealousy could become an everyday norm for Lena, another thing she has to battle with her anxiety, and my regret grows for wanting a job that would cause her pain.

My optimism now gone, I default, once again, to silence.

CHAPTER 21

Lena

IT'S the perfect day for a picnic, as if the Rileys placed a special order and paid extra for cloudless blue skies, low seventies, and zero humidity.

The Riley Trust Family Picnic sprawls across the campus' main lawn, a scene from a Hallmark movie. Food trucks and massive grills line the parking lot on the outskirts. Multiple tiki bars spread strategically across the landscape serve beer and mixed drinks. Occupying the left field, bounce houses, a petting zoo, small amusement park rides, and carnival games keep the kids entertained. On the central lawn, a band plays pop hits on a stage, surrounded by dancing couples and a campground of lawn chairs and picnic blankets. To the right, tented shelters overflow with families eating and enjoying the band. It's a perfect setting for fun and relaxation, a stark contrast to my unease.

Meeting the Rileys and Ben's potential workmates *en masse* knots my stomach into an aching, anxious ball, like I'm pregnant and in labor with it. I'm seriously going to have an anxiety baby right here on the lawn.

The funny thing is, I'm not anxious about meeting new people. Peopling is a part of my business where I excel. I'm not even that worried about meeting *these* people. I don't particularly relish the idea of seeing Lauren again, but the rest were once Ben's secondary family. Getting to know them might reveal insights about him, and maybe I'll get some fun Ben stories out of it.

For once, what bothers me is Ben. He returned home from his working interview more sullen than ever. He eventually revealed that it was a positive experience, and he leaned toward taking the position. Despite my best efforts, he didn't go into detail.

Instead, he discussed Matt Kirby and the invasion of our privacy by the movie studio. Over the last week, he's taken extra shifts at work, and when he is home, he thwarts my efforts to spend time with him. Instead, he's overrun by the smallest frustrations.

Me getting Ruthie to preschool ten minutes late...

Me talking with Matt Kirby (we've had a few light conversations in passing)...

Me "letting" the movie people block the driveway once...

Me "letting" the movie people spook the horses...

Lately, Ben seems hellbent on finding fault with me. I don't understand why.

Dot thinks Ben's on a perpetual period—"man-menses," she calls it.

Cherry suggests he's having a mid-life crisis—the first stage toward utter destruction.

I believe he's finding excuses to push me away. Whether away from him or the things he needs to say or both—I don't know. But I don't deserve it.

So, today, I feel the pressure. I'm finally spending time with my husband, and hopefully, being a gold-star wife will break him from his awful mood. I'm running out of viable ideas, even after reading every article from Cherry's influencers and sporting Avery's sexy lingerie.

We stand at the outskirts of the party, taking it all in.

Ruthie gushes at the attractions. "That first. No, the bouncy castle. No, wait! I wanna ride the ponies."

"We'll do it all. Don't worry." I turn to Ben, my good hand slipping automatically into his. "This looks fun. And this place is amazing—not like a bank at all. It'd be a cool place to work."

"A definite upgrade from a patrol car." With an almost imperceptible smirk, his eyes meet mine. "I want to show you around."

"I'd love that." My words get drowned out by his name sounding across the lawn.

My head turns toward the noise, and Ben's eyes follow—I wonder if he heard it. A small horde moves through the crowd toward us, reminding me of the slow-mo scenes in *Twilight*. Ah, the cool vampires have arrived.

Ben drops my hand.

An elegant blonde woman in her sixties leads the pack. She wears a flowing silk kaftan in Bermuda blues and a sweet smile identical to Lauren's.

She ignores my extended hand and goes directly for a hug. She smells like roses and expensive spa treatments. Cherry, Dot, and I had a spa day once—nothing is funnier than watching Dot get a pedicure.

"You must be Lena," she says, pressing her softness against me. "I'm Jillian Riley, and I adore you already. If you won Ben's heart, you've won mine."

"Oh, thanks." *If?* "It's a pleasure, and that's a beautiful dress."

"Ah, bless you, dear," she returns, sounding almost humble. She pulls back, keeping my one good hand in hers. She holds it out and takes a long look at me. "You're so sweet, and what a pretty, um…"

She looks a little baffled at my outfit.

"It's a romper. Walmart couture." My attempt at humor falls flat, though I guess it's not funny—my romper *is* from Walmart. We both glance at my sage green one-piece. I try to stay confident—I got it approved. Jaye helped me through my closet crisis and said its spaghetti straps and scooped neckline showed just enough skin without seeming desperate to impress. She shared a pic with Dot and Cherry. Both gave an enthusiastic thumbs-up.

But now, under this scrutiny, my confidence dips, especially when Lauren edges in beside her. Her silky blue top and scalloped tan shorts give off a sexy girl-next-door vibe. I feel like Luigi standing beside Beachtime Barbie.

"It suits you." Jillian's eyes fall to Ruthie, and she beams. Her French manicure rises to her mouth, and tears speck in her eyes in joyful wonder, like love at first sight.

My daughter *is* adorable but *what the fuck?*

"Oh, Ben… She's perfect," she coos as if Ruthie's the prized granddaughter she never had. "Ah, she has your eyes. Oh, and that serious look of yours. How lovely."

Her hand goes to her heart as if she's holding it in.

Ben and I exchange awkward glances before I say, "Ruthie, say hello to Mrs. Riley."

"Hello," Ruthie says. "Can I ride the ponies? They aren't doing it right."

"Of course!" She holds out her hand to Ruthie. "May I escort you?"

Ruthie looks at me. I look to Ben. He nods hesitantly. She happily pulls Jillian along like a puppy on a leash.

"Sorry about that." Lauren moves in. "You know how Mom is."

Ben shrugs, watching Ruthie drift away from us.

"Lauren, it's nice to see you again." I offer my hand.

She shakes it tenderly, gives me a curt once over, and then remembers her vampire-esque entourage. Introductions follow—their names jumble in my head, but I smile wide and give vigorous handshakes.

Finally, she introduces her father, John, who steps between the others, like Moses parting the Red Sea.

He is a silver fox—fit, gray, and charming.

"Lena." He says my name like it's the title of an amazing rock ballad. "I've been dying to meet you. Saddletree is the kind of homegrown, family-friendly, local business we started Riley Trust Bank to support."

They never would've given me a loan for Saddletree. They turned me down with my first bakery. "I love a bank that looks out for the little guys."

He chuckles. "That's us. I can't wait until you reopen so I can see the magic for myself."

"Saddletree *is* magic. Thanks. It's a lot like this. A place to connect."

"It's more than that," he gushes. "*NC Magazine* calls your cinnamon rolls legendary."

"Wow, you've done your homework. They're very popular," I say, now feeling pseudo-humble myself. In Dot's language, my cinnamon rolls are *da bomb*.

"Being married to Lena means doubling my workouts," Ben says.

Everyone laughs while I gape with pleasant surprise at my charming husband.

Someone seeks John's attention nearby, but before he leaves us, he says, "Make yourself at home. Give Lena the grand tour, Ben."

"And Lena, save me a dance, huh?" Dr. Rob Riley coos, following his brother.

"Not a chance, Rob," Ben tacks on, making them laugh again.

I feel like I've been electrocuted. Ben's being outgoing without being prodded? *Who is this man?*

I spot Ruthie through the crowd. She's perched on a dark brown pony, attempting to get the poor animal to canter despite protests from the woman holding the lead. Mrs. Riley sticks to her side, and Lauren soon joins her, as if a four-year-old is a fun novelty, like Spanx or BMWs. I wonder if they know what they've gotten themselves into.

I take advantage of the free babysitting and lean into Ben. "Dance with me?"

His eyes narrow skeptically.

"Ah, come on. We used to do it all the time," I remind him, smiling and edging closer. "On rainy days in the carport."

"Sometimes, I wish we could go back to those days," he says, his big hands slipping around my waist.

"Me, too."

"Sorry for being a dick lately."

"Good, you should be," I say lightly. His blanket apology feels half-hearted, though he seems sincere. "You've had a lot on your mind."

"That's no excuse." He takes a breath, his grip on me tightening. "Change is… difficult for me."

I nod, though I'm unsure exactly which change he means. The movie people? The career switch? Something else?

"I don't react well to it, and my history with the Rileys dredges that up." The words emerge slowly and uneasily like he's pushing a heavy cart up a flight of stairs one step at a time. "There's a lot of uncertainty right now."

"You helped me through the most uncertain time of my life," I remind him, resting my cast on his shoulder. "It's my turn to help you… but you have to let me."

"It's just—"

"Ben Wright—the man of the hour!"

A booming voice cuts through his words, leaving me hanging. Ben drops his hold on me and moves aside for a rotund man in his sixties and a petite brunette beside him—Larry and Jenny Tenor. We chat casually and easily for a suitable amount of time before Ben says, "I want to take Lena on a tour."

Larry pulls a security badge from his shirt pocket with a magician's flair. "I thought you might. I took the liberty of creating your access card."

Ben nods, taking the badge. "Thank you, sir."

Larry slaps his back proudly. "Eh, one less thing I'll have to do later. It'll get you anywhere you want to go. Be sure to check out your office."

Your office, like it's already decided. Maybe it is, and I'm the last holdout. I can't deny that Ben seems lighter and comfortable here. Why doesn't he feel this relaxed at Saddletree? I think about what he said the night of my accident—that he loves Saddletree but doesn't belong there, *professionally*. Maybe he doesn't feel like he belongs there at all. It's more of a burden for him, a source of frustration and stress. Like me, it seems lately. And the movie people are a constant reminder.

Larry and Jenny leave us for dancing, and I automatically scan for Ruthie again.

Ben takes my hand. "Ruthie will be fine. Come with me?"

A familiar spark pings between us, like he's taking me on an adventure. I've missed that spark. I nod automatically, and he leads me toward a glass-heavy building.

"They have their own restaurant, cafeterias, dry cleaner, and yoga studio—"

"Are you into yoga now?"

He scoffs. "No. But it's here. You could do it if you wanted—families are welcome to use the amenities, too. There are many opportunities here."

"There's yoga every Thursday morning at Saddletree. I'm good."

He swipes his badge at the door and holds it open. We enter a lobby with high ceilings, marble floors, bright chandeliers, and leather seating, very hotel-like. We lean against the back wall inside the elevator, watching the lighted numbers change over our heads.

"I like the romper."

His eyes catch mine, and I break out laughing while he smirks. *This is my Ben.*

"Walmart couture… funny," he adds as the elevator pings. He takes my hand, locking it surely in his, and leads me down the hallway.

CHAPTER 22

Lena

"WOW, BEN." I stand at the window wall in his *potential* office, overlooking a delicate rock, sand, and stone garden below. Flashes of orangey gold catch my eyes as koi skim through the pond. Box turtles bake on a staged log. "Ruthie'll love the view. This office is swanky."

"I don't need swank, but I like the minimalism and efficiency of it." He adjusts a light switch near the door, and the recessed lighting dims.

I move toward the room's center and lean against the desk. "I can picture this for you. You deserve swank and dimming lights and a koi pond. What are you thinking?"

He leans beside me, folding his arms. "The decision is harder than it should be. One minute, I've decided. The next, I don't know."

"Well, what excites you about it?"

"The schedule and managing my time *my* way. The money. No-limits healthcare. Working with John. The minimal bullshit," he lists off quickly.

"What's holding you back?"

"Handing in my badge. Giving up the larger community." He pauses, glancing at the dark tile floors beneath us. "The Rileys. You."

"Me?"

"I don't want a job that will cause you anxiety."

I chuckle. "You mean more anxiety than you being a police officer?"

"You know what I mean."

"Yes, I do." I push off the desk and twist to stand before him, straddling his extended legs. My cast arm rests on his shoulder while the other lands on his chest. He unlocks his arms and slides them around me. "I won't worry as long as we have this… you and me together, talking, as long as we're *us* again. Are we?"

"Yes." His forehead presses to mine. "We're always us, even when it feels like we aren't."

"Then, I'm with you, whatever you decide to do." A soft kiss bridges the gap between us. "Tell me why you're reluctant about the Rileys."

His shoulders bounce. "How about I show you?"

He doesn't explain as we leave the office, travel down the hall, and up the elevator again. His badge grants us access to a posh suite with John Riley's name on the door. Everything is dim and quiet, and it feels slightly wrong to be here, like snooping in someone's medicine cabinet.

But Ben is undeterred.

He doesn't turn on the lights—they aren't needed with sunlight pouring in from the floor-to-ceiling windows. Mr. Riley's workspace is larger than the dining room at Saddletree, and I can't fathom the cost of the leather sofas, handmade desk, or modern art.

Ben motions toward a display of pictures elegantly centering a glossy wood-paneled wall opposite John's desk and plush seating. I move closer, and that's when I see Ben's army photo amongst the others.

A breathy sigh escapes me, taking it in, and I'm bum-rushed with feelings, good and bad, not knowing which to latch onto. It's the same portrait on our family wall at home.

Finally, Ben says, "I feel like the prodigal son, and this offer is my return to the fold. Maybe it doesn't matter—a job's a job—but it's wrong. Leaving the Rileys behind wasn't me avoiding or wasting my life… it was me *finding* my life."

His eyes lock on mine like he wants to study me. He'll see only love in my eyes now that his words have broken through my crowded emotions. *God, I adore him.* I've always known this about him, but it strikes me, once again, how thoughtful and intelligent Ben is—he doesn't say much, but he thinks about everything. And this insight into his relationship with the Rileys is a profound one.

He shrugs lightly, shoving his hands into the pockets of his khaki pants. "I could be overthinking it."

"You're not. Trust your feelings, Ben." I nod toward his picture. "This is… strange."

"It's a symbol of respect. He's always viewed me as a son."

"You aren't, though… I don't want to overthink it, either. Or dissuade you from something that could be amazing. Military service is important to them, and so are you. They want to showcase it—no big deal, I guess."

"But?"

"But, do you think that attitude comes with… expectations?" I ask, my mind spinning over what it could mean.

"That's why I'm reluctant. I don't know." He runs a hand through his short hair. "They want to pick up where we left off, and that's challenging after…"

I know better than to ask what happened. I don't want to push him when he's *finally* opening up. But his furrowed brow makes me hurt for him—it was no ordinary break-up.

"So, accepting the job feels like stepping back into your old life?"

"It suggests I want that life back. I don't." He winces. "I want the job as I am… not who I was. If that makes sense."

"It does." My good hand goes to his arm for a gentle squeeze. "When you know, you'll know—that's what Mom used to say. It's like falling in love. I loved Mark, but always tried to make us fit when we didn't. I didn't know any better until you came along. Don't try to make anything fit. It either will or won't. When you know for sure, that's your answer."

He smirks briefly and nods. "So, wait?"

"I think so. All you have to do today is enjoy the picnic and spend time with Ruthie and me. Right?"

He gives me a short kiss. "Right. We should get back to her before she runs away with the ponies."

I laugh as his hand slides into mine and folds through my fingers. Before we reach the door, I nod toward his handsome portrait. "It must be shitty for Lauren, walking into her dad's office every day to see an ex in a place of honor on the wall. The first thing Mom did when I left Mark was take down every picture of us—I found the stack buried in her closet after she died."

Ben's brow pinches, considering my words. "I hadn't thought of that. Trying to make me feel sorry for her?"

"I'm not trying to make you feel *anything* for her… but seeing that, I kinda do," I shrug, pulling him to the door.

Ruthie races full speed across the lawn when she sees us. Ben scoops her up, and she straddles his side. "Dad, I rode the ponies four times. They were a little slow for me, but that's okay. There's a cotton candy machine!" Her eyes look like green golf balls.

"How about some real food first?" I say.

Mrs. Riley lumbers over, winded and sweaty in her museum-worthy attire. "Ruthie, you got away from me again."

"Sorry, Jillian. She tends to do that."

"I love her independent spirit," she puffs. "Reminds me of Freddy and Omar. Course, we didn't have them at her age."

Her pointed expression makes it a complaint.

"Let me introduce you to some of Riley Trust's families, huh?"

She steps between us, linking her arm to Ben's like a move she's done a thousand times. With Ruthie in his arms and Jillian on his free side, I fall behind them—a tagalong afterthought.

She leads us to the calmer right side of the grassy area, away from the food trucks and children's spaces—where a lovely picnic-scape hosts the Rileys and their special guests. Colorful awnings tied to posts provide ample shade for blankets, pillows, Adirondack chairs, and tables with food and drinks. It could be a magazine spread in *Coastal Living* under the headline—"Outdoor Dining with the Upper Crust." This is *their* space—and though it's not roped off, it feels like the red-carpet section where one must be invited in, which makes me think of vampires again.

Ruthie slides off of Ben and takes my hand. "I'm thirsty."

I lead her to a serving table and pour her some lemonade. She's flushed and already tired. When Ruthie goes full force, she crashes quickly. So, I think of finding a quiet spot where she can settle before her next round of fun.

But Lauren's laughter lures me back to Ben. A gold-star wife wouldn't leave her husband alone in such an important social situation. Ruthie and I wedge next to him as best we can.

Jillian and John introduce us to other members of upper management. John brags about Ben's workday at Riley Trust and how he prevented a homeless invasion near their property line—a story Ben neglected to share with me, but it sounds like they were under a zombie attack with them scaling the fences and gnashing their teeth to hear them tell it.

God, what is with me and the zombies and vampires today?

Ruthie leans against my leg, sipping her drink. New to cups without lids, she holds it precariously in her stubby hands, sucking from the rim instead of tilting it back. I scoop her up carefully, shifting her against my right hip so I can balance the cup for her with my cast hand.

"So, Lena, I hear Hollywood has taken over your little business," Jillian says. "What's that like?"

Little? Okay, that's the route we're taking? "Um, different, but exciting."

"My grandsons love that *Hunter* movie," Jenny Tenor chimes in. "Have you met Matt Kirby?"

I nod, shifting Ruthie's weight as she leans against me. "He's nice, very down-to-earth."

"Is he as handsome as he is on TV?" Jenny asks. "I always think those actors must be air-brushed."

"Um, he's alright," I answer diplomatically. "He's not air-brushed."

"He's been raving about Saddletree on Insta," another woman says. "I loved this pic of you two." She holds up her phone and pans it around to the crowd. Jaye took the image of Matt and me in front of a hay bale. I couldn't dismantle it with the pitchfork one-handed, and he came to my rescue. "Positive publicity," Jaye called it.

Judging by the sudden divot on Ben's cheekbone from tightening his jaw, I imagine he'd call it something else.

"Oh, right," I say weakly. "Everyone loves farm chores, especially when they don't have to do them every day."

"Well, he adores the place. He posts more about Saddletree than he does the movie," she says, tucking her phone away.

"Must love the free advertising," John Riley says, tilting his beer.

"I liked him in *Nightshift*. What about you, Ben? Are you a Matt Kirby fan?" Larry asks.

A beat passes, making me think Ben didn't hear him.

"Ben's not into horror movies or crime shows—he gets enough of both at work," I say, shifting their attention back to me.

"That's funny," Lauren says. "You used to love horror movies. Remember our *Halloween* and *Friday the 13th* marathons?"

"I only watched them because you liked them," he says.

Lauren goes doe-eyed over his romantic admission while Jillian says, "Aw, how sweet."

"Now, you're watching one in your backyard," Larry laughs. "What's this one about? Demons? Ghosts?"

"Witches. Jim Hunter is saving a family from an ancient coven trying to steal their souls." *A coven not unlike the Rileys, I think, watching Lauren stare at my husband. Stop with the monster thoughts.* "It's a twist on your classic ghost story."

"Well, hopefully, it won't haunt your business," John says. "It's risky, closing for two months. Most businesses would find that difficult to recover from."

I wonder for a moment if Ben has shared his concerns with them.

"I have a strong and loyal community base." I hoist Ruthie more securely against me. She's getting heavy, and my wrist twinges with pain under my cast from the effort. "After my accident, it makes sense. I want to do some restructuring anyway. Ben's helping me make Saddle-tree run more efficiently."

My voice upticks on the last part—a gold-star wife would obviously promote her husband's skillset to the people interested in hiring him.

Ben sighs. "Lena's a talented baker but a disorganized manager."

Hello, bus. Didn't think I'd get run over by you today.

John beams proudly. "A business can't be successful on cupcakes alone…"

An internal cringe restarts my earlier tension like a stalled motor running again. *What's happening? How'd this turn around on me?*

"I didn't know you were business-minded, Ben."

Ben's long pause encourages me to answer for him. "He's *management*-minded," I say, just as Ben starts to speak. He closes his mouth and gives me a bothered look.

Still, I add, "A quality manager can manage any business, right? Cupcakes or not."

Cold lemonade drizzles down the front of my romper. Ruthie startles awake. "Mom, potty."

Ben leans in, easing the nearly empty cup from her hands and whispering sternly in my ear, "Stop answering for me."

His soft, even admonishment comes out in a hot breath and makes me cringe. I don't think anyone hears it, but I feel his irritation with me, and because my face is a human emoji board, others see it. A tiny smirk carries Jillian away from us while Jenny shoves napkins at me unsurely.

My forced smile emerges again, weaker this time. "Um, we better get cleaned up. Please, excuse us."

Jenny points me toward the nearest bathroom, a mile away. I trek across the lawn, holding Ruthie tightly so the lemonade puddling in my bra won't travel to my underwear.

Ruthie does her business in the family bathroom while I strip down to my boutique lingerie (I had high hopes for today) and use the hand dryer on my damp romper. She giggles at my ridiculous display of black lacy-covered butt and boobs—I suppose it is funny, but I don't feel like laughing.

Have I been answering for him?

My anxiety bitches are quick to show me where I've gone wrong on replay. The Matt Kirby question. The business-minded remark. Wearing a romper. *Damn it.*

The wet spots dry, leaving stained rings on the top of my outfit. I redress with a huff.

"Buck up, buttercup," Ruthie says suddenly.

I gasp. "Where'd you hear that?"

"Aunt Barb."

"Huh, your grandma used to say that, too." Over the river of my anxiety issues and through the woods of my terrible first marriage, Mom must've said that to me a million times. Hearing Ruthie say it makes me want to cry over how much I miss her.

I imagine her now, serving up her best Ben-advice between asking me questions about Matt Kirby. What would she tell me to do? Buck up? Stand up? Give up? I let so many things slide with Mark just to keep our peace. Toward the end, I hung on to our pseudo-marriage by frayed threads tied to my finger, libel to break any second. And they did, of course. Putting up with his shit only delayed the inevitable and made me feel like a human doormat. I can't let that happen with Ben.

"Mom, cotton candy. Remember?" She climbs the step stool to wash her hands. "I'll have a hot dog first, if that makes you happy."

"Um, it would. Yes." I push off the subway tiles, straighten my back, and switch into mom mode. This isn't the time for Mom memories or Ben-worries.

But.

Emerging from the bathroom, I look for Ben. He's easy to spot in a crowd, and I'm desperate to apologize for conversationally overstepping him.

"Where's Dad?" Ruthie asks.

I scan the red-carpet area and don't find him. "I don't know."

I spot John and Jillian—he pulls his wife closer by the waist, and she leans her head on his shoulder. They're looking toward the stage, where the band plays a soft pop ballad, and just below, I spot my husband.

He's dancing with Lauren.

CHAPTER 23

Ben

LENA CARRIES Ruthie awkwardly to the bathroom. I'm compelled to follow and lend a hand.

I've never spoken to her like that and regret it immediately, but my harsh reaction felt necessary in the moment. I don't need her to talk or hear for me—*not yet*. At Saddletree, she intercedes on my behalf frequently, and I've never objected. It's a noisy environment there, and her help prevents me from making apologies and asking people to repeat themselves.

It's surprising how often that irritates people.

The only difference is that she did it here, around people I want to impress, a distinction that's unfair to her.

Guilt settles on my shoulders the further they get from me. I turn, determined to follow.

Lauren's hand slips around my bicep like a hook, stopping my forward motion.

"You okay?" she asks. "Mom said—"

"Everything's fine. They might need help."

"Are you kidding? Lena's got this. She's handled this a million times —that's expert-level momming."

I groan, not needing Lauren to tell me what a good mom Lena is. I know firsthand. But since she's operating one-handed, I want to help and deliver my apology. I turn toward the lawn and no longer see them through the dense crowd.

Lauren's head tilts toward me—part pained, part curious. "Did you *really* watch those awful movies for me?"

"Yes." I scan the area, wondering if they're inside the restroom yet. I could wait for them outside if I knew which bathroom they entered.

"Gosh, Ben. I wish you would've said." Lauren's voice is like a fly buzzing around my ear. "I didn't like them either."

"What?" I demand, my eyes landing on hers. "*You* wanted to watch them."

She shakes her head before I get the words out. "No… I mean, yes, I suppose it's my fault. But Uncle Rob told me if I wanted to get close to you… watch a scary movie."

That fits. Rob's good at two things—gross doctor stories and making moves. It sounds like his bad advice.

Still, this new information amuses me. "So, we watched movies neither of us wanted to see?"

"He was only on his second wife then… I still should've known better than to listen to him." Her tone shoulders bounce in a sheepish shrug. "Good memories, regardless."

A smile emerges, remembering her face buried in my shoulder and me, eyes closed, trying to be "the man" and not cringe every time a knife plunged into a victim. I hated those movies and still have a problem with gratuitous violence.

I wonder how Lena and Ruthie are faring.

"Lena's amazing," Lauren says, returning my attention to her. "And beautiful."

"Yes."

When I don't engage, Lauren launches into a long-winded oration about her boys and how violence in movies increased their aggression as middle schoolers. I zone out.

More regret bombards me. The other night, Lena suggested we watch the first *Hunter* movie together. I made a snide remark about getting enough of Jim Hunter already and went to bed early, claiming a migraine. It felt easier.

Standing here, shooting the shit with Lauren when I should be chasing Lena to apologize, also feels easier.

But that's not the only reason I stay.

I glimpse John and Jillian watching from several yards away. A familiar warmth rekindles in me. I recall my homecomings. Lauren would drop everything for my return, commit all her time and energy to me, knowing every second was a countdown before another long stretch apart. *Disappear with me*, she'd say. Her complete attention kept me going until my last tour. I lived in two worlds; in hers, I found incredible comfort, zero pressure, and love.

Until I didn't.

"I wonder how else he steered me wrong," she says.

"Who?"

"Rob." Her dainty head tilts, contemplating me. "Where were you just now?"

"What do you mean?"

Her finger twiddles around my face. "That faraway look of yours, like the old days."

Her inside knowledge unnerves me. "I wasn't anywhere. Here. Thinking about Lena."

She nods, glancing at her feet, and I feel sorry for my curtness, especially after Lena's insights in John's office. The Rileys pressured her about everything—her appearance, education, job choices, relationships. That pressure surely extended to me. Even now, maybe.

"I was… thinking about your great-aunt's questionable potato salad and your grandmother getting pissed at Rob for that awful joke he made at my last going-away party," I say.

Her entire demeanor lifts. Even her feet rise onto her toes. "Oh, gosh, I remember. The potato salad was crunchy—what the hell made it crunchy? Oh, and Rob… you'd think a doctor would refrain from dirty jokes."

"Rob doesn't refrain from anything."

She laughs.

Glancing over my shoulder, she mumbles a quick, "Oh, shit." She reaches for me but thinks better of it. She cowers instead, peeking carefully over my shoulder on her tiptoes. "Not again."

"What's wrong?"

"Ryan from accounting." She huffs and rolls her eyes. "Don't look."

I look.

Behind me, thirty yards and closing, an average-looking guy in a flamingo shirt scans the crowd.

Lauren edges closer, using me as a human shield and pleading with her gray eyes. "We went to dinner once, and he's weirded me out ever since."

My brow furrows, and I prepare to have a word with him.

Lauren slaps my chest in amused protest. "Ben. Relax. He's a decent guy, just not for me."

"Situations like that escalate."

"He doesn't need a talking-to. He means well, but… is there any way you might dance with me?"

"No."

"Ben, I'm not asking you to enjoy it," she grins, "just help me out. If he sees me with someone more… impressive… he'll get the hint and back off."

I nod, reminded of Rowan Mackey and her similar trouble once. Lauren pulls me toward the stage, and music echoes through my hearing aids like I'm in a cave. Trapped. My hands find her waist but barely hold on, as if that makes this better.

The determined man detours when he sees me, confirming her story. It's Lauren Riley, after all. Unwanted suitors must be a daily problem.

"Thank you." Her hands slide up my chest and circle my neck.

"Can we stop dancing now?"

"Another minute, please."

"Obsessive men are a problem for women," I say, trying to be conversational. "I see it often. It's a wonder women still tolerate men at all. Evolution should have done away with us by now."

She laughs, though I don't mean to be funny.

"Be direct with him next time," I advise. "Tell him you're not interested. He could be emotionally disturbed and should be taken seriously. A friend of mine settled for a man she considered decent, and he turned violent. She has facial scars from a burn injury she sustained as a teenager, and he used them to manipulate her self-worth. Now, she's with someone who loves her as she is."

I shut my mouth—I'm talking too much.

Lauren huffs, her pained irises drifting toward her feet. "I fucked up, Ben. You don't have to remind me."

Shit. Scars. "I wasn't."

"I'd do anything to change what happened." Her voice is stern but shaky. Her glassy eyes find mine again. *"Anything."*

I don't like the desperation in her eyes. I don't like *many* things about this. My hands fall off her waist like freed weights. Stepping on this conversational landmine was not my intention—explaining

Rowan's situation was meant to encourage her not to fall into the same trap. *That's* all.

But I see the unfortunate parallel between our stories and wish I'd said nothing. This is why I don't talk much.

Lauren's soft gaze tugs gently on the tight locks that keep the past contained. Her expression is identical to the first time I kissed her. I'd been nervous, but she made it easy with the same sweet, wanting, and patient look she's giving me now.

She read me like a book she never wanted to put down.

That was the best thing about Lauren—she was easy. Not in a derogatory sense, of course. Just in the way that I became the axis on which she rotated, and she never required anything of me except my attention. She hung on my words, clung to my arm, and devoted herself to my happiness. Completely uncomplicated.

I thought she was it for me.

That's why what happened to us destroyed me with such totality— that memory slips through the locked door, too. To her, I was broken. And my love for her shattered with the cold wince of her eyes. The IED taught me pain, but Lauren wounded me.

Wounds I'm now grateful to have endured since they led me to Lena.

"It can't be changed, and I'm exactly where I want to be," I finally say, hating how the memory still tightens my throat. "Excuse me."

"Ben, I'm just—"

Her voice disappears as my attention diverts to the crowd. I look for Lena's green romper and catch a glimpse before she moves behind a food truck.

Several minutes later, I find Lena and Ruthie sitting under a sprawling magnolia on the far west side of the party, opposite the Rileys' camp. Ruthie munches on a hot dog while Lena stares off, pensive and bothered. I don't know if she saw me dancing with Lauren —*God, I hope she didn't.* But she's upset. *Shit, she probably did.*

She doesn't look at me when I sit beside her.

Ruthie holds up her hot dog. "Dogs are pretty good, Dad. You should get one."

"Maybe later."

"Well, you can't have cotton candy without having real food first," Ruthie reasons. "Then, I'm going on some rides."

"That's our plan." Lena stays even-toned and refuses eye contact. "You should mingle. We're fine on our own."

She's telling me to fuck off. Her supportive enthusiasm has vacated the premises. This is Pissed-Off Lena.

She wipes ketchup from Ruthie's lips and brushes the crumbs off her dress. They stand, and Lena tells Ruthie to toss her garbage in the nearest receptacle. I rise, too, the magnolia leaves brushing my shoulders as I slump underneath them.

Lena huffs when I don't take off. "You should rejoin the Rileys. We'll be fine."

"I know. I don't want to miss the cotton candy."

She's unamused.

"I'm sorry," I say.

"Oh? For which part?"

I meet her narrowed gaze and stumble over my words. "For all of it."

She groans, returning her attention to Ruthie and making me feel worse than I already do. She said all the right things earlier when we were alone—exactly what I needed to hear.

How did I repay her support?

With anger, humiliation, and dancing with my ex.

I silently align with her, determined not to leave her side. Ruthie chomps on cotton candy as we explore the offerings. She has her fill of the rides, and the Ferris wheel turns her a worrying shade of green.

Lena suggests leaving soon.

Her hand slips easily into mine as we cross the lawn to the Rileys' opulent corner, and she gushes with her usual smiling warmth as we deliver thanks and goodbyes.

But the ride home is unnervingly silent.

Ruthie falls asleep in record time, less than two minutes, a preferred outcome to the potential alternative—hot dogs and cotton candy bits all over the backseat.

Lena languidly fixes her eyes on the passenger window. I feel her disappointment, and it makes me want to shrink into my self-hatred and disappear.

Still, I manage to say, "I'm sorry for being short with you about speaking for me… and for dancing with Lauren. It wasn't—I didn't want it to happen."

She doesn't respond and keeps her eyes directed out the window. Her good hand fists her pant leg, and I wonder if she's staving off a panic attack.

"Are you okay?"

"No, I'm not okay." Her voice shakes with emotion. "I'm sorry for bulldozing you in the conversation. I do it all the time, and I shouldn't. But I worried you couldn't hear them and thought you might want me to step in like I *always* do. Maybe I deserved your pushback, but it felt sharp and humiliating. And that's *after* feeling like a jealous shit over you suffering through gruesome horror movies with Lauren while refusing a mid-level one with me the other night—"

"Lena, slow down. Please."

She takes a breath, twisting in her seat so I can read her lips and hear her better. She repeats herself before saying, "You danced with her, Ben. Fucking danced with her. How should I feel?"

"Upset, like me over your hay games with Matt Kirby."

She glances at Ruthie, still asleep in the backseat, and leans closer to me. "I've never fucked Matt Kirby... and I wouldn't. And don't want to. It's not the same."

I take a breath, my grip white-knuckling against the steering wheel. "You're right. I'm sorry."

"You *hurt me* at every turn, Ben." Her voice becomes breathy and strained. I glimpse her purple cast moving toward her face. She covers her mouth with her hand. "Pull over... Can you pull over? Please."

With a sharp turn into the empty parking lot of a closed CVS, Lena bursts from the Jeep and throws up into overgrown bushes. I rush to her, hand going to her back. She coughs and spits as I hand her a napkin from my pocket.

Soon, her nausea subsides enough for her to stand upright. "I'm not pregnant."

"I didn't suggest you were."

She breathes into the napkin like she might hyperventilate. "I was too nervous to eat at the thing. Or before it. The pain pills didn't like that. Plus anxiety. Sorry."

"Stop apologizing. Everything's okay."

Lena's disorder often leads her to bad decisions, like not eating out of fear that her anxiety will upset her stomach. Still, it adds to my guilt that this event agitated her nerves and worse for not noticing. I usually pay attention.

I go to the Jeep's tailgate and return with a water bottle. She takes manageable sips, and her color returns slightly.

"We passed a McDonald's. Want fries and a shake?"

This earns me a short smile. It was her go-to craving with Ruthie.

"Okay," she says, breathy and uneasy. She leans against the Jeep. "One more minute."

"Take all the minutes you need." I nod toward Ruthie, who has her head back and mouth open in a deep sleep. "Our passenger doesn't mind."

Lena smirks again.

"I don't mind, either. I'm sorry I keep hurting you. I don't want to. It just happens," I say, pinching my temples between my fingers. "I understand why you speak for me, and it helps. But sometimes, you overcompensate, making me feel incapable, and here, I wanted to make a good impression."

"You did," she says weakly. "I'm sorry for helping too much. I'll try not to take over so much anymore."

"Sorry about the dancing, too. I didn't want to. She was trying to avoid 'Ryan from accounting,' an overly determined suitor," I say, though my excuse sounds inadequate.

Lena chuckles, rolling her sapphire eyes knowingly. "Ah, the old fake-dance trick."

I give her a stunned look. "Fake? What do you mean?"

"We used to do it at high school dances with guys we liked. *Oh, please, kind sir, will you dance with me so so-and-so thinks I'm unavailable and stops bothering me?*" She uses a high-pitched voice. "It always works on the good guys."

I groan. "It seemed legitimate."

"Maybe it was," she allows. "But I didn't like it."

"Understood. It won't happen again."

She nudges my shoulder as we lean against the Jeep, and I rest my head on hers, her wild tendrils tickling my chin.

"I don't like how things have been with us lately. Up and down and… tense."

My chest tightens with nonsensical pressure, hearing her say that. "Me, neither. It's my fault. My indecision. My…"

"Please, talk to me, Ben." She edges in front of me, much like in John's office, studying me with her huge eyes. "What's making you so angry?"

My mouth feels full of sand, dry and uncooperative, but I push the words through. "I hate that my life continues to revolve around one damn day in Afghanistan. I keep reliving it. That day stole everything from me, and I'm afraid it's happening again."

"No, we won't let it." She wraps me up awkwardly around my folded arms. "You are not your circumstances."

I unlock my arms, pulling her into me as her words—my words to her years ago—resonate.

"You're more than that day, Ben. More than your injuries. More than your hearing," she says as I bury my face in her neck. "I love you, no matter what. You're safe with me. Safe and loved and never alone. Whatever happens, we'll face it together."

Her words pull me closer to her than anything has in ages, like she's my anchor, holding me in place.

A long beat passes before she says, "Do you think we should see someone?"

She is as gentle as possible, but I jerk back like she's sprung it harshly. "What? Like who?"

"A therapist? For couples? Maybe Dr. Reese—you like her." Her brow forms that hard *L* again. "We keep having setbacks, and I worry that…" Her voice trails off. "Am I overreacting?"

The idea irks me. My hands clench at my sides, and my eyes close to the noises in my head. I spent years on the proverbial couch.

During the army.

After the army.

After Lauren.

Times since.

I've done my fucking time. Needing help makes me feel weak, incapable, and vulnerable. But for Lena…

"No. I'll make the call Monday."

She wilts slightly as if she hoped I'd refute her. I can't play my usual role—strong, stable husband, calming her in her distress, confident that nothing can break us.

I know better.

So, does she. She nods. "I think I'm ready for fries now."

"McDonald's it is."

I escort her to the passenger side in case she feels additional weakness. Before I close the door, her hand falls on mine. She nibbles her bottom lip like she wants to say something but can't find the words—I relate.

I wrap my sausage fingers around her dainty ones. "Everything's okay."

And she nods and smiles like she believes it.

Ruthie stirs in the backseat. "Did someone say McDonald's?"

CHAPTER 24

Lena

TWO WEEKS LATER, I climb into the passenger seat of Dot's work van, plagued with nerves. Why should this plan be any better than the handful of others I've attempted since the picnic? Ben's admission about his unresolved anger over the IED and its aftermath felt like a breakthrough, the same as telling me about his anger toward Lauren at gatorpark. He's letting me in one admission at a time—a strategy that'd be fine if it happened more often. Instead of the door inching open bit by bit, he cracks it and shuts it again. The girls and I've worked extra hard to create time for us. Ruthie's had plenty of play dates and sleepovers so I could arrange the same for Ben and me, both spontaneous and planned, and they always fall through. *He's working. He's not up for it. He's got a headache. He's got things to do.* Every excuse hurts a little more than the one before, which is why I'm so nervous now.

Thanks to the family calendar, I know his plan today, and I hope to join him.

If he'll let me.

It's a big *if.*

"Thanks for doing this," I say, buckling my seatbelt.

"No prob," Dot says, blowing the cloud from her vape pen out the window.

Jaye stands with Elsie Todd near the carport, reviewing today's schedule—a meeting I usually attend but can't this morning. Dot nods quickly in Jaye's direction, earning her a coy grin and a wave.

"How's that going?" I ask as she rumbles down the bumpy driveway.

"I did it." Dot blushes.

"Did what?"

"I did *it.*"

She looks like she's trying to share a secret with me telepathically, her eyes sparkling mischievously. Then, it hits me.

"You asked her out?" I gasp. "She said yes, right?"

"Better than yes."

"What's better than yes?"

"Only that we asked each other out at the same time," she beams. "She said yes to dinner *after* inviting me to Wilmington Comic-Con on Saturday. She'll be there signing her graphic novels. Anyway, she's got us all tickets. Please, say you'll come."

"Me? To a comic-con?" I wince. "Ruthie mentioned it. Adam's going as Spiderman, and she automatically wants to do whatever he's doing."

"She can dress up, too." She turns her dark eyes toward me, rubbing her chin thoughtfully. "Maybe you can go as Chewbacca."

"I am *not* dressing up."

"But you'll go with me, right? Hang out with me while she's doing her thing? Ben can come, too. He'll make a perfect robot."

"Hmm, worth a shot," I say, adding it to the family calendar. "But I won't get my hopes up."

She side-glances me. "How'd counseling go?"

"I'm working on active listening and facing problems head-on. He's working on communication and trying to stop practicing avoidance—no more extra shifts or turning down my offers to spend time together."

Dot looks skeptical. "How's that working out for you?"

I shrug lightly. "It's not. I haven't seen him much. We'll see how today goes."

I fidget with the hem of my sundress and nibble the inside of my mouth. I knew counseling wouldn't magically fix us overnight—it's a process that requires work and time. But Ben didn't want to be there. I did ninety percent of the talking—no surprise—and even Dr. Reese, who knows Ben well, couldn't crack his code of silence. Counseling won't help if he's unwilling to give it a chance.

"Lena, babe. Here's one way you can face problems head-on. Tell him not to take the job. That's where the problems started—"

"No, we had problems before that. That's just when I started to see them."

"Still… it's okay to say you have a problem with him working with his ex—*anyone* would. Maybe that's what he needs to hear."

"*Or* he'll think I'm robbing him of a great opportunity, want the job even more, and resent me for keeping him from it. Then, he'll take the job to spite me and run straight into Lauren's open arms."

"Dude, Ben's *your* husband. He'd do anything for you and Ruthie. If you tell him the job's a bad idea, he'll listen."

"I don't want to be *that* wife," I say, glancing at my outfit again. "Without Ben, I never would've dreamed of Saddletree, let alone pulled it off. Hell, he *lives* in my dream and supports me at every turn. How can I stand between him and a job he wants?"

"You and Ruthie are his dream, Lena. And Saddletree. He wouldn't be so involved in making changes if he didn't care about the place. He's on the fence about the job. All I'm saying is to help him off the fence. Gently."

"I don't know. Maybe. But that's not what today's about," I say, straightening my dress again.

Dot side-eyes me. "Are you nervous?"

"Yes."

She scoffs. "Why? It's Ben. It'll be fine."

"I don't know how he'll react… Can you stick around until I give you a thumbs up? Just in case he hates that I'm there?"

"He won't hate—"

"Dot, please. I honestly don't know anymore."

She catches my stern tone and nods dutifully. "There's something you're not telling me. What is it?"

"Nothing."

"Tell me."

"You want me to make something up? I told you, it's nothing."

"Then, there *is* an *it*. What?"

I huff, loving and hating how well she knows me. "I don't want to talk about it."

She slams on the brakes, sending us both forward with an uncomfortable jolt. "Holy fuck, Dot!"

"Has he hurt you? Physically? Or verbally? Or anything like that? So help me God, I'll—"

"Dot, no! Absolutely not! Nothing like that!"

Cars honk around us, but Dot ignores them. She takes a deep breath to quell her sudden fury. "You said you didn't know how he'd react, and my brain went to red alert."

"I get it. I'm sorry. But I promise—Ben would never."

She nods. "Yeah, I didn't think so, but had to make sure."

A light chuckle escapes at her overzealous protection. "I appreciate it, my personal Zena Warrior Princess."

"Damn straight." She starts driving again while reaching for her vape pen. "Only a sword won't fit with my murder plan."

"What murder plan?"

"Oh, Cherry and I have talked about it at length. Not murdering Ben, but her ex or any guy in general. We have a solid plan that prevents us from getting caught, should we need it. It's quite clever."

This information doesn't surprise me, and I don't doubt it either. "I'd like to hear this plan."

"No. Tell me what *it* is."

"I fell asleep on the couch waiting for him to come home last night, and he didn't wake me up." My shoulders bounce with the quick explanation that sounds so small and insignificant. "He just went to bed without me."

"Maybe he didn't want to disturb you," she tries.

"That's what he said this morning, but it's bullshit. I've fallen asleep waiting for him hundreds of times when he works the split shift. He always wakes me, usually with a kiss. Sometimes, he carries me to bed. He's never left me there before. No, he didn't want to talk to me. It was easier for him to sneak off to bed than to have a conversation."

Dot groans. "So much for avoiding avoidance. Am I right?"

"Yeah… I'm losing him. The harder I try to connect with him, the more he pushes back. I'm starting to think… Ben's falling out of love with me, Dot. Little by little, he's slipping through my fingers. I feel him pulling away, see it when he looks at me. I'm not even sure he realizes it yet."

I droop in my seat, the admission zapping my energy. I needed to hear myself say it. Last night confirmed my worst fear—he'd rather be without me.

"I don't believe that's true," she says, "but let's put it to the test. He won't want you here if he doesn't love you. I bet he won't turn you away when you show up… I'll even go as far as to say he'll be glad to see you. When I win, you must promise to stop talking like that, okay? Ben loves you. You must know that."

I sigh, knowing how easily that can change. "What if I win?"

"Then, I'll let you and Cherry do that fucking makeover on me that you've always wanted to do, dresses, heels, make-up, the works—*that's* how damn sure I am."

I laugh at our preposterous makeover plans concocted over too much wine one night. We would never change Dot. But her willingness to risk being turned into a girly girl speaks to her confidence and upticks mine slightly.

"Fine. Deal. But promise me, you won't take off to force his hand. Crying my ass off while waiting for an Uber will be extremely humiliating."

"I'll wait for the thumbs up. Promise." She puts on her calm voice, and once she pulls into a space street-side in front of the clinic, she parks and turns off the motor to satiate me.

Still, my anxiety surges.

Ben's blue Jeep isn't here yet—I made sure to arrive twenty-five minutes early so there was no chance of him entering the building first.

I take cleansing breaths, watching the gentle sway of the multi-colored crepe myrtles lining the street.

"Ben *isn't* Mark, you know," she says after a few silent minutes. "There's no falling out of love with you. It's a rough patch. That's all."

"Then, tell me why I feel this way?" I return, measuring my breaths to avoid the panic in my chest.

"It's your first storm. You're scared. You both are."

Across the street, Ben's Jeep pulls into the small parking lot beside the building, and he backs into the first space. My fears compound, making me second-guess my *brilliant* idea to show up for him. He doesn't like surprises.

"This was a bad idea," I sputter.

"No, it wasn't. Go get 'em, tiger." Dot gently shoves my shoulder and motions to Ben, who heads to the front door.

I topple from the van, adjust my skirt, and clop around the sidewalk.

"Ben!" I call out as he approaches the stoop. When he doesn't stop, Dot lays on the horn. "Ben!"

Our eyes lock, and I wave timidly. He looks confused but meets me on the sidewalk, where I tiptoe on my wedges to give him a short kiss on the cheek.

"Hey," I say. "Fancy meeting you here."

"I have an appointment. What're you doing here?"

"Um, going with you to your appointment. If you'll have me."

His hesitation spikes my already-primed anxiety and assures me that asking Dot to stay was a good plan. Her engine starts and revs behind me, waiting for the signal, and I pray she doesn't leave yet.

"Is this okay?" I ask and sign together, my fingers trembling with nerves.

His hands rest on his hips as he scans the perimeter, perhaps searching for a way to escape me. My heart sinks with every passing second. It feels like last night, waking up to a dark living room with the TV off and realizing he'd left me there by choice.

My inner hollow grows as I scramble to fix yet another mistake. "Um, if you don't want—"

"Lena."

CHAPTER 25

Ben

KEEPING my distance from Lena protects her. I can't stand hurting her, and I can't stand myself for being unable to stop it. So, I've gotten small lately.

Still, my heart skips to see her here.

I'm sick with myself that she expects my rejection. Dot's van idles at the curb across the street, probably awaiting an all-clear to leave. My wife anticipates me not wanting her here, and I can't blame her. All I've done is reject her. She's overcompensating for me, tiptoeing around me like something delicate that might break if she makes one wrong move. Lena's made every conceivable effort to spend time with me, but the harder she tries, the worse I feel. The pressure mounts with every effort, keeping me from complying, and my guilt compounds with her disappointment when I refuse her.

She shifts on her feet, swaying her little dress and awkwardly fidgeting as she awaits my answer.

This is what I've reduced us to—instead of calming her, I cause her anxiety. Exactly what I never wanted. Our marriage has switched from me living in her periphery to her edging around mine. And I know that won't change, especially after the inevitable news we'll receive at today's appointment.

This'll get worse before it gets better. If it ever does.

I wonder how long it'll be before she stops trying.

Last night replays in my head. It had been a long shift, longer than usual. Tedious nothingness was bookended by bullshit—belligerent shoplifters at the mall and a drunk who spewed all over my backseat on purpose. It took me over an hour to clean it up, and the cleansers instigated a migraine.

I wanted to wake her when I got home. I always wake her. Groggy Lena is soft, lovable, easy, and comforting.

But she would've known immediately something was wrong and jumped into Busy Lena to take care of me. I don't want her taking care of me. Or asking questions I wouldn't want to answer. I've hurt her enough already.

It was easier to let her sleep. I left her there for a cold, empty bed and put off her inevitable disappointment until this morning. She stirred on the couch when I made coffee, and the hurt and confusion on her face when she realized I let her sleep there made me feel like I'd betrayed her.

Her shoulders slump. "Um, if you don't want—"

"Lena." Over her shoulder, I wave to Dot, freeing her to go. Her thumbs up out the driver's window stays as she pulls off the curb. "It's good you're here."

Her full-bodied relief makes me smile, and not much does these days.

"Thanks for putting it on the family calendar," she beams.

I slide my hand over hers and escort her to the building.

Janice, the audiologist who works with Dr. Lin, greets me by name and brightens at the sight of Lena. "Brought your A-game today, huh, Ben?"

"Yes. Lena, my wife," I clarify.

"I remember. Good to see you, honey."

She leads us through the small office into the exam room. It's minimally decorated and dimly lit. Most importantly, it's quiet. Lena sits in the corner while I perch in the exam chair. Dr. Lin rushes in—he always acts like he's late, even when he isn't.

"Ah, Mrs. Wright, glad you could join us today. It's a big one. Let's see what we're working with, eh?"

Lena looks confused—the family calendar didn't report the significance of the appointment, only that I had one. But as my omissions don't surprise her, she says nothing.

Janice greets Lena with the same welcoming smile she gives her customers. "They've got some tests to do. How would you like to experience hearing from Ben's point of view?"

She perks up. "Really? You can do that?"

Janice nods. "Come with me."

Lena follows her to another room. Dr. Lin grabs his otoscope. I remove my hearing aids.

He examines my ears through the otoscope, periodically typing notes into his computer and making noises of interest. I don't hear him like I once did, but I catch his reactions by watching and feel grateful that he's not one for chitchat. I go through the usual tests in the sound booth to determine if my hearing has worsened since my last appointment.

I already know the answer.

Once the tests are complete, Dr. Lin leaves me to examine the results. I'm putting my hearing aids back in when Lena slips inside, leaning against the closed door behind her. Her gaze holds mine, surprising me with her determined smile.

She crosses the room in two steps and crushes her lips to mine, making me laugh at her sweet aggression. I respond in kind, gripping her against me and letting my hands wander. My hard edges soften with her affection.

"What's all this?" I ask, breathless and barely able to stop kissing her long enough to talk.

"I just got to know you better. It's a good day."

I used to say that to her all the time, but it's been ages.

Janice probably gave her a simulation of hearing loss via headphones and a computer. Her reaction is a relief. Fondling my wife in a doctor's office is much preferred to dealing with her sympathy or sadness.

I couldn't handle that. Not today.

As my fingertips skate down her neck, hope replaces my earlier hesitation.

"It is a good day," I repeat. "No matter what he's about to tell us."

She nods, biting my lower lip in a playful kiss. "No matter what."

She's like medicine finally hitting my system, easing the pain and pressure.

A light rap on the door ends our moment.

They enter, bringing a mood that makes everything feel quiet and discontented. I sit in the exam chair, and Lena takes my side, resting her hand comfortably on my shoulder.

Dr. Lin glances at the file he carries but then tosses it on the counter. "Ben, there's no easy way—"

"Just say it," I interject.

"Your hearing number is seventy-six." He makes eye contact, saying the words slowly so nothing is lost on me. Then, he looks to Lena. "That's significantly worse than our last check and only a few decibels from *profound* hearing loss. With the migraines and now the balance issues—"

Lena's arm tightens against my shoulders—she doesn't know about that. Another omission.

"Surgery is our next best option, and your tests indicate that you're an excellent candidate."

"Cochlear implants?" Lena says, her voice thankfully absent of emotion. "Can you explain what's involved with that option?"

Dr. Lin breaks out his ear chart and details the procedure—ENTs love their charts. It's a routine outpatient surgery with minimal risk.

"Once the internal implants heal," Janice chimes in, "we'll turn his devices on, and I'll work with Ben to learn how to interpret the sounds."

"What do you mean?" Lena asks.

"I'll have to relearn how to hear," I say. "It won't be the same as normal hearing."

"But it will be better than hearing aids in the long term," Dr. Lin adds.

Lena's arm tightens again. "How long will it take to get used to the implants?"

Janice and Dr. Lin share a look—they know this is a sticking point for me, even more than the idea of implanting magnets in my skull.

He says, "Six months to a year."

"I see… What are his other options?"

Dr. Lin shrugs. "Status quo—continue with the hearing aids indefinitely and manage the migraines and balance issues with medication. The deterioration could level out, and your symptoms appear manageable."

Lena shakes her head. "Ben deserves better than *manageable*. What else?"

Dr. Lin puts up his hands. "When his hearing aids fail to help, he could accept deafness. That should reduce the migraines and balance issues naturally. You've already acquired many skills—ASL, reading lips and facial cues. It might mean a career shift, but people do it all the time."

Lena's eyes land on mine, sizing me up.

But I'm a stone. None of this is news to me.

Outside in the sunlight again, Lena takes my hand as we stroll toward the Jeep. I expect a thousand questions, but she only has one.

"Want to go to lunch?"

I take her to a downtown restaurant, and we sit outside, facing the Riverwalk and overlooking the Cape Fear River. She mentions our first date away from Saddletree—a night branded into my existence so deeply that it's legend. I knew long before then that I loved her. But her unequivocal acceptance that night solidified it.

I close my eyes and still see her adoring expression when she took in my scars the first time. She loved me, no matter what. When I die, that's the memory I want to go out on.

She made a promise that night. *Whatever your reality, I'm with you, and I'll try to make it better.*

Today, her promise feels reaffirmed.

We spend our lunch discussing Ruthie and Saddletree. Lena gushes excitedly as she outlines the changes she's implemented. I love seeing her like this. It reminds me of Saddletree's early days, when she operated on hope and creativity and loved lassoing me into her decisions. She ran everything by me then, not because she needed to—she wanted to. We were partners.

We aren't anymore, not like then. But it's my fault. Her dream is too big for one person. She's been in a rut caused by stress and overwhelm. I've failed to offer the support and encouragement I used to. Throwing tasks at her isn't the same as helping. I haven't given her enough credit. She's a good boss, capable of change, not a frazzled woman running a dog park.

This Lena—my Lena—wouldn't be a difficult employer.

"Oh, and I've decided on a new car," she says, nibbling on a fry.

"Yes?"

"I don't want a new car," she returns. "I'm a farm girl. I want a truck. A Chevy Colorado, I think. Something big and rugged. What do you think?"

I smirk, imagining it. "Yes, that would suit you. Plus, the safety features—"

"Ugh, Ben. Don't ruin it. Tell me it's badass."

I comply, chuckling. "Want to go for a test drive before we pick up Ruthie?"

She gasps. "Yes!"

The pot-bellied salesman at the dealership eyes Lena in a way I don't like. *At all.* He speaks in mumbled Carolinian when I ask about the vehicle's features. When I ask him to repeat himself, he jokes about "cleaning the wax from my ears." Lena doesn't interject or speak for me but signs the information so that I understand. Randy turns red at his ignorance—I hope that means he won't ridicule anyone else for having trouble hearing.

"It's still a good day," she says when he leaves to retrieve the keys.

I have to agree. Lena drives the truck like a professional, whipping around corners and merging in and out of traffic. She loves the truck.

But when we return to the dealership, she hands Randy the keys with a firm "No, thanks" before pulling me to the Jeep.

"I thought you liked it," I say.

"I love it, but I'm not buying it from that guy. Did you see how he looked at me when we got here?" She shivers. "Creepy."

I laugh. This is my favorite Lena—*my* Lena. Present, funny, loving, and the only woman in existence who knows what I need without words. She seems to understand that this is what I need today.

Not career advice.

Not rehashing my hearing options.

She doesn't even mention our therapy session, though I displayed minimal effort and need to do better.

We pick Ruthie up from preschool, and she shares a dramatic account of her day while I hold her mother's hand across the front seat. I long for home and a quiet evening with Lena curled up on one side of me and Ruthie on the other as we watch TV.

But arriving home, any plans for a relaxing evening are upended.

Cars line the country road, haphazardly parked along our outer fence. A camera-toting crowd assembles at the foot of our driveway, blocking the path. I lay on the horn, whipping the Jeep around Officer Bennett's patrol car, already stationed where I want a gate. The studio's few security guards stand with him, keeping a weak barrier.

"What's going on, Dad?" Ruthie asks.

"Paparazzi… it's a funny word for pushy photographers," I say.

"That is a funny word," Ruthie says after failing to say it properly. I don't correct her. It's not a word that should be in a four-year-old's vocabulary. "Take Ruthie home. I'll deal with this."

Lena obeys, crawling into my seat when I exit. The Jeep peels down the lane as I approach Bennett.

"Hey, Ben." He shakes my hand. "Got ourselves a nuisance here. They're mostly behaving, but the security team caught a few wandering the property earlier and called me for backup."

With Bennett at my side, I approach the line and demand their attention.

"I'm Lieutenant Ben Wright, Wilmington Police. This is private property. Remove your vehicles before I have them towed. You have ten minutes to comply." I hold up the timer on my phone. "Step on our land after that, and I'll have you arrested for trespassing."

The group confers, assessing their surroundings. With the Harveys' cornfield towering across the street and our pastures taking up this side, there's nowhere to park without infringing on private property. Country roads don't have shoulders to pull onto or nearby parking lots.

With no options, the group disbands.

Officer Bennett promises to increase patrols, but his department is small. We confer with Elsie Todd, the production manager, who apologizes and claims that a top-notch security team arrives in the morning.

"For a few paparazzi?" Bennett asks. "Seems like you should've already expected this."

"Um, we did. But there's something else." Ms. Todd leans closer. "Jaye's received disturbing fan mail lately, creepy enough not to ignore."

"Understood. I want access to the fan mail," I say. "I want to talk to the security team when they arrive. I also suggest moving the trailers horizontally with the fence line to create more of a barrier and less access for the cameras."

She nods and immediately delivers the instructions in her walkie. Bennett and I walk the perimeter, finding another cameraman hiding in the bushes near Matt Kirby's trailer. He's arrested and taken to the local station. Ms. Todd forwards Jaye's fan mail. An emotionally disturbed person claims that Jaye is demonically possessed and needs cleansing via holy water, fire, blood-letting, acid bath, or death. The unpleasant reading prompts me to suggest that she change hotels and use an alias or, better yet, relocate to a more private residence altogether.

"I believe Dot and Mrs. Moore have an extra room," I advise, knowing they'd happily accommodate her. Jaye seems willing to consider it.

Inside the house, laundry is going, the dogs are eating, something is baking, and Ruthie is occupied with homework at the kitchen island. Busy Lena has returned. She looks defeated as I enter, probably in expectation of my anger.

I *am* upset. But not at her. Even I wouldn't have foreseen this.

Her teary eyes catch mine. "I'm sorry. I'll get the fence and security cameras installed. I've left a message for the company you recommended."

Her words come quickly as if cutting me off from my usual irritation. I step to her side of the kitchen island, where ingredients and utensils are scattered beside a cutting board and casserole dish. She huffs, trying to open a jar of roasted red peppers by bracing it with her cast. I pry the jar from her grip, open it, and set it on the counter.

"Come here," I say, holding my arms open.

Surprised and relieved, she falls against me, wrapping her arms as best she can around my neck to tighten her grip. I love the way she fits me and how her wavy hair tickles my cheek.

"It's still a good day," I assure her, and despite the bullshit—mine and Saddletree's—I feel better about us.

CHAPTER 26

Lena

AN ORGANIZED BUSINESSWOMAN should have an organized office. With Ruthie on a playdate with Dot and Ben at work, I spend the next afternoon clearing out my messy barn office. The more I clear out and file away, the better I feel. Ben was right—the restructuring of Saddletree is long overdue, and finally getting my shit together feels amazing.

Thinking of him brings another smile to my face. Things feel better between us. I still feel his tender goodbye kiss this morning before he said his usual, "See you later." I can't wait to show him my progress when he gets home.

My phone pings—a text from the new security team manning the driveway.

Lauren Riley?

I stiffen. *What the hell is she doing here?* I type back a reluctant thumbs-up emoji.

Lauren's white BMW gleams as she drives toward the barn. She exits the car, flipping her perfectly straight blond hair off her shoulders, and extracts a large planter buckled in the back seat.

Hugo and Penelope greet her—they love surprise guests. She dances around them, trying to satiate them with smiles and awkward head pats. She's clearly not a dog person.

She approaches like a catwalk model—all legs, poise, and elegance in her black heels, steel-gray pencil skirt, and soft teal top. Meanwhile, I'm fully decked out in country-chic: cut-off jean shorts, a low-cut Metallica tank, and my signature black-skulled rubber boots. This is me in my element—she's the outsider—yet I feel small and out of place by comparison.

A bracing inhale squares my shoulders.

"Lena, hi," she greets, her voice villainous with good cheer. "I hope it's okay that I popped in like this."

"Sure, but Ben's not here."

"Oh, I know," she says. "I'm here to see you."

She hands me the gorgeous blue ceramic planter bursting with a mature rosemary plant that tickles my senses as she passes it over. I baby it in the crook of my good arm. "That's for you. It's from my grandmother's garden—you met Mamma Riley, right?"

"Um, yes, I must have. That's very thoughtful."

"Ah, well, least I could do. She's quite the gardener and has loads of it. Ben mentioned you loved herbs."

"I do, yes. Thanks."

She stands there, awkwardly shifting on her heels to prevent them from sinking into the dirt, and I take a breath, trying to remember polite protocol in this situation. "Um, would you like to come up for coffee? Or something? Ruthie and I baked banana bread last night."

"Oh, yummy, but no, thanks. I can't stay long, and I know you'll be fixing dinner for the family soon," she coos like this is the greatest thing ever or my only station in life—it's hard to tell.

Regardless, I don't know what to do now. I set the plant on the spiral staircase by the barn door to give my arm a rest. "It's sweet of you to come all this way to bring me rosemary."

Her sculpted arms bounce in a shrug. "I've been meaning to stop by since the picnic, to be honest. It means the absolute world to me and my family that you and Ben are considering Riley Trust."

"Oh, yes, I, um, gathered that. Ben has the greatest respect for your father."

She smiles knowingly. "That's definitely mutual. We're interviewing other candidates, just in case, but it'll break Dad's heart if Ben doesn't take it. Larry's heart, too."

"Well, he certainly doesn't want to disappoint them, but he's still weighing his options. Law enforcement is what he knows, and he's exceptional at it. He loves the community. It's not easy to give that up."

Her head tilts curiously. "Oh, Ben said that *you* were the reason he's reluctant to accept our offer."

"Me?" The word spits out like I'm choking on it. *Hello, bus. Didn't expect you to mow me down today.*

"Believe me, I understand." She lightly pets my arm like I'm a cute farm animal. "Ben and I share an incredible history. We were together for a long time. It must be so weird for you."

"Um, it's—"

"It'd be weird if it wasn't, right?" She chuckles. "Well, I hope I can put your fears to rest."

So, I'm the problem? I tuck my fidgeting fingers behind my back.

"It's strictly professional," she says in a tone that suggests it's a public service announcement. "Ben and I have made that clear to each other…"

They had to clarify it?

"And you two are so happy. Obviously, you have nothing to worry about."

Obviously? Her words feel laced with sarcasm, as if she's privy to our marriage issues. Who knows? Maybe she is.

I laser in on her icy gray eyes. "I'm not worried. Certainly not about Ben. But *'strictly professional'* seems inaccurate unless Riley Trust typically drops in for home visits on potential candidates… three times."

Smirking, she shrugs again. "You're right. Ben isn't just another candidate. After his injuries, he needed us, and we failed him. I don't want to fail him now, not with more changes ahead regarding his hearing. It's an outstanding offer. He deserves an easier life. My family will take care of him."

"No—*his* family will take care of him. He's done just fine without the Rileys."

"Yes, of course, he has. Ben always does *just fine.*" Her perfect face crinkles like the words are taboo. "But he could do so much better… I don't want to upset you. I'm Ben's past. You're his present. But we both want what's best for him, don't we?"

Double score for Lauren for making me feel like a petty, unsupportive, selfish hag-wife, all while she smiles, looks gorgeous, and drips with concern for Ben. I should expect nothing less from the woman with zero qualms about tricking my husband into dancing with her.

"All I'm asking is that you don't keep him from the care and support he's going to need, especially if he gets the implants. It'll be a long recovery. With us, he'll have job security. Larry's agreed to stay on through Ben's recovery, part-time, full-time, whatever he needs. Ben saved Larry's life once… Did he tell you that?"

My agape expression reveals my utter cluelessness. I rein it in, growing irritated. "No, but he never spoke of you, either. Ben doesn't live in the past."

Her porcelain face flashes with surprise and hurt that he'd left her out of his history, the same way I felt learning about her existence.

"Oh, right. I know. He's a present-thinker," she recovers weakly. "And a planner. Knowing him, it won't take nearly as long as the doctor claims to recover. Right?"

"Um, probably not," I mumble the words like my lips are sticky.

"He won't find the support he needs anywhere else, and having a position of authority, an income, a… mission… will help Ben through what's likely to be a tough transition mentally. I don't want him to lose that because of me."

My head spins—anxiety, confusion, anger, and weirdly, appreciation. Dr. Lin's yearlong recovery time gongs in my head, and my purpose-driven husband will need a positive focus that makes him feel valued. Early retirement or a desk job won't do that.

Even so, I hate that she's educating me about *my* husband. It's a good thing I don't know Dot and Cherry's jail-proof murder plan.

Lauren beams. "I'm glad we got to talk, Lena. Enjoy the rosemary."

She front-steps away, careful of her stilettos.

CHAPTER 27

Ben

THE FAMILIAR SCENT of hay and horses greets me at the barn. Lena tacks up Shadow, tethered in the alley. The dogs, always quick to announce my arrival, don't distract her from her task.

All day, I've longed to see her. But the sweet lightness of yesterday is lost on her now. She's busy and upset.

"What's wrong?"

"Lauren Riley paid me a friendly visit," she says in a way that doesn't sound friendly at all. "I want to discuss it, face my problems head-on, yada yada, but I need to calm down first. Ruthie's upstairs with Dot. Dinner's in the oven. I'm going for a ride. I need to think and clear my head."

She heaves the saddle onto Shadow's rotund midsection but struggles with the girth, one-handed. I assist, securely tightening the thick strap's belt latches so the saddle won't slip.

"Thank you," she breathes, reaching for the leather bridle. She eases the bit gently into Shadow's mouth and attaches the headgear over his ears. He grunts and flaps his thick lips. She secures his reins in her casted hand while I take hold of the other.

I caress her fingers between my hands, gently insisting on eye contact. She gives in, but anxiety pumps through her like pressure through a hose that's liable to burst.

"I'll get River. Let's ride together," I say, leery of her riding with an injury and in this worked-up condition. Horses play off their riders' emotions.

She huffs. "*Now* you want to ride with me? Is this what it takes for you to opt in? Me getting upset? Or are you simply curious about Lauren?"

Her harsh look softens with immediate regret. She takes a breath and forces a smile. "See? This is why I need to calm down."

"Let me come with you. We don't have to talk until you're ready... Please."

She nods reluctantly. She doesn't want me to accompany her, but once again, she's accommodating me.

Thirty minutes later, we ride side-by-side at a slow, walking pace down the lane toward the outer trail. Production has shut down for the day, but hollow-eyed, pale-faced, and black-garbed witches remain throughout the woods, suspended from intricate pulleys. The trees no longer resemble typical pines but blackened obelisks, bleeding through their bark. Gauzy drapes form thick cobwebs between branches, entwining mummified corpses. It's a much different riding experience than usual. But the change of scenery is enjoyable, especially with the sun setting behind the branches and glowing against the gold in Lena's hair.

Touring the property on horseback reminds me how much I adore Saddletree and what she's created here.

What *we've* created here.

"You should take the job. It'll be good for you."

Her calm tone surprises me. She even sounds encouraging. "I'm confused."

"Why? I've thought it through. That's why I needed the ride—to consider the pros. There are so many pros... I mean, if you *want* my opinion."

"Yes, I do, but tell me about Lauren's visit."

"She popped in, brought a plant, and reassured me that... It's the right thing." Her voice cracks slightly on this last part. I study her as best I can from my side angle. She glances over with a soft smile, and the *L* clear between her brows.

A downed tree blocks the path, staged for the movie. She steers Shadow over it, and he grunts his disapproval at having to jump. River picks up his pace, wanting to jump it. I pull the reins back, navigating around it instead.

When Lena and I merge together again, she says, more sincerely this time, "If *you* want it, *I* want it."

"I don't know what I want."

"Ben, you can't turn down this job because of me. You *can't*."

"There are multiple factors. We discussed this. What does this have to do with Lauren?"

"Let's wait and discuss that part with Dr. Reese. Things have been better for us lately... or, at least, yesterday they were. I don't want to..." She takes another calming breath when we lock eyes. "I don't want to argue."

"We won't. Just tell me what happened."

With a long exhale, she says, "You spoke to Lauren about your prognosis. They already have a generous recovery plan for you. They truly want to support you through this. With them, you'll have the best of everything. It sure as hell beats early retirement or working with me, right?"

A wary smile escapes as she swallows her emotion. She's done this often lately, pushing down what she usually purges. I don't like it. It's not her, and it doesn't help us.

"I want this job for you, Ben."

"Then, why does it hurt you to say it?"

She nods, amused at how well I read her—it's not hard.

"I *am* hurt. You're right. Again."

A lone tear skitters down her cheek. She swipes it quickly, holding tight to her calm. I reach for her reins and tug both our horses to a stop to see her lips and expressions clearly.

"Tell me why."

"*We* haven't discussed the implants yet. I don't even know if that's what you want, let alone have a plan for your recovery. But *I* should be your plan, whatever you do. *That's* what I want. But I'm being sidelined for the Rileys. It *hurts* that she shows up knowing more about you than I do. It *hurts* that you'd share your prognosis with her and make plans without talking to me first. It *hurts* that you'd confide to her that *I'm* the reason you haven't taken the job yet. How could you... betray me like that?"

"Wait. What? I didn't confide *anything* to her."

She waves her hand dismissively. "How would she know these things if you didn't tell her?"

"My communications have been with John and Larry. *Not her*." I slide my phone from my jeans and offer it to her. "My texts will prove it."

Her eyes flicker between the phone and me in a debate. "I'm not reading your texts, Ben."

"I informed John and Larry about my situation in case they wanted to retract the offer," I explain. "Instead, they devised a recovery plan. I didn't solicit it. I didn't indicate *any* decision because you and I haven't made it yet."

Her shoulders release their pent-up tension in a breath. "Shit. I let her get to me again. Didn't I?"

"Yes."

Her face relaxes into pained relief, as if ashamed for believing it. "Sorry, Ben. She was so confident and informed. She looked me straight in the eye and told me *you said* I was holding you back."

My stomach knots. "I said that, just not to her."

Her relief is obliterated.

"Oh, I see. So, I *am* the problem? And everyone knows it." A sardonic laugh funnels through her obvious distress—she does this sometimes when her emotions come on too strongly for her to contain. "I've been as supportive as I know how to be."

"Yes. I shouldn't have said it. I'm sorry."

She shakes her head, tears dripping now. "Did you blame it on my anxiety or my insecurity about Lauren?"

My head hangs. "Lauren."

She manages a wry smile. "Bet she loved hearing that."

"It wasn't for her to hear. I felt pressured to explain my indecision, and it slipped. Lauren *is* a difficult factor in this—we both have concerns about her."

"Yes, but you blamed those concerns *on me*. That's unfair. What about the rest? Not wanting to give up the badge, the community, and so on. Did you discuss those, too?"

"No." My head droops again—blaming Lena felt easier at the time. Now, her disappointment guts me.

"What're we doing here, Ben?" she asks, her voice tired, edging on defeated.

The horses grunt simultaneously as if bored.

"I'll call John first thing tomorrow and refuse the offer. It's not going to work."

"No, you won't. If that's what you wanted, you would've done it already. It's not about the job. This is about us."

I huff and roll my eyes. "It isn't."

"Yes, it is." Her voice is eerily calm, as if she's too exhausted to be angry. "You've blamed me for everything since this started. You lied about the interview and Lauren because *I'm* difficult to talk to. You told me *I'm* too busy for my family because *I'm* a shit businesswoman. You fault me at every opportunity for the studio decision, though I only did it to spend more time with you, time you've mostly rejected. At the picnic, you snapped at me, embarrassed me, and chose Lauren over me. And your new 'work family' thinks *I'm* so insecure that I'd keep you from your dream job, which isn't true. It's one hurt after another, like you want to push me away."

"I don't. I've apologized for all those things. I'm sorry for hurting you again—I don't mean to. It's unintentional... like my frustration naturally funnels in your direction. It's not a reflection on you or us."

"Ben, it's *all* a reflection on us. You're caught between two worlds, and *I'm* the one you're pushing away. What does that tell you?"

That this isn't the world I want? No. Unacceptable. Untrue.

"I want you, Ruthie, and Saddletree—that's *never* been the issue."

"If that's true, why won't you spend time with me? Or talk in therapy? Or do what Dr. Reese said?" Her tears stream now. Shadow shifts uncomfortably under her, like he's pissed at me, too. She wipes her cheeks with the back of her riding glove and takes a breath. "You can't even *talk* to me, Ben."

"I can. I want to. It's difficult for me," I defend weakly. "Some things are just... hard for me to say."

She nods, freeing more tears. "I know, but I need you to say the hard things. I need a little mercy..." Her voice trails off in a small sob. "I overheard you with Rob. Lauren's waited for you to come back to her *all this time*. She'd be with you in a heartbeat, and *you* know it. *Everyone* knows it. And you can't even talk to me about her. It's like you're letting me fear the worst because... the worst is true."

"No! It's not that at all! That's your anxiety talking—not me. Stop putting your shit on me!"

We're both stunned by my anger. So much for not arguing. I don't know even where my anger toward her comes from—she and Ruthie are the best parts of me. And yet, I *am* pushing her away.

Finally, she shakes her head with a knowing, tearful look. "My fault. Again. Got it. This was a bad idea."

Then, she yanks Shadow's reins and takes off through the woods, kicking her heels into Shadow's sides for a strong canter. River shifts under me like a revving race car, but I'm not a good enough rider to follow suit.

"Whoa," I say, struggling to hold him back. But the reality of my wife's accusation hits me in a wild rush of fear and anger. Lena believes my distance and indecision are about Lauren.

"Fuck!"

I dig my heels into River's sides, though he needs no encouragement. He takes off as soon as I stop resisting his antsiness. The ride is clumsy, too fast for comfort, and incredibly unsafe, but I reach the barn as she dismounts.

She puts up a hand. "If you can't even understand my feelings, let's wait for Dr. Reese—"

"No," I return, sliding off River and not even bothering to gather his reins. The horses mingle at the mouth of the barn, attempting to eat grass between their bits. I stand in front of Lena, winded and angry.

"Lauren rejected me," I say finally, unable to meet her eyes for the tears flooding mine. "Six weeks after the IED. Two weeks after being honorably discharged. We were finally together, and the woman who claimed to love me cringed when I took my shirt off. She could barely look at me. Couldn't touch me—"

"Oh, God, Ben, I'm so—"

"Stop." Tears stream down my cheeks, hot against my flushed face. I meet her gaze long enough to see her agonized sympathy—a look I never want to see. "Can't you see why I wouldn't want to tell you this? That someone else found me repulsive, so weak and broken she physically recoiled? Does this make you feel better?"

"No, I'm heartbroken—"

"Don't do that," I cut her off sternly. "You want to know about Lauren, so here it is. She immediately apologized, saying it was only a reaction. But reactions are truth, aren't they? Love can happen in a moment and be destroyed just as fast. *That's* what happened. She did everything she could to fix it. But I couldn't get past it."

I pause, trying to swallow the hard lump in my throat while forcing myself to keep going, to purge the toxic parts that have eaten away at me all this time, if only to satiate her.

"But the truth is, I didn't want to get past it… because six weeks earlier, lying in the sand, bleeding, burning, ears ringing, head pounding, sure I wasn't getting out of there just like the guys next to me, I ached for what Lauren would go through, losing me, but… I also felt fucking relieved. Expendable. I didn't want to go back. Didn't want… her. Then, I felt ashamed for not loving her the way I-I thought she loved me."

My head droops, and tears fall, thinking about everything I went through then and all I put Lauren through, too. I square my shoulders, determined to get through this for Lena's sake.

"When I was safe aboard the Blackhawk that rescued me, I vowed to return home and keep my promises. She'd waited for me, loved me, for ten years. I wanted to do my duty and make her happy. That's why her rejection gutted me so badly. Here I was, patting myself on the back for being so goddamned noble, and I was too fucked up for her. Her rejection hurt me, but it also freed me—it took a lot of therapy to realize it. *That's* why she never heard from me again. I knew I could've gone back to her. I still know it—you're right. But why would I give up the life I want for the one I didn't? I loved her, but something was missing. I never understood what until five years ago when fate and Alice Harvey brought me here. To *you*."

She reaches out, but I gently bat her arms away. I don't want to be touched or consoled. Another pause brings silence as I boil in a debate I never wanted to have, let alone like this—under pressure in the court of Lena's anxiety. But I also know there's no getting around it, especially if she's hellbent on believing there's something between Lauren and me.

Lena stares up at me, eyes glistening with fresh tears for me. Her sympathy pisses me off—*this* is what I never wanted.

"What happened with Lauren still angers me. Not because I love her —I don't. But because…" My words sound haggard, like my mouth's full of sand. "You say the right things and put on your fake smiles and your busyness, but *I know* that one day you'll look at me like she did… not over my scars, but over something—frustrations over our communication or the burden I'll become. You're already accommodating me at every turn and making decisions to suit me. Goddamnit, Lena. See? *This* is why I never wanted you to know. I want your truthful reactions, not your sympathy or accommodation. It's bad enough dealing with this shit and all the pressure over the job and my future—*our* future— without reliving it every time I look at you, too."

My index finger rises between us. "I won't say this again—I don't want to talk about it."

Her riding boots scrape the brick walkway as she moves back, and her sympathy shifts into anguish. I've hurt her—again.

But somehow, I don't care.

I gather the horses' reins and move them into their holding stations. "I'll take care of the horses—"

"Let me help."

"No. Leave me alone." I take a breath, already regretful about my anger, my tone, everything. "Please, Lena."

Though it goes against every fiber of her overthinking, sensitive being, she does.

CHAPTER 28
Lena

CLASHING LIGHT SABERS, incredible costumes, and a mishmash of beeps, buzzers, and zippy music greet us as we enter the double doors leading to the main convention center. An imperial soldier shoots me with a Nerf gun.

"Die, rebel scum!" he shouts before rushing away.

I'm not in the mood for this.

Ruthie squeezes my hand, ballerina-stepping in her bright pink boots. Her Toadette hat and pom poms bounce with her, emphasizing her excitement. "Mom, I wanna go there. And there. Where's Adam? Do you see him yet? He's Spiderman. Remember?"

"I remember. We'll find him."

"Let's get eyes on Jaye," Dot says. "I want her to know I'm here."

She claps her hands together like she's about to feast on a buffet. Like Ruthie, she's also made an effort with her wardrobe. Long black jeans accent her shiny black Tims. Her *Nightmare Before Christmas* t-shirt is tucked in and secured by a silver-knotted belt—Dot has a waist! Silver studs weave around her upper ears, and her black hair is artfully twisted away from her eyes with dagger bobby pins. A smudgy black eyeliner highlights her piercing eyes, making her look vixen-like. She's not even wearing flannel.

"I want Jaye to see my costume," Ruthie agrees.

"Lead the way, Dot," I say.

She eyes the event map on her phone and points down the middle lane like an air traffic controller. Darth Vader breezes by, making Ruthie gasp in trepidation. He's followed by a swarm of fairies and a Batman. We pass game tables, eclectic fan art, comic books, and a wall of Funko Pop figures, weaving through thick crowds. My grip on Ruthie's hand tightens to keep her close. Dot grabs her other hand as backup.

At the end of the row, the space opens. Celebrities line the back wall at tables, signing wares for fans. Hundreds wait their turn, the lines stretching and crossing into the aisles. It's organized chaos, difficult to make our way through, let alone see where we're going.

As we look for Jaye among the other artists, actors, and authors, Ruthie squeals and rips away. I bolt after her, using my weaponized arm to push through the crowd, not caring about the lines I'm cutting or the complaints I hear. Her pink-domed head bobbles in and out of sight before I catch up to her.

She plops into Jaye's lap with a victorious, "I found her!"

I go to my knees before them both and grab Ruthie's hands. "Never do that again, Ruthie. Never run away from me in a crowd."

My stern voice carries, though I'm not yelling. Ruthie's face flushes before tears fall.

"It's my fault, Lena. I spotted her and waved her over. My bad," Jaye explains, and my whole body slumps when Ruthie buries her face in Jaye's expensive-looking winged shrug over her black tube top.

I pull her off Jaye's lap and smile as I capture her teary eyes. "Ruthie, I'm sorry, but you scared me, sweetheart. It would help if you stayed with me and Dot in this place. You might lose us."

"Sorry, Mom." She shrugs and purses her lips.

"It's an exciting place. I get it. But better together, right?"

I bop her nose, and her domed head bobs while she giggles. She tumbles into my arms for a reassuring hug I'm happy to give.

"There you guys are! You lost me!" Dot squeezes through the crowd.

"See?" I smirk at Ruthie, and she giggles.

Jaye rises from her seat, kissing Dot's cheek. "Wow, you look amazing."

Dot's blushing face rivals the bloody designs on Jaye's graphic novel covers. She cuts me a glance, making sure I saw that. I give her an *I-told-you-so* grin. Jaye smooths her slinky black one-piece as she returns to her seat and picks up her Sharpie.

"Hang out with me?" she asks Dot, who then stands, sentry-like, behind her.

Signing her next book, Jaye catches Ruthie's eye and motions left. "Look who I found, Ruthie."

Yards away, positioned against the wall, stands Ben. It's a surprise to see him—he lists his shifts on the family calendar, but never where he's assigned.

His eyes dart between us and the crowd. He looks stiff and alert, though he's sporting his more casual class-B uniform. A quick wave in our direction has Ruthie rushing from my arms again straight into his. He leans down, admiring the homemade Toadette costume they made together last Halloween from felt and craft foam. That's when I learned that Ben can sew.

"Hi," I say unsurely. "I didn't know you'd be here."

"I knew you'd be." He holds up his phone. "Family calendar."

My brief smile fades fast. Things have only gotten worse between us.

I cried myself to sleep that night after learning what happened between him and Lauren. I felt—*still feel*—his devastation in my soul. I can't imagine what it would've been like—suffering from trauma and heartbreak at once.

Now, I understand why he was nervous about me seeing him for the first time. He'd almost methodically worked up to it—first telling me about the IED, then his concerns about his hearing and his future, and even giving me a heads-up about his scars before I saw them. Ben needed me to know what I was getting into so I wouldn't hurt him like she did. *Oh, Ben.*

I hate that he thinks I'll *pull a Lauren* (that's my mental phrase for it now) one day, but I understand his fears. It's just like me when I didn't believe he could truly love me until shit happened and my trust grew. It should be a milestone for us—his beautiful vulnerability.

But Ben has a *real* problem with vulnerability. He's embarrassed, angry, and avoidant. He doesn't want me to see him like this, the same way I felt ashamed of my roof leaks, unemployment, panic attacks, sudden onset crying, and scrounging for money in couch cushions five years ago. It's his turn for a shitstorm, and he's struggling to hold onto his umbrella—me.

That night, I didn't harp on it or ask questions. I only thanked him for telling me and reiterated how much I love him. Simple. Easy. No pressure.

Even so, the last few days haze together like a weird nightmare.

Waking up to a cold, half-made bed the morning after he opened up to me.

Him telling Dr. Reese that he needs to be seen alone.

Ben keeping his distance like I'm the new fucking Covid. An irony since the pandemic brought us together.

I've tried to be there for him in the gentlest way, but he's not ready yet.

Knowing we'd be here, it's a wonder he accepted this assignment. Our interactions have been reduced to run-ins at the coffeemaker and brief family dinners that'd be quiet if not for Ruthie. Like I told Dr. Reese, I no longer know what to do. A feeling she validated when she advised patience.

Now, he holds Ruthie's attention. "Mom's right about not running off. It's unsafe and inconsiderate."

She nods. "Sorry, Dad."

His attention returns to me, and there's a smile there like he's happy to see me.

My return smile twinges with concern when I notice his shaded green eyes. "Feeling okay?"

He rubs the scarred side of his forehead. "I have a meal break soon. Maybe we could—"

Ben's eyes turn stony at something over my shoulder. Before I can ask what's wrong, his hand wraps my waist, pushing me aside. "Stay behind me."

I scoop Ruthie into my arms as Ben's tall, wall-like frame moves between us and the crowd. His head tilts briefly to the walkie clipped to his shirt.

He intercepts a lanky, clean-cut teenager in khakis and button-downs, reaching nervously into a backpack as he approaches Jaye's table.

"Stop!" Ben yells as the boy extracts a glass jar, flinging it.

"Repent! Repent!" he yells as the glass shatters against the cinderblock wall near Jaye's head.

Screams. Shuffling feet. The crowd shifts like a wave, amassing. Holding Ruthie to my chest, I cower against the wall. Peeking over Ruthie's head, I see Dot shielding Jaye behind the table.

Ben hooks the offender around his chest and yanks him to the ground—a decisive move that happens so fast my brain barely registers it. Holding the perpetrator down, Ben shoves the backpack aside and unholsters his taser.

"Don't move," he warns, and the assailant complies. Ben's voice breaks through the crowd's distress, silencing even them.

"Daddy!" Ruthie screams, her voice shaking with fear, and her legs latched tightly to my torso.

"It's okay, baby. We're all safe," I whisper, rocking her gently.

Ben side-glances us, ensuring that we're okay.

Officers surround the scene and take the suspect into custody.

"Holy shit! That was fucking awesome!" Dot cheers, hooting and clapping. The crowd joins in, none louder than Jaye. Ruthie shimmies down and rushes to Dot, probably to scold her for her bad words. Onlookers praise and applaud Ben while recording with their phones.

Relief and pride overwhelm me when our eyes meet. Of course, he's great at his job—his calm but strong demeanor assures it—but I've rarely seen Ben in action and never like this. I long for *An Officer and a Gentleman* moment, him scooping me up and carrying me away for fun, sexy times—I've missed our closeness so much lately.

Instead, he retreats to my side, looking sheepish and uncomfortable.

"You okay?"

"Hell, yes! That was amazing!" I'm a flushing, grinning, lovesick mess over him, and his light smile assures me he likes it.

He gives a manly, one-shoulder shrug. "All in a day."

"How'd you see it coming?"

He shrugs. "Jaye's received some distressing hate mail. When I noticed the religious icons on his bag and how nervous he was, I suspected—" He blinks a few times before wobbling. He catches my shoulder to steady himself while my arm slips around him.

"Ben! You okay?"

"Dizzy."

"Dot, take care of Ruthie. Ruthie, don't leave Dot's side," I order, locking eyes with them as Ben leans against me. They salute me almost in unison. I curl under Ben's arm. "Let me take you somewhere quiet."

CHAPTER 29

Ben

LENA DIRECTS us into the first empty room—the back entry to a dimly lit conference area. Anger and embarrassment overtake me, forcing me to pull away from her grip.

This was not the fucking plan.

When I saw the Wilmington Comic-Con on the family calendar, I arranged to work the event. I wanted to interact with Lena and Ruthie in a neutral setting, something fun and engaging, to counter the tension that I've inadvertently created at home. This week has been rough, especially for Lena.

I know she has a million questions and things she wants to say. She's glimpsed parts of me I don't show anyone, not even her, and as Dr. Reese said when we met privately, "There's a lot to unpack here." But including Lena is difficult until I learn how to handle my emotions better.

She fell in love with a stable, understanding, patient man who had his shit together. That's not who I am right now. And I don't want to put us more at risk.

Today was meant to remind us of us. I intended to take an extended break to enjoy the convention as a family. With my uniform and responsibilities as a shield, I'd hoped she'd be reminded of the capable, steady, and dutiful man I am. Or try to be.

She sees the worst of me instead.

"Fuck!" I yell. I can't help it. I sink into the nearest chair, hiding my face in my hands. I'm flushed with anger on top of adrenaline and reeling with shame. I can't even make a simple collar without falling apart. Tears blur my vision. A migraine threatens. I hear a voice, but not what she says. A gentle hand falls on my shoulder, but I jerk it away.

"Go!" I tell her.

She doesn't move.

"I'm fine! Just go!"

She remains.

I make eye contact, no longer giving a fuck if she sees the mess I've become—it's too late. "I don't want you here!"

But she doesn't leave.

Pain and frustration overtake me. I lean over, elbows to knees, face in my hands, hiding the rage that's seeping from me in tears. *I'm fucking sobbing.* She's never seen me like this. I've rarely *been* like this, and I hate it.

Hate myself. Hate that day. Hate so many days since. And my chronic hatred culminates into this—my wife rubbernecking my damn breakdown. I can't take it.

"Please, Lena," I beg, weaker now. "Please, go."

I don't look up, don't want to see how I've hurt her again. Moments ago, she couldn't have been prouder of me. I ruined it. Now, she sees the truth about me—weak, angry, deficient—and I can't handle more of her disappointment.

The pressure compounds. I can't keep on like this. Can't do the fucking job I love. Can't stay calm and controlled. Can't be the man she needs.

I am defeated. Broken.

Alone.

Not alone. Her stomach grazes my head as she moves in front of me. Her delicate fingers slide over my shoulders, curling in an invitation. Testing me, inching me closer.

I latch onto her, and the dark thoughts recede. Tightly, so tightly. My face crushes to her soft stomach. Her fingers rake through my hair, nudging me even closer.

"Shit, Lena. I'm sorry."

"Everything's okay, Ben."

Her words, her softness, and her acceptance unlock the aching tightness in my chest. I bury myself against her, hiding my tears but letting them come. It's freeing and frightening at once.

I'm reminded of the night I came home after finding Adam, and she held me like this, accepting me completely in silence. Letting me hurt. Letting me feel. Why must I always be at my worst before opening up to her?

Time is lost on me—I don't know how long we stay like that. But when her fingers softly massage my temple, I confess, "I don't want this for you."

"*This* is you right now. *I* want this for me. Always." Her deep breath lulls me.

"It's getting worse. Every day," I whine. "It's not fair to you."

"You never need to worry about me. We've prepared for this, remember?"

I shake my head, dragging away from her. "No, we didn't. Not enough. There's no contingency plan for me falling apart."

"*You* are going to be fine. I promise." She sighs, her breath a warm blanket drifting over me. "You had a dizzy spell. It happens. You still kept everyone safe. You're a hero—"

"No, I'm not."

"Yes, honey. You are. You saved Jaye from being attacked, and Ruthie just got to see her dad take down a bad guy. You help people every day. And what you did for Adam—"

"Lena, I almost missed Adam." The words fall from me like loose bricks tumbling down a wall and shattering between us. She holds my gaze, confused, but stays close, edged between my legs like she's locking me in place. "I almost didn't save him."

"What do you mean?"

"He was inside that trailer, trapped in that damn crate, crying for help, and I didn't hear him. I just walked away."

"But you must've come back." Her brow crinkles into the letter *L* again as she assesses me. "What happened?"

"I got lucky." Her fingers delicately wipe my tears away. "The forecast called for storms, and I noticed a kid's backpack on a picnic table. I went to move it inside the screen door so it wouldn't get ruined. It wasn't until I went to the door a second time that I heard..." My voice trails off as I bury my tears in her stomach. She rubs my head, pressing me closer.

"If I hadn't gone back... if I hadn't seen the backpack... if it hadn't been about to rain... I would've left him there, tortured and alone, all because I couldn't fucking hear him." I peer up at her, desperate for her to understand. "He was there the whole time, and I couldn't hear him. *I* couldn't *hear* him, Lena. I came so close to failing him, and every time I think about the horrible shit he went through, I feel sick and disgusted with *myself*. I can't do this job anymore. I just can't. Not if I can't respond to a call confident that I'll fucking hear someone crying for help."

Her hand grips my chin, bringing my eyes to hers. "But you *did* hear him, Ben. A million ifs don't change the truth—Adam is safe because of you."

"I can't risk it."

"Everything's a risk," she says after a thoughtful pause, "and no one's infallible. For every person who could've saved Adam, another could've missed him for one reason or another. Hell, most people wouldn't go back for a kid's backpack. It does no good to deal with what-ifs. You can't put that kind of pressure—"

"All I feel is pressure," I say, gently moving her away to stand up. "I've always been the strong one, steady and calm, the one that people rely on, count on for support. I need to be that for you, but I'm afraid I can't be anymore—"

"You *are* that for me. And Ruthie. *Always*, Ben. We don't need you to be a cop or a hero or anything. *You* are enough. *You* are all we need." Her hand loops around my arm, holding me in place. Then, she presses it to the middle of her chest. "Breathe. Just breathe."

I do as she says, closing my eyes and taking deep breaths to match hers. Lost in the time warp of her comfort again, I don't know how long I stay there. But the pressure relents with each exhale.

"I love you," I say, like I can't help it. "Thanks for staying."

"You'll never get rid of me, Ben Wright. I'm yours, always. No matter what." She tiptoes up to me for a kiss, soft and sweet, like she wants to seal her promise.

If only I could believe it. God, I want to believe it. "Um, I should get back."

"Okay, but can we talk more tonight? We'd be in a much better place if we were there together. Please."

My hesitation disappoints her. I envision her freed to launch into her million questions, breaking me down further, and her gushing with encouragement and platitudes to rebuild me again.

But some things are beyond her control. She can't give me my hearing back or stop the changes ahead. She can't control her inevitable disappointment or reaction when I become the burden I fear. I dread that day more than death.

The pressure returns tenfold just thinking about the conversation. Still, I can't refuse her.

"Tonight. Yes."

Logically, it's a good plan. Identify the problem through calm communication with her and Dr. Reese. Solve the problem with support, assistance, and workable strategies. Simple.

Well, bordering simple.

It's the best course of action. For the moment, anyway.

She and Ruthie rejoin the comic-con. I call my captain, admit my difficulty with today's event, and request to be taken off patrol after this shift. He says he'll have a new assignment for me starting Monday. At a desk, probably.

Rejoining my fellow officers in the arena to finish dealing with the situation, I notice Lena and Ruthie meeting up with the Mackey-Grahams. Jack Graham slips his arm around Rowan's waist while she mindlessly rubs her basketball belly. I almost don't recognize Adam in his full Spiderman costume. He crouches around Ruthie, shooting her with imaginary webs from one hand and clicking his flashlight at her with the other. *My flashlight.*

Guilt and shame hit me again like a blisteringly cold wind through the arena.

Stop thinking and do your fucking duty.

But Adam bolts through the crowd when he sees me, and my bad feelings mount into an avalanche. He grabs onto me, gushing about his costume and the event. Holding him reminds me of the first time and how emaciated and scared he was. He's much healthier now, though still slight. His family and mine follow, and light conversation ensues.

Under it all, the pressure grows. A glance at Lena's soft, loving, but concerned eyes tells me she sees it.

So, when Jack invites me over for a drink later, I agree, and Lena's smile disappears in her disappointment.

CHAPTER 30

Lena

IT'S NEARLY eleven when my phone indicates an arrival through our new electronic gate, and my entire body sighs in relief. Perhaps it's unwarranted tension. I witnessed the plans Ben made with Jack, so I knew where he was. But an undercurrent of anxiety has run through me since the Comic-Con.

He's avoiding me. Again.

Stepping outside to the front deck, it's not Ben's Jeep pulling in beside my truck. It's Jack's Tesla. Barefoot, I race down the spiral staircase and reach the passenger door as Ben nearly spills out.

"Sorry, Lena. Too many whiskies," Jack apologizes, rounding the car to help.

Ben laughs, red-faced. "Not enough whiskies."

Jack edges his shoulder under Ben's arm, supporting his bulky frame like a crutch.

"He didn't want to come home," Jack tells me, his brown eyes pinched in concern.

Shit, I pushed too hard. I tuck that pain away for later and position myself on his free side. "Ben, let's go upstairs, huh?"

His feet move unsteadily beneath him, and he laughs again. "See, Jack? I've got a hot wife."

"I know, bud."

"A really amazing wife." His voice almost sounds sad and apologetic. "Think she'll be mad?"

"I'm not mad, Ben," I say beside him.

He twists in surprise, as if seeing me for the first time. "Hey."

"Hey."

"Come on, Benny, ol' boy. Use those tree trunks of yours," Jack urges as we circle the spiral staircase, one step at a time.

A snorting chuckle spurts from him. "Tree trunks."

He stumbles through the front door, ramming my casted arm into the doorjamb, fingers first. I wince but bite my lip to avoid cursing.

"You okay?" Jack asks.

"Yep." *Not okay. Definitely not okay.*

Ben stares at me, confused.

We get him to the couch, where he plops down with a loud thud that makes him laugh again.

"Shh, Ruthie's sleeping," I say, leaning down to remove his shoes.

Jack grabs water from the fridge and hands it to him. "Drink up," he orders.

I walk Jack to the door. "Sorry about this."

"No apologies. It was nice that he finally let his guard down with me." He hovers in the open doorway, running a hand through his shaggy brown hair. "Listen, Lena. You should know that he's, um, not himself."

I lean against the opposite side, folding my arms and fighting tears. "I know… How can I help him, Jack?"

"If this were a novel, I'd say…" He rubs his stubbled chin. "Give him a holy-shit moment that lifts him into a better perspective and shows him what's right in front of him. In real life, though, that's a lot of pressure and hard to do—"

"He gave me fireworks once. Surprised me with them after I'd had a terrible day, right out there, over the pond. That was the first time I thought this place could be… well, Saddletree."

Jack's eyes go wide with renewed admiration. "Ben Wright did that? A fucking grand romantic gesture? Ah, damn, that's my boy. That's what you need, Lena. Ben's version of fireworks."

"That's what closing Saddletree was meant to be. Epic fail. It's only made him angrier."

"Yeah, he's mentioned it… try something more subtle. It's all change and indecision for him right now. He needs to feel secure. That's all."

"Secure. Okay. Thanks for bringing him home and for the advice."

"No problem, but I'll be stealing the fireworks thing for my next book. I took his keys. My neighbor Vern and I will bring his Jeep over in the morning."

"I'll have a batch of Rowan's favorite double chocolate chip cookies waiting for you."

"Hell, yes... Oh, and how 'bout we take Ruthie for the day? We're doing the Children's Museum and Airlie Gardens—it's free day. Might give you some time to create some fireworks, eh?"

I chuckle. "She'll be ready. Thanks again."

He tosses a wave before heading for the stairs.

Ben rests his head on the back of the couch, eyes closed, and I assume he's asleep. But as my shadow crosses the room, he sits up.

"Lena." He sounds somber again, as if sucked into whatever black hole he climbed into by tossing back whiskies.

I go to him, grabbing his thick hand in mine. "Feeling okay?"

"I'm okay."

"How about a sandwich? You'll feel better with—"

"I'm not hungry."

I take a breath, trying to decipher his tone. It sounds like regret. "Ben, it's okay. Everyone gets a little hammered occasionally, and I'm sure Jack made it easy. You're off tomorrow. We'll talk then."

"I don't want to talk."

"Um, let's go to bed," I say, signing the words as I say them.

His hands shoot up in a rapid-fire response. "I don't want to go to bed."

"What do you want? Tell me, Ben." I try to be soft and understanding, but his clear frustration is pooling and seeping over to me. What happened to the jovial drunk of a few minutes ago who laughed at Jack's every word? He doesn't even seem drunk anymore, just bothered and restless.

"I don't want to talk," he repeats, running his hands over his head in frustration. "I want... this rock in my gut and this fucking battle in my head to go away. It's making me... second-guess everything."

"Second-guess what, Ben?"

"The damn job. My fucking hearing. Hell, you."

The word runs like a dagger through me—*you*—then it twists and deepens, splintering my core, with his glassy-eyed glare. But I think of what he's been through, what he's still going through, and dredge a secret strength from some dark reserve and bury my feelings. Again. I have to.

I take a breath and manage a smile, thinking of that day Ben showed up as I created my first garden, affectionately called my *Middle Finger Garden*. I tried to get rid of him, warned him that I was all anxiety and bullshit, not worth his trouble—a sentiment I replayed often in our early days. He stayed anyway and kept showing up. My inner struggles made more sense to Ben than they did to me then. That's what he needs now—someone who gets it. This is anger, anxiety, and alcohol talking— not Ben Wright.

"Second guess, if you want. But I love you no matter what. Cop or not. Hurting or not. Hearing or not. That won't change," I say, slow and clear. "Whatever our reality, remember?"

He softens, but I can't predict him—his expression lands somewhere between crying and screaming. The starbursts around his eyes melt into gentle lines as he takes me in. His hand goes to my face, almost roughly, and cups my cheek before pulling me to him.

Then, his lips take mine, desperate and sudden.

"I… want… you." The words straddle kisses and come out like a command—to me or himself, I don't know. But he repeats it in a sad whisper that he probably can't hear, but we both feel.

I think of saying it back to him, more surely, but I nearly slip from the couch edge as his strong kisses push me against it. "Ben…"

His lips curve over my chin and down my neck, clumsy but deter- mined. Hands grip my back, tugging me closer as he lowers onto me. My legs circle his midsection to keep my balance and draw him closer. *I've missed this.* He fumbles with the straps of my cami when one tangles with his watch—a mishap that'd usually have us giggling. But he isn't even smiling, as if the joy is lost. He seems bothered and hurried.

"Ben," I say louder this time. He stops, hovering with concern as he watches my lips. "Are you sure you're up for this? You're, um, okay?"

He whips us both upright, me straddling his lap. The kitchen light illuminates our faces as we consider each other.

"I'm fine," he says softly. "Truly. Are you okay with this?"

A vigorous, automatic nod hides my hesitation. I want him, but I'm unsure I want him *like this*. The whiskies have worn off enough—he's lucid and serious. And we both need the connection. But it feels more like a diversion than the sexy, fun times we're used to.

Still, I deliver a quick, "Yeah, okay," desperate for this not to turn out like the morning of my accident, when this nightmare started with an insensitive glance at the clock.

Besides, he's second-guessing me? Like a product, he's considering returning to the store? I don't want to disappoint him. I can't deny him this. Or anything. Or miss a chance for him to feel close and secure.

He gives me a tender kiss, as if he can read my mind and wants to offer reassurance. "Hold on to me."

I lock my arms around his neck, and he lifts us both, taking my breath away at how easily he does it. There's no drunkenness in his manner as he carries me down the hall, either. His eyes laser to mine, even when he kisses me, as if afraid to look away.

He gently eases me onto the bed, disrobing me in seconds. Then, he takes me in. Slowly. One curve at a time, like he's mapping a trail through the wilderness. I want to joke—*you've seen it all before, hon*—but his expression stops me.

He's locking me into his memory like I'm a phone number he never wants to forget. Worries start to crowd me. Then, he collides with me. Full on. Heavy. Handsome and all-consuming.

I barely get his clothes off—a push-and-pull tug-of-war, like his body is an afterthought. And when we're both there, naked, I shift on top of him, letting him see me fully because he seems to want to, and easing him into me like we're in slow motion.

He cries out, closing his eyes. But only for a second.

Hands grip my ass hard, guiding me to the perfect rhythm. Despite his eagerness to do this, he wants me slowly, savoring each thrust.

His hand finds me, touching me as I move over him, but his accuracy is off. It's an awkward, hit-or-miss endeavor. I go with it anyway—this is for him, not me—but I can't fool him. Soon, he flips me on my back and crams his mouth between my legs like he has something to prove. It's rough, almost frustrating, but wild enough to make me come quickly.

He groans when he enters me again, deep and fast, and I cry out this time. He hits the end of me with a vigor I'm not used to. Fun and gentle lovemaking is replaced by rough, hard, and determined sex. I wonder if this is the real Ben—aggressive and strong—and what else he's held back from me.

He pins my hands over my head, regardless of my cast. As he rams against me, my eyes devour him like a feast. And the part of me that worries, that thinks too much, disintegrates into aching, loving, sweet pleasure.

"Holy shit, I'm going to come again," I spit out because I can't help it.

"Hold on," he says against my lips. Watching me. Waiting. Steadily moving into me until his eyes close, and I can't hold on anymore. My contractions pull him into me, and he breathily moans my name as he finishes.

We stay there, suspended, foreheads pressed against each other. I smile up at him, kiss his lips, then his chin, and plant soft pecks over his cheeks and scar, needing him to feel loved and secure. Needing the same myself.

But the comfort I need isn't there. And I don't want to be tricked into believing anything's different.

He soon shifts away, lying on his back and staring at the ceiling.

I leave him for the bathroom and cry silently on the toilet.

CHAPTER 31

Ben

I **DON'T STIR** and keep my eyes shut when I feel Lena get out of bed the next morning. Or when she sneaks to my bedside and takes my phone. She expects me to be hungover and commandeers my phone like I've done to her when she needed sleep.

Only I haven't slept all night.

I feel Ruthie's heavy feet thump through the house when she wakes and the closing door when she leaves with Jack. I vaguely hear movement in the kitchen—dishes, water running, clinks and thumps of Busy Lena.

When I finally emerge from the bedroom, dressed and prepared, I find her exactly as I expect to—engrossed in busy work.

She smiles warmly when she sees me. "Hey, good morning. Feeling alright?"

My throat nearly closes. "What's all this?"

"Oh, a surprise for you," she beams coyly. "Let's go off-roading. I'll drive. We'll picnic on the sand, hang out, swim, relive that beach kiss, remember?"

"Lena, I can't." My army-green duffle drops to the floor by my feet, and I drape my dry-cleaned uniforms on top. I avoid eye contact as I cross the room and grab my keys and phone from the island. I prompt my screen and send a hurried text before tucking it in my pocket.

"Why not? What're you doing?" She stumbles around the island, nearly tripping over her feet and looking desperate as her eyes go from my bag to me again.

I manage the words I've prepared, but they come out weakly. "It's not good for me to be here now. I need time. Away."

She waves off my words like a fly buzzing near her face. "No. It's Sunday. Let's spend the day together. Just you and me. I made us a picnic. I promise not to interrogate you or be pushy. We'll sit in the sun and watch the waves."

"That won't help."

"Yes, it will." Her lips curve into a strained smile and her eyes flood with tears, as if part of her understands what's happening while the other is still catching up. "The beach is always a good idea. That's where I first told you about my dreams for Saddletree. You helped me believe it was possible. You're making decisions about your future, so it's fitting to do it there, right? We don't have to talk if you don't want to. We can just... be there together."

"I'm telling you we can't be together right now. Every time we're together, I hurt you." I step closer, hands rising submissively like I'm about to talk her down from the ledge. "I'm sorry. It kills me to say it. But I have to go."

Her head bobs in a weird half-shake, like the words don't make sense. "You're leaving me?"

She winces slightly when I take her hands. I hold up her casted arm, and seeing her bruised and swollen fingers from last night's stumble at the door makes tears fall from my eyes. "I can't keep hurting you."

"You're hurting me now," she cries.

"It's best for us—"

"No! What's best for us is being together," she says. "That's what you've *always* said to me."

I swallow like I'm choking and stop myself from crumbling into her. "I love you. Please, try to understand that this is different—"

"No, Ben. It's a rough patch. That's all. You can't leave. Please."

"I'm sorry. I see how hard you're trying. I know you'd do anything for me, that you love me. Love isn't the problem. I am. It's unfair for me to stay, unfair for me to heap blame and frustration onto you like a fucking packhorse. All I do is hurt you. And last night..."

I falter then, bowing my head to the pain forcing its way through me. She cups my cheek, bringing me back to her. "What about last night?"

"I broke our trust," I manage, my voice cracking. "It's one of our rules… If we're both not all in, it shouldn't happen. I knew you weren't all in, but you'd give in to me, anyway. I took advantage—"

"No, you didn't. I wanted to—"

"You cried in the bathroom. Didn't you?"

She doesn't answer.

"You know *that* wasn't us. That was… you accommodating me, forcing a smile, holding me all night even though I hurt you. Over and over again. I can't…"

I succumb to my emotions, sobbing into the space between us.

"I can't let you lose yourself in me like you did with your mom and Mark. I can't be Mr. Wickers, dependent on you for my well-being while you force your smiles, mediate my conversations, and stay busy to make me happy. I can't be the husband you need, either. I'm not sure he even exists anymore. Please understand. It's just too difficult to be here now."

She nods. "I'm too much. I've always been too much. I'm sorry. I'll keep my distance. You don't have to leave. I'll sleep on the couch—you can have the bedroom—"

"Stop being so fucking accommodating, please. That won't work."

"Tell me what will work, Ben? Something that will keep you here. If you go, you won't come back—I know you won't. You can't do this. Please, don't do this."

Her pleading eyes almost do me in, especially when she pushes into me and kisses me with anguished desperation. I want so badly to say, "Fuck it," and take her to bed like last night. But it won't make things better. I gently pull away.

"You'd do anything for me, right? I need you to let me go," I say, and her hands fall away like she can't help it.

She curls into herself, hand to mouth in a vain attempt to stifle her sobs. It takes every ounce of my remaining fortitude not to comfort her.

"Let you go? How? How can you even ask me that? That's the worst thing you've ever fucking said to me." Her fingers tremble, and her breathing becomes labored and quick as she tries to form words. "Does this mean—? Are you divorcing me?"

"Lena, breathe. It doesn't mean that. I don't want it to be forever. It just means I need time."

"A day? A week?"

"I don't know."

"What about Ruthie?" she says, crumbling with the words.

"I will be here for Ruthie," I say sternly. "I'll keep up my usual schedule with her, and whatever else you want me to do. I'm not leaving you alone to parent our daughter without me. I promise."

"But Ben, what will I say to her when you aren't here tonight?"

"I'll talk to her and tell her the truth, in simple terms—that I'm having a hard time and need extra help to fix it. That's my plan, Lena. With some distance, I think I can break this cycle of hurting you and figure my shit out. I've consulted Dr. Reese about adding more individual sessions, and I'll continue with our couple's appointments."

"How can we work on our relationship if you aren't here?"

"Dr. Reese will help us figure that out. Please, try to understand— I'm doing this for us."

"Bullshit," she cries. "This is about Lauren, isn't it?"

"No. It has nothing to do with her. I promise."

"Where will you be?"

"Becca's."

My guilt compounds with each tear she sheds, and they stream in long bands down her cheeks. "Please, Lena. Tell me you'll be okay."

She takes a breath, seeming to compose herself before she glares at me. "No. I've always told you the truth. I won't lie now. I'm *not* okay with this. I'll *never* be okay with this. It's *not* the right thing. You're so worried about changes and me having to take care of you that you're pushing me away—*that's* what this is. You're pulling the fucking fire alarm!"

The memory makes me take a step back and shake my head, as if I might rid myself of it. When I was a middle schooler struggling with dyslexia, I'd pull the fire alarm to escape the pressure in my classes. I said the exact words to Lena five years ago when she panicked and nearly walked out on me. Sometimes, the pressure builds until you must take drastic action to relieve it.

My eyes close tightly, sending fresh tears down my cheeks. She's right—I'm pulling the fire alarm. Her world, her emotions, her love— it's all too big for me, and I need to get small. To protect her, I have to.

I lean close and kiss her cheek. "I love you, Lena. Always. But I have to go."

The front door opens, and Dot rushes in. "What the fuck, Ben? What's wrong? I got here as soon as I could."

"Lena needs you." I gather my bag and clothes and assure Lena, "I'll call you tonight."

Quick, long strides bring me to the front door, brushing by Dot and ignoring her heavy *what-the-fuck* look. Then, the door clicks closed behind me.

I get as far as the Harvey's driveway before I have to pull over. I break down, unable to stop it, but determined not to cry like this again.

Pull it in. Drink water. Drive on. Do your fucking duty.

Relief sneaks in where my emotions dwell. It's done, and the worst is over. The pressure relents the further I get from Saddletree.

CHAPTER 32

Lena

IT'S the car accident all over again. I took things too fast and didn't steer right. Now, I'm spinning out of control, unable to prevent the crash or the damage. I only hope I survive it.

That *we* survive it.

Long-dead beliefs resurrect. *Nothing ever works out for you.* And like I once predicted, Ben Wright makes the list.

I thought I knew despair. Leaving Mark hurt. Losing Mom hurt. But this pain blasts the others to laughable bits as it rips through them. My leftover hope vanishes into a gnawing, aching, unbelievable sadness. In my acute emotional trauma, Dot rushes to my side. Words I never thought I'd say spill from my mouth through choking, desperate sobs. "He's left me, Dot. Ben's left me."

She glares at me like she might jump in her van, hunt him down, and bring him back to me, hog-tied if necessary. If anyone could, it'd be her.

But in a nanosecond, she softens, gripping my neck and yanking me into an embrace whether I want it or not. Her strong arms wrap around my torso, holding me up. She doesn't try to talk to me, thank God, but drags me to the bedroom and pushes me, gently for her, onto the bed.

That's where I stay, sobbing until I can't anymore.

The setting sun sends gold bands across my bed when Dot opens the door. "Ruthie'll be home in twenty minutes. Get your shit together. This isn't the end of your world—I fucking promise you that. You're needed, loved, necessary, and a badass who doesn't give up on anything."

She shuts the door, her words banging around in my head. But it's hard to feel those things when devastation runs the show. I feel carved out. Empty. A ghost drained of living blood. I curl into Ben's pillow, wondering how long it'll be before I no longer smell him on it.

I've failed him, and he's failing me, too.

But Dot's right—I won't give up and must be strong for Ruthie. For Ben. For myself.

I get up, clean up, and amble into the living room. Bright lights and the smell of something baking hit me first.

Then, a welcoming cheer greets me—Dot isn't the only one here.

She meets my eyes near the kitchen island and shrugs. "I called for reinforcements."

Jaye, Cherry, and Mrs. Moore move across the open living room and beeline toward me.

"Everything'll be okay," Jaye says as she embraces me. "We've got chocolate, Cheetos, and mac-n-cheese in the oven."

"Oh, that's sweet," I say, weakly.

Cherry grabs me next, yanking me into her rose-scented perfume. "And wine. Lots of wine."

"Good."

Mrs. Moore's delicate frame warms me in an instant. "We're here for you as long as you need us."

"And when you don't," Dot calls from her kitchen station. "You're stuck with us."

A chuckle escapes, and it surprises me to hear it. "Thanks… I would cry, but I'm all dried up."

Cherry pushes chardonnay toward me (definitely a Texas pour). "Let me help with that."

Mrs. Moore leads me to the living room and motions to my spot on the couch. I sit, curl into the blanket she hands me, and take a deep breath. It's nice being cared for like this. Not just nice, but necessary. I feel loved and supported like my personal rescue team is removing me from the wreckage. They gather around me, and I tilt my glass toward them before taking a long sip.

"You've done everything right, Lena. Compromise, communication, therapy, keeping your body tight and the wrinkles at bay. The odds must be in your favor," Cherry says, typing into her phone. "Let's see the stats on reconciliation with therapy and after someone moves out."

"He hasn't moved out," Dot defends. "He's on a… hiatus. That's all."

"Eesh." Cherry puts her phone away. "Never mind. You'll beat the odds anyway. I mean… as long as… are you sure he's not cheating?"

"He's not cheating," Dot and I say together, and she continues, "Oh my God, Cherry!"

But how can I be sure of anything now? "I mean, he said he wasn't."

"Then, he isn't," Jaye offers. "He doesn't seem the type."

Cherry's brow cocks. "Did you install that tracker app like I suggested?"

"No."

She shakes her head disapprovingly, her dark curls bobbing with her. "See how useful that'd be now? That and Penis-Dar."

"Penis-Dar?" Jaye repeats.

"Oh, that's the penis activity tracking app Dot and I are working on," Cherry says. "It'll be big, and we're looking for investors."

Jaye smirks. "Not a bad idea."

"Well, the sooner you know, the better. That way, you can shed your tears and move on with your life. There's no coming back from that."

"He only left a few hours ago. Maybe it's too soon to talk about moving on with my life. And that's not the problem, anyway. He needs me to be less… me."

"Is that what you *really* think?" Dot shoots back as she waves a hot pad over the mac-n-cheese she's just pulled from the oven.

"That's what he said, pretty much. It's what I've always feared. I'm not enough, and I'm too much…" A loud sniffle separates my words. "I don't know what to be anymore."

"This isn't your fault," Mrs. Moore says, sitting beside me. "He needs a minute to get himself together. A reset—that's all. He's losing his hearing and grieving for it. Who here wouldn't fall apart over something like that?"

"What do I do?" I ask. "How can I be what he needs?"

Mrs. Moore's pale face eases into a wide smile, and her gray eyes twinkle. "Just be the woman he fell in love with. Be *yourself.*"

Tears spill over my eyes, especially when her soft, bony fingers slip over mine. She pats my hand like one would a baby's back. At my new tears, the women rush over to me. Love surrounds me on all sides like a blanket, making me warm again.

CHAPTER 33

Ben

I NEARLY TURN around six times before I reach Becca's house. Exhausted, I try to sleep in her guest room, but it doesn't go well. It's not home. I know I'm doing the right thing, that I need this. But why are the right things always the hardest?

I text Dot for updates on Lena's condition and find solace in the fact that she's not alone.

After a tense dinner with Becca's family (she's none too pleased that I'm here), I FaceTime Lena.

She answers after the first ring. A weak smile accompanies her distracted greeting. "Hey, we just finished eating."

Her hair is pinned up in that soft way she does when she's cooking, but loose bits fall around her face, waving as she moves through the kitchen. Her eyes look puffy, but she isn't tearful or upset. For that, I'm grateful.

Her swimming pool eyes take me in, but only for a second. She's probably ensuring I am where I say I am, which is why I made the call in my sister's unmistakable yellow kitchen in front of their family beach portrait.

"Everything okay?" I ask.

Her lips perk weakly, like she wants to smile but can't. "Want to talk to Ruthie?"

She doesn't wait for an answer. The screen moves from her face to the floor and into Ruthie's chubby fingers.

"Dad." She pushes her face into the screen way too closely. "You won't believe my day."

Ruthie carries me around the house as she tells me about it. Her. Adam. Jack and Rowan. The Children's Museum. Airlie Gardens. They picnicked under the "ginormous tree" and "pretended to be herons and turtles." It's not until she exhausts her story twenty minutes later that she takes a deep breath and asks, "What're you doing at Aunt Becca's?"

"I'm staying here for a while. Remember when I went with Grandpa to his cabin to help him re-shingle the roof?"

"Yep."

"Well, it's like that. I have a problem that requires extra help to solve, so I'm spending time here to fix it," I explain, wishing I'd rehearsed this better.

She giggles, scrunching her nose. "So, you're fixing your roof?"

"Something like that. We'll talk more about it when I see you."

She shrugs, thankfully not sensing a problem.

Our conversation continues until she tells me she has a date with her bath toys.

"Be good for your mother," I say, though she always is. "I love you."

"Love you, Dad. Be home soon. Miss you. Bye."

Regret hits me, especially when Lena takes control again.

She flashes her soft, warm smile at Ruthie. Only I see the pain in her eyes. "Go pick out your toys for bath time. I'll be right there, okay?"

"I've got it, Lena," Dot chimes in, and Lena nods.

I hear little thuds of Ruthie's bare feet across the wood floor. When Lena's eyes return to mine, her smile falters. "That was... inventive. Thanks for keeping your promise to call."

"Of course. How about I take her to preschool in the morning?"

Her eyes narrow, and her forehead scrunches with worry lines. "I'll do it. And I'd rather not start talking schedules and who gets her when yet. It's too hard just yet."

There's no anxiety or anger in her voice, just sadness that I don't want to make worse.

"No, of course not. I'm sorry."

She forces a smile, but her demeanor cracks. "Are we done, then? With the call, I mean?"

"One more thing. I made an appointment with Rob for ten to check your hand. You can go after dropping Ruthie. I think you should have it—"

"My hand is fine."

"Please." My voice falters this time, and I turn the phone away. I take a breath, trying to ignore the despair that emanates from her like a damn toxin. "Lena, look I'm—"

"Fine. I'll go to the appointment." She takes a breath as if bored, but the soft shudder in her voice reveals the emotion she's trying desperately to keep in. "I'll go."

"Want me to meet you there?"

"No, I can handle a doctor's appointment. Anything else?"

Her attitude surprises me. She's curt and, more surprisingly, together. But what do I expect? Lena is the strongest person I've ever met—of course, she's okay. I'm the one who isn't.

"Um, I guess not," I say when the silence is too much, even for me.

She nods. "Okay, do what you need to do."

The line goes dead, and instantly, I ache for her and Ruthie.

But lying in bed that night, I know the ache will lessen with more time apart. Getting small will help me see what's important. Then, I expect clarity and renewed focus.

I'll decide about the job.

Decide about my hearing.

And decide, once and for all, if I'm better off alone. Or rather, if she's better off without me.

CHAPTER 34

Lena

I AWAKE EARLY Monday morning to black skies and Mrs. Moore's words. *Be the woman he fell in love with. Be yourself.* Maybe it's good advice, but the truth is, I'm no longer the woman Ben fell in love with, and I don't want to be again. That woman was sad, lonely, spastic, and lost. She barely functioned on a mental diet of anxiety and self-doubt. And while those aren't the parts that Ben fell for exactly, *that* was me back then. I'm lucky he saw through my bullshit to love the real me.

Maybe that's what I have to do for him now.

Being myself is better advice. I roll over in my empty bed, staring at lights through the woods. Filming has started early today, and shadows cross the deck and bedroom ceiling. Tears wet my pillow again. It's been an on-and-off production all night—me waking and crying over missing him and feeling sorry for myself.

But present-day Lena can't believe this is the end for us. Dot and the ladies gave me time to wallow, and that time is over. For now, anyway.

So, on my damp pillow, I ask myself, since Ben's not here for me to worry about winning over or tiptoeing around, what would I like to do today? It's a selfish attempt at self-preservation, but necessary, because present-day Lena doesn't sit around waiting for shit to happen. This Lena makes shit happen.

With the dogs at my heels, I take my coffee outside my bedroom, where set crews work to maneuver the eerie witches and emphasize the blood-stained trees. The sun rises behind me, sending delicate bursts of orange light across the sleeping pond like soft touches, waking it up. Mom's tree gets the spotlight next and seems to wave good morning with its drooping Spanish moss.

I adore this place. It comforts me. Even now.

When Ruthie wakes, I'm in the kitchen decorating a dozen white and cream cupcakes for her preschool class with jellyfish, sea stars, and whales. It's ocean week. My skills aren't quite the level I'm used to with my sore, injured left hand supporting my right, but it'll do. They're bonus cupcakes anyway—I needed to bake something.

I went somewhat overboard on batches, trying to get them right—trays of cupcakes cover the enormous kitchen island. And though my decorating skills are off, the taste is on point. I went all out with the flavors, doing my best to recreate saltwater taffy—a distinctly beachy candy.

Ruthie's ecstatic when she sees them—I love her no-holding-back excitement. It reminds me of Ben's when he first sampled my bakes. He ate them in almost one bite. Ruthie nibbles the icing first when my phone alights beside her. It's Ben, and she answers it herself.

"Dad, Mom made *the* best cupcakes," she says, panning the phone around the room.

I expect a remark about cupcakes for breakfast, but he says, "She always does... Ready for school?"

Ruthie takes the phone around the room, sharing her to-do list. It's a thing they do when getting ready. I wonder if this is how it will be now—co-parenting our daughter via FaceTime.

But that's a worry for later.

It takes several bins to house the cupcakes, but I have them stacked and ready to go when Ruthie pushes the phone to me. I twist it around to me while telling her to get dressed.

"Hey," I say.

"Good morning. Just wanted to remind you about ten o'clock."

"Ben, I got it."

"Will you let me know what Rob says?"

His concern should relieve me, but it doesn't. Still, I assure him I will before ending the call.

I meet with Jaye and Elsie Todd while loading my cupcakes into the passenger seat of my new truck. Ruthie chases the dogs badly in rubber boots, her backpack flopping as she bounces.

Jaye puts her arm around my shoulders. "Doing okay?"

"One hundred percent," I lie. "I'll be gone most of the morning."

"The paparazzi are back," Elsie reports, "but the security team is controlling it. We'll be filming in the main house most of the day."

"Stop by when you get back," Jaye says. "You won't believe how freaking awesome the place looks inside. I'll give you a tour."

"Maybe," I return, waving Ruthie to the truck. "Gotta go... Oh, here."

I hand Jaye a bin of oceanic cupcakes. They gush with thanks before enthusiastically sharing them with their team.

The security guys and the paparazzi at the end of the driveway also receive cupcakes. Who knows? Maybe I can convince them to behave with sweets.

I drop Ruthie at preschool and make charitable rounds, leaving cupcakes with Myles Drake at the assisted living center, Olivia Jones at the group home, and Rowan Mackey-Graham at Coastal High.

I make my appointment with Dr. Rob Riley with a few minutes to spare. He isn't as charming without Ben and isn't with me long. He tells me what I already know—my arm is fine, just bruised.

I exit the building, mid-texting Ben with the update. But glancing up to see where I'm going, I see him. He leans against his Jeep, parked next to mine. A smile crosses my face—I can't help it. It's only been a day, but it feels like forever since I've seen him.

"Checking up on me?" I ask when I get closer.

He smirks. "What'd Rob say?"

"Bruised. I'm supposed to ice it, take ibuprofen when needed, and continue my exercises," I report, showing him the text I was composing before putting my phone away. "The cast comes off in two weeks."

He nods, relieved. "Thanks for keeping the appointment."

A weak smile precedes a wave of sadness. I want to cry for the strange tension between us. Then it hits me. Holy shit, we're *estranged*. I always thought it was such a weird word, but now I get it. Neither of us knows how to be around each other in this situation. At least, I don't. *What's allowed? What does he need? What's the best way to handle my husband, who's left me, when he shows up at my doctor's appointment?* Finally, I push my anxiety bitches aside and decide to be myself.

I shrug, catch his eyes, and ask, "Ready to come home yet?"

A crease forms between his brow. "I can't," he says, sounding regretful. "I'm meeting with John Riley and Larry Tenor Friday to discuss their proposal to support my recovery. I'm close to accepting the position. It's the most viable solution to support my family."

I nod, though the knot inside me tightens. "*I* can support our family… but I understand."

"Is that okay with you?" He looks unsure, asking the question.

That he cares about what's okay with me feels confusing. His leaving certainly wasn't. "It's *always* been okay with me, Ben, if it's what *you* want."

The confused crease on his brow reappears. "I'll add it to the family calendar, along with my schedule and other appointments. Perhaps we can discuss time with Ruthie… when you're ready."

"Yeah, sure." *Estranged. That's what estranged couples do.*

"Our appointment with Dr. Reese is Wednesday," he says.

"I'll be there."

He nods.

"Oh, Ben… I have something for you." I unlock the truck and hand him my final bin. "I went a little cupcake crazy this morning. I thought your coworkers might enjoy them."

A real smile stretches over his tight mouth. "Like the old days."

"Yes, like the old days. It's a new recipe I'm considering, so let me know what everyone thinks."

"Will do. Thank you, Lena."

It's good he has his hands full—it prevents me from trying our usual goodbye. Instead of a quick hug and kiss, I offer a timid wave and leave him.

At home, Jaye waves me to the main house as I exit the truck. I half-wonder if Dot has asked her to keep an eye on me today. Cameras and other equipment nearly block the path through the sliding glass doors. She leads me inside the café, where the serving counter and coffee stations lie dormant and dim. Seeing the display case empty is strange when it's usually filled with colorful cakes and treats. It makes me sad to see it like this.

If it's possible to feel even sadder.

My dining room of eclectic chairs and tables salvaged from my parents' hoard of hand-me-downs is gone and replaced by an average-looking living room, like a set-up one might see at a furniture store.

Except for the Ouija board on the coffee table.

And the pale-faced, black-eyed child mannequin with tar-like ooze around his mouth perched on the ceiling beams. I gasp when I spot him.

Jaye chuckles. "Sorry, I should've warned you. That's Edgar."

"It's like walking through a haunted house."

"That's the idea." She elaborates on the story and how the elements fit together, but I zone out. I once had a massive roof leak where Edgar hangs, like he's the ghost of my former life here, when I was broke, alone, and trying to make do with duct tape and Flex Seal.

God, why don't they make Flex Seal for people? I could affix Ben to me and make us divorce-proof.

Focus, Lena. Breathe.

They've transformed the sitting area in the middle of the house into a study. A large wooden desk houses a lawyer's green desk lamp and stacks of books and papers. It sits facing the large double window, once the location of the ancient couch that comprised my makeshift bedroom.

"Dr. Hunter discovers that the man of the house, Mr. Bonner, has become obsessed with local history. His jaded curiosity incites the evil coven," Jaye explains. "Some history is better forgotten."

Remembering the nightmares I used to have in this room, I agree.

They haven't changed Mom's room much; just added creepy elements and mood lighting and used different bedding than my hotel-style linens. It's a beautiful bedroom with a fireplace, plenty of windows, and sliding glass doors leading to the wraparound porch.

But being here today fills me with sadness, remembering those last few weeks with Mom. Her frequent bouts of dementia. Not being able to wake her. Waiting for ambulances and trying to calm us both when they arrived. Living here then was one trial after another—I felt so scared and alone.

Ben's left and those feelings penetrate me as sharply as ever. I'm scared and alone and frustratingly powerless. Then. Now.

No surprise—I wake up screaming later that night. Heart racing. Body flushed with sweat. Hand reaching for the phone to call for help, like I once did over nightmares after Mom died.

I come to my senses when Ruthie appears in my open doorway, rubbing her eyes. "Mom? You okay?"

Not okay. "Sorry, baby. I'm fine. Just a bad dream."

She climbs into bed with me and does exactly what we do with her when she has a bad dream. "Go back to sleep, sweet girl. I'll keep you safe."

CHAPTER 35
Ben

THE THREE-STORY BEACH house looks the same as I remember. I can't believe I'm here. The meeting with Larry and John ended with John extending a dinner invitation. "You, me, and the grill tonight. How 'bout it?"

When I hesitated, he said, "Bring the family. Seven o'clock. I won't take no for an answer."

Not only have I shown up against my better judgment, but I haven't brought the family. I didn't even log the event into the family calendar. I tell myself that my omission is out of respect for Lena, but it's cowardice. Dot reports that it's been a difficult week for Lena and that I need to "get my head out of my ass ASAP." But our separation has given me room to breathe. To think. To consider. And kept me from continuing the torturous cycle of giving her hope only to dash it again.

It's better this way. I think.

The Rileys are here in full force, judging by the driveway full of Land Rovers, Teslas, BMWs, and a…McLaren. *Who the hell drives one of those?* Then I notice the license plate, *DRROB*, and shake my head. I park off-shoulder by the road to ensure a quick exit. I grab the expensive cabernet I bought at Sunny's—a favorite of Jillian's—and go inside.

They greet me with the same joyful enthusiasm as they did in the concert booth.

"Where's Lena and Ruthie?" Jillian asks.

"Other plans." I hand her the bottle.

"Oh, well." She reads the wine's label. "Ah, Ben. You remembered. Come help me get this open."

She doesn't need my help, but latches onto my arm and takes me to the kitchen anyway.

The interior decor has changed over the years—stark-lined sofas and chairs have replaced the cushy sectional I remember. New artwork and knickknacks have been added, but the bright, casual atmosphere remains unchanged.

I assist Jillian with the wine, make small talk, and joke with Rob. It feels normal. No pressure. It's always been that way with them.

Lauren and I once studied at the same rustic table in the dining room. She sits there now, reviewing a file. Her smile when she looks up at me makes my heart quicken with pleasant memories.

She closes the file and holds it up. "Ben, I have the paperwork for your health insurance options and deduction options for the Lauren Project. I know you like taking your time with paperwork, so I thought I'd give it to you early. That way, when you're ready to say yes to Riley Trust, you'll already have it done."

"That's considerate. Thank you."

"Take your time with it," she says, rising to meet me. "I'll set it by the door to grab on your way out."

"Thanks."

I follow to see where she puts it on the entryway table. She wears a soft sundress today, and I see the ties of her bikini top at the base of her neck. Lauren lived in a swimsuit as a teenager. "Always ready for a swim," she'd say. I joined her on multiple occasions. There was something beautifully freeing about stripping down on a whim and diving into a wave.

I never do that anymore.

Our spontaneous swims mimicked the feeling of my homecomings. Losing myself in her was a full-bodied relief. Easy. Familiar. Uncomplicated. A way of getting small, I realize now. It was called *leave* for a reason—I left every difficulty behind.

I take a sip of wine—too sweet for my taste—and catch a picture collage on the high wall near the front door. The family portraits have always been here, but many new pictures have been added. I scan them, hunting for Lauren.

Her standing proudly in front of scenic mountainscapes. Surrounded by children in what looks like schools and orphanages. With doctors in makeshift hospitals. The pictures change in the subtle ways she has over the years, revealing that she returns to these places frequently, committing herself to bettering others.

But in the pictures of her and her boys, she is most happy. Camping. At the beach. At school events. Basketball games. Her between them in Eagle Scout uniforms, both kissing her cheeks on either side.

She breathes a soft sigh beside me. "They're my life."

"I misjudged you." The words emerge like heavy weights hitting the ground when my arms are too tired. "I was angry then. I said things I didn't mean. I'm sorry."

She nods, tears glassing her gray eyes. "We both messed up. I'm sorry, too."

"If I'd been a better man, I would've... done things differently."

She shrugs, and a tear slips out. She motions to the pictures. "I'm glad you didn't. We were needed elsewhere."

"Agreed." I nod to the images again. "You should be on your father's wall in his office. Not me. Your service is equally commendable."

She pushes into my arms with an emotional surge. I don't initiate it. I don't know what to do at first. But hearing her soft "Thank you" in my ear, I accept her affection.

As she slowly pulls away, we understand each other. Her reaction to my scars no longer carries the pain it used to. Her expression makes me think she feels better, too, like the dark cloud of our breakup has finally dispersed.

She lingers in the inches between us, meeting my eyes with a hopeful question in hers. Her hands rest on my chest while mine slips over her back. It's familiar but strange, too. It's like hearing the instrumental of an old song and not being able to put a title to it. Not that I want to remember it.

She's not Lena.

I step away so abruptly that she pitches forward in my absence. Then, I lose myself in the crowded living room.

At eight, I retreat to the beachside deck to call Ruthie and say goodnight. No one is out here, but inside enjoying dinner. I use the ocean as a background for the FaceTime call.

"Where are you, Daddy?" Ruthie asks, eyeballing the screen.

"The beach. I went for a walk."

"When are you coming home? I don't like it when you're not here for bedtime."

"I don't know."

"Mom says you're figuring things out," she continues. "But I don't understand. You're not lost. You know how to get home, right?"

"Yes. That's not it."

With a weepy voice, she says, "You can't stay at Becca's forever. We miss you."

My hand rakes through my hair in frustration. I glance up from the phone, trying to find words.

Lauren stands on the open threshold of the sliding glass door, aghast over what she's clearly overheard—my daughter in tears over my absence. She retreats inside with the refreshed wine glass she probably meant to hand me, mouthing an apology.

Fuck.

"Ruthie…"

"Dad, it's not fair."

I almost tell her that life isn't fair.

"I know. I'm sorry, but I'm proud of you for being brave and patient with me. I'll try to be there for tomorrow's bedtime, okay?"

"Okay," she returns grumpily.

"Start thinking about what you want to do on your sleepover this week. I love you. Be good for your mom."

I don't wait for Lena to get on the phone but hang up as soon as she says, "Okay, Dad. Love you. Bye."

Avoidance isn't the answer. But it's the only thing I have right now.

The call with Ruthie tightens my chest. I return to the gathering for an acceptable amount before claiming the need to leave for an early shift tomorrow.

That's a fucking joke. My new assignment puts me to sleep. I've been assigned to the desk unit, answering phones and managing walk-ins.

Lauren walks me to the door.

"Everything okay?"

"Yes."

"If you need to talk…" Her voice trails off. She hands me the file folder, pushing it softly into my chest. "Why don't you bring these by my place Friday night? We can go over them together."

Her body language tells me that meeting her there would mean more than paperwork, and I feel uneasiness rise in my stomach at the invitation.

Mainly because I don't say no.

CHAPTER 36

Lena

THE SECOND FRIDAY after Ben left (because that's how I measure time now), I stand on our upper deck with a dozen hopeful, somewhat pitying faces staring at me. It's our Friday meeting—the first one in a while because I haven't felt up for it.

Don't think about that now.

I hold my clipboard to my chest like a shield as everyone settles in the mismatched patio furniture I've dragged together. They help themselves to lemonade and lemon-mint cupcakes, another new creation that tastes of summer. Though it's not anymore. It's fall. October. Still warm, but less humid. Behind me, beyond the pond, color bursts from the changing trees amid the static pines. Reds, oranges, and yellows remind me of nutmeg, cinnamon, and allspice. It's like the woods are coming to life, but they're actually dying, a final burst of vivid expression before the end. The cold emptiness of winter soon will turn the world bleak.

My world's already there.

A centering breath brings a weak smile as the chatter softens. "Thanks for meeting me. I have some big changes to announce."

But my voice hitches when Ben and Ruthie round the corner of the house. He's early. The second surprise is his friendly demeanor, light smile, and gentle wave, as if all is well.

"I'll get my teapot," Ruthie says, realizing she's made it just in time for my *sometimes*-weekly meeting. Her boots flap as she races inside.

Ben doesn't disappear like I expect. He leans against the outside wall of our bedroom—*my* bedroom, now—and signs for me to go on.

I hesitate. We've gone from *estranged* to *strangers* the longer we've been apart. Now, I'm nervous when I see him, like I might fuck up and do or say or be something that ends us once and for all.

It used to be *this* place that edged on brokenness toward being unlivable.

Now, that place is us.

On the first appointment with Dr. Reese since he left, he said he'd accepted the job, he only had to sign the contract and undergo training before starting the position in the new year. Not only that, he's excited. He's been spending more time with the Rileys—events not shared on the family calendar. He says it's helping him remember who he was before he sustained his injuries, and it's been almost a relief. For him, anyway.

So, while Ruthie and I have spent our evenings tackling farm chores and eating dinners alone or with Dot and Cherry, he's reunited with his former second family over seafood nights and fancy dinners.

It's hard not to feel betrayed by my husband's happiness without me, as if I've been holding him back—a sentiment I shared tearfully when Dr. Reese asked how this made me feel.

When she asked Ben his response to my feelings, he said, "Yes. Saddletree, Lena's anxiety, and her busyness sometimes feel all-consuming. Her world often feels too big for me."

There's that fucking bus again, honking as it peels away from my trampled body.

In the second appointment with Dr. Reese since he left, he admitted to enjoying his independence. He claims it's curing his indecisiveness.

I told him it was selfish—a word I wanted to rescind as soon as I said it. But how could I not feel angry and hurt?

Ben's making me feel like we're a lost cause. And it's killing me.

Staying busy is the only choice. But his being here, mixing in with the only thing besides Ruthie that's kept me going, blurs the lines he's established, making me nervous.

Worse, everyone sees it.

After an unbearable pause, Trisha says, "Lena has mastered our new software!"

She claps, and the group joins in, snapping me out of my dysfunction.

I chuckle with a weak bow. "I've started calling it my bitch—that's how well I've mastered it. Our records are now dancing around in the cloud and have shared some surprising insights into Saddletree…"

I clear my throat, glancing at my notes and finding a weak footing in my mental fog. "Um, first, Saddletree's profits could be much better if I pared down my menu to my top sellers and seasonal favorites. I've provided a new sample menu for when we reopen—"

"When are we reopening?" Mr. Wickers asks.

"December first. The studio will make its grand exit by Halloween—"

Mild applause.

"And I'm hoping for an amazing Thanksgiving. Lucas, Drew, and Luna might fly in—we're in talks. Ben's family, um, maybe." My eyes catch his, only for a second, lest I fall apart. "Anyway, December first."

Ruthie spills from the sliding glass doors of our bedroom, barely managing her teapot full of lemonade. She starts doing her rounds, making me smile. She had her first sleepover with Ben at Becca's house last night.

The house felt so quiet I wanted to scream. And I did, a little.

"Wow, this menu is short and bakery-forward," Tessa points out, glancing up from her iPad.

"We're focusing on what we're best at—baking. I'm cutting out most soups, all casseroles, and half the sandwiches. We'll stick with typical café fare and picnic foods, but I want to concentrate on special orders again."

"Wait, where are the bran muffins?" Mr. Wickers eyes the screen over Trisha's shoulder.

My nose scrunches. "Sorry, Mr. Wickers. Bran muffins didn't make the cut."

"No one likes those muffins, Gus." Trisha taps his knee to soften the blow. "Lena, I love this menu."

With a smiling nod, I glance at my guests and nearly choke when I remember the woman beside Alice. "Oh, damn. Sorry, everyone. Where're my manners?"

I motion toward her. "Alice brought a friend today. This is Marnie Strange."

The gorgeous, petite redhead stands and offers a bubbly wave. "Hello, everyone!"

"We're in talks to feature Saddletree's baked goods at her grocery store."

"Well, not *my* grocery store. But yes, we'd love showcasing Lena's treats. Thanks for including me today," Marnie says. "It's fascinating, like joining Mr. Wonka to tour his chocolate factory. I can't wait to work with you… and please, don't let me interrupt any further."

When Alice introduced us earlier, I sized her up immediately. She's a yes-person. No excuses. No complaints.

Just yes.

Yoga at dawn?

Yes.

Round up for charity?

Yes.

Can you… will you… have you… Yes, yes, yes.

And not dutifully, but in an affirming way, like life's a great adventure. Her positivity drew me in and warmed me in its wake.

I only hope my new friend doesn't catch on to the tension suffocating me.

I take a deep breath. *Focus.*

I motion to Shakespeare and his friends, occupying the settee to my right. "We have our van! Shakespeare is our official driver, hayride tour guide, and delivery guy. Martin and Rick will handle dishwashing and farm chores. Plus, Shakespeare will secure extra help for Alice."

"I'm the man with the van and the plan to lend a hand," he coos, bowing his head.

"I'm ready to put Shakespeare and friends to work on holiday orders," Alice says.

"Perfect, we can schedule everything via the app," I say, holding up my iPad, "and he'll know where he's needed and when."

"Nothing to fear, Shakespeare will be there." He holds up his phone with a woot-woot of triumph.

Marnie claps at his enthusiasm.

I motion toward Ben. "Thanks to Ben for coming up with the van plan."

He gets brief muted applause since Dot and Cherry refuse to clap—they aren't fans right now. But he nods slightly and says, "It's no trouble."

I refocus on my notes. "Other changes… Oh, this is a big one. I won't be replanting the garden next spring."

Alice's gasp sounds like a gunshot. She even grabs her heart, like she can't handle the news. "Your beautiful garden?"

My brow pinches, and I wonder if Mom would've had the same reaction. I started that garden because of her, the seeds she sent for my birthday, but it's become too much for me to handle.

"I hate losing it, too, but it's not profitable and difficult to manage. I'll create a smaller kitchen garden on the less populated side of the main house, but it won't be open to the public."

"Lena, babe, how 'bout I make you some window boxes for the wraparound deck?" Dot suggests. "It'll add a garden vibe without the heavy labor."

"I'd love that. Thanks, Dot."

"It's a brave decision," Mr. Wickers says, "letting go of the old to usher in the new."

"Um, thanks. It's not brave but necessary. Change is good if it's for the right reasons." My voice falters—too many things are hitting close to home, and they're made harder with him here. "It's more important to me to be a better manager and more available to my family than keeping a garden… That's why I'm also reducing our schedule. Saddletree will be closed Mondays and Tuesdays."

"Geez, Lena. It's like a total Saddletree makeover," Cherry says, "but I agree. It's just like with dating. You don't want to be *too* available."

"Leave it to you to put it into dating terms, but yes," I chuckle.

"That'll be much easier for me with school," Tessa says.

"I want more time with you, Tessa. So, if you're free on Tuesday afternoons, we can bake without distractions."

She sits up in her lawn chair with a half-eaten lemon-mint cupcake in her hand. "Yes, perfect. I want to experiment with you. These things are amazing!"

"Delicious!" Marnie chimes in.

"Thanks. We'll do all sorts of creating. I've left an opening on the menu for a bake of the day—that's for us, Tessa."

The way she beams fills me with joy I haven't felt in a long time. It takes a minute to compose myself and keep from crying.

"But it's not all about downsizing." Ruthie hands me a tiny cup, and I pause for a dainty sip, pinky out. "Thanks, honey. I'm expanding one aspect of Saddletree. The support groups."

I can't help but look in Ben's direction—his arms are folded, but his brow perks up.

"There's not a huge profit in it," I continue. "But it builds our customer base. It's little work for us, and nice for them to have a comfortable, safe space. Thanks to the studio, we have a new meeting space. Dot and I are planning another structure and an expanded playground where the garden is now. So, with two new spaces, we can accommodate more groups."

"What about scheduling?" Trisha asks.

"With the new software, they book themselves. Trisha and I will approve any new groups that want to use the facility. Once approved, they're given an access code for scheduling, select refreshment packages, and pay online. Our app will let us know what's on that day's schedule. It's hands-off for me, which means less chance of mistakes. I've contacted more support groups. Soon, we'll have two UNCW dog training classes here, Pets for Vets, and WPD's mounted police division doing their annual safety training at Saddletree. We always envisioned Saddletree as a retreat and place of connection for groups that need it. This move will prioritize them and get us back to our roots."

Applause breaks out, filling me with relief and pride. Saddletree's future feels hopeful, even if other parts of my life don't. Still, I glance at Ben, standing opposite me by the house, and I nearly fall out.

A warm smile stretches over his lips, and he drops his folded arms to sign, *"I've never been more excited for Saddletree. Excellent work. I'm proud of you."*

With the group distracted by chatter and unable to understand us anyway, I sign back, *"Thanks for helping me. I couldn't have done any of this without you."*

Warming admiration flashes over his face like my words have stirred forgotten feelings. He signs, *"It's no trouble."*

A brief chuckle escapes, and my fingers work furiously to ask, *"Ready to come home yet?"*

His brow pinches with surprise, even though I ask it whenever we're together, in case he wants to but can't say it. His face quickly morphs with pity—a look I hate from anyone, most of all him—and my sadness compounds like blood thickening around my heart.

Still, I wait him out, staring until he answers the question, however much it hurts. I think of Dr. Reese's advice at our last session that I shouldn't hold back, that Ben needs my openness. I sign exactly what I'm thinking. *"Please, Ben. You are killing me. I love you, and you're killing me."*

He breaks eye contact to stare at his boots—that's my answer. But then, as hope oozes from my pores with my anxiety sweat, his hands move again. *"Let's talk after."*

"All of this is well and good, Lena," Alice says, breaking my trance, "but will you still host Jack's poker nights? If he's not helping you with spring planting—"

"Don't worry," I say, perking up. "I've already scheduled some groups as recurring bookings, including poker night."

She sighs. "That's a relief. Thanks, dear."

Now wanting to end this meeting as soon as possible, I continue, "The app is ready for scheduling starting in December, so until then, we'll continue training, fine-tuning the menu and staff, and advertising our grand reopening. I want to do a huge social media kick in November to excite people. I'll also be looking for ideas on how to make Christmas at Saddletree very special this year… so think about it."

Murmuring starts between the tables.

"What about the new logo?" Trisha asks between conversations. "We'll need that for social media."

"Cherry has her portfolio with her." I motion to the large leather binder propped against the railing. "Let's see it."

Her eyes cut to Ben, but she squares her jaw, slaps the leather binder on the table, and unzips it. She extracts the large, penciled sketch, holding it up for everyone to see.

My breath catches, and my heart quickens.

It's the perfect logo for Saddletree.

Almost. As beautiful as it is, what's missing is obvious.

Mom's tree, outlined in apple green, stands out against a gold half-moon. The artful lines of the detailed leaves and Spanish moss give the impression of movement—it looks like it's swaying in the breeze. A pink swing hangs from its thickest branch, holding a little girl wearing distinctive rubber boots. Leaning against the tree trunk is a stenciled version of me, one knee up, hair waving. It's Ruthie and me sharing a tree moment, as we've done hundreds of times.

Trisha gasps. "It's beautiful."

"It's Saddletree," Mr. Wickers agrees.

"Gorgeous, really. It makes me so happy, I could cry," Marnie gushes.

"I love it," Alice says. "Such happy colors."

"Pink, green, and gold. It'll never get old," Shakespeare says.

"The colors are nice, but it's, um…" I suddenly feel hot, like it's high summer, and I'm mid-marathon. "Um…"

Ruthie hops closer. "It's me! And you, Mommy. But where's—"

"Ruthie," Ben's voice is sharp. He waves her over, and she quickly complies.

Out of the corner of my eye, I see him leaning down to Ruthie's level, talking, but I focus on the group. "It's not right, Cherry. It's missing Ben."

Dot and Cherry stand like a united front, pulling me into their circle.

"I didn't include Ben for a reason," Cherry argues in a heated whisper. "You don't want a logo that doesn't fit anymore."

"Cher has a point, Lena, babe," Dot says. "This is about the *future* of Saddletree."

Panic rises at the idea that this could be my future—a life here without him. It's certainly my present. *But he wants to talk. And he belongs here. With us. With me.*

"I don't care," I say between labored breaths. "Saddletree is *our* story. His, mine, and Ruthie's. I want him in the logo."

Dot and Cherry give me a stare-down before Cherry shrugs. "Fine."

She pulls out a second drawing, identical to the first, but with Ben beside me, his arm perched against the bark, leaning close like he's telling me a joke.

It takes my breath away.

"This is the first one I did," she explains, "but I wanted to see if you'd go for the revised version for your own sake."

"That's Saddletree," I tell her, smiling through fresh tears.

I look for Ben over the gathered crowd as they wriggle in to see the other design. But he's gone.

Ruthie bobbles over, sloshing her lemonade.

"Where's Dad?"

"Had to go," she says.

I circle to the front of the house, but it's too late. His Jeep bumps quickly down the driveway. So much for talking later.

I end the meeting, and the group lazily disbands, offering muted encouragement and brief congrats on the changes, while I nod, smile, and secretly fall apart.

Alice leaves last, giving me a pointed look. "Hang in there, Lena. The world ain't over until we see the zombies or feel the blast."

I nod. "Might be soon."

"Okay, well, find us in the basement… you know the door, right?"

"Yes, thanks, Alice. You've never steered me wrong."

She smiles. "No, I haven't. You remember that." She squeezes my hand before leaving.

In the barn's open doorway, I watch Ruthie play with dogs and try to bring my roller coaster emotions back into the station. My feelings aren't my reality.

But it's no use.

A dark, unthinkable reality strangles my leftover hope. The longer he's away, the more I know my worst fear is coming true.

Ben's not coming back.

CHAPTER 37

Ben

PULL IT IN. *Drive on. Get small.*

Four miles away, I pull into the dusty lane between cornfields. I clench the steering wheel until my hands pop and ache. My heart races, and fluttering palpitations make it difficult to catch my breath. I'm gasping and sweating, and my hands tremble with the surging energy.

A fucking panic attack.

I almost laugh at the damn irony. I've spent years gently staving off Lena's panic, and providing a calming presence amid her worst storms. I've got it down to a science with her—I can see her anxiety rising and regulate her breathing in minutes.

I can't do it for myself, though.

Just breathe. Breathe.

I exit the Jeep and inhale the earthy air, willing myself to slow down.

But the pressure built over the last months compounds, a rock heavy on my chest. *I'm killing her. She loves me, and I'm killing her.*

I can't pinpoint what set me off exactly. Her words. How lovely and strong she looked. Missing her. That she's changing for the better without me. My chronic need to avoid talking.

Or maybe it was Saddletree's logo.

I couldn't have imagined a more perfect visual. Saddletree has always been Lena's dream, successful because of her. Her talent and warmth bring people in and keep them coming back. She's the heart of the business. Her mom's tree represents its foundation. And Ruthie's future will be shaped by it, one way or another.

But it confirms what I know and fear—I don't belong. I'm the guy in the background, unable to talk to people or smile or be warm and approachable. I'm on the outside looking in, a truth that will worsen as I do.

Lena and Saddletree are better off without me.

Falling sunlight flickers over the corn stalks, dancing in my eyes. I lean against the driver's door, taking long breaths and massaging the pressure points in my wrists. One then the other. Easing myself down with tears specking my eyes.

My phone rumbles in my pocket, and with a still-shaking hand, I extract it. A text from Lauren.

> Looking forward to tonight. What time will you be over?

I scoff. I'd completely forgotten the invitation that I neither accepted nor refused. I text back as fast as my jittery fingers will let me.

> I love my wife. That'll never change. Not for you or anyone. Think about what you're asking.

I don't expect an answer. My response is terse, direct, and probably mean. But I know Lauren, the games she's played, and I want to be clear.

The ellipsis engages immediately.

> We aren't kids anymore. I know what I'm asking, but I'll clarify. One night, just between us. I want to right my wrong. Nothing more.

"Fuck me," I blurt with irritation and disbelief. My panic upticks with her absurd suggestion, and I refocus on breathing.

But when my phone buzzes again, I can't help but look.

> I know you're hurting. Disappear with me, Ben.

Tears spit from my eyes. I lean over, bracing my body against my knees. She used to say it when I came home on leave whenever I had that faraway look on my face, lost in thoughts about the last deployment or the next one. *Disappear with me.* And I would. Sweet and innocent in the early days, that meant diving into waves, off-roading to the furthest points on the island, camping, or hiking. When we got older, that meant losing ourselves in each other.

She let me get small between battles, I realize now.

I don't answer her text, but a wicked game ensues, daring me onward.

What if I leave this cornfield?

Then, I do.

What if I head toward her neighborhood?

And I turn in her direction.

What if I pull up to the gate outside her community and give my name?

And somehow, that happens, followed by them letting me in.

I bring the Jeep to a slow stop at the curb across the street from Lauren's cape-side home. It's the same house she lived in when we were together—a small, three-bedroom craftsman. I recall her excitement in purchasing it "on her own" and how I stopped myself from mentioning the sizable down payment her grandparents gifted her to make it possible. It's the house she hoped we'd share, and we did when I was on leave. It's also where we came to a crashing, devastating end.

Shattering glass echoes. My hands strangle the steering wheel.

But the agonizing panic I felt earlier has left me.

I'm killing her. She loves me, and I'm killing her.

My what-if game turns into a dare, sickening and tempting.

Walking into Lauren's house means walking out on my marriage permanently. Lauren says *just between us*, but I couldn't live with that secret and Lena together. Certain things can't be forgiven, not that I'd ask or deserve it. I wouldn't forgive myself for it, either. I'll forever be small, protected from Lena's larger-than-life life, and sentenced to handle my traumas and deficiencies alone.

But it'll end the indecision for us both.

No more couples' therapy.

Or confusion over where things stand.

This one decision will make them all.

Total destruction.

Then, reinvention. We'll adjust to the new us. Lena won't be saddled with caring for me or obliged to accept my mistreatment. I'll never be her burden; she'll never become jaded over my inadequacies or permanently stuck on Busy Lena to take care of me. I won't be weighed down by her pain—*eventually*. She'll recover. She's a survivor. A warrior. Today proved it.

And this moment proves I don't deserve her anyway.

I stare at the house, gripping the steering wheel until my fingers hurt.

I don't love Lauren. But somehow, that makes this seem easy.

Only it isn't.

I've responded to many domestic disturbance calls regarding infidelity. The guilty party always makes cheating seem par for the course, like a mess you fall into accidentally or an event attended unintentionally via a wrong turn or detour. For some, it just happens.

Not for me. It's a decision. A difficult one. Certainly not a fly-by-my-dick whim. It's premeditated destruction. A Molotov cocktail thrown into a relationship, rendering a painful but quick death.

Lena and I need a quick death because the suffering has become unbearable. In that way, this'll be a mercy.

My shoulders jerk when my phone rings. My heart races as if the caller knows where I am and what I'm about to do. I take a deep breath, attempting to exhale my fucking guilt.

I answer Alice Harvey's call with, "Yes, ma'am?"

"Don't *yes ma'am* me, Benjamin Allan Wright," she snaps. "What do you think you're doing?"

My free hand rakes through my hair as I assess the empty street, half-expecting her to peek out from behind a palm tree. Can she see me? "Nothing. My middle name isn't Allan."

She guffaws. "I don't care. I needed a full name to scold you properly. How can you do this to Lena?"

I twist around, but again, I don't see her. "Do what?"

"Leave her! You saw her today—she's devastated."

That's partly why I'm here, not that I care to explain that to Alice. Lena amazed me earlier. Watching her lay out her plans for Saddletree reminded me of the confident, intelligent, hopeful woman I married. I've always loved her ingenuity and creativity.

Lena shines best in her worst darkness.

That makes her my hero because it's so unlike me. The last five years, I've put up a good front for her, but the truth is, hard times bring me to my fucking knees.

This moment is a good example.

"We're both devastated," I say after a pause.

"But *you're* causing the devastation. Is it the seven-year-itch come early? A mid-life crisis thing? What's the meaning of all this, huh? I've never seen Lena so broken, and I was there after her mom died... with her excessive wine boxes lining the counter and mice running over the floor. For goodness' sake, Benjamin Alexander Wright, the other day, Jack caught her bawling her fanny off on a tree stump—not sitting on the stump, leaning against it on the ground, like she done fell out. She didn't even stop when he approached her, like a wild animal in a fit. Is *that* what you want for her? Feral tree stump crying in the woods?"

I take a breath, unhappy with this information.

"No. I don't. But it's temporary—"

"Temporary? Do you *know* Lena? If crying were an Olympic sport—"

"It's... none of your business, Alice."

"Lena *is* my business. So are you. I'm worried about her, and if you have any heart, young man, you would be, too. She can't take much more of this."

"I know. But she seemed fine today," I say, though it's untrue. She put on a face. That's what she does. Ruthie revealed that she's having nightmares again. Her hurt and disappointment are wrecking me. "It'll pass."

"She's far from fine, and you know it. Look, Ben," Alice says. "Tell me how we can help. Whatever you're going through—"

"Take care of Lena," I say quickly before telling her I must go and hang up.

A cleansing breath alleviates some irritation. It's not the first time Alice has called. I've also received numerous calls and texts from Dot, Cherry, Jack Harvey, Mr. Wickers, Jack Graham, Mrs. Moore, and Lena's brother, Lucas.

Everyone thinks they have a say in us, but no one gets it. Pressure mounts from all sides. I need to breathe again.

To disappear.

As the sun vanishes, the streetlights blink to life, and I take in Lauren's house. I glimpse her moving across the front room window, preparing for my arrival. I take another breath, my anxiety rising.

Lena thinks I'm pulling the fire alarm on us—an accurate assessment. But it's what I must do, if only to end her obligation to me.

"Are you telling me you left her *because* you love her?" Dr. Reese asked during our last private session. "You understand the faulty logic there, right, Ben? Why deliberately hurt someone you care so much about?"

"Because I don't want to *keep* hurting her. She deserves better."

"Better than you? She'd disagree… and isn't that what she once said to you?"

"Yes. This is different. Lena could improve her circumstances. I can't. I don't want to be her burden."

"Burdens are *unwanted*, Ben. Lena wants you, no matter what your hearing number is." She leaned forward and stared me down so her words would resonate. "Lena will *never* do to you what Lauren did."

My throat constricted uncomfortably. I shook my head at Dr. Reese. "I know. I won't let her."

"Martyring your marriage won't change your hearing loss. It'll make it harder and hurt everyone involved."

"Only in the short term."

"That's erroneous, too. You think her heartbreak will be easy for her to get over?"

"No, but being angry will help."

I shut my eyes, ending the memory.

Once it's done, it's done. This will end our unbearable limbo. Tasks will fall into place after tonight. Me officially moving out and starting procedures—all before the inevitable bullshit happens with my hearing. Lena will stop hoping for us; her anger will subside into resignation and even contentment when, six or so months from now, she realizes that she dodged a fucking bullet. It's hard enough to communicate now. When we're reduced to sign language only, it'll be harder. Combined with the appointments and adjustments—it's better not to put her through it.

I can't handle the pressure, anyway. I want to be the man before the IED. Before my life fucking exploded. But since I can't, I'll get small and disappear.

All I have to do is walk through that door, and Lena will never ask if I'm ready to come home again.

CHAPTER 38

Lena

BEN MEETS me outside Becca's two-story colonial when I drop off Ruthie for another sleepover. It's Saturday afternoon, and Ruthie has been an adorable hive of excitement over their plans—movie night with the cousins, blueberry pancakes for breakfast, and Sunday at the beach.

He's been diligent about spending time with her, going out of his way to be there for pick-ups, drop-offs, and downtimes—as he should. The other night, he asked to stay and put her to bed for me—a good thing because that's been the most difficult time of day. She's gotten teary in her bath when I can't do her dad's play-voices right with her toys.

And teary again when I tuck her into bed. Alone. I didn't report this to Ben, but maybe Ruthie did. I didn't want to make things worse, especially after Dr. Reese assured me he was working hard to "find his place again."

His place is with us, I told her.

Now, Ruthie bobbles to him, barely managing her overstuffed backpack. "This is going to be epic, Dad."

He chuckles, giving her a quick side hug, and she rushes into the house without looking back at me.

Our eyes meet after the front door slams, and an awkward beat passes. He looks unsure.

"You left before we could talk yesterday," I say.

"Sorry, we should talk." His eyes narrow. "I'd invite you in, but with everyone, it's—"

"It's okay. This is weird, so that'll be even weirder," I blurt with a sardonic laugh. I'm trying desperately not to cry—I love this man, and he's treating me like his daughter's chauffeur, not his wife. "It's hard getting used to this. But I guess we have to, unless…"

I hesitate, knowing I need to stop asking. "Unless, are you ready to come home yet?"

His brow pinches, and I know the answer.

"That's okay. Take your time. I know how hard you're trying." *Don't cry. Don't cry. Don't fucking cry.* "I just want you to be happy, Ben. Truly. Happy. I'm sorry for losing sight of what you needed. I wasn't there, even when I was. By the time I realized it, it was probably too late."

Every word is true—something I realized this morning when Mr. Wickers showed up at my door with a bin of badly executed homemade cupcakes—lemon with cream cheese frosting and purple smiley faces adorning their messy tops. They reminded me of Millie Davis's cupcakes that smeared my windshield in the accident.

I thought of her divorce, too. The sexless marriage she didn't notice until it was too late.

Mr. Wickers's cupcakes were delicious, regardless of their style. And I appreciated the gesture.

He handed them over and said, "You showed up for me, Lena, at one of the toughest times in my life. I'm here for you now."

"I can always count on you, Mr. Wickers," I cried.

"Yep, I learned long ago as a mailman. Consistency means everything. There's nothing like a sunny day and hitting your usual route."

I broke into tears then, remembering how Ben showed up for me at my worst time. No matter my mood. No matter the awful state of me or my house. No matter what we were doing—sometimes nothing at all. Ben was there. He made me feel human again, worthy and capable, and after that, he made me feel so loved and safe that I thought I could do anything—*and I did.* I did the impossible, all because of him.

Ben made everything better just by being present.

I failed to do the same for him. I remember after he found Adam—I *knew* something about it had cracked his typically rigid surface. That event hurt him, made him question his future, and dredged up his past. And what'd I do? I went to work, baked hundreds of cookies and cupcakes, and never pressed him to talk. Or even spent time with him. I waited too long to be present—that's all Ben really needed from me.

Hope drains now, and I'll soon follow—turning into mush in my boots that Dot'll have to suck up with her wet vac.

When I cared for Mom, I let tasks take priority. My quest to make *one* thing better helped my anxiety, but at a cost. Tasks don't equal happiness. I kept myself busy when I should've spent more time with her… with him… Now, it's too little, too late.

Now, Ben stares at me with what looks like sympathy and confusion —I don't know anymore. His lips part as if he wants to speak, but nothing comes out.

I wave him off. "Sorry, I didn't mean to…This is our new normal, right?"

I sling the tote from my shoulder and hand it to him. "Ruthie's extra dresses, normal shoes, and sandcastle gear. Oh, and your vitamins, protein powder, and migraine prescription refill. I was at Sunny's, and it was ready, so…"

"Thanks." He sets it by the porch. "I want you to be happy, too."

I smile weakly. "Without you? No chance. But I'll make do… Oh, and we're not going with the logo you saw. I told Cherry it can't represent Saddletree without you in it." I slide out my phone and show him a picture of her first version with him leaning beside me by the tree. "That's the one we're using."

His Adam's apple bobs in a heavy swallow. "The one with you and Ruthie is better, Lena."

I shake my head. *Don't cry.* "No, it's not. Saddletree wouldn't exist without you. It's where you belong. I'll never stop hoping you'll come home to us. When you're ready…"

"Lena." My name hooks on his tongue like it doesn't want to come out. "There's something I need to tell you."

When he pauses, I flash my usual smile of encouragement, hoping to help his words come easier. But the longer he takes, the more my anxiety grows. His tough-guy stoicism is gone, replaced by what looks like exhaustion and devastation. Ben suddenly looks like a man who hasn't slept in days—and can't, like he's tormented by Jaye's witches whenever he closes his eyes.

Or something worse.

"You can tell me anything," I say softly when the silence feels stifling. I step closer and think to run my hand over his arm like I've done a million times. But I stop myself, unsure.

His arms fold, creating a muscular barrier between us.

Suddenly, I realize that whatever he wants to say is not what I want to hear. He knows it, too—that's why he hesitates. He's *afraid* to tell me.

"Go ahead. Say it." My voice is stern but not unkind, despite how my anxiety bitches launch their attack. *He's ending it once and for all. He's going to say the d-word. Divorced again. Nothing ever works out for you.* Every good thing I've worked for comes at a price. My first marriage. Mom. Now him. My life is a monkey's paw, cursed.

A tear slips down his cheek.

I nod, and tears escape me, too. "Is this the final push?"

"What?"

"The final push that gets rid of me? Is this it?"

He looks stunned. "I'll never want to be rid of you."

"Just not married to me anymore, right? Or is it that you don't want *me* married to the deaf guy?"

I step closer, scraping tiny bits of strength together and staring up at him with nothing but love and sadness in my eyes. "Tell me the truth, Ben. *That's* what we're about, remember? Whatever you've planned to hurt me with… tell me."

His voice cracks when he says, "I went to Lauren's house last night."

Everything inside me shatters like his words are bricks through a window. Still, I conjure his famous calm from some deep reserve of strength I didn't know I had. "The woman who rejected you because of your scars? Who took one look at you and turned the fuck away? You went to *her*?"

He pushes his shoulders back, maybe surprised that I don't believe him. "Yes."

"And what, Ben?" I push, anger rising despite my best efforts. I lock eyes, studying him. "You what? Kissed her? Fucked her? Pledged your love to her? What?"

"I'm telling you, I went to Lauren's last night. What does the rest matter?" He stumbles over the words like his tongue is too big.

"You've made it this far. Why not tell me *all* the fucking details, so I'll believe it? Rip our marriage to pieces in one quick pull, like a band-aid."

"I'm not—I can't do that." He swipes at tears like annoying flies landing on his face. "I won't."

"Why not? Have too much integrity to cheat and tell?" I scoff. "Tell me how you laid naked in her bed, her fingers strumming the scars on your chest that once repulsed her while you discussed ending things with me. Did she make you promise to do it today?"

"Stop it. It's done. It's over."

"I don't believe you," I say with more confidence than I should have. "I don't believe it."

"Fine," he snaps. "Yes. I kissed her, fucked her, conspired against you. It's true. Is that what you want to hear?"

His emerald eyes look like cold stones, twisting into my soft places. My heart stops in his iciness. *Is he telling the truth? Holy fuck. It is true.* My eyes close in acute agony—I can't look at him. My hands fist. One of them, anyway. Nails dig into my palms. Panic surges with anger like a surfer riding the perfect wave.

I hear Mom's voice. *You deserve better than this.*

I don't even realize I'm hitting him at first. His chest becomes a punching bag—my emotions have nowhere else to go. Fists and forearms. My cast whacking against him with whatever force I can. Anything to hurt him, though it's nothing compared to how he's hurt me.

He doesn't fight back or try to stop me. He stands, tall and strong, before me, hands at his sides as he accepts the blows.

"You're a fucking liar," I breathe out finally—a truth, either way. "How could you do that to us? To me? To Ruthie? That's not who you are, Ben."

He doesn't answer but turns his eyes to the ground between us. His coldness hits me with a new truth—*I don't know this man.*

About to hyperventilate, I back-step. I glance at Becca's house, hopeful that no one has witnessed my anger. *This isn't me.* Seeing no faces peering through the windows, I take a deep breath, determined to regain some semblance of control.

"This is what you wanted," I decide. "The fire alarm wasn't enough of an escape to make you feel better, more in control? So, you fire-bombed us to bits instead? Just like the damn IED—irreparably broken and safely alone for the aftermath."

"You don't know anything about it." He drags his hand over his face before shaking his head and saying, "This conversation is over."

"It's over when *I* say," I correct sternly but with remarkable calm as if my subconscious (or perhaps my anxiety bitches) prepared me for this. "If it's true, tell Ruthie you're not coming home before returning her to me tomorrow. Tell her *why*, Ben, and don't you *dare* blame me. Understood?"

I don't wait for a response but race to my truck.

Two blocks later, I pull over. Uncontrollable sobs force me into a McDonald's parking lot. My purge takes so long that an employee taps on my window, asking if I'm okay.

Not okay.

I don't remember the drive home. Or the hour I spend on farm chores. Or going to Mrs. Moore's house.

Hugo and Penelope race from the truck when we arrive, their barks waking me from my numb stupor. Dot greets me for our prearranged girls' night with Cherry and Jaye. I feel drained—nothing but a skeleton, wobbly and bare, going through the motions. There, but not really. Maybe it's my ugly denial again, and I'm shoving the truth away like food on my plate that I can't stomach, but I don't tell them what happened. Admitting that Ben's a cheater after all will only tug the last string of my marriage apart. I can't. Yet.

When they ask if I'm okay, I tell the truth. "I'm tired."

Even so, dwelling in misery doesn't work with this crowd. Cherry makes pink champagne margaritas, and we feast on Mrs. Moore's famous mac-n-cheese casserole and crab dip that's so hot, it burns my tongue but, so good, I keep eating anyway. We play poker with the antique cards Dot bought for her birthday. I do terribly, but I laugh, get tipsy, and somehow enjoy it even though my world is burning to ashes.

Mrs. Moore gets loads of laughs over her funniest teaching moments. Cherry has us on the floor with her worst dating stories. Jaye regales us with hilarious, jaw-dropping tales about Hollywood and the graphic novel business. And Dot chimes in with experiences that are so ridiculous that I wonder if they're true.

I don't care. True or not. Truth is a murky puddle these days, anyway. Laughing feels good, releasing the pressure behind my eyes and choking my heart. I need this. I need them. And sometimes, laughing is the best—*the only*—thing to do.

On Mrs. Moore's front porch, I FaceTime with Ruthie around bedtime. She's sleepy from movie night but happy. Ben hasn't told her anything yet.

"Good night, sweet girl. Love you. Be good for your dad," I say before she hands the phone to Ben.

"I'll have her there at three tomorrow," he says, brow pinched.

"Yes, I saw the calendar."

"You okay?"

I hang up before he says anything else.

Reentering the living room, Jaye says, "The way Ben swooped in there and saved the day puts anything Hollywood might make up to shame."

Mrs. Moore smiles. "Jaye was just telling me what happened at comic-con."

"He started with holy water, but he had pig's blood in his bag," Dot says. "Can you believe *that* twisted bullshit? Pigs fucking bled for that?"

"'The world is full of misguided people who make terrible mistakes," Mrs. Moore quips dryly.

"Wait, do you mean the stalker or Ben?" Cherry asks, chuckling. "What's the status on our hero-boy, huh?"

A weak smile emerges. "He's having movie night with Ruthie."

"You know what I mean," Cherry balks. "When's he coming home?"

I take a breath, my hands fidgeting under the table. "He's not."

Dot gives me an angry look. "What did I tell you about talking like that?"

"I'm not talking *like* anything. I'm presenting facts. He told me today."

They stare like this doesn't compute, and they require more input. I don't give it to them, though. I don't share Ben's final push simply because I can't handle them knowing yet. Not with Dot's murder plans and Cherry's man-hate.

"God, are you okay?" Cherry asks.

"I'm letting go." I force a short smile. "I have to. For his sake. For our family's sake."

"What about *your* sake, huh?" Dot demands. "He's your fucking husband. You can't accept that bullshit."

"I don't have a choice. I have to make the best of things for Ruthie. It's bad enough that he doesn't love me anymore—I can't handle him hating me. That's what happened with Mark. It'll break Ruthie's heart if her dad despises me. No matter how hurt I am, I refuse to let that happen."

Even Dot fails to argue. Cherry and Dot aren't mothers, but they love Ruthie like we all gave birth to her.

"Now, whose turn is it to deal?" I choke out. "And how about another margarita, huh?"

Jaye grabs the cards. Cherry takes my empty glass for a refill. Dot leaves the table, probably to vape on the porch and perhaps to consider her murder plan.

Mrs. Moore's delicate hand falls on mine, catching my tearful attention. "This too shall pass," she says, words Mom said often. "Loving *is* losing, eventually… but I don't believe all is lost yet."

She pulls me into her pink floral cardigan and circles my back as I cry into her shoulder.

CHAPTER 39

Ben

MY PHONE FLASHES to the home screen with a definitive beep. Lena hung up on me. I deserve it. It was a dumb question, anyway. *You okay?*

Of course, she isn't.

I'm not, either.

After she left, I fell apart. Knowing I couldn't face Ruthie or anyone, I texted Becca to watch her and took off running. Soon, sweat hid my tears as the miles moved under my feet. I pushed myself, hoping my heart would explode with the effort.

I didn't have a destination in mind—just wherever the sidewalk took me. But on the other side of Wilmington, I came to a huffing stop in front of my former residence—the craftsman cottage I bought after Lauren, a fixer-upper to focus my energy. It's where I spent seven years getting my life back together, where I planted roots for the first time in my adult life, where Lena and I spent our first night together.

Memories swirl like a home movie projected in front of me.

Us walking up the sidewalk after a strange discussion about sharks and gators.

Me asking her at the first step if she was sure she wanted to spend the night.

Her hopping up a step in the affirmative before asking me the same.

Me taking all the steps at once to assure her I was.

Then, me coming clean about my scars at the doorstep, suddenly fearful and nervous that she'd recoil at the sight and change her mind.

She didn't. And that night, I told her what I'd wanted to say for ages. I loved her.

I stare at the house, noting the differences from when I owned it—a swing set in the yard, an unfamiliar car in the driveway, plants across the front porch, and a cat sunning in the front window. I put it on the market as soon as Lena and I moved into the barn house, and it sold the same week. I had zero hesitations signing it over—*that's* how confident I was in us. The money went to Ruthie's college fund, our savings, and Saddletree's farming vehicles.

I said *all in*, and I meant it.

Then, I considered my relationship with Lena a delicate operation that needed care and precision. I showed up, built her trust, and eased us together slowly. She was my heart's mission. Merging our lives together marked that mission successful.

Only my commitment came with limits. I helped her through her anxiety, uncertainty, and grief without showing her my own, making me a hypocrite from day one.

I hate that I was never truly *all in* with her like I wanted. Like she was with me.

Lena's right. I've fire-bombed my marriage to escape my fears and self-loathing, to get small and minimize my pain. But it's done the opposite. I'm Godzilla, bulldozing over what we've built, the monster in me taking over.

From the sidewalk, I called Dr. Reese for an emergency session. I talked her through everything that had happened. And during the ten-mile walk back to Becca's, she guided me through my self-hatred toward the truth.

That day in Afghanistan and its aftermath.

Almost missing Adam.

The return of the Rileys.

Lena's accident.

I distorted these events into one singular, crippling fear—that luck runs out. And when it does, it takes every good thing with it.

I subconsciously set out on a mission of preemptive destruction. And I succeeded. There is no coming back from this.

Now, still staring at the screen as it goes dark, that reality hits me even harder. She gave me her heart, and I blew it up. And it's too late to save it.

CHAPTER 40

Lena

DOT'S VOICE cuts through a strange haze between nightmare and reality. "Lena, I can't wake her."

"What?"

"Aunt Barb. I can't wake her."

I sit up, pushing the throw blanket off me. I'm on the couch in their living room. Cherry sleeps in the recliner beside me, curled in another throw. The dogs cuddle by the unlit fireplace. Jaye's probably in the guest room. Grayness seeps in through the curtained windows. It takes me a minute to remember that it's Sunday morning, Ruthie's with Ben, and I crashed here last night.

Mrs. Moore went to bed around nine. "Too tired for any more fun," she said with a laugh. "But you girls carry on for me."

Now, I stare down at her in the dim light of her bedroom. She wears a floral print nightgown, her crocheted duvet tucked up over her chest where her hands rest, knotted together. She's as peaceful as I've ever seen her.

I reach for her pulse—her hand is cold. I feel nothing beneath her soft skin. Dot awaits my verdict in anguish. All I can do is pull her to me with one hand and call nine-one-one with the other.

The next call I make when I'm able is Ben. He answers on the first ring. "Lena, everything okay?"

"It's Mrs. Moore." My voice cracks and sounds childlike. "She... passed away in her sleep last night."

"Lena… I'm sorry," he says with a ragged sigh. "Are you okay? What can I do?"

"Keep Ruthie until I can come pick her up? Dot needs help with the arrangements, and I don't know how long that'll take."

"Of course. Want me to tell Ruthie?"

More tears. "Um, no. Have you told her about us yet?"

"No."

"Don't, please. It's too much. Not with this…" My voice trails off as tears take over, imagining how sad Ruthie will be about her Aunt Barb. "I shouldn't have put that on you, anyway. When the time comes, we'll talk to her together."

"Lena—"

"Just give her a good day, like you planned. I'll break the news when I pick her up."

"When you get here, we'll tell her together."

"Okay."

"Is there anything I can do for you? I-I… want to help."

Sobs break through the last of my seams. I'm flooded with smart-ass answers, but all that comes out is a weak "I have to go" before I hang up.

The next hours pass in a haze. Consoling Dot as she cries. Meeting with the funeral home. Discovering, much to our surprise—not surprised—that Mrs. Moore made her arrangements, from the flowers to the guest book. This, of course, makes Dot break down again. But truly, it's a miracle.

No one wants to pick out caskets and burial plots for someone they love.

Dot, Cherry, and I spend hours on Aunt Barb's front porch. We share memories. We discuss details. But the most important thing is that we're together, absorbing the truth. She's gone, and she's not coming back.

Jaye shows up early in the afternoon with catered food. She seems almost as upset as Dot, tearfully grabbing onto her like they're each others' life preserver. "You okay? I need you to be okay."

Dot nods. And Cherry and I witness the most amazing thing—a first kiss. Born from sadness and despair, but also love. Jaye edges into Dot like she can't help it—primal and necessary. Cherry and I both gasp from the sidelines at their tangle of lips and love. It's what I've always hoped for her. Love as I've known it. Love—pure and simple.

And it makes me miss Ben.

Then, I feel wrong for missing him, like what he's done should've instantly turned me to the Dark Side. No love. Only hate. But that's not what I feel.

He texts me.

> I'm taking Ruthie home. Meet us there when you're able.

That doesn't happen until after dinner. The dogs and I find Ruthie and Ben snuggled on the couch, watching TV. The kitchen is clean. I hear the washing machine rumbling in the background and hope it's Ruthie's dresses. It feels almost normal.

Ben flips the TV off when I come in, and I take my usual side of the couch. I tell Ruthie what's happened, nearly breaking when her bottom lip quivers and she bursts into tears. Ben holds her to his chest while she cries and pulls me toward him, too.

"Aunt Barb's in heaven with Grandma Ruth now?" Ruthie whimpers.

"Yep. Best friends forever," I say from the other side of Ben's chest, our tears pooling on his t-shirt.

"Everyone dies, Ruthie," he says into the air between us, "and we'll miss her. But we can honor her by being brave and living fully like she did."

My hand grips his like a lifeline as the tears flow. I'm grateful that he had the right words because I don't.

Ruthie cries herself to sleep, and soon, Ben carries her into bed. She tucks in with barely a murmur.

Nothing tires like grief.

We reenter the living room. I'm exhausted and weak, totally spent. All I want is to crawl into bed and bury my face in the pillow. His pillow, if I'm honest. That I haven't washed and still barely smells of his aftershave.

Ben stands by the kitchen island, looking unsure.

"Thanks for bringing her home," I say, "and doing that with me."

He nods as I lean against the counter opposite him. "Whatever you need."

"She went peacefully in her sleep. That's all anyone can hope for, really," I say, the words avalanching from my mouth. "I should've known it was coming. She told me she loved me last night... between asking if I'd remembered to check the mail and if I thought Dot and Jaye would make it."

"What'd you say?"

"Yes, I remembered the mail. Yes, Dot and Jaye will make it. And yes, I loved her, too. She also said… Loving is losing, eventually. Didn't know she'd provide the evidence so soon, not that I needed proof."

He looks unsure. "I'm sorry, Lena."

"Me, too," and then feeling bad about my jab, I add, "You were her favorite opponent in cards."

He looks shocked. "Really? You think so?"

"She said so. Best poker face ever," I grin, "and best strategist."

He smiles—the first I've seen in so long that it hurts. "That means a lot… and thanks for not shutting me out."

"I'll never shut you out, Ben. Ruthie needs you. I… "

Tears flow again as if my body's sprung leaks that won't be stopped. I want to beg him to stay, to ask my usual question, but knowing he doesn't want to and what he's done, it'd only make me feel more pathetic. This is how he wants it—hands off, feelings off, on to someone else. Sadness tugs at my weaknesses like a sweater about to be undone.

"You should go," I manage.

"If you need anything, let me know. I mean it," he says, slow and stern. Then, he leaves.

The days blur together like a hazy sunset. Dot's estranged family reaches out, curious about the will, and I steer her through that drama like a captain, ready to go down with the ship. We were relieved, but again, not surprised, to discover that Mrs. Moore left Dot everything—her beautiful farmhouse, everything inside it, and even her cute MINI Cooper.

Both having cried ourselves out, we sit through social calls and death details in numb stupors—zombie women. I mourn her and my marriage together like they're a packaged deal. I mourn Mom again, too. She put the pieces of me back together after my last marriage failed. She's not here to puzzle me together this time.

I take care of Dot and Ruthie as best I can. In quiet moments, I bake and ride—the same joys that got me through Mom's death.

My cast comes off in a quiet appointment with Dr. Rob Riley. He spends five minutes with me while my head spins with anxiety. *Does he know? Do all the Rileys know? Are the Rileys giving themselves high fives and back pats over Lauren and Ben's reconciliation?* Rob doesn't say anything, but my imagination feeds my anxiety bitches plenty of material. Ben doesn't show up to my appointment this time.

He texts often to see how I am, even on days we're not exchanging Ruthie, but I only manage quick answers, like he's an addiction and I'm in a difficult recovery. Ruthie doesn't notice our strange situation—it's too strange a time. We're off our usual schedule, Ben is still "fixing the roof" at Becca's, we're sad and mopey over Mrs. Moore, and there are witches in the woods around the house—nothing is normal.

But that'll soon change.

After the funeral, we'll sit down with Ruthie to explain it as gently as possible to a four-year-old. I imagine he'll start proceedings, and there'll be lawyers and custody agreements—all the sad rigamarole of separating our lives. He slept with someone else—there's no coming back from that. *Is there?* When I think about them together, I flush with anger, but I can't stay that way long.

Sadness takes over every time.

I still haven't told anyone. It's not the right time, and the pathetic truth is, I'd still take him back. It goes against my female identity and all the strength I supposedly have to admit it, but I would. I'll never be Cherry, pinning Ben's face to a dartboard and cackling while I throw darts at it. I'll never move on to male nurses and dating apps, hardening my heart with each emotionless encounter. It's fine for her, no judgment, but it's not me. There's a huge difference between Cherry and me—she wasn't meant for Warren, but I was meant for Ben. I still am.

We just failed. I failed.

CHAPTER 41

Ben

I SIT in the Riley Trust Bank parking lot, tightening my hands around the steering wheel until my knuckles crack. My appointment with John should've started five minutes ago, but I can't exit my Jeep. I stare at my phone, perched on my dash, hoping the screen will alight with a notification. The text I sent to Lena twenty minutes ago, asking how she's doing, if she needs anything, remains unanswered. Though reason assures me that she's doing as well as can be expected and probably busy caring for Dot and Ruthie, awaiting her response puts me in agony. An agony that's swollen with additional brokenness, like Lena's hand after the accident. Brokenness I caused, and that's sharpened since losing Mrs. Moore.

I need to know she's okay. Need this shred of connection to remain intact. Need her to know that I'm here.

Despite the destruction I've caused, I long to be with my family. Especially now.

Instead, I'm here, and late to a meeting for the first time in memory.

My phone pings. A text from Lena.

> We're okay. Shopping for funeral dresses. Are you okay?

That she asks makes me tear up. I don't deserve her concern. But that's my wife—always prioritizing her love over her pain.

I stare up at the glass building, blurry in my tears, and my resolve solidifies. I know what I have to do. I've known since holding my girls to my chest as they sobbed over Mrs. Moore; a realization that came too late, but I owe them the follow-through regardless.

My first instinct is to respond that I'm fine. It's my go-to answer. But I delete it and try again.

> I'm hurting for you and Ruthie. I'm here for anything you need.

She reads the message but doesn't answer. That's okay.

I exit my vehicle, ready for this meeting.

John Riley greets me with a beaming smile when I enter his office moments later. Lauren sits on the leather couch, opposite Captain Tenor. Between them, champagne chills in a silver ice bucket and crystal glasses await pouring on the coffee table. I shouldn't be surprised that they've turned my contract signing into a celebration.

"There you are!" John says. "We were starting to wonder about you Ben."

"A whole ten minutes late," Larry chuckles good-naturedly. "Must've been that Wilmington traffic. Eh?"

"No." I approach John's desk as he moves from behind it. "I can't accept the position."

My announcement is stern and clear, but John freezes, like he doesn't understand, and he's waiting for a punchline.

"Ben, no." Lauren drops the paperwork she's holding onto the coffee table. "What do you mean?"

"I apologize for letting it get this far," I say, "but recent events have brought clarity, and this won't work for me or my family."

"Nonsense," John says.

I stave off his upcoming argument with, "I appreciate the opportunity, Mr. Riley, but it's not going to happen."

John glares at me, hands on hips, and his eyes narrow like he's strategizing his next move in a chess game.

"Well, Ben, that breaks my heart," Larry says, coming over and giving me a gentle back slap. "But you know best. You've got to do right by your family. You take care."

He shakes my hand before leaving.

"Ben, don't do this. You need us." Lauren steps closer, like she wants to reach out. Her stony eyes glisten as they water. "I thought we—"

"You thought wrong," I insist, returning my gaze to Mr. Riley. "I'm sorry I wasted your time."

He huffs, shaking his head. "Lauren, give us a minute."

She rushes at his command like just another staff member, closing the office door behind her.

Mr. Riley replaces his disappointment with a knowing smile, firmly squeezing my shoulder.

"Ben, let's sit down. You owe me that at least. I understand what's going on."

Respectfully, I comply, though I doubt he understands anything. Nor do I feel he's owed. He takes the couch opposite me.

"This isn't the time for second thoughts or cold feet." With a deep breath, he leans forward, conspiratorially. "Lauren shared your recent home situation with me. I can't say that I didn't see that coming. How's Ruthie handling the separation?"

"She's fine," I manage, defenses rising.

"She's such a beautiful little girl. Jillian and Lauren couldn't stop gushing about her after the picnic," he smiles. "Kids are resilient. I know you wouldn't leave Lena without strong reasons, and I hate that you're struggling. We can help you."

"Help me?" I repeat dumbly before assuming he means with the counseling and mental health services described in the company's policy manual.

"Of course!" He goes to the bar and pours whiskey into two crystal tumblers. I accept the glass he hands me, but I don't drink. "You know me, Ben. I take care of my own. Whether you take the job or not, you're family. Lauren never stopped loving you—"

"I stopped loving her. I don't love your daughter. This isn't about Lauren," I say, unease percolating beneath my rigidity like lava inside a mountain.

A disappointed twinge shadows his expression that he quickly bypasses. "No, you're right. It's about you and Ruthie for now. I want to support you in this. You've already accomplished the hardest part of the mission. Leaving took courage. Now, let my lawyers handle the details. They're top-notch, and they'll get everything you deserve. Half the assets. Custody of Ruthie. Lauren says you have dogs. Hell, we'll get them, too."

He laughs, a sound as devastating as it is familiar.

I hold tight to my calmness like a shield, though every muscle in my body tenses with disgust. That he offers lawyers rather than help, that my portrait still hangs on his wall at his daughter's expense, that he laughs over the dissolution of a marriage and the ruthless dismantling of Lena's dream—I'm hit with a truth that I've always known but somehow ignored for the security they could provide me.

The Rileys are *small*.

In integrity. In kindness. In everything that matters.

"Has this been the main objective all along?" I ask as their collective manipulations pile together in my head.

"The objective was to offer you the job you deserve. Secondary to that, we want to see you happy. It's all been for a good cause, Ben," he argues lightly. "We failed you after your injuries. I promised myself I wouldn't fail you again. For your sake and Lauren's. Ruthie's, too. We can give her the best of everything. Let us give you your life back."

I stand, setting my glass down before shaking his hand across the table. "Thank you, Mr. Riley."

"You're more than welcome. I'll call my team now—"

"No, that's unnecessary. Thank you for validating my decision not to take this job. I already have a family, and they're what's best for me."

He scoffs. "*You* left them, Ben. You're not with Lena anymore because you can do better. Lauren *is* better. Stop punishing her already. She was devastated when you didn't show up the other night."

I cringe with shame that I even considered it. More regret clouds me over letting Lena believe it. Sparing her a future with me seemed right at the time. Now that I know better, gluing the broken pieces of my marriage back together seems an impossible task. Not everything that's broken can be fixed.

Not that I'll ever stop trying.

I lock eyes with him, determined to finish this. "No one is better than Lena. My love and loyalty belong to her forever. I'd rather spend the rest of my life alone, broke, Deaf, unemployed, and whatever else life decides, begging for Lena's forgiveness and restoring her faith in me, than live a half-life in your superficial, manipulative, entitled family."

The ease of my delivery surprises us both. I feel unstuck. Clear. Focused. Recycling some of the same words I used on Lauren when we broke up feels cathartic. This time, they aren't said in anger but in truth and acceptance. I did the right thing then; I'm doing it now. I feel ashamed for judging Lena for her forced smiles while I fell so easily for their fake ones. How could I have been so damn gullible?

One long stride brings me to the pictures on his wall, where I remove my portrait and tuck it under my arm. "I don't belong here."

As I move toward the door, Mr. Riley shakes his head in disappointment. "You're making a mistake, son."

His parental stare-down takes me back to times when he could guilt Lauren with a look over subpar grades or speeding tickets. My respect for him made me hellbent on never inspiring his disappointment.

Now, I no longer care.

At the door, I say, "*Everyone wants the wins, but the losses… those make us who we are.* That's what you said. Remember? Your family lost me, and now I see *exactly* who you are. I want no part of it. And don't call me son."

I jerk the door open, and Lauren stumbles inside.

A weak smile emerges from her distress. "Ben, don't let Dad scare you off. We can work this out, just the two of us."

I huff and push by her, done with them.

But as I near the elevator, she calls out, "Ben, don't go. It's not my fault."

"Nothing ever is." I slap the elevator call button repeatedly.

"It came up one night at family dinner—"

"I don't care."

"I told him that you're the only man I'd ever marry," she smiles like it's an endearing anecdote.

My irritation only grows.

"So, when this happened, Dad took those words to heart. We all did. I'm sorry, but we were so happy once. Remember? It can be like that again. I still have hope for us."

Long shadows of anger stretch into my present, recalling her cringing expression at my scars. That same dismissive attitude toward anything that doesn't fit into the Rileys' plans is still there, hidden. My injuries didn't fit. Neither did my wife. Her condescending encounters with Lena, her scheme to get me to dance, her inappropriate invitation, and total disregard for my marriage and family all prove it.

The door pings open. I step inside, blocking her from joining me.

"We aren't kids anymore, so let me be clear," I say. "There is no *us.* There will *never* be an us. And if ever I waste a thought on you again, it'll only be in vague gratitude for *one* thing."

Her arms fold over her chest as she glares, her fake smile retreating behind a scowl.

"Leaving you led me to Lena. She's everything I need, all I'll ever want. She's where I belong." I smirk, amused by the sharp irritation etched on her face. "Oh, and Lauren, get a life… stop trying to fuck with mine. Don't come near my wife or Saddletree again."

Her mouth drops with my warning, just as I free the door and let it shut between us.

A profound sense of satisfaction fills me as I watch the floor numbers decrease. I finally did the hard thing—I said what I needed to say. It was exhausting and exhilarating, and revealed truths I've struggled to see. Not only is turning down the Rileys in every respect absolutely the right decision, but turning Lena away wasn't. I didn't cheat, but I betrayed her all the same.

The elevator pings open on the first floor, and I emerge renewed with one hope—getting Lena back.

CHAPTER 42

Lena

SATURDAY, the morning of the funeral, I wake feeling anxious and queasy after a fitful night. Nightmares rattled me between crying—mostly for Ben, who once made my peaceful sleep his personal mission. I wonder if I'll ever have a good night's sleep without him.

I take my coffee on the back deck. It's overcast, and rain threatens—funeral weather. Saddletree is quiet. Jaye made sure that the studio wouldn't be here today. Their equipment sits dormant, waiting for action that won't be until Monday. I get caught up in the quiet, staring off at Mom's swaying tree, and when I finally go inside, I have to rush to get us ready.

Ruthie refuses to wear the dark blue dress I bought her for the occasion. "Aunt Barb loved me in pink," she argues, and I relent. She goes full-on pink—dress, leggings, and cardigan—like she's a walking advertisement for Pepto-Bismol.

I wear a snug black dress with sheer long sleeves and dotted with white and brown dogwood flowers. I rip my stockings, putting them on, so I go without. Who cares? My high heels click across the hardwoods as I gather our things. I promised Dot I'd be there early—a glance at the oven clock tells me to hurry if I expect to keep it.

Rain starts, so we take the mud room stairs, spilling into the barn to stay dry. "Oh, Ruthie, I forgot the umbrella. Stay here."

"I have one."

Ben stands inside the barn entrance, umbrella tucked under his arm.

His Jeep idles close behind him, lights on and wipers flipping. He's in his dark suit—the same one he wore the day of my car accident. He steps closer, watching my expression like a pressure gauge nearing the red zone.

"You're here," I say dumbly.

"Yes. I told you it wouldn't happen again."

"What?"

"Pulling a no-show when you need me."

I nearly fall apart—that's what he's doing every day he's not here. I'm confused and nervous. I almost wonder if Lauren sits in the passenger seat as his plus one, but I can't see behind the rain's glare on his windshield. *Would he do that?*

I feel like I have marbles in my mouth when I say, "I, um, need to get there. Dot's beside herself. Her parents are coming—she hasn't seen them since she had to move in with Mrs. Moore." My eyebrows cinch together. "Did you want to take Ruthie?"

"I want to drive you both. We could go together," he says, "if that's alright."

A mental debate happens in a breath—angry me versus me who still loves him. But it's no contest.

"Yes," pushes from me, remembering his hospital promise and ignoring the irony—*Ben still keeps promises?*

"You look lovely," he says, green eyes moving from me to Ruthie.

"Aunt Barb loves me in pink." Ruthie holds out a spray of wildflowers. "She loves flowers, too. I'm bringing these for her. I picked them yesterday."

"Very thoughtful." He leans down to sniff the messy bouquet that instantly makes him sneeze.

I chuckle lightly. He extends his arm, and I link my hand comfortably around it. Suddenly, we're a family again—a thought that both delights and scares me. I'm Cinderella, waiting for the clock to strike midnight.

CHAPTER 43

Ben

LENA AND RUTHIE huddle under my umbrella to the church breezeway, where Dot, Jaye, and Cherry await us. Dot paces, her wet black boots squeaking along the pavement. She looks uncharacteristically nervous, fisting rumpled index cards in one hand and waving a stack of programs with the other.

Her brow cocks upon seeing me. "Good, you've finally come to your senses. Make yourself useful, huh? Hand these out in the lobby?" She pushes a stack of programs into my chest.

"Guess you were right to go with the family logo, Lena. My bad. I honestly didn't think you'd be back," Cherry adds, turning to me.

My eyes cut to Lena, taking in her worry with her *L* brow and nibbled lip. She mouths words no one else sees. *"Not now."*

She hasn't told them about Lauren.

I accept the programs, relieved that she's spared me from her best friends clawing my eyes out on sight. *For now.*

But I ache, too. Lena's lived with this information for over a week, hoarding her pain with no one to help her through it so that she could be strong for everyone else. *Shit.*

"Whatever you need," I tell them before leaving for my assignment.

Forty minutes before the starting time, the church is empty. The front altar and side tables are adorned with flowers—so many that the air is thick with their scents—and pictures. Large collages of Mrs. Moore's life

287

line the front. There's no casket or urn—Mrs. Moore donated her body to one of her loves, science.

I take my position at the lobby doors. I mentally prepare for the inevitable backlash. The community may not want to see me. Lena is their sweetheart, everyone's daughter, sister, and best friend. And they all know I've hurt her.

Dark clouds, heavy and angry, linger outside the main doors as the first vehicle arrives—Mr. Wickers's Prius. Trisha emerges from the passenger seat and dashes through the rain to the Fellowship Hall with a covered dish. Mr. Wickers makes his way toward me.

"Welcome," I say, handing him a program.

"Ben."

"Mr. Wickers."

Though the entire sanctuary is available, he plops into the pew beside my post. He swipes his bald head free from the rain and cleans the drops from his glasses with his tie in silence.

I've always appreciated his word economy.

I watch for more attendees through the church's glass doors, but the driving rain pelts the gravel lot, and I expect people are waiting it out.

"Lena saved me," Mr. Wickers says. "Everyone knows that."

Pause.

"What they don't know, and she doesn't either," he starts again, "is how true that statement is. Two months after my retirement, on a Thursday morning, she visited my house with her little bin of cupcakes and interrupted, well... let's say I was about to take another early retirement."

My pinched eyes dart to his.

"Ben, I'm fine now. I promise," he says, amused at my concern.

It's my job and responsibility as a human to be concerned—I don't see what's amusing.

"Better than fine. When I think of all I would've missed..." His head shakes like he's ashamed.

"It was the right time to retire from work. Things started to slip, you see. My energy, motivation, and speed weren't there anymore. You do a job for fifty years and get tired of the grind. I wanted to hang up my blues."

He chuckles, though again, I don't know what's funny.

"Little do you know how much of your self-worth is tied to work. How much purpose it gives you. When the novelty of having all that time on my hands wore off, I looked around and didn't find a purpose anymore. I didn't know what to do with myself. And thought I'd be better off… well, you get it."

I do—after Adam, I lost my purpose.

He stops to rub his hands along his legs like he's warming them up. "There she was… She asked how I was doing, she hadn't seen me in a bit. Made chitchat, like she does."

I nod.

"I said to her, what made you think to visit me? She said, 'When you love someone, you show up. Ben taught me that.'"

A soft sigh puffs out as I try to remain unmoved.

I taught her to show up, but I haven't been here.

I taught her to rely on me and failed her repeatedly.

I promised always and wrecked us the moment things got hard.

Mr. Wickers fiddles with his tie knot, taking it from straight to crooked. "She didn't stay long, but handed over her cupcakes and invited me to the café. I'm always there, bright and early, she said. Come anytime. So, I did. I had a purpose again. She made me see that my worth wasn't in a job. Or a paycheck. I'm worthy just being me."

Lena's words from comic-con whisper through my thoughts. *"We don't need you to be a cop or a hero or anything. You are enough. You are all we need."*

"I've treated her horribly," I say, the words rising from some deep pit inside me. I don't say things like this aloud. I don't *talk* to people. But where has my silence gotten me?

"She'll forgive you."

"I don't deserve it."

"Let her decide."

"She needs more than I can offer her. She needs me to be strong enough to be vulnerable. I've spent my adult life serving and protecting. I fear I won't be able to do that for my own family."

He nods, soaking up my words like a dry sponge. "Son, you do that just by showing up. You wouldn't be here if you didn't know that already." His hand lands gently on my arm. "Don't let go because you're afraid to hold on."

His words rattle around in my head like loose bolts. "It's too late."

"You're here. She's here. It's never too late."

He rises weakly and finds a better seat near the front.

When guests arrive, I do my duty, my guilt and shame gnawing at me relentlessly. Neighbors and friends greet me with smiles and kind words as if nothing's happened, and I absorb their collective warmth like a campfire on a cold night.

A woman I don't recognize rushes in wearing an elegant black dress and rain boots, which she quickly changes out of while leaning against the wall beside me. When she's ready, I hand her a program.

"Can you point me toward the church's pianist? Mrs. Moore called me last week to perform a special song for her funeral. I had no clue it'd happen so fast." She scans the program. "Okay, I'm there, at least. I need to coordinate with whoever does the music."

I direct her to the fellowship hall. She quickly weaves through the growing crowd and disappears.

Moments before the service begins, Lena texts.

> Can you hand off the programs to someone else and join us?

I quickly obey, asking Jack Harvey to take over.

I find their small group in a nervous huddle in the fellowship hall while Reverend Jenkins watches in helpless resignation.

"I don't want them here," Dot says with irritation. Her eyes lock on me as I enter the room. "Are they here? Did you see them?"

"Your parents?" I ask, trying to catch up. A mental scan of guests in my head stops on strangers who most resemble Dot. "Yes."

She scoffs and rolls her eyes dramatically.

"Would you like me to ask them to leave?"

The ladies turn to me, stunned, but I don't see what's surprising. *Identify the problem. Solve the problem. Simple.*

"Would you really do that?" Dot asks, almost dreamily.

"Yes."

Lena smirks, knowing I mean it, and I feel superhuman.

"We generally don't turn away mourners," Reverend Jenkins says, looking worried. "View it as an opportunity for reconciliation."

Dot scoffs again. "Forget it. Let them hover and judge. Let's just get this over with."

I turn to exit and find a solo seat in the crowded sanctuary, but Dot's brash voice stops me with, "Where do you think you're going?"

"Ben, sit with us, with the family," Lena explains.

"Yeah, besides, what if I change my mind about you bouncing my folks?" Dot adds with a shrug.

I take a position next to Lena. Ruthie reaches out, her tiny face drooping with sadness. I lift her into my arms, and she rests her head softly on my shoulder. We file into the sanctuary and take the reserved section up front, me on the very end near the outer wall.

Rain hits the church roof, a fitting drumbeat to the occasion. Reverend Jenkins gives a warm welcome, shares about Mrs. Moore's life, and peppers his sermon with Bible verses she provided in her detailed instructions.

After a prayer, the normal pianist moves aside for the woman in a rush earlier—one of Mrs. Moore's former students, Reverend Jenkins introduces. At the piano, she performs "Ode to Joy" from Beethoven's Ninth Symphony. I'm grateful that I can still hear the music, but mostly, I feel it in my chest. It stirs my emotions, kicking up everything that felt settled at the bottom. My hand slips over Lena's beside me—I can't help it. Her cast is gone, and I run my fingers over her delicate fingers, wrist, and arm, where her newly exposed skin feels strangely softer, if possible.

She *should* reject me. That's what I expect. She believes I've committed the worst crime in a marriage. To her, my affection must incite betrayal and anger.

So, when her fingers interlock with mine, her wedding rings sliding between them, my breath catches and holds in amazed disbelief. She still loves me. Even now. She's said it all along, but in that simple action —letting me hold her hand—her promises finally crystallize into absolute truths.

Whatever your reality, I'm with you, and I'll try to make it better.

You belong here. With me.

I'm yours, always. No matter what.

You *are enough.* You *are all we need.*

The revelation astounds me—that she could love me *that* much, even after the million and one ways I've hurt her. It's like… damn, *fireworks.* My throat constricts, and wetness dampens the corners of my eyes. I glance at our joined hands and then at her, her glassy blue eyes catching mine like a light through a long, dark tunnel. The song nears its crescendo, but more powerful is her thumb running softly over mine and the small smile she offers me.

Dot pulls her attention away from me, and a whispered discussion ensues between them. I refocus on the music to keep tears from falling. The music soon ends, and generous applause shakes the small sanctuary despite being a funeral. Mrs. Moore would approve, I think.

Reverend Jenkins clears his throat, giving Dot her cue to come to the podium for her eulogy.

But nothing happens.

Lena's gentle coaxing doesn't get Dot to her feet. At first, I think it's nerves about seeing her dismissive, intolerant parents. But, leaning over, I read her lips as she says, "This is the last thing I'll do for her, Lena. The last thing."

Identify the problem. Solve the problem. Simple.

I stand and approach the podium.

The room quiets. Dot and the rest stare up at me with gaping apprehension. Dot mouths to Lena, "What's he doing?"

The truth is, I don't know. But when Lena smiles reassuringly and says, "Giving you time, Dot," purpose and duty drive me onward.

I clear my throat. "I'm not much of a public speaker… or even a private one."

Laughs.

"But for Mrs. Moore—a mom to Lena for the last five years, to her niece Dot much longer, and a surrogate grandmother to Ruthie—it's not difficult finding words, even for me."

Laughs.

"Mrs. Moore was a mean card player. That's how I best knew her. I looked forward to our canasta nights and planned my gameplay against her with military precision, knowing she was a keen strategist. She would disarm me with her dainty smile and incredible crab dip before going in for the kill, winning most of the time."

Laughs.

"One night, a terrible migraine threatened to end our game early—I get them often. Standing in Mrs. Moore's kitchen, she said, 'Most troubles, we can't change, but we can count it all joy, Ben.' I disagreed at the time but said nothing. It felt impossible to find joy in a migraine. Sometimes, pain takes over, graying what's usually so vivid and clear and making it hard to feel anything else. Now, I understand what she meant —finding joy within the troubles… It's holding on to what you love through the pain instead of giving in to it. That's what life is—an ode to joy."

My eyes fall to the podium. I take a deep breath, centering myself. Returning to the crowd, I find Lena, her encouraging smile beckoning me on, as it has a thousand times. Only this time, my words come easily.

"We just heard "Ode to Joy" from Beethoven's Ninth Symphony. He was almost completely deaf when he composed it, and it's said to be his greatest masterpiece. When he conducted it in Vienna, he couldn't hear the applause."

My throat tightens. A beat passes.

"I'm nearly deaf—a circumstance that has troubled me and caused uncertainty and hardship for those I love most. I have not handled myself well, something I will forever regret and strive to rectify. I am surrounded by a community, neighbors, friends and family, like Mrs. Moore, who have loved and supported me without hesitation while I've failed to count it all joy."

"Lena," my voice hitches when I meet her eyes. "I love you, and I'm sorry. You and Ruthie are my joy."

She dabs her eyes with a handkerchief while Dot, no longer a nervous wreck, wraps an arm around her in consolation.

I take a breath, refocusing on the crowd. "Mrs. Moore only added "Ode to Joy" to the program the week before she passed. Ever the strategist, she understood that it was what we needed to hear today. What *I* needed to hear. The song is her message to us—to celebrate her, each other, and count it all joy. The night before she left us, she told Lena that loving was losing, eventually. That makes us all joyful losers today."

Laughs.

"This isn't the last thing we will do for her," I say, looking at Dot. "She's engaged us in a mission to live fully, love completely, and seek joy in everything."

Mild applause ensues. Mixed in, I hear Alice Harvey coo, "Oh, Ben," while Jack bursts with an, "Amen." Mr. Wickers calls out, "Well said, son."

Dot gives me a smirking thumbs up, and it's clear that she's ready. I nod and leave the podium as she takes her place.

"Wow, Ben. I've never heard you talk so much," she says, earning more laughs.

"Don't get used to it," I return before sitting down to more chuckles.

Dot gives a heartfelt, humorous eulogy. She describes Mrs. Moore as her savior—the only person in her life at the time who loved her for who she was.

I relate, especially when Lena's hand clasps mine and doesn't let go.

Dot is her usual self—blunt and vulnerable in her honesty in a way I aspire to be. When her parents leave somewhere in the middle of her gushing about Mrs. Moore's "unconditional acceptance," she smiles with satisfaction.

During the reception, I watch Lena move through the crowd. She is beautiful. Stunning, really. Smiling with tears in her eyes. Kind and open to everyone. She keeps her eye on me, floating to my side more often than she should. She includes me in warm conversations as if nothing's happened.

But I know it's only temporary.

At the end of the reception, I wait by the glass doors, umbrella in hand, for Ruthie and Lena. Most people have left, and everything has been done. The women huddle in what's become their usual, tight-knit circle, Ruthie between them.

"Ben, get your ass over here," Dot orders loud enough for me and anyone in the vicinity to hear.

I close the distance, merging next to Lena, unsurely.

"Thanks for what you did," Dot says. "Who knew you were such a good public speaker?"

"I didn't," I admit, "but it was no trouble."

"Dot asked to take Ruthie tonight for an epic sleepover," Lena explains. "Is that okay with you?"

"Yes. Thanks for asking."

"Give her a goodbye kiss then," Lena says, "and then take me home?"

I say goodbye to Ruthie and extend my final condolences to Dot.

"Will we see you later?" Jaye asks Lena as we start to walk away.

"Um, I don't know. I'm running on empty. I'll text you after farm chores."

It's a quiet ride home. Lena leans against the side window, her tears mirroring the rain slipping down the glass. The after-funeral letdown—I know it well. She's broken but not defeated. It reminds me of when I met her and fell in love. She's so much stronger now, though.

She's made me stronger, too.

Everything I need to say surges in me until the air inside the Jeep feels heavy, ready to burst. She's the one person I want to talk to, yet I struggle. Words get stuck in my throat like a vehicular pile-up on the interstate—the way forward is blocked in tangled destruction.

Destruction I caused. *How could I hurt her so terribly?*

The rain picks up angrily and loudly, affecting my visibility. The Jeep splashes through the driveway despite going slowly. I park close to the barn.

"I'll come around for you," I say, but she's already out the door. I catch her at the barn's entrance, thankful that her high heels limit her speed. "Lena."

"You should go," she says, her voice weak and trembling. "I'm sure you have…"

"I don't have anything."

"Please." Her shoulders bounce in a tired shrug. "I'm so heartbroken, Ben. I can't keep pretending or putting on a brave face. Please. I can't hold it together another second longer… even for you."

Her pain and vulnerability feel like iced daggers penetrating me—*I did this. To her.*

"I lied to you," I blurt urgently. "I didn't sleep with Lauren."

"What?" she scoffs. "Why should I believe—"

"I swear, I didn't. I went to her house but never made it to her door."

She shakes her head in renewed anguish. "Don't do this. You're not making sense. You destroyed me. Why would you lie?"

"You were right—I fire-bombed us to avoid what I was going through and stop hurting you over and over. I stupidly thought that one huge hurt would protect you from a lifetime of smaller ones—a damn explosion rather than a slow death. I don't expect forgiveness or understanding. Hell, I don't understand it completely. I've had a dozen sessions with Dr. Reese just to get here today. She thinks nearly leaving Adam behind triggered my PTSD and survivor's guilt from that day in Afghanistan, and Lauren's reappearance made it worse. I tried handling it all alone because that's what I've always done. I get small, tightening all that shit into an impenetrable ball deep inside me. It's worked before. But not this time. It's not just me anymore—and I don't want it to be. I *need* you to know that *Lauren and I didn't happen.*"

I'm out of breath, my confession so labored and agonizing but so intensely necessary that my heart rate skyrockets. She glares, eyes glassy with tears and mouth parted in anguish, just as hurt as the day I told her that awful lie.

"I'm sorry, Lena. So fucking sorry." Mr. Wickers's words skip into my thoughts. "I let go because I was too afraid to hold on. I love you, Ruthie, and Saddletree. I just got… fucking confused.

"But not anymore. I turned down the job, even commandeered my portrait. It didn't belong there, and neither do I. If you give me another chance, I'll never let go again."

Her brow forms a wonky *L* as she takes in my words. Her hands slip behind her to hide her growing panic. "I've been in *misery*," she mutters weakly as if actively trying to extract herself from it but failing. "You *hurt* me. *On purpose.*"

"Yes," I admit, hanging my head. "I'll spend a lifetime making it up to you, whether you take me back or not."

"Take you back? How am I supposed to trust you? What happens if you get small again and don't come back?"

"That *won't* happen. Lena, I promise," I say, shaking my head as the words come out. "I know my promises don't mean shit right now, but… you held my hand. That meant everything to me. It must mean there's hope. All I can ask is that you try to believe me. I'm at your mercy. Now. And always."

Her face seems rigid with hurt, and my desperation sinks into resignation.

"I don't want you at my mercy. I want… I can't… It's too much," she finally says, her breath quick. "I need time."

I nod. It's all I could ask for, given everything I've put her through, especially as she tries to regulate her panic. She puts her hand up, stopping me from helping. I back away, leaving only because she *needs* me to.

The rain hits me like a waterfall as I push through it. I slump in the driver's seat. Her pain—the pain I've caused—reaches out, pulling me to her.

But she wants me to go.

And I should. She's heard me out and knows the truth. Hopefully, she'll join me for counseling this week and for as long as it takes for Dr. Reese to help us work through the damage I've caused. Leaving now doesn't mean there isn't hope for us.

I put the Jeep in drive, easing off the brake.

A shadow moves through the pouring rain. She stands at my headlights, arms outstretched as if she might physically prevent the Jeep's forward motion.

She mouths the words, "Don't go!"

I exit the Jeep and meet her there. Her sapphire eyes lock on mine. "I held your hand because… for better or worse, *that's* what we said. This is just… *worse*. We made a promise. *You* promised *me*, Ben. We said for better and worse. I don't care if it's worse from now on, I still want you. Need you."

Her voice gets lost in her sobs.

"Don't go," she repeats, yelling over the rain. She's soaked and desperate, holding onto my arms like she can't stand on her own. "This is the last time I'll ask you. Are you ready to come home, Ben?"

I drop to my knees in the mud at her feet, like I tried to do the day I asked her to marry me. She wouldn't permit it then, but she does now. Rain hides my tears as I fist her hands between us. For better or worse. Her words bulldoze every barrier I've thrown up, freeing me.

"Forgive me, Lena," I beg, my desperation puddling at her feet. "Forgive me for being so fucking scared."

I expect her to recoil at my weakness. I am exposed. Vulnerable.

But her smile is instantaneous. Soft and reassuring. "I'm scared, too, but let's be scared together. What scares you?"

"*Everything*. Everything is changing—I'm changing. I'm scared you'll lose that fucking adoring look on your face, like when I collared that perp—I can't do that shit anymore, Lena. I want you, *need you*, to be proud of me. What if you can't be? I'm fucking terrified that one day I'll lose your love and adoration because I'm no longer the man you married. My bullshit will chisel away at you, and I'll feel worthless because I can't be what you need. I'm petrified that I won't hear your voice one day. Or Ruthie's. Or know when you need me. That I'll be a burden—"

"Never, Ben." Her serene expression leaves me breathless. "Even what's bad will be better with us together, remember? I forgive you, just come home."

"I am home."

I bury my face in her stomach, sobbing with relief and holding on to her midsection like a life preserver.

My shields dissolve into the dirt, merging with my foolish pride and anger. I've never felt more vulnerable or more alive. Her delicate fingers trace my cheek and rake through my hair. The rain baptizes us, renewing us, and she holds me there, understanding everything. Fear is something I've always hidden—as a kid with reading problems, as a high schooler figuring myself out, as a soldier, as a husband and father, as someone nearing deafness.

I don't have to hide anything from Lena. I've always known that, but now my oneness with her snakes through my body like blood. She's here, no matter what I am.

"Enough already," she cries and chuckles at once. "We're soaked, and you're ruining your suit."

"I don't care." I stand at her request but refuse to release her. My large hands wrap around her like a gift I long to open.

"Promise me one more thing," she says before I can kiss her.

"Anything." I kiss her anyway, soft and quick.

"That you tell me what's going on with you *as we go*. No matter where I am or what I'm doing. Please don't wait until it's too much. You always know when I'm anxious and never let me deal with it alone. I need a learning curve with you—it's hard to tell when something's wrong. So, if you're angry or depressed or—"

"Right now, I'm happy. No. Better than happy. Overjoyed," I say, taking her bottom lip into mine. "I promise—no holding back."

She grins and sighs softly. "No holding back."

Then, I show her I mean it.

CHAPTER 44

Lena

HE HOLDS NOTHING BACK. *Nothing.*

Right there at the Jeep, in the rain, soaked and starving, he lavishes me with overdue kisses and touches, melding into me like we're one.

We are one. But Ben needed to fight through his shitstorm to believe that again. He needed to see that this is where he belongs, not just here with Ruthie and me but, here, at Saddletree, with this community and our extended family. Miraculously, the funeral gave him that.

And it gave me another beautiful insight into him. He astounded me today—showing up for us and standing up for Dot and Mrs. Moore. If asked this morning for a list of things Ben Wright would *never, ever* do, delivering an impromptu speech for a crowd would've ranked high. Showing up at the funeral at all was risky—for all he knew, I could've told everyone about his final push and turned them all against him. But he came anyway. It proves what I've always known—*this man would do anything for us.* Even leaving was his misguided way of saving me. *Aw, Ben.*

I'm breathless with relief and desperation. I've fallen in love with him all over again, only stronger, if that's even possible.

I've been with Ben hundreds, maybe thousands of times. Gosh, I wish I could go back and keep a sex journal like people do for food they've eaten or books they've read. I'd call it Sexy Encounters of the Ben Kind, and there'd be many volumes with notes and crude drawings with lots of exclamation points and smiley faces. Today's entry would take many detailed pages, and I'd never get it right.

But that's okay. It's a cornerstone memory burned into us like fireworks, our wedding, Ruthie's birth, and now, our toe-curling reconciliation.

The first time we made out in this barn, I couldn't break from my anxiety long enough to enjoy him how I wanted and ended up crying in his arms.

This morning, I felt even sadder without him.

Now, it's all joy, overflowing and spilling onto him.

The rain picks up, and somehow, he drags us inside. His deep kisses and roaming hands press me to the nearest wall. Thunder crashes through the driving rain outside, giving a fitting soundtrack to the storm of his affection. He is all over me. His mouth is all over me. I cry out like it's new—it is, in a strange way. It's been too long without him.

A breathless search for a way to rid me of my dress ends with him gently gathering the hem and slowly easing it over my head. In nothing but black heels and lace, he moans at the sight of me—his green eyes wide and glowing with want.

Pressing his body fully against me, his hand grips my face almost roughly. "You are beautiful."

He takes one hand in both of his, letting his fingers skim my soft skin all the way to my shoulder, followed by his lips. "And amazing at *everything* you do—I mean it."

I laugh at this, though tears speck my eyes again to hear him say it.

He peels out of his suit jacket, dropping it atop my dress. He kisses me hard and deep before trailing his tongue down my neck and nibbling my protruding collarbone. Looking up from the curves of my breasts, he says, "You *are* my wife," recalling my tearful words at the hospital. I melt at those words like he's setting them in stone.

He's down on his knees again—so much for the suit—watching my expression as he gently eases one leg onto his shoulder and then the other. I go from relief to curiosity to *holy shit*.

My body flushes hot in a second as he fingers my panties aside and kisses me. Hoisted against him, back against the wall, exposed to the coolness, he takes me ravenously. Supporting and seducing me. Wrecking and rebuilding me. With his hands tight to my thighs, I come so deeply that I cry out, and my entire body shakes. All that tension without him. My nightmares, fears, anger, and love release into the musky barn in this glorious, intense moment.

He slows, breathing against me as my thunderous cries reduce to a soft, satisfied whimper.

Then, he starts again.

When he's done with me there, my muscles feel like noodles.

He eases my legs from his shoulders, setting my heeled feet on the dirty brick floor one at a time. His strong hands knead my legs, calves, and thighs, sparking life back into them as he stands.

"You've totally undone me," I say, breathless. "And you haven't even loosened your tie."

He yanks the tie off and tosses it aside.

"I've missed you like crazy." A devilish smirk appears on his handsome face. "I want every inch of you, as many times as you let me."

"Take me here. Now." A giddy laugh rolls off my tongue. "Then, take me upstairs, and let me get you out of that suit."

"Yes, ma'am." Smirking, he hoists me against the wall when my legs wrap around him.

In the next moment, he's inside me—my legs pulling him into me for that first, aching thrust like water for the thirsty. His deep moan joins my higher one. My bare back scratches against the barn's shiplap, but I like the roughness. His hands claw me as they explore—my face, neck, chest, pressing me into the wall, pressing himself into me.

"I'll never get enough of you," he says, reading my mind.

With the next thrust, he says, "You are my wife…"

And another.

"For better or worse…"

Another. *Holy fuck.*

"Till the day I die…" His words sound breathy but stern, and his sultry green eyes fix on mine, piercing through me. Watching me, he moves in and out slowly, dipping himself in before a full dive.

And it's making me quiver for how good it feels and how desperately I want more.

"I promise… your bed will never be cold or your nightmares uncomforted again…"

"Holy shit, Ben, please."

Deeper now.

"I promise… my heart, thoughts, and all the words I don't say…"

Deeper again. I cry out.

"The entirety of me…"

A bit deeper.

"From this day on…"

Oh, shit.

"If you'll still—"

"Yes! God, yes!" I sputter as I convulse with him inside me, pulling him deeper.

"Forever then," he says, determined.

"For-fucking-ever," I cry as he releases in me. Eyes wide and watchful. Body pressed. Hands holding me to him. And I melt in our oneness. I collapse against his shoulders like a marathon runner through the end tape.

"I promise I won't disappoint you again," he whispers, nuzzling his forehead to mine. "I'll make it up to you."

"Good," I say, smiling. "You can start by joining me in the shower, and then in our bed."

He releases me gently. "Yes, ma'am." He scoops up his discarded jacket, tie, and my dress, flings them over his shoulder, and then does the same to me, making me laugh hysterically as he gently slaps my ass. He carries me to the loft that way amid my relentless giggling. I love his playful side, and it's been too long since I've seen it.

At the top of the stairs, he sets me down, and meeting his eyes again, my laughter melts into his seriousness. He tugs me close, my nearly bare skin pressing against the soft, dampness of his shirt, and his fingers thread through my hair.

"I'll miss your laugh when my hearing goes," he says with a small smile, not in a woe-is-me way, but with gratitude and reverence, like he's glad to have heard it at all.

"You'll always have it. You'll see it," I say, tracing the soft lines around his eyes before placing my hand against the rock-hardness of his chest, "and feel it."

A coy side smile eases up his cheek as he takes me in. "I'm a lucky man."

Hearing those words brings a wide smile. The despair I've seen in him over losing his hearing is replaced with something more Ben-like. Acceptance. Gratefulness. And especially joy.

"We're both lucky," I say.

He hoists me on his shoulder again, forcing choking laughs, and carries me to our bedroom. He releases me near the bathroom doorway and kisses me until I'm pinned against the doorjamb. It reminds me of the first time we were together like this, how we barely made it to the room at all, and how we stopped at the bed to see each other naked for the first time. "You're breathtaking," he said then.

He says the same words now once he strips me down. I peel him from his suit as fast as my fingers will work—*not fast enough*—and he laughs at my urgency.

We shower together, and our sweet reunion becomes a sex marathon, ending with us damp and breathless on the bed a while later. Beside me, he drapes his arm across my belly as we catch our breath.

Tears slip from my eyes as I bask in the loveliness of us together again. He perches on his side, locking eyes, his deep greens penetrating me. He doesn't ask why I'm crying. I think he knows—sadness for Mrs. Moore and relief for us. Instead, he smiles and wipes my wet cheeks with his thumb.

"What can I do?"

"You've done it. You're home," I smile. "This is all I need… and my phone. I should check in with Dot."

He leaves me for the living room, retrieving my phone from his jacket pocket. When he hands it over, he grins. "Before today, I had a feeling she wanted to murder me."

"Oh, she did. Dot and Cherry have a plan. I'll tell them I can't make it over—"

"Wait. Let's go over together." He sits up slightly. "We'll check that all is well, and I'll find out more about this murder plot."

"Careful. Learning about the murder plot risks plausible deniability."

He waves this off. "It's okay. Soon, I won't be a cop anymore."

He pats my ass and leaves me for the bathroom. I stare at the ceiling, saddened by the thought.

Ben detours to Sunny's on the way to Mrs. Moore's country cottage —now Dot's. When I ask what for, he only says, "A peace offering." I let him keep the mystery.

At the house, he meets me on the passenger side with his wide umbrella, and, shoulder-to-shoulder, we rush through the puddles and steady rain to the front porch. We find everyone in Mrs. Moore's quaint living room. It's like walking in on an adult slumber party, with one cute exception, of course. Jaye sits, laptop open, at the table by the window. Cherry is curled under a throw on the couch with her phone. Dot and Ruthie are on the floor, with photo albums, books, and old boxes between them. Nirvana plays softly in the background to the gameshow applause on the TV.

I understand why she'd want a full, noisy house tonight. It reminds me of how empty the house felt after Mom died. Lights and noise helped.

The group looks up in unison when we enter the living room.

"Mom, Dad, Aunt Barb left me *all* her science stuff." Ruthie holds up a magnifying glass almost as big as her face and peers through it. "I'm going to be a scientist when I grow up."

I chuckle, mentally adding it to the long list in Ruthie's Future Game.

"Why wait until you grow up?" Ben says. "Be a scientist now."

Ruthie nods, a determined smirk rising on her cheek. She jumps from her seat and sweeps across the room with the magnifying glass at the ready, like a detective searching for clues.

When attention returns to us, Ben addresses my friends almost like he's standing at the podium again. "I apologize for causing distress. It won't happen again." He holds up a grocery bag. "Hungry? I'm making Reubens."

I laugh-blush, gaping up at him. He made Reubens on our first night together at his place—his only specialty, he said. His eyes catch mine, and I love the subtle smile on his lips.

Another truth about marriage is how it changes. Long gone are the days of spontaneous fireworks (and barn escapades, I would've thought). Now, romance is soft, subtle, and sweet in the little things. Even so, when it happens, it's just as big as fireworks for the love and warm feelings it reenergizes. Somehow, the sweet, small things matter more these days.

Showing up.

Holding the umbrella.

Holding hands.

Making Reubens like our first date.

Ben Wright promised to always romance me. Tears spring to my eyes that he's returned to keeping it. *He's back. He's really and truly back.*

"Aw, he's making you sparkle again," Jaye coos, her hand going to her heart.

Dot eyes me critically before saying, "Fine… extra sauerkraut on mine."

"Oh, can I help?" Ruthie asks.

"Yes." He heads to the kitchen with his daughter bouncing beside him.

CHAPTER 45

Lena

MONDAY MORNING, I host a full kitchen at home. Ruthie chomps down on blueberry pancakes next to Dot, who's doing the same. Jaye enjoys coffee beside her, laptop open. Cherry picks at oatmeal and fruit, sipping chai tea and skimming her phone. I fan a tray of cinnamon rolls, hot from the oven, to ready them for icing.

Ben peeks out from the hallway with a quick "Lena" and waves me over.

He nods toward his outfit. Gray pants and a blue button-down. "This okay?"

I fiddle with his collar only because I want to touch him. "Handsome as ever. Very business casual. The cinnamon rolls are almost ready."

"Good." He checks his watch. "Leaving in fifteen." He disappears to the bedroom after a short kiss.

He almost looks nervous, though meeting with human resources at the police department to discuss job opportunities that fit his unique situation shouldn't cause distress. Nor should the lunch meeting he has with a friend in private security to see what else might be out there for him. He shouldn't be nervous but excited.

Unless it's not what he wants.

We spent Sunday doing relaxing family things—church, lunch, walking the property, and enjoying our horses, dogs, bunnies, chickens, and each other. Though the studio would return Monday morning with its usual noise and drama, Saddletree felt like home again.

We talked about the future. Indecisive Ben has retreated—he's returned to his former *always-have-a-plan* self. That means sorting out his career before undergoing his cochlear implant surgeries next year. It's a comfort seeing him forging ahead to find his new purpose.

"You're my purpose," he told me yesterday when I said that to him. "You and Ruthie… but I want a job, too."

Now, watching him disappear behind our bedroom door minutes before he's due to leave, I feel uneasy. I don't know why, other than, *hello, anxiety.*

I distract myself in the kitchen. I place the naked rolls in a pink box before dousing them in my signature cinnamon-brown sugar icing and roasted pecan topping.

"Mom, I don't have any room for those rolls," Ruthie declares, rubbing her belly as she pushes it out.

"These aren't for us. They're for Dad's workmates," I say before explaining to the rest, "He's interviewing with HR for other positions in law enforcement."

"Wow, he moves fast," Cherry says. "But I say, *sayonara* to Riley Trust."

"Seconded," Dot says as Ben enters the living room. "Yo, Ben, I could always use a hand on my truck."

"Oh, and I'd love a PA," Cherry grins.

"I bet you'd make a pretty good editor," Jaye offers, not to be left out, and they all laugh.

Ben smirks. "All good offers, but I'll pass, thanks."

He grabs his keys, wallet, and a file folder from Mom's refinished hutch before heading to the kitchen. He reaches for a travel mug. "Rolls almost ready?"

"Almost." I drizzle faster.

"Your weird neighbor sent out a text alert yesterday. Did you see it?" Cherry asks, reading the message. "*To the family and friends of Lena Buckley-Wright*… with a picture."

Ben and I lean in to see us sharing a smiling kiss by the Jeep before heading inside for church yesterday morning. Since Alice Harvey brought Ben into my life in the first place, I can't be upset with her for publicizing our reunion. I guess.

Ben smiles easily. "Good picture."

Jaye and Dot crowd around Cherry's phone as she scrolls through the follow-up messages.

"She also shared a picture from your wedding," Jaye coos. "Aw, you did it at the tree. How perfect."

"That was a fun day," Dot says. "I was the Best Woman—my version of her maid of honor."

Wedding memories warm me with joy and gratitude, making me beam. Ben's hand circles my side, and I lean into him.

"You should do more weddings here," Jaye says. "It's an incredible venue. I wouldn't mind getting married here." A tiny smile creeps up her cheek as Dot turns bright red.

"Um, yeah, weddings make bank, Lena, babe," Dot recovers. "I picture a gazebo by the pond."

"Draped in peonies and lilacs," Cherry chimes in.

"And twinkle lights," Jaye says, like it's a game. "To mimic the stars, and—"

"Fireworks," I say dreamily. Ben's hand tightens against my waist.

"We'll happily host your happily-ever-after, Jaye," I say with a wink, "but not everyone's. I can't add another thing to Saddletree's workload. I'm busy enough already."

And refuse to let work come between Ben and me again, I think, but don't say.

Cherry moans. "But Lena, even *I* love a good wedding. It'd fit your vibe and your new logo."

"I'm pro-weddings, too. With proper planning, weddings could be high-profit, high-publicity, with minimal work and time... They're sweet, too," Ben adds with a light smile.

"I don't know. I'm setting boundaries. I'm already expanding the groups."

"Dad *loves* the groups," Ruthie says, running her fingertips through the leftover syrup on her plate. "It's his favorite thing, after us. And the dogs. And the horses. And our bunny friends."

Ben goes to Ruthie, kissing her forehead before taking a wet towel to her fingers. His green eyes land on mine as he works. "I'll help if you want to consider it."

"Thanks, I'll think about it." My anxiety upticks again, especially when Ben announces that he should go. I finish the cinnamon rolls and secure the lid on the pink box.

With a deep breath, I hand it over and smile through my growing anxiety. "I'm sure you'll find something you love, Ben."

His broad shoulders shrug lightly. "A job's a job, but thanks. Let's research wedding venues tonight. I have some ideas."

A weak nod suffices as my answer. He gives me a soft kiss and a smile, "Love you. See you later."

"Love you, too."

The door clicks shut. Ruthie rushes to her room to finish getting ready for preschool. Jaye closes her laptop and steps aside for a phone call.

Cherry and Dot stare at me like I'm naked, and they're stalkers outside my window, in full ogle. "What?"

"A job's a job?" Dot repeats Ben's words. "Eesh. That's depressing."

"Right?" Cherry scoffs. "He got more excited about hosting weddings."

"Yeah, like me when I get a new project," Dot says, "or fix something better than the other guys."

"Or when I get creative tingles seeing a space for the first time," Cherry says. "It makes me giddy."

Dot laughs. "Who knew Ben could almost sound giddy about something?"

Their eyes fall on mine expectantly, and lightbulbs flicker on in my head.

I race for the door. Ben's Jeep leaves his space beside my truck. I take the spiral staircase two steps at a time, nearly tripping. Spilling out at the bottom, I topple into Elsie Todd with her clipboard and dart around the set crew, moving gear into the barn. He's already on the driveway next to the main house when I dash across the lawn in my rubber boots that aren't getting me there fast enough.

A simple text could've prevented my frenzied chase. But that's the thing about frenzied chases—it's hard to think of anything else but what the universe demands. Still, I feel my pockets for my phone. It's not there, of course, but on the kitchen island, where it served as my baking timer. I take the alley between the main house and the driveway, gaining on him.

Then, I pivot right and jump in front of the Jeep. It jolts as Ben slams on the brakes. Hands against the grill, I lean over, catching my breath and watching dust clouds flitter from his tires.

"What's wrong?" Ben asks, getting out.

"Sorry," I pant. "Don't go."

"Why not?"

"I don't want you to take a job just to have a job," I admit. "We said no holding back, and I've been holding back."

"Um, okay. But why?"

"You loved your job, but it's time to move on. I don't want you to settle for anything less than a new dream, Ben, and I don't think you'll find that in HR or security."

"My dream is to support my family the best I can," he counters.

"Then, I have a better offer." I take a breath, nerves rising. "Manage Saddletree."

His brow furrows.

"Hear me out. I know you said you couldn't work for me—I get it. Chaos. Dog park. Whatever. Saddletree was a mess. But that's not true anymore. By implementing all the strategies that *you* suggested, Saddletree will reopen with more efficiency, more help, and higher profits. If you'd give it a chance, I believe you'd enjoy managing what you started. I don't want *you* to work *for me*, Ben. I want you running Saddletree."

A tiny smile appears, encouraging me to continue.

"I want to be in the kitchen, experimenting with recipes and mentoring Tessa, or out in the dining room, talking to people without worrying about falling behind schedule. I want to do more special orders and vet treats and expand that side of the business because *that's* what I'm good at. With you in charge—and I mean it, *you'd* be in charge —we could both focus on what we love. People and baking for me. Management and groups and, hell, weddings if you want, for you. What better way to support your family than to turn Saddletree into a true family business?"

Over Ben's shoulder, moving shadows catch my attention. Dot, Cherry, Ruthie, and Jaye stand at the sidelines of the driveway, holding coffee mugs like they're watching a parade. Ben doesn't notice their arrival, thank goodness. I don't want him to feel any more pressure. His green eyes fixate on mine in deep contemplation.

Though his lingering silence unnerves me, I say nothing more but give him the space he needs to think. Ben doesn't make snap decisions.

He sighs and checks his watch like he's worried about being late. My heart sinks.

But then, he grins and latches onto me. "You had me at *don't go.*"

CHAPTER 46
Ben

THERE IT IS. *That look.* Adoring. Proud. I live for that look. Joy erupts inside me like fireworks.

She falls into me, full-bodied and tearful, like I'm her damn hero.

I'm not.

She's saving me. She saves me every day without even knowing. I've put her through hell the last two months, but she muscled us through it with that Herculean strength of hers, never giving up on us.

Lena Buckley-Wright is the hero of my story forever.

She could've asked me anything, and I would've said yes. But I'm happy it was this.

Yes. *Happy.*

Though our weekend discussion helped me conclude that I needed to put myself out there and explore other opportunities, it made me uneasy. I barely slept last night, trying to pinpoint my distress.

Now, I understand that Lena's been the source of my hesitation. She loves what she does. It motivates and excites her. She's been right this entire time—I want a job that makes me happy. Saddletree became my dream almost as soon as it became hers.

Now, I get to live that dream, too.

Her relief and love wrap me tightly, and I feel complete. I lift her off her feet to bring her even closer. She laughs in my ear and then pats my back to set her down. She motions behind us.

We have an audience.

Ruthie laughs as she signs, "We snuck up on you."

"Congrats, boss man," Dot says while the others hoot and clap. "Don't let it go to your head. The ladies will always be the real bosses around here."

I nod. "Understood."

Matt Kirby approaches cautiously, arms oddly folded over his gathered shirt.

"Sorry to interrupt, but..." He maneuvers to reveal a tiny head. "I found this little guy foraging under the catering table in the tent."

"Ross!" Ruthie screams and bum rushes the actor, snatching her pygmy bunny from his hands.

I can't fucking believe it.

"Oh, thank you!" she gushes. "Thank you!"

"Happy to be of service, Miss Ruthie." Matt Kirby bows dramatically.

"Let's get that little fella home," Jaye says, motioning Ruthie to the pen.

"Yes, he wants his friends," Ruthie coos. "They've been so sad without him."

"Thanks, Matt." Lena flashes her grateful smile.

"Yes." I step to the Jeep's passenger side and retrieve the cinnamon rolls. "Cinnamon rolls. For your trouble."

"Sweet." His eyes look lustful. He's sampled Lena's baked goods before. "You're wrecking my diet, but these are too good to care."

"Oh, I know, right?" Cherry steps closer. "If I'm here too much, I double up my Pilates classes to burn the extra calories."

"A small sacrifice for friendship. It's working for you." He smiles, shamelessly glancing her over.

Dot sighs and says what I'm thinking. "Geez." Leaving Cherry to her flirting, Dot follows Jaye and Ruthie.

Lena tugs at my arm. "Drive us back home?"

I comply, opening the passenger door for her before taking the driver's seat. I put the Jeep in reverse and carefully steer it toward the house.

"Do you really mean it?" she says in the quiet of the Jeep. "You *want* the job?"

"Yes."

"You're not doing it to make up for things or because I asked? You're doing it because it'll make *you* happy?"

"Yes."

"You truly want to do this?"

"Yes."

She sighs, studying my face like she's looking for dishonesty behind my well-practiced facade.

She won't find any.

"Sure you're okay handing over control?" I ask.

"God, yes! I'm a baker and a badass entrepreneur, but I hate the day-to-day details. It's all yours."

"We'll have to discuss my terms… and the benefits package you're offering." A smirk edges my mouth as I park beside her truck.

She giggles and bats her big blue eyes at me. "I look forward to our negotiations."

I exit and meet her at her side, taking her hand as she slides from the Jeep. "I'm a skilled negotiator."

"*That*, I know."

She leads me up the spiral staircase, lightly twiddling my fingers with hers.

"Before those talks begin, I'd like to propose another idea."

She doesn't elaborate as we reach the top deck. On the right side, we witness Ruthie reintegrating Ross into the rabbit pen. Lena fiddles with her fingers as we overlook the scene, looking serious, almost anxious.

"Tell me your idea," I urge after a long silence.

A light October breeze makes her hair dance around her pensive face. She takes a cleansing breath.

"Next year, things will be different." She locks eyes, her hands moving furiously. "We have time and money. Before we jump back into Saddletree, let's pull Ruthie out of school, take a month, and do everything we want. Together, as a family. Road trips with the music blasting and us singing… beach days with waves and birds and coastal breezes… mountain hikes with gushing waterfalls… movies and concerts… camping with a crackling fire… let's tell bad jokes and funny stories and laugh until our sides hurt—"

"A last hurrah for my hearing?"

"If I'm being insensitive, please say so," she says. "But you haven't lost your hearing yet, Ben. Let's take advantage and make so many incredible memories that you don't feel like you're missing *anything*. And every year after, no matter the changes, we'll make it our family tradition—"

A determined kiss breaks through her signing and stops her frenzied explanation. I love the way she relaxes in my arms, accepting my kiss as freely and easily as she does me. I picture everything she describes, and it gives me renewed purpose.

"May I plan it?" I ask against her lips, unable to entirely pull away.

She laughs. "Of course."

"May I do the packing?"

"Definitely."

"When can we leave?"

She sighs, her smile and sparkling blue eyes filling me with unbelievable joy. "When you decide where we're going first."

I am smitten.

The fear that drove me away from her, I no longer feel because of her. Life is sweet, and love abounds.

CHAPTER 47

Lena

SADDLETREE REOPENS on a brisk but sunny Saturday in December, and we've never been busier. It's a good busy—not the crazy-busy mess it once was when I needed codes to take breaks or free myself from conversations.

Trisha runs the dining room (with Mr. Wickers). I run the kitchen. Ben oversees everything.

Cars line the country road waiting to get in—Mr. Wickers, Jack Graham, and his neighbors volunteer to direct traffic for opening day. They have a surprisingly well-ordered and professional system with bright neon vests and lighted cones, like those used by air traffic controllers. Jaye Kent, Matt Kirby, and other celebrities from the *Hunter* series show up for pictures and autographs. Shakespeare's hayrides boast a waiting list as he drives groups through the woods where *"Dr. Jim Hunter puts up a good fight against the evil witches causing a fright."* His poetry clashes strangely with the hayride's Christmas theme, but patrons enjoy it anyway. Seats in the café and wraparound porch also have a wait, but with the Taylor sisters gone (early retirement) and more professional servers at work, no one minds the wait or has to wait very long.

Not that I have anything to do with that. My focus is in the kitchen, where Tessa and I, a new hire, Rosa, and our dishwasher, Rick, handle orders with precision and low wait times.

I even have time for breaks (Ben calls them code sevens).

Outside, Hugo and Penelope greet me with excited barks and follow as I stroll the busy property.

Under the carport, Cherry hangs out at Matt Kirby's table, where he flashes his actor smile at fans between offering his real smile to her. Something a little magical is happening there. She accepts his attention coyly, like a skittish cat, unsure if she can trust him. But Dot says they've been inseparable since they met. He's asked her to redesign his Manhattan apartment, and she's helping him find a beachfront property here. Matt let Cherry install a tracking app on his phone, and Cherry took down her online dating profiles and changed her Facebook status to *it's complicated.*

Dot and Jaye's romance is less complicated—they've been *all in* since that kiss. No drama. No bullshit. All love, as if their relationship always existed and kissing clicked into its intended place. Dot stands, bouncer-like, beside Jaye's signing table, occasionally dropping her hand on Jaye's shoulder. The satisfied grin stretching up Jaye's high cheekbones assures me she's in love with my best friend.

I find Ben at Mom's tree, busy on his phone while Ruthie and Adam take turns on the swing. He doesn't notice me as I cross the lawn toward him, weaving around picnickers and lawn chairs.

In the new shelter, a local band called The Hurricanes plays classic rock hits. After their set, another group will take over, and the music will continue all afternoon and evening. Saddletree's opening day will end with sparklers, small campfires, hot chocolate, and fireworks. Wanting a real celebration, Ben planned it all. The families stretching across the field laugh, smile, clap, and dance, clearly in favor.

Saddletree is finally, once again, the happiest place.

I eye my tall, bulky, handsome husband and want to climb him like a lustful monkey—a plan for later. For now, I take him in with so much love in my heart. He looks serious and determined, dressed in his business casual button-down, vest, and khakis and wearing his reading glasses as he operates his phone.

His demeanor changes when he sees me. His dashing, full smile reaches his eyes as he slides his phone away. He looks coy, like he might want to climb me, too. A tongue-laced kiss greets me—I could get used to code sevens like this.

"You were right," I say, remembering this morning when our alarms sounded together, and after both hitting snooze, we turned to each other, and he signed, "It's a good day" in the small space between us.

"How do you know?" I asked. "It hasn't started yet."

"They're all good days with you," he said before kissing me, and then… well, let's say I no longer think about the clock when sexy, fun times kick off. That's one perk of having a good manager.

Another is his unabashed excitement. It's no surprise that he's good at this job. All that self-discipline, efficiency, and hyper-planning—how could he not be, right? What I didn't expect was his devout enthusiasm. This is not just a job for him. During our epic road trip, he started a notebook of Saddletree ideas, like hosting outdoor movie nights and optimizing seating in the dining room. Ben manages with wholehearted belief that anything is possible here. More support groups. Community festivals. Weddings. Car shows. Holiday celebrations. Christmas light shows. Corn mazes. Anything. And he wants to try it all. Ben lives, breathes, and loves managing Saddletree.

"We've already exceeded today's projected profits," he tells me at the tree. "Tomorrow might be even bigger." He motions to a camera crew from the local news setting up near the concert venue. "Have time for an interview?"

I grimace and step away from him. "Oh, I have to get back to the kitchen. Those rolls won't bake themselves."

His green eyes narrow, catching my sarcasm. He grabs my hand and pulls me to the less-populated side of the sprawling live oak. He eases me against the rough bark with soft kisses.

"On second thought," I say a little breathless, "I'll do whatever you want, boss."

With a throaty chuckle, he says, "That's better."

I've learned a few bonus lessons about being married to Ben Wright lately. I don't call him *quiet* anymore—maybe he is with other people, but not with me. His stoicism acts as a shield that he drops with us, like kicking off your shoes when you get home. And his minimal conversation doesn't mean he doesn't have a lot to say. He's always thinking. Always measuring his words and actions. Always thinking of us.

Therapy has continued to help us communicate, and practice makes perfect. The more we share and connect, the easier it becomes and the closer we feel.

Marriage has levels. We aren't the same people who met five years ago or stood at this tree and said I do. We lost sight of our love and connection. But getting through it means leveling up in the depth of our commitment. Bad shit happens, but there's no one I'd rather be with when it does. Ben loves me now more than ever. Standing by him, him coming back to me, and choosing forgiveness over hurt, love over anger, and reconciliation over giving up has solidified the real us like poured concrete, turning stronger with every passing moment in place.

Love is weird like that. Just when you think you can't love someone any more than you already do, you do. Love grows like a tree, thickening at the base and spreading nonsensically in directions you'd never thought it'd go. Big. Beautiful. Love.

And I love that there will always be more to learn about Ben Wright.

Like how he's still able to surprise me.

"Got you something." He pulls a small ring from his top shirt pocket. He gingerly slips it onto the ring finger of my right hand, opposite my fireworks engagement ring and the simple gold band that followed. "Technically, I can't marry you again. I would, though. Again and again. Everyday. For better and worse, forever."

He's all serious and nervous in a way that makes me want to launch a full-fledged kissing attack and wrap my legs around his midsection.

I take in the simple band of garnets, pearls, and emeralds—our three birthstones—and gush, "It's Christmas."

He smirks. "A pleasant coincidence. You're my favorite gift."

Pushing up on my toes in my rubber boots, I kiss him, laughing and crying together. "What's with you giving me rings at this tree, huh? You're spoiling me. It's beautiful. Thank you."

"Thanks for making everything better," he says, his forehead resting against mine.

I'm about to offer his typical "It's no trouble" response, but my words get lost in his kiss.

Fall in love with Lena and Ben all over again in their origin story, *One Thing Better*.

Access *Every Good Thing's* deleted scenes, Dot's Soulmate Recipe (a short story), and read *Every Good Thing's* follow-ups—their epic road trip & other surprises—in Ben and Lena's BONUS EPILOGUES, free for subscribers!

Scan the QR code below for access to all of my books (including signed paperbacks), bonus content, and more.

bio.site/authorjessicasherry

Writing a sequel to *One Thing Better* probably wasn't the *best* business decision. For all its accolades (a Kirkus starred review) and love from readers (I've met so many incredible people!), that story takes place during a difficult time, the pandemic, and many readers (and agents and publishers) weren't down for that.

But that's okay—I *needed* more Ben. The quiet, gentle giant of *One Thing Better*, who spoke few words but always the right ones and made Lena feel loved *just* as she was, has become a forever favorite.

But, damn, he was challenging to write!

From the start, I wanted *Every Good Thing* to be *his* story, and I hope I did him justice. I found it a stretch to understand a man with such a calm, controlled, and unemotional exterior, battling internally with mental health issues, and struggling to communicate them, especially from *his* point of view. I found myself just as frustrated with him as Lena was. *Talk to me, Ben. Just talk to me.* He listened, eventually.

His story serves as a much-needed reminder to me that just because someone *seems* fine doesn't mean they are. Often, the only way to get those *keep-everything-close-to-the-chest* people to open up is by being available, listening, and meeting them where they are.

No one should struggle alone. Between the two books—Lena's story and Ben's—I hope I've conveyed that simple truth. Real strength comes in vulnerability and honesty; real love is shown through acceptance, just as we are. As Ben said in *One Thing Better*, "We're us. You and me. We *should be whatever that is and never feel bad about it."*

So, maybe these books won't make any bestseller lists, but if they encourage even one person to reach out for help during a tough time, then they've made a meaningful impact.

As always, my big-hearted thanks go out to everyone who made this book possible. Firstly, the hopeless romantics, anxiety sufferers, Ben-crushers, meaning-seekers, and all-around lovelies who not only read

One Thing Better but rated, reviewed, talked it up, and reached out. You're the reason I dared to write Ben's story.

Thanks to Julie Mianecki from Reedsy for her thought-provoking edits. My beta and arc readers for their excellent feedback.

Thanks to Sam Palencia at Ink & Laurel for this amazing cover that reflects their angst, but also their love and passion for each other.

Thanks to Jenny Austin for her detailed final edits that shaped the story to its best, and for her overall enthusiasm and inspiration that truly make me want to write many more books as fast as I can. You mean so much to me!

Thanks to Tabitha for her insightful advice and for inspiring me to write chapter forty-one. You came into my life at exactly the right time!

Endless love and appreciation go to Julie Ward. I thank my lucky stars every day that our move brought me to you. Thanks for all the walks, talks, and free therapy.

Finally, Joe. My dream wasn't working out for me until you made it yours, too (Yes, just like Lena and Ben—I see it now). There's so much more to putting great books out there than writing them—it's too big for one person. You've always helped and supported me (nearly thirty years strong now), and you still manage to make me laugh in the process. Since going ALL IN with me on this, things keep getting better, thanks to you.

You, our family, and every good thing we've built together fill me with joy and gratitude.

Now, on to the next one.

Big Hugs,

Jessica Sherry